More advance praise for Sherri Wood Emmons and PRAYERS AND LIES

"*Prayers and Lies* is a sweet, revealing tale of family, friendship, long-held secrets and includes the all-important ingredients of forgiveness and love."
—Kris Radish, author of *The Shortest Distance Between Two Women*

"A strong debut . . . Emmons has a rich voice that pairs well with the earthy setting . . . and the characters are wonderfully drawn."
—*Publishers Weekly*

"When I was reading *Prayers and Lies,* the voice was so genuine, so sincere, I felt like Bethany was standing right before me, barefoot, earnestly telling me her story, alternately laughing, crying, wondering, confused, and scared. I was on the edge of my seat, listening, every scene coming in to full, bright, Technicolor detail as one prayer was heard, one lie was shattered, one family's raw, haunting life laid bare. I loved it."
—Cathy Lamb, author of *Such a Pretty Face*

"Prepare to stay up all night reading! Sherri Wood Emmons perfectly captures the devastating impact of family secrets in her beautifully written—and ultimately hopeful—debut novel. With its evocative setting and realistically crafted characters, *Prayers and Lies* is a must read for fans of rich family drama."
—Diane Chamberlain, author of *The Lies We Told*

PRAYERS AND LIES

SHERRI WOOD EMMONS

KENSINGTON BOOKS
www.kensingtonbooks.com

KENSINGTON BOOKS are published by

Kensington Publishing Corp.
119 West 40th Street
New York, NY 10018

All Kensington titles, imprints, and distributed lines are available at special quantity discounts for bulk purchases for sales promotion, premiums, fund-raising, educational, or institutional use.

Special book excerpts or customized printings can also be created to fit specific needs. For details, write or phone the office of the Kensington Special Sales Manager: Attn. Special Sales Department. Kensington Publishing Corp., 119 West 40th Street, New York, NY 10018. Phone: 1-800-221-2647.

ISBN-13: 978-0-7582-5324-8
ISBN-10: 0-7582-5324-9

First Kensington Trade Paperback Printing: February 2011
10 9 8 7 6 5 4 3 2 1

Printed in the United States of America

To Kami—
you are my sunshine

ACKNOWLEDGMENTS

Let's start with two clichés that happen to be true. First, writing is a solitary venture. Second, it takes a village to raise a child. I alone wrote this book, but I was not alone in the process. I am grateful to so many people who helped along the way. And so . . .

To the members of my writers' group—Gail Whitchurch, Egan Dargatz, Ron Shipman, Ploi Pagdalian, and especially Kathleen Martin—who saw the potential in this story before I did, thank you.

To Steven Scholl, Janice Lineberger, Steve Brite, and Beth Browne, whose careful readings and thoughtful critiques helped shape the story, thank you.

To my agent, Judy Heiblum, and my editor, John Scognamiglio, who took a chance on an unknown and whose suggestions and ideas made the story so much stronger, thank you.

To Joy Simpkins, whose attention to detail and thoughtful copyediting should win an award, thank you.

To my dear friend Tina Burton, who read every word of every draft and who fed me body and spirit during the writing, thank you.

To my children, Zachary and Kathryn Spicklemire and Stephen Emmons, who put up with my long absences and wild mood swings, thank you. I am so proud of the terrific people you have grown up to be.

To my husband, Chris, who loved me through it all and still does, thank you. I can't imagine it all without you, and I don't even want to try.

From my grandmothers, Minnie Chafin and Irene Wood, I learned to work hard and love fierce. Their lives stood as testimony to the power of perseverance and family.

Finally, thank you to my parents, Thomas and Peggy Wood, who taught me how to pray.

I love you all.

Prologue

The Bible says that the sins of the fathers are visited
upon the sons to the seventh generation.
But I believe it's the daughters who bear
the brunt of most family sins.
At least that's so in my family.

1

The Kiss

We always knew when Bobby Lee came home. Folks up and down the Coal River Valley heard the roar of his motorcycle on the gravel road long before he tore around the final bend, turning so sharp he lay nearly sideways on the ground. Sometimes he'd be gone weeks at a time, sometimes just a few days. But his homecoming never changed.

He rode into the valley like a conquering hero. And Jolene, his wife, would come flying out of their shabby cabin, long red hair streaming behind her, just as Bobby Lee pulled into their little dirt yard. He'd be off the huge bike in a flash as she ran down the two broken and patched steps and into his arms. And then there would be the kiss—scandalous for that rural West Virginia community in the 1960s. We children would stand on our own porches or in the road, gaping at the two of them, our mouths and eyes wide.

Usually, Reana Mae was waiting on the porch, too, but Bobby Lee didn't notice her right off. His wife was such a whirlwind of red curls and short skirts and hunger that their daughter—thin, freckled, and silent—went unnoticed. After the kiss would come gifts, if his haul had been a long one. Sometimes, Bobby Lee drove his rig all the way from Charleston to California, and he brought Jolene and Reana presents from places like Los Angeles and Las

Vegas. Usually a toy or coloring book for Reana. For Jolene, he brought clothes—shocking clothes. Like the halter top and hot pants he brought from San Francisco. Or the lime green minidress from Chicago. Jolene strutted around like a peacock in them, while the rest of the valley folk shook their heads and whispered to one another over their fences and laundry lines. Jolene was the first woman in the valley to go braless, her round, full breasts barely contained beneath the tight T-shirts and sweaters she wore.

After the gifts and the hellos and the "What's happenin' in the world?" talk, Jolene would send Reana Mae off to her great-grandma's, then disappear into the house with her husband for the rest of the afternoon. Sometimes, Reana spent the night at her Grandma Loreen's before Jolene remembered to come for her. Loreen would make up Jolene's old room, and she'd fry pork chops and boil potatoes with green beans and bacon fat like Reana wanted, and she'd sing her the lullaby she used to sing to her own babies. And so, on those days, Reana Mae got cherished a little bit.

Jolene wasn't from the valley, though her people were. She'd spent most of her childhood up north in Huntington with her mama, EmmaJane Darling. Her father, whoever he might have been, was long gone before Jolene made her appearance at Our Lady of Mercy Charity Hospital in Huntington. Jolene came to live with her grandparents, Ray and Loreen, after EmmaJane died, and she was a handful.

But Bobby Lee fell for Jolene the first time he laid his eyes on her, the day she came to the Coal River. She was just twelve years old then, but she looked sixteen in her tight black skirt, low-cut blouse, and bright-red lipstick. And Bobby Lee told his little brother, "I'm gonna marry that girl." Five years later, he did. And don't you suppose Ray and Loreen were relieved to have Jolene married off? They fairly beamed at the wedding, didn't even bat an eye when Jolene wore a short blue dress to be married in instead of the nice, long white gown with lace that Loreen had offered to make for her.

"At least," my Aunt Belle had whispered, "it ain't red."

They were scandalous, those two, even in a valley that tolerated a good bit of questionable goings-on. Times were hard, after all, and people had to take their happiness when and where they found it. Folks in the valley were philosophical about such things. But Bobby Lee and Jolene Colvin, they pushed it too far by half.

They didn't go to church, for one thing. Everyone else in the valley spent long Sunday mornings at Christ the King Baptist Church, praying for redemption, hearing the true gospel, and assuring their eternal salvation. But not Bobby Lee and Jolene.

They sent Reana Mae to church, though, every Sunday morning, scrubbed clean and wearing her one Sunday dress, her spindly legs bare in summer and winter alike. Folks sometimes said Jolene sent her daughter to church just so she could lie abed with Bobby Lee, desecrating the Lord's Day. And the church folk were sugary sweet to Reana on account of it. But she never even smiled at them; she just stared with her unblinking, green cat-eyes and all those brown freckles. Not a pretty child, folks whispered. Small, knobby, wild-haired, and so quiet you'd hardly notice her, till you felt her eyes staring through you. You couldn't hardly tell she was Jolene's daughter, except for those eyes—just like Jolene's.

Reana Mae sometimes sat with my sisters and me at church, and she never wrote notes on the bulletin or whispered or wriggled or pinched. She just sat with her hands folded in her lap and stared up at Brother Harley preaching. Sometimes her lips moved like she was praying, but she never said a word. She didn't even sing when Miss Lucetta started up a hymn on the piano.

Christ the King Baptist Church was the glue that held that community together. The weathered white house of God had married and buried valley folk for longer than anyone could remember. Brother Harley, the pastor, was a heavy-jowled, sweaty, balding man who liked a good joke and a cold beer. When he didn't wear his black robe, he donned plaid shirts with a breast pocket, where he tucked the white handkerchiefs he used to wipe the sweat from his forehead and neck. His daddy had been the first pastor of Christ the King Baptist Church, and he was hoping his grandson, Harley Boy, would take the pulpit when he retired.

Brother Harley was great friends with my Great-Aunt Belle. Often on quiet summer nights, you could hear his belly laugh echo all through the valley when he sat on Belle's porch, drinking beer and sharing gossip. His tiny, sharp-eyed wife, Ida Louise, didn't join him at Belle's. Folks sometimes wondered, quietly over their laundry lines, just why Brother Harley spent so much time with a rich widow and so little time at home. "But"—Loreen would sigh to my mother, her head bobbing earnestly—"knowing Ida's temper, maybe it ain't such a wonder as all that."

Aunt Belle—Arabella was her Christian name—was born and bred in the Coal River Valley, the eldest of the three Lee sisters. My grandmother, Araminta, was the youngest. Arathena, Bobby Lee's grandmother, was the middle child.

When she was nineteen, Belle caught the eye of a much older and very wealthy man. Mason Martin owned a chain of drugstores in East Virginia, West Virginia, and Kentucky. He'd come to the valley to look into property, before deciding the community was too small to support a drugstore. He left without a store but with a beautiful young wife. The couple settled into a fine house in Charleston, and for eleven years lived happily together.

At thirty, Belle came back to the valley, widowed and childless. Mason had dropped dead in his rose garden at the age of sixty-two, leaving Belle the sole heir to his drugstore wealth. They'd had just one child, a scrawny son who died of whooping cough before his first birthday.

When Mason died, Aunt Belle had her big house built and proceeded to buy from the Coal River Excavation Company as many of the small riverfront cabins as she could talk them out of. These she sold to the families who had long lived in them, for monthly payments of about half what their previous rents had been. It was Belle who waged war with the electric company to get the valley wired in 1956, and Belle who hired the contractors to install plumbing and septic tanks for her little houses a few years later.

Aunt Belle always sat right up front at Christ the King Baptist Church, marching in solemnly, winking sidelong at friends, just as the first hymn began. When we first started coming to the river, she and my mother had battled fiercely over whether we would sit with her.

"Pride of place," my mother said softly, in that velvety firm voice that brooked no argument, "does not belong in the house of the Lord."

"You all are my family," Belle had hollered. "You ought to be up front with me. What do folks think, you all sitting way at the back of the church, like you're ashamed before the Lord?"

But my mother would not be moved. Aunt Belle had all the resources of her drugstore empire and the indebtedness of an entire valley, but they were nothing in the face of my mother's rock-solid belief in the rightness of her faith.

That was always the difference between valley faith and my mother's. Valley folk took their religion tempered with a hard dose of pragmatism. If Brother Harley spent more time than was absolutely seemly with Arabella Lee . . . well, look at his wife, after all. If the mining men drank too much beer or even whiskey on a Saturday night . . . well, didn't they earn that privilege, working underground six days a week? If Reana Mae had been born only six months after Bobby Lee and Jolene got married . . . well, at least they made it legal in time.

My mother's fiery faith allowed for no such dalliances with the Lord and His ways. There was no liquor in our house, no card playing, no gossip. And there was definitely not pride of place; no, ma'am, we would not sit up in the front pew with my Aunt Belle, no matter how loudly she argued. We sat quietly in the back, with Reana Mae.

Most of the valley kids teased Reana Mae, but my sister Tracy was the worst. Tracy seemed to really hate Reana. I wasn't sure why, but then I didn't understand a lot about Tracy in those days. She was purely mean most of the time, and poor Reana Mae bore the brunt of it when we came south. I wonder sometimes that Reana didn't fight back earlier. Later, much later, she learned to hurt Tracy more than Tracy ever hurt her. But in those hot and sticky days of the 1960s, she only took whatever Tracy gave and came back for more.

"Why doesn't your mother get you some clothes that fit?"

Reana Mae looked down at the faded yellow swimsuit that hung from her shoulders, her cheeks reddening. She shrugged and lowered her head. We were building mud and sand castles at the strip of cleared land that passed for a beach.

"I guess she doesn't want to waste her money," Tracy continued, shoveling dirt into a pink bucket and smashing it down with both hands. "Why, it'd be like dressing up a scarecrow. Like putting Barbie dresses on a stick doll. Ain't that so, Bethany?" She paused, looking up at me expectantly. I didn't make a sound, so Tracy went on. "I guess she wants to keep all Bobby Lee's money for herself so she can buy those trashy dresses she wears, the ones that show her butt."

Reana Mae just stared at the ground, her small frame slumped and still.

"My daddy says people down here breed like rabbits," Tracy continued, "but your mama and daddy just have you. How come?"

Reana shrugged her shoulders again, still silent. She shoved her dirty-blond hair back from her freckled face with a muddy hand.

"I guess when they saw how ugly you turned out, they didn't want any more babies." Tracy smirked.

Still, Reana Mae said nothing, and neither did I. At least Tracy wasn't focused on me.

"What's white and ugly and disgusting to look at?" Tracy continued.

Neither of us said anything.

"A pile of maggots . . . and Reana Mae's face."

Tracy's laughter rang shrill up and down the river. Reana Mae looked up at me, to see if I would laugh, too. She looked like a dog waiting to be kicked.

"Shut up, Tracy," I heard myself say out loud.

Tracy's eyes widened in surprise, then she snickered. "Well, I guess you finally found your *real* sister, Bethany-beanpole-bony-butt-baby. You and Hillbilly Lilly must have come from the same garbage can. That's where we found Bethany, you know." She turned to Reana Mae now that I was the target. "She was crying in a garbage can and Mother felt sorry for her and brought her home. She's not our real sister. Mother has to pay people just to be her friends." She laughed again, her brilliant hazel eyes sparkling mean.

Reana Mae stared directly into Tracy's beautiful, hateful face and finally whispered, "I think you're the meanest girl that ever was."

Tracy stopped laughing abruptly and hurled the contents of her bucket at the two of us, drenching us both with wet sand and mud.

"You two are just alike," she hissed as she rose. "You're the trash-can twins."

With that, she picked up her bucket and ran up the road.

We sat there silently for a moment, dripping and muddy and miserable. Then Reana said to me, smiling shyly, "Well, I guess I always wanted a twin anyhow."

I smiled back at her. All my life I'd had three sisters—three strangers I lived with but never really knew. Sitting in the mud on that muggy day, I found my real sister. I was seven, Reana Mae was six, and I had no way of knowing just how intertwined our lives would become. But from that day forward, Reana and I were connected in a way I've never been with anyone else. Her story and mine got so tangled up together, sometimes it felt like I was just watching from the outside, like she was the one living. Sometimes, I hated her for that. But mostly, I loved her.

❧ 2 ❧

Strangers in a
Strange Land

We weren't from the Coal River Valley, really. We only spent our summers there, my mother, my sisters, and me. Nancy and Melinda—the older girls—never let anyone forget that, either. They were *not* hillbillies. They were northerners, from up in Indianapolis, Indiana—which was a real city, as anyone could tell you. People up north in Indianapolis, Indiana, didn't talk like trailer park trash, or listen to Tammy Wynette, or cook with lard, for heaven's sake. My big sisters hated coming to the valley—or at least they pretended to.

Tracy, of course, played both sides of the record. When she was south, she talked incessantly about how much better, cleaner, and more modern things were back home. But when she was back in Indianapolis, she affected a Southern accent and bragged about her family's "vacation place" down south.

My mother really did hate coming to West Virginia, though she was born and raised in Charleston and had been coming to the Coal River Valley since she was just a small girl herself. But when she married, my mother wanted to get as far away as she could from the bluegrass music, the coal mines, and the grinding poverty of her childhood. It was hard on her to have to come back every summer, but she had no choice. My daddy wanted it. And what my daddy wanted, he usually got.

My parents met in the valley in 1946. Daddy's people lived on the river. His mother—my Grandmother Araminta—had married a valley boy named Winston Wylie and then moved north to Ohio, where Winston found work in a mill. But Winston was killed in a car accident at twenty-four, leaving Araminta with two small children and no drugstore wealth to fall back on. So she came home to the valley and stayed on in one of Aunt Belle's little cabins for a while, taking in laundry, sewing, and baking bread to support herself and her babies.

My father was just two then, and he was the prettiest baby the valley had ever seen—everyone said so. His reddish-blond ringlets, dark brown eyes, and childish lisp captivated his Aunt Belle. Before a year was out, he had moved into Belle's big house to live with her.

"After all, Minta, you ain't exactly got the same resources I got," Belle had argued to her sister. "I can raise Jimmy up right, like he deserves."

And Aunt Belle did raise Daddy just like he was her own. Since her son had died so young, Belle had always wanted a boy. My grandmother also had a daughter, but Belle never offered to take DarlaJean. She only wanted my daddy. Soon after my father moved in with Belle, Araminta took DarlaJean and moved on south to Florida, and they never came back to West Virginia except once, for my parents' wedding. Araminta hovered at the edge of our family's consciousness, like a specter instead of a real person.

Aunt Belle, on the other hand, taught me to make spoon bread and whiskey balls. Aunt Belle switched my legs raw when she caught me playing on the railroad tracks. Aunt Belle bought me my first high-heeled shoes. Aunt Belle was my family.

Belle's house was a showplace, fitted out with all the bells and whistles a chain of drugstores could afford. The three-story, yellow Victorian stood right at the river's bend. Sitting on Aunt Belle's porch swing, you could see up and down the river for miles. I loved sitting there and watching the barges glide back and forth from the mines, empty or loaded down with coal. It seemed like the safest, most comfortable spot in the world. And I could not understand, as a child, why my mother hated it all so.

Mother had spent her own childhood summers farther downriver, staying with her grandparents, who kept a boardinghouse for miners. Mother came every year to help in the kitchen and breathe cleaner air than they had back in Charleston.

When she was fifteen, Mother spent an entire year on the river with her grandparents, the year her own father went on a seemingly permanent bender before finally disappearing for good. That's when she met my father.

Daddy was sixteen then—tall, freckled, and handsome. He was so smart, folks knew he wouldn't stay in the valley and work the mines. Mother was tiny and pretty, with curling dark hair and flashing black eyes. She had a quiet manner and a fiery faith in Jesus Christ. She caught Daddy's heart right away, and she loved him fiercely.

Three years after they met, my parents got married in a big church up in Charleston—Mother in a demure, white gown and Daddy sweating nervously in his first real suit. They moved away from West Virginia the very next day.

Daddy studied at a college in Oberlin, Ohio, while Mother typed away in a doctor's office. As soon as my father graduated and got a sales job with Morrison Brothers' Insurance Company, my mother quit her own job, got herself pregnant with my sister Nancy, and set to work making an orderly, clean, and quiet home for her family. She never once wanted to go back south. Even when her own mother died in 1957, she only drove down for the funeral in Charleston, then came home the very next day.

I was two years old when my father was made a regional director at Morrison Brothers'. As a regional director, Daddy had to travel, and the summer months were the busiest. So he decided, rather than leaving us alone in Indianapolis, he would leave us with his kinfolk for the summers. And Mother knew better than to try to argue him out of it.

My sisters might have copied her disdain, but I loved the Coal River Valley right from the start. I loved the way the steam rose hazy off the water in late August. I loved the way the muddy river bottom suddenly dropped out from under your feet if you stepped in the wrong spot. I loved the nasal twang and sleepy drawl of the voices around me, the fiddling, the innumerable cousins, the smoky kerosene lamps, and the mossy dark woods that crowded in around the row of small, clapboard houses. I even liked the outhouse behind our cabin, gray and white with a tiny window box planted with petunias under a painted-on window.

There was so much life in that valley. Babies were born and old folks died in those houses by the river. Our own cottage had seen weddings and births and even a death or two. The red-checked curtains in the bedroom I shared with Tracy were hand-sewn by my Grandmother Araminta when she was young and newly widowed. The sagging porch out back was where Joe Colvin first kissed my Great-Aunt Arathena. The weathered picnic table in the kitchen had groaned under more Thanksgiving turkeys than I will ever eat. It was my family's place, even if they didn't seem to know it.

It was home.

I don't think Reana Mae ever felt at home in the valley. The dense woods and muggy heat were suffocating to her. As a small child, before she could even read, she spent hours at her Grandpa Ray's little grocery, paging through the same old *National Geographic* magazine—one with vivid photographs of a gloriously blue sky somewhere over Montana. And it seemed to Reana Mae that a person could probably breathe out there in the West, and maybe she wouldn't feel so afraid under a great big sky like that.

Reana Mae was born in the little house Bobby Lee bought from Aunt Belle when he and Jolene got married. Jolene's labor went so fast, they didn't have time to drive to the hospital at St. Albans, so Bobby Lee sent his kid brother running to Belle's, to ask if her housekeeper could come quick. Donna Jo Spencer had tended to women birthing in the valley for years, and she delivered the baby without a hitch—though Jolene swore the process nearly killed her. Her Grandma Loreen told folks later she'd never heard a woman carry on so over a few labor pains, especially since Reana Mae was such a tiny thing—barely five pounds, after all. But Jolene had hollered so you could hear her half a mile down the river. Poor Bobby Lee, smoking unfiltered Camels on the porch outside, could hardly stand it.

After the birth, Loreen carried Reana Mae out to meet her daddy, wrapped tight in a blue flannel blanket. Bobby Lee grinned at the baby and asked, "Boy or girl?"

Loreen shook her head. "I'm afraid it's a girl, Bobby Lee . . . an itty-bitty little girl. Ain't she just the scrawniest thing you ever laid eyes on? I'd never even guess she was Jolene's baby," she clucked, pulling the blanket from the baby's head. The cool air on her scalp made the baby squall, and Bobby Lee brushed past Loreen and into the cabin.

"I'm sorry, Bobby Lee," Jolene said, wiping a hand across her eyes. "I know how bad you wanted a boy."

"That's all right, sugar," he crooned. "We'll get us a boy next time."

Jolene dropped her hand from her eyes and stared up at her husband with wide eyes. "You listen here, Bobby, and you listen good. I ain't never doin' that again. I done gave you a daughter, and you'll just have to make do with her."

All the while, Loreen stood on the porch with the tiny girl already forgotten by her parents and screaming at the world into which she'd been born.

❧ 3 ❧

Essie Down Under

Reana Mae and I spent the sticky summer months of 1969 hunt-ing for garter snakes, swimming, digging tunnels in the mud at the river's edge, carving out a clubhouse in the dense bushes, and mothering her dirty little doll, Essie. Essie had a lumpy cloth body and a rubber head, hands, and feet. Her hair and face were painted on, and she had one yellow-flowered dress to wear. I had a much prettier doll at home, but my mother didn't let me bring her to the river. There wasn't room in the car, she said, and she didn't want me to lose my best doll. "I'll get you another doll when we get there." She sighed, kissing my forehead.

"But there aren't any other dolls like Patsy," I wailed. "And she'll be lonely without me."

But Mother would not be moved. Patsy was left in her pink flan-nel nightgown, tucked safely beneath the quilt on my bed back home, her beautiful blue glass eyes shut beneath her real eyelashes. I hated Mother that day.

I didn't tell Reana Mae about Patsy. She loved Essie, and I didn't want her to know how much nicer my own doll was. So we played that summer with Essie, carrying her out to our clubhouse in the bushes, making her a bed from leaves and soft, dry grass, feeding her with an old baby bottle Cousin Lottie had outgrown in the spring.

One morning in early July, I was lying on my back in the sun on the small porch behind our cabin, listening to Mother and Jolene talking in the kitchen over coffee.

"I'm going over to St. Albans tomorrow, Jolene. Do you need anything?"

"Thanks, Helen, we're fine. Don't you worry 'bout us."

"Well . . . I was thinking I might pick up a doll for Bethany while I'm there, since she forgot hers at home."

Forgot? Was my mother telling a lie? I leaned against the wall and listened intently.

"And I was thinking I could get one for Reana Mae, too." Mother paused briefly, then continued in a rush. "That way the girls would have matching babies to play with."

"No, thanks, Helen." Jolene's voice was flat. "Reana Mae's already got herself a baby doll. She wouldn't know what to do with a brand-new one."

"I just thought . . ." my mother began, but Jolene cut her off.

"That girl is the most careless child you ever saw. What she don't ruin, she loses. She don't need a new doll, Helen. When she does, her daddy and me'll get it for her."

Mother gave up, and I never got a new doll that summer either. But I understood why she wouldn't let me bring Patsy to the valley. It was the same reason I didn't tell Reana Mae about her. Neither of us wanted Reana to know how little she had. She loved Essie, and that would have to be enough.

What I didn't understand in those days was why Mother took such an interest in Jolene and Reana Mae. They were the very picture of all the things Mother despised about her West Virginia childhood. Jolene was nearly illiterate, slatternly, and mouthy—often profanely so. Moreover, she was overtly, even brazenly sexual—reveling in her marriage bed and flaunting herself shamelessly to young men and old alike. And poor Reana Mae was purely odd—everyone said so and even I saw it. She hardly talked at all; when she did, it was in a nasally half-whisper. Her face and hair and clothes alike were mostly dirty and disheveled. Worse, she sang to

herself almost constantly that summer, a tuneless, wordless hum-
ming she seemed unaware of. From near silence to constant hum,
no one seemed to know why she was the way she was. She was just
odd.

But Mother doted on Reana Mae in ways she never did on her
own daughters. We all saw it, and we all resented it—even Nancy,
who didn't seem to worry about what Mother thought most of the
time. But for Tracy, it went way past resentment. She hated the attention Mother paid Reana Mae, and whenever she could, she
made Reana pay dearly for the smiles and quick hugs she received
from our mother. For Reana Mae to receive so freely what Tracy
fought so hard for must have been a fine torture to her stunted
soul.

That day on the back porch, I understood why Mother would
lie to Jolene about me forgetting my doll at home. She wanted to
get Reana Mae a new one.

But the two women soon began talking about other things—like
hemlines. In 1969, ladies' hemlines were a topic of great contro-
versy. Just now, my mother was opining that they couldn't get any
shorter without God himself sending down another flood, and Jolene was laughing that she planned to take all her dresses up another two inches that very week.

I gave up listening and rolled off the porch onto the damp
ground below, and then on down the hill to the river's edge. I didn't
care about hemlines or God's wrath, either.

Reana Mae was out with Bobby Lee that morning, on a rare
father-daughter outing. He had been home almost a week—a
nearly unheard-of break during the summer months—and Loreen
had pestered him into taking Reana to St. Albans to get an ice
cream. I watched them roar off on the motorcycle just after breakfast, Reana Mae clinging to her daddy's back and grinning from ear
to ear. Usually when Bobby Lee took them anywhere, Jolene rode
behind him on the bike—her short skirts hiked up over her thighs,
her arms wrapped around his waist, her hands resting in his lap—
and Reana rode in the small green sidecar. But this morning Jolene
had stayed home.

"I got cramps," she told Bobby Lee. "You go ahead and take Miss Mouse."

So Reana got to ride behind her daddy that day. Which was all fine and good for Reana Mae, but it left me with nothing in the world to do.

I lay on my stomach, throwing sticks into the water and watching them swirl downstream, wondering what to do next. Then I heard the low rumble of a car and saw Aunt Belle's long white Lincoln Continental pull up in front of the cabin. If I went up to the house now, Mother would make me come inside and sit quietly, to "pay my respects" to my elders.

Now, most times I adored being with Aunt Belle. When it was just her and us kids, she'd laugh loud and tell silly stories and bad jokes and give us Oreo cookies and cashews and spicy-strong ginger ale.

But around my mother, Aunt Belle seemed to lose some of her steam. Mother was insistent that her girls behave like ladies, and she disapproved of Belle's great horselaugh and off-color jokes.

Even Arabella Lee Martin didn't stand up so well in the face of my mother's disapproval.

Sighing, I threw another stick into the water. Now I was stuck. I couldn't get up to the road without Mother seeing me, and I couldn't go anywhere down on the bank. The riverbank was overgrown with weeds and brambles. Gnarled ancient trees stretched out over the water, and thin reeds crowded the shore. A few folks had cleared their portions of the lower bank. One or two even had swings or old furniture set down by the water. And my Uncle Hobie had built a small dock on his property and kept a rowboat tied there. But mostly the area along the riverbank was wild. Our own portion had been cleared, so we could sit with our feet in the water and cast fishing lines out into the river. A tiny path ran from our cabin's back porch to the bank below, but mostly we just rolled or slid down the hill on our backsides.

Bobby Lee had built a stone stairway behind his house down to the bank, which Jolene boasted of up and down the river. "Thirty-two steps he put in, all by hisself," she crowed. But the stones were steep and unsteady, and Reana and I usually just slid down their hill, too.

I sat with my chin on my knees, staring at Uncle Hobie's boat. If only I had a boat like that, I could row it down to the beach. But Uncle Hobie and Mother would have my hide if I used that boat. I glared up at the house and sighed again. Was there ever a day as boring as this?

Finally, I decided to practice my spying skills. Reana Mae and I had been playing spy all summer, crawling on our bellies, sneaking up under windows, listening to people's dinner-table talk. Not that we heard much to interest us. Ida Louise yammering at Brother Harley about new choir robes. Aunt Loreen clucking over Bobby Lee's younger brother, Caleb, who had just been kicked out of high school again—this time for pulling a knife on a teacher. And once, Bobby Lee and Jolene in their bedroom, in the middle of the afternoon, sighing and cooing and then moaning.

Reana Mae had run down the hill with her hands over her ears. After that, we'd given up the spying business.

But I was bored and feeling a might desperate.

Silently—or as silently as a child of ten could be—I climbed the hill, cursing as the thistles scratched my bare legs. I crawled back onto the sagging porch and set to listening under the open window again.

"I just don't know what Cleda Rae's gonna do with Caleb," Aunt Belle was saying, her voice grim. "What with Noah gone off like he did, it's all left on her shoulders."

"That boy was always trouble," Jolene said shortly. "The day I married Bobby Lee, when I was getting dressed for the wedding, I caught him peeking in at the bedroom window, watching me."

"Well." Aunt Belle sighed heavily. "Caleb's a spirited boy, that's a fact. But Bobby Lee could always keep him in line. And Caleb, why, he just worships Bobby Lee.

"Probably," she added, "that's why he was peeking in at you."

"Is that so? I thought it was so he could see my tits," Jolene said.

Even from outside I could feel my mother's dismay, see her lips forming a tight, thin line.

Aunt Belle burst into a great laugh.

"Probably some of that, too," she admitted. "He's all boy, that one."

"What did you do?" Mother asked. "When you saw him at your window, I mean."

"I told him if he didn't clear off, I'd tell Bobby Lee on him. That made him run, I can tell you."

"Did you tell Bobby Lee?"

"No." Jolene sighed. "Didn't seem any point. Bobby loves that kid, even though he is a pain in the butt. Besides, I knew he'd be going off to Dunbar with Noah and Cleda Rae right after the wedding."

"With Cleda Rae, at least," Belle added.

"I cannot imagine what possessed Noah to leave his family," Mother said.

"A hundred and one pounds of fun, I guess," Jolene said.

"Oh, Jolene, don't say that. You don't know that."

"I do know, Helen. I know it for a certain fact. Cleda Rae told me when he left, he took his little Pop-Tart with him. It near to broke Cleda's heart."

"I had no idea," my mother said.

I imagined she was shaking her head now, the way she did when she was confounded by the sins of the world.

"Poor Cleda Rae . . . and now to have so much trouble with Caleb."

"Oh, Cleda will get by," Jolene said firmly. "She always does. When push comes to shove, she just pushes and shoves whatever it is off on someone else."

She paused. "I just hope she ain't planning to push Caleb off on me and Bobby Lee. I already told Bobby, I ain't havin' trouble like that in my house."

She sighed loudly. "But you know how Bobby Lee is about Caleb. He thinks the sun rises and sets on that kid."

Now, all of this was more interesting than pitching sticks into the river, but only just barely. I slid back down the hill again—my shorts were nearly black with dirt by now.

Mother did not allow us to walk along the river beyond Uncle

Hobie's property. After that, the bank was uncleared. But last summer, Reana Mae told me that she and Harley Boy had cleared a path almost all the way to the beach. Maybe I could find it.

I stared up at the cabin again, then set my shoulders the way I'd seen my daddy do when he started a big job.

If Reana Mae could do it, surely I could.

The way was easy at first. I took a big stick with me and used it to swat at vines and low-hanging limbs. The mosquitoes and brambles were bad—my legs would be a scratched-up mess when I got to the beach—but I plowed ahead. Pretty soon, I'd get to Bobby Lee and Jolene's place, and their land was cleared, so that would be a break.

As I pushed on through the brush, I thought how impressed my sisters would be if I could make a path from our cabin all the way to the beach. It was nearly a mile, after all, by road. But going by the river would cut the walk almost in half. At least that's what Aunt Belle had said when she tried to convince the county government to put in a paved walkway. She didn't win on that one, but she gave it a good try.

I could tell I was getting close to Bobby Lee's place, because the river curved inward slightly. I peered ahead, looking for the clearing I knew would come up soon. But when I spied it, I stopped short.

In the clearing, just coming down the stone steps from Bobby Lee and Jolene's cabin, I saw Tracy.

What was she doing here? She knew Bobby Lee and Reana Mae had gone to town. She'd pitched a fit with Mother that morning about not getting to go along. Tracy adored Bobby Lee—he flirted with all us girls. And when Mother explained that Reana Mae needed some time just with her daddy, Tracy had stalked out, slamming the screen door behind her with such force it rattled the whole house.

I crouched in the tall brush, watching my sister as she crossed the cleared area onto the lower bank. She was carrying something small in her arms. I couldn't tell what.

I watched in dumb fascination as she knelt in the mud at the edge of the river and began digging with a plastic shovel.

When she had a hole big enough to satisfy herself, she threw the shovel aside and rocked back on her heels. Then she picked up the small bundle she had carried and carefully unwrapped it from a tattered green receiving blanket. My heart missed a beat then. I knew that blanket. It had been Cousin Lottie's, and now it was Reana's. She used it for her baby doll—for Essie.

What was Tracy doing with Essie?

Tracy grasped the doll's lumpy waist and shook her so that her tiny head and limbs jerked in a grotesque dance. Then she dropped Essie into the hole and began shoveling dirt onto the doll. She looked around now and then, but she didn't see me there, watching her.

When she had filled in the hole, Tracy threw the shovel far out into the water, picked up the receiving blanket, and rose to her feet. Below those angelic hazel eyes, her lips formed a smile that was wicked. Her cheeks flushed bright red.

I must have made some small noise then, because she looked straight into the bracket and our eyes met. Her smile froze, her nostrils flared, her eyes widened. I backed away, but she charged into the bushes, grabbing me by the hair and dragging me into the clearing.

"What are you doing here, maggot head?" she hissed furiously.

"I was just going to the beach," I whispered frantically. I didn't want to cross my sister in this mood.

"You're not allowed to go that way," she said, smacking at my head. "I'm gonna tell Mother on you."

"Well, I'll tell what you did to Essie," I blurted out.

Immediately, I wished the words back. Tracy was a whirlwind of scratching claws, kicking feet, and biting teeth.

"Oh no you won't, you little bitch! Because if you do, you'll pay for it. Do you hear me? I'll make you so sorry, you'll want to die."

She was hissing as she pummeled me.

"Don't you think I know where you keep Patsy? I'll chop her into little pieces, and then I'll do the same thing to you! Some night while you're asleep, I'll get Mama's big kitchen knife and I'll chop you up with it."

I stared into her red, angry face—her eyes wild and mean, her mouth a furious grimace—and I believed her to my very core.

"Don't, Tracy," I sobbed. "I won't tell. I promise I won't tell anyone, ever."

"Swear it," she demanded, holding tight on to my wrist. She wrenched me to my knees. "Swear it on Daddy's life, and seal it with blood."

"I swear on Daddy's life," I sobbed, "I won't tell anyone."

"Now seal it."

She pulled a small penknife from her pocket, the one Daddy had given her last time he came to visit. Smiling coldly, she held it out to me. "Go ahead," she spat. "Seal it with blood."

Squeezing my eyes shut, I drew the little knife across my fingertip and squeezed a drop of blood onto the ground. "I seal it," I whispered.

"Just you remember," she hissed, grabbing back her knife. "You swore on Daddy's very life."

Then she turned and ran toward the hill, climbing the stairs two at a time.

I sat on the ground, trembling and sobbing.

I cried till my stomach hurt. Then I slowly climbed the thirty-two stone steps and headed for home, kicking small stones before me and cursing my sister with every step.

That evening, I sat at the picnic table in our kitchen, staring sadly at the food on my plate.

Mother had fried small cubes of Spam and potatoes in bacon fat—usually one of my favorite meals, topped with ketchup.

But tonight I felt as if a stone sat in my stomach. I pushed the little squares of meat and potato around in a puddle of grease and ketchup, listening to my two oldest sisters chatter.

Nancy had heard a rumor just before we left Indiana that Paul McCartney's wife was pregnant. Melinda indignantly pointed out that the latest *Tiger Beat* magazine had profiled Linda McCartney, with no mention of a pregnancy. Nancy said *Tiger Beat* wasn't a reliable source.

Glancing at my mother across the table, I felt like I could read her mind. How had she raised such a mindless, thoughtless group of chattering, noisy girls? Lord knows she tried hard to teach us. She took us to Sunday school and church every blessed Sunday, she read us Bible stories and parables, she prayed with us morning and mealtimes and night. What more could she do?

She caught my eye and smiled, reaching across the table to push my bangs from my forehead.

"What's the matter, Bethy? Aren't you hungry?" she asked.

I shook my head.

"My stomach hurts," I lied, glancing at Tracy sitting beside me on the picnic bench.

My sister was not having any trouble with her dinner. She was on her second helping of Spam, licking ketchup from her finger tips. She met my eyes briefly, then looked at Mother.

"Did you talk to Daddy today, Mother?" she asked sweetly.

"No, honey," Mother replied. "You know I talk to him on Saturdays."

"I hope he's all right," Tracy said, her brow creasing slightly.

"Why, of course he's all right, Tracy. He was just fine on Saturday. He said he was going up to Chicago this week. That's just a short trip."

Tracy set her fork aside and used her napkin to dab at the corners of her mouth.

"I just don't want anything bad to happen to him."

She kicked me under the table as she said it, but her eyes never left her plate.

Mother patted her hand.

"He's fine, Tracy. You don't need to worry. Your daddy is just fine."

I rose suddenly, feeling like I was going to throw up.

"What's the matter with you?" Tracy asked. "You look like you're going to puke."

"Tracy! Please don't use that word!" Mother rose and came around the table to me. "Are you all right, Bethany? You do look pale."

"Can I be excused?" I asked, not meeting her eyes.

"Surely, sweetheart. Why don't you go lie down in your room for a while?"

Before I could move, the door to the house swung open and Reana Mae burst in.

We all stared in openmouthed amazement. In 1969 in the Coal River Valley, one simply did not burst into another family's house—and we had never known Reana Mae to burst anywhere at all. But there she stood, red-cheeked and grinning.

Then, noting my mother's look, she stammered, "Oh, I'm sorry, Aunt Helen. I forgot to knock."

She backed toward the door, her cheeks growing redder by the minute.

"Nonsense, Reana Mae. Come in, don't be shy. Family doesn't have to knock."

Tracy's fork clanked against the pine floor.

"But, Mother," she protested, "you always tell us . . ."

"Hush, Tracy," Mother snapped. She walked toward Reana Mae, her arms opened. "Come in, sweetie, and tell us all about your day in St. Albans. What have you got behind your back?"

Reana was clutching a wrinkled paper bag behind her.

She ran into my mother's open arms and they sat on the worn, plaid sleeper sofa.

"I brought you something," she whispered.

She reached into the bag and pulled out a flat, white box tied with silver ribbon.

"Why, Reana Mae, you didn't need to bring us a present." Mother smiled.

She took the box from Reana, but before she could untie the ribbon, Reana said, "It's a box of chocolates . . . from Fannie May's. I knew you liked 'em."

"Well, yes, we do, Reana Mae. We surely do." Mother kissed the top of Reana's head. "Thank you, sweetheart. What a lovely thing to do."

Mother opened the box, and we could see the assortment of chocolate candies laid out so prettily inside.

"Who wants a chocolate?" Mother asked, still smiling.

Melinda and Tracy crowded in to choose a piece. Nancy hovered, declaring she would not have any. She didn't want to gain weight before cheerleading tryouts in the fall. But she finally was prevailed upon to have just one piece, since Reana Mae and Bobby Lee had brought them especially for us.

I stood by the table, staring as Tracy chewed the chocolate-covered caramel she had chosen.

I couldn't believe she could eat Reana Mae's chocolates after what she'd done to Essie. Yet there she was, chewing noisily and eyeing the box hungrily, spying out which piece to have next.

Reana looked up at me eagerly. "Ain't you gonna have a candy, Bethany?"

I shook my head, unable to open my mouth for fear I'd scream.

"Bethany has a tummy ache, Reana. We'll save her a piece for tomorrow." Mother's hand still rested on Reana's shoulder.

Reana Mae suddenly bent forward, rustling in the bag again. "I almost forgot. I brought these, too," she said, holding up several magazines. "Daddy thought you all might want 'em."

Nancy and Melinda eagerly snatched the magazines. "*Photoplay*," Melinda squealed, "and *Teen Beat*! Thanks, Reana!"

The older girls soon disappeared up the ladder to their loft with another piece of chocolate each and the magazines. I knew we wouldn't see them again for the night. Mother didn't even remind them to wash the dishes. She sat smiling on the couch with Reana Mae and Tracy, letting her girls enjoy the small holiday.

"Tell us about your day, Reana Mae," she said.

Reana stared adoringly at her.

"Well, we went to the movie theater and saw *Chitty Chitty Bang Bang*. And Daddy bought us some popcorn and Jujubes and Coca-Colas. And we had lunch at Woolworth's. And he bought Mama some fabric to make herself a dress and one for me, too. And he bought me a comb and brush set. You got to see it, Aunt Helen. It's powdery blue, and the brush is round and soft, and it's so pretty. And then we had us some ice cream cones at the Tastee Freez and came on home. And Daddy took the turns so fast on the road, we almost touched the ground. But I didn't squeal or nothin'; I just held on real tight to him, like I seen Mama do. And he said I was almost as brave as Mama!"

Reana beamed proudly, and my mother touched her hair softly.

"You are a good, brave girl, Reana Mae," she said.

"Shoot, I guess anyone would be brave with Bobby Lee," Tracy spat. "Anyone can see he's a safe rider. What's there to be afraid of?"

"I think I'd be afraid." Mother laughed lightly, but I could see she wasn't pleased. She never let us ride on the motorcycle with Bobby Lee, although sometimes she let us ride in the sidecar. "I hope he didn't ride too fast with you, Reana."

"Oh no, Aunt Helen. My daddy's a real good rider, you know."

"Of course I do. And I'm glad you had a fun day together."

"Lord God in Heaven." Reana stood abruptly. "I gotta get back home. I promised Mama I'd help her put supper on the table."

She skittered to the door and was gone in an instant, leaving behind chocolates and ribbons.

When Reana Mae had gone, Mother made me lie down in bed while she and Tracy washed the dishes. I heard them clatter around the small kitchen, Tracy chattering about what she would do on a day in St. Albans.

I was still awake when Tracy came in. I lay quietly as she pulled back the covers and crawled into the double bed beside me. She sighed, pulled the quilt up over her head, and almost immediately fell into the deep, regular breathing that told me she was asleep. Whatever she did or didn't do during her days, my sister's conscience never kept her awake nights. She always slept the sleep of the innocent.

I lay quietly beside her, wondering what I could possibly do. I couldn't tell anyone what Tracy had done, that much I knew for sure. But what would Reana Mae do without Essie?

I shuddered, thinking of poor Essie buried under the black mud by the river. I couldn't leave her there. I would have to go get her . . . that was all there was to it.

It seemed like hours before I heard my mother pull out the sleeper sofa in the living room and blow out the kerosene lamp. It was quiet in the house then—quieter than it ever got at home in Indianapolis, where there were always street sounds outside.

Still I waited, because I knew Mother was at her prayers now. I couldn't see her in the dark, but I knew she was kneeling beside the sofa, her face buried in her hands, her lips moving silently as she talked to her God. She did this every morning and every night, and woe to the little girl who shouted or laughed or disturbed Mother's conversations with the almighty Lord.

At long last, I heard the creaking springs of the sleeper as Mother climbed into bed. And a while after that, I heard her gentle, regular breathing.

Now there were only the sounds of sleep in the dark little cabin by the river. Tracy wheezed slightly beside me, Mother snored softly in the living room, Melinda and Nancy slept silently in the loft above. Now it was time to go, before I lost my nerve.

I crept into the living room, fumbled for the key on the hook by the door, turned it in the lock, and slipped out onto the porch. I closed the door again, slid the key under a large rock by the steps, and then I was running down the dirt road, my bare feet slapping the ground, my heart pounding.

The night sky was lit by a nearly full moon, but below lay a silent, palpable, living darkness. No streetlights shone along the river, no porch lights, no spotlights from car dealerships, no traffic lights. The moon was bright, but off the road on either side, the woods closed in darkly.

I had never been out alone at night, and I slowed to a walk when I got past Uncle Hobie's place. I felt brave and shivery and very alert, seeing the familiar houses locked up and dark. The air on my skin was cool and damp, and I stopped for a moment to enjoy the strange sensation of being alone in the night. Everyone I knew, everyone who knew me, was asleep. I felt like I might be the only person awake in the whole wide world.

Down the river somewhere a dog barked, shaking me from my reverie. I had to get done what I needed to do and get home before I was missed.

I ran along the road, swift and sure. I knew every bump and

rock, where to stay on the dirt, where to run in the grass alongside. It took only a minute to reach Reana Mae's house. It was dark like all the others. Bo, Bobby Lee's big coonhound, lay sleeping on the porch. I worried briefly that he would bark at me if he woke, but he only sighed in his sleep as I passed. I knew Jolene kept Buttons, her little white muff of a poodle, inside at night, for which I was grateful. Buttons, I was sure, would have barked her fool head off.

I slipped around to the back of the house and stopped at the top of the hill, undecided about how to go down. Usually, Reana Mae and I slid down to the bank below. I didn't think I wanted to try that in the dark, in my white cotton nightgown. But I surely did not want to navigate those thirty-two uneven stone steps in the dark. I stood, frozen in indecision, my stomach clenching, my palms sweating.

I sat down at the top of the hill, staring at the steps, those uneven steps. How could I do this in the dark, Lord? After all, I was only ten years old—much too young to do something like this. And yet, how could I not rescue Essie?

Finally, I scooted slowly toward the edge of the first step, then bumped down on my bottom to the next. I would scoot down this way, one step at a time. And I wouldn't look down at all, no matter what.

One step after another, I bumped my way down. Halfway down, I stopped to say a quick prayer.

Lord, just help me get down okay and get Essie out of the mud. That's all, Lord, just that. If you'll do that, Lord Jesus, I promise I'll be good from now on. I won't ever tell a lie again, and I won't fight with Tracy, and I won't try Mother's patience. Only just get me down without falling.

I waited for my heart to stop pounding so loud, then I slid to the next step, and on down—slowly, one uneven step at a time—till I got to the bottom, where I sat gratefully for an instant, saying thank you to the good Lord, not thinking of how I would get up again.

It took only a moment to find the place where Tracy had laid poor Essie in the ground. The dirt was mounded slightly, and I knew she wasn't buried deep. Using my hands, I dug as quickly as I could until I felt Essie's smooth rubber head. I pulled the doll from her shallow grave and hugged her tightly to my chest, heaving gratefully.

Clutching the wet doll in my fist, I started the long, slow climb up those thirty-two steps. My heart was pounding so hard it seemed I could hear it beating like an Indian's tom-tom.

Then quietly, under my breath, I began to sing: "Amazing grace, how sweet the sound that saved a wretch like me. I once was lost, but now am found, was blind, but now I see."

By the end of the third verse, I had dragged myself onto the top step. Looking back over my shoulder, down the long flight I had climbed, I swayed. My head swam dizzily and, for a moment, I thought my knees would buckle under me.

I turned away and walked unsteadily to the front of the dark cabin, where good ole Bo still slept. I laid Essie on the step to the porch, then turned and ran as fast as I could toward home, and my bed, and my mother's gentle snoring. As my feet pounded the dirt road, I prayed with every step, *Dear, sweet Jesus, let them still be asleep. Please don't let them wake up till I'm home.*

I reached the cabin porch, cold and sweating, and as I knelt to retrieve the key from beneath the rock, I realized I was covered with mud; my hands and face, my feet, and my white nightgown were all a black, muddy mess.

I walked around to the side of the house, slipped off the nightgown, and shoved it deep into the bushes, resolving to wash it in the river in the morning, before Mother saw it. Shivering in the cool night air, I ran to the pump in front of the house and pumped icy-cold water onto my hands, my face, my feet and legs.

Then, clenching my teeth to keep them from chattering, I unlocked the cabin door, crept inside, hung the key on its hook, and padded to my room.

Heaving a huge sigh of relief, I pulled a clean nightgown over my head and crawled into bed beside Tracy. Then I snuggled myself around her curled back, thankful for the heat from her body. Tracy may have been as mean as a cornered possum during the day, but she put off heat like a cookstove and she slept like a bear. On cold winter nights at home, I often left my own bed in the converted attic that was our room and climbed into bed with my sister, soaking up her warmth. And in all the years of our childhood, she never woke or complained of it. For that, at least, my sister was a blessing.

As my body warmed against hers and my teeth stopped clattering, I finally relaxed into the pillow and allowed myself to drift off to sleep—secure in the knowledge that I had fixed the wrong Tracy had done, without bringing a curse down upon myself or my father.

But my sleep was restless and filled with dreams. I dreamed that Reana Mae was buried up to her neck in thick, black mud by the river. And Tracy, smiling wicked, was shoveling dirt onto her head. In the dream, I couldn't move, couldn't help Reana, couldn't make a sound. And all the while, Reana Mae screamed.

4

Signs and Wonders

I struggled to wake myself from the awful dream.
Finally, I opened my eyes to see the sun just peeking through the parted curtains of the little room I shared with Tracy, who still slept soundly beside me.

But the screaming continued, even when my eyes were wide open. I was not dreaming. What was happening?

I slid out of bed and ran into the living room, just in time to see Mother fling open the front door and run out onto the porch. I followed her as she ran down the step, into the yard, and out to the road, her blue housecoat flapping behind her, her hair still pinned to her head with a small army of bobby pins.

I didn't call to her as I ran; I simply followed her as best I could, racing down the road in my nightgown for the second time in eight hours, wondering at the sight of my mother out in public in her bobby pins.

As we passed Uncle Hobie's, I saw Aunt Vera peek through the curtains at us, then pull them shut again.

The screaming continued. I knew it was Reana Mae. We rounded the curve in the road and I saw her on the sagging porch of her house, crouched down, her hands covering her head.

"No, Mama, don't!" she was crying, over and over. "Don't, Mama, please don't!"

Jolene stood over the small, huddled body. She was still in her nightgown—a tiny slip of pink-flowered nylon—and she held one of Bobby Lee's belts by the buckle. She smacked the belt against Reana Mae's back again and again. Her face was mottled crimson, her red hair fell in tangles over her nearly bare shoulders, and she shook with rage as she swung the belt. Her mouth hung slightly open. She said nothing.

I stopped in the road, transfixed at the sight of her. But Mother ran into the yard, letting the wooden gate swing shut behind her. I don't believe she even knew I was there.

"Jolene! Stop it! What are you doing?" she cried.

Jolene did not look up. She just kept hitting Reana Mae. The belt made a sickening smack each time it met with flesh.

"You stay out of this, Helen," she said. "This don't concern you."

"But what happened?" Mother stood at the foot of the porch, just out of range of the swinging belt. "Why are you doing this?"

Reana Mae had stopped screaming now and was huddled in a small, sobbing heap.

"She went and ruined her own doll baby," Jolene yelled, bringing the belt down hard on her daughter's back. "The one her daddy brung her all the way from Atlanta. The one he paid for with good, hard-earned cash money. Look at it!" she screamed, pointing at poor Essie sprawled on the ground by the porch stop. "Look at what she done to her doll!"

"No, Mama!" Reana Mae cried out. "I didn't do that! I didn't, Mama."

"Don't you lie to me!" Jolene screamed, swinging the belt again.

"Jolene, stop it!" Mother was on the porch now, grabbing at Jolene's arm. She wrested the belt from Jolene's hand, pushing her backward into the wall of the cabin.

"Stop it now." Her voice became quiet, soothing. "Where's Bobby Lee, Jolene? Is he at the store? Is he coming back soon?"

Jolene didn't answer. She jerked away from Mother, righted herself, and stood silently for a long moment, staring at my mother in obvious rage, her fists slowly clenching and unclenching. I thought she was going to hit Mother, but then she turned abruptly and walked back into the house without a word, slamming the door behind her.

Mother crouched down by Reana Mae, wrapping her arms around Reana's shaking body and lifting her up.

"Get the doll, Bethany," she said to me quietly.

Reana Mae's arms curled around her neck, Mother carried her out of the yard and down the road, crooning softly all the while. I followed, holding poor Essie by the arm. Of course, in the moonlight I had not seen it, but the doll was a wet, muddy mess. I held her small cloth body to mine and walked miserably behind my mother, trying not to cry.

When I raised my eyes from the road, I saw Tracy standing at the bend. She stared at Reana Mae, her face white, her eyes round. Her fist was shoved against her mouth and she was visibly shaking. On down the road, Melinda and Nancy were standing on our porch in their pajamas, hair still wrapped around the orange juice cans they slept in each night.

"What's happening, Mother?" Melinda asked.

"Come inside, girls," Mother said quietly. "Let's get ourselves dressed and have breakfast. Everything is fine. It's going to be all right."

She walked past Tracy into the yard, up the steps, and into the house. In the road, Tracy stood absolutely still except for the shaking. I thought she might shake herself completely into pieces. I stopped beside her, still clutching Essie.

"Look at what you did," I hissed.

She raised her eyes to mine and stared mutely. I had never seen her look like that. She looked younger and helpless and completely lost. She stared for a minute, then turned and ran toward the beach. I watched her in disbelief. Should I go after her? I had never felt sorry for Tracy before, but right then I did. Even after what she had done to Essie, I felt sorry for her. But I didn't go after her. I looked down at poor Essie, dirty and wet in my hands, and went into the house to be with Reana Mae.

She was sitting by Mother on the couch, still crying. I heard Melinda and Nancy in the kitchen, getting out bowls for cereal.

"Hush now," Mother crooned. "Everything is going to be all right. You're all right now."

Looking up, she nodded at me. "Bethany, why don't you get dressed and find something for Reana Mae to wear."

She took Reana into the bathroom, and I heard Reana cry out as Mother dabbed Mercurochrome on the open welts along her back and legs. Then Reana Mae put on my nicest sundress, and we all sat down to Cheerios and toast. Mother didn't ask where Tracy was; I'm not sure she even noticed Tracy was gone.

Reana spent the whole day with us. We listened to the radio, threw sticks in the river, ate bologna and cheese sandwiches, and cut out paper dolls. Tracy showed up late morning, silently dressed herself, and went to bed, where she stayed till lunchtime. After lunch, Mother took her and Reana and me to the laundromat in St. Albans and bought us Snickers bars while she washed a load of permanent press shirts and Essie in the big washing machine. Reana Mae and I pushed each other in the rolling laundry baskets. Tracy sat quietly on a metal folding chair beside Mother, clenching and unclenching her hands, watching us play.

When Essie came out of the washer, she was sodden and heavy, but clean as ever. Mother wrung out her cloth body and handed her to Reana Mae to hug.

"I'm afraid to put her in the dryer," she said, "but I think she'll dry out by tomorrow."

She put Essie's yellow-flowered dress in the dryer with the shirts, then sat back down with her *Ladies' Home Journal*. Reana Mae and I took turns pushing Essie around in the laundry basket, and still Tracy sat silently, watching us.

When the drying was finished, we all helped to fold. Then we climbed back into Uncle Hobie's Chevy, which Mother had borrowed for the day. Reana and I sat in the back, with Essie on the seat between us. Tracy sat in front with Mother. I saw her lean over and whisper to Mother, then saw Mother smile and nod. Tracy turned to the backseat.

"That old doll needs a new dress," she said. "We're gonna stop at Woolworth's and get one for her."

Reana Mae smiled at Tracy hopefully.

"Will you choose one, Tracy?" she asked.

"Yeah." Tracy shrugged her shoulders. "I'll find her a good one."

Mother smiled at her. I wanted to scream, "It's her fault! It's all her!" But I sat still, holding Essie's little plastic hand, and wondered at my sister.

When we got home, I had even more cause to wonder when I saw Tracy take a dollar from her dresser drawer and hand it to my mother, in payment for the doll's new pink dress. Mother smiled down at her and kissed her soft auburn hair.

Would wonders never cease? Tracy Janelle Wylie buying a dress for Reana Mae's doll. Not only that, she actually sat and played dolls with Reana that afternoon.

I lay on the couch, watching them in wonder. I was stunned that Reana Mae would even want to play with Tracy. I couldn't understand why she would, since Tracy was nothing but mean to her most of the time. I wished mightily that I could tell Reana—and Mother, too—that it was Tracy who had nearly ruined Essie. But of course, I couldn't. I'd sworn on Daddy's life.

I wondered, not for the first time, why Tracy was so mean. Nancy and Melinda were sometimes thoughtless, but they weren't mean. Daddy and Mother certainly weren't mean. No one else I knew was that mean. Well, maybe Jolene was mean sometimes . . . but not like Tracy. Tracy was mean for no reason. Sometimes she was downright vicious.

And then, just when I thought she couldn't possibly get any meaner, she would go and do something kind . . . like buy a dress for Essie.

I shook my head as I watched my sister playing dolls with Reana Mae. Tracy was, indeed, a mystery.

After supper, just as it began to get dark, Jolene knocked at our door. Without a word, Reana Mae picked up the pink-frocked Essie and her old, yellow-flowered dress and followed her mother home.

Tracy and Mother and I stood on the porch and watched them go. Jolene's arm draped lightly across Reana Mae's shoulders.

We didn't know where Bobby Lee had been that day. Jolene never said. And we didn't know then just how often Reana Mae took treatment like that from her mama.

Later, we learned it all. But that day, we thought the storm had passed.

5

A Harsh Mistress

Jolene loved Bobby Lee, that's for certain. No one could say she didn't love her husband. But it was a grasping, sucking kind of love that didn't leave room in her life, or in his, for anyone else.

I suppose she loved like that because she didn't get a whole lot of love herself when she was a little girl.

EmmaJane—Jolene's mama—had run away from home a week after her seventeenth birthday, leaving her own parents, her job, and her steady beau behind. She'd been working downriver for the summer at the boardinghouse where my mother worked. And then, just like that, she was gone. No one in the valley knew why, though a lot of people weren't so very surprised at her sudden disappearance.

"Always trouble," Aunt Belle said of EmmaJane. "Too pretty for her own good, and raised by a damned fool."

Folks speculated that EmmaJane had run off with a man from the city, but no one knew for sure. And because they didn't know for years where EmmaJane had gone to or what she'd done, the stories that circulated ranged from the exotic to the ludicrous. Her mama was convinced she'd been kidnapped by white slavers. Some people said she'd gone off to Hollywood. Others whispered that she'd drowned herself over a failed love affair. Her forlorn beau waited almost two years for her return, before finally marrying a girl from St. Albans and moving away.

The truth was that EmmaJane had got herself pregnant and gone off to hide her shame. She took the bus up to Huntington, rented a cheap apartment, and found a job in a hair salon, setting herself up as a single mother in a time and place where that wasn't so fashionable as it is nowadays.

Jolene was left pretty much to raise herself, coming home from school to an empty apartment in an old brick duplex by the train yards. She learned early to rely on herself. And she learned how to get what she needed from men. She learned that skill at the knees of a harsh mistress, indeed. Even all those years after EmmaJane died, Jolene remembered how cold her mother had been. "A mean bitch" is what she called EmmaJane, a term that made my mother blush.

One day, EmmaJane came home from work in the middle of the day, fired from her job for sassing the boss.

She gave Jolene a dollar and told her to go to the movies. As she left, Jolene heard her mother opening a beer.

When Jolene came home, she found her mother's body sprawled dead on the couch, four beer cans and a bottle of bourbon empty on the floor alongside a smaller but equally empty pill bottle.

It nearly broke Loreen's heart for her only daughter to die like that—by her own hand and alone in a cheap city apartment. Of course, Loreen never would believe that EmmaJane did it on purpose. No, Loreen insisted to her dying day, EmmaJane had died by accident, or maybe even been murdered.

When EmmaJane's landlady had called to tell them their daughter was dead, and would they come get their granddaughter, Ray and Loreen drove right up to Huntington, even though it meant borrowing Brother Harley's Buick and closing the store for a whole day. And even if it was the first time they even knew they had a granddaughter. Jolene was twelve when she came to the valley to live with Loreen and Ray. And by then, folks said, it was too late. She'd been city-spoiled. She cried for missing the radio, and a telephone in the house, and the bus to go shopping. But no one ever saw her cry for her mama—not even at the funeral. Oh, she'd been a handful, all right. She smoked and she swore and she stole from Ray's store. She skipped school, she got into fights, and twice she ran away—one time getting all the way up to Huntington before Ray found her and brought her back home. She was hard and smart-mouthed and sullen. Just like EmmaJane. Nearly drove her poor grandma to distraction, even after she married Bobby Lee.

The only person Jolene ever really listened to was my mother. Probably that was because Mother really listened to her, too. It was a puzzle why Mother was so patient with her. She was almost old enough to be Jolene's mother, but she acted more like a sister to her. Even when we were in Indianapolis, Mother worried over Jolene. She sent her letters and coupons and gifts, and she tried to show Jolene how to be a mama.

One thing was certain, though—Jolene never learned to be a mama. But Reana Mae did have some family who loved her. Loreen fussed over her. Ray was quietly fond of her, letting Reana Mae spend her days at his store, reading to her from the *National Geographic* magazines he collected, and teaching her to read and write before she was even five.

And then, of course, I loved her. Between the two of us, we made a sisterhood of misfits that sustained us both for a long time.

❧ 6 ❧

A Time to Give Thanks

We tumbled out of the wood-paneled station wagon, cramped and tired from the eight-hour drive, and stared at the scene before us. The valley looked like a picture postcard—a soft-focus watercolor of rural Appalachia. The hills and trees and bushes, the cabins and outhouses, the pumps and split-rail fences were frosted white. I had never been to the river in winter before, and the landscape I knew as well as I knew my own name looked foreign, the familiar markers blanketed in snow. Even our cabin looked strange under a foot of snow. But someone had shoveled a path to the front door for us.

"Okay, girls, stop gaping and start carrying," Daddy hollered, opening the tailgate. "No one uses the bathroom till the car's unloaded!"

"Now, that's some incentive you got goin' there!"

We turned to see Bobby Lee in the open door of the cabin, laughing.

"I got you a fire goin'." He grinned. "Figured you'd need it after the drive."

Daddy strode onto the porch and shook Bobby Lee's hand. Mother hugged him. "Thank you, Bobby Lee. How thoughtful of you. Is Jolene with you?"

"I'm here, Helen." Jolene was just inside the door, a blue apron tied around her waist. The smell of fresh cinnamon rolls wafted from the cabin. Mother's eyes widened in surprise—Jolene was not known for her domestic skills. But she smiled and hugged Jolene tight, then reached for Reana Mae, standing just behind her mother, clutching a wooden spoon. The front of her gray sweatshirt was dusted with flour, and she was smiling shyly.

"Come on, girls. Let's get moving!" Daddy returned to the business of unloading the car. Bobby Lee and Reana Mae joined us, carrying the suitcases, boxes, and bags into the cabin. Mother and Jolene stayed inside, unpacking groceries in the kitchen. Bobby Lee and Jolene always opened the cabin for us when we came down, but never had they been such a welcome sight. The kerosene lamps and fire in the wood-burning stove made a small oasis of light and warmth in the frosty late afternoon, and as soon as we had brought in our luggage and made our hurried visits—clutching a roll of toilet paper—to the outhouse, we unwrapped ourselves from layers of coats and mufflers and hats, and gathered around the stove.

Mother made coffee for the grown-ups and cocoa for us. Jolene passed around cinnamon rolls warm from the oven. We were home for the holidays, spending Thanksgiving at the river. Best of all, Daddy was with us to stay for the whole week. I thought I would split my face open from grinning so wide.

Reana Mae was showing me the new dress and coat, with matching hat and muff, that Loreen had sewn for Essie, when we heard the tramp of boots on the back porch. The door swung open and the frame was filled with a bearlike shape, bundled head to toe in dark wool. The creature was carrying a huge armful of firewood. I shrank back into the couch behind Mother.

"Here's more wood, Bobby," said the bear, dropping the wood onto the pile by the stove. Now I could see it was a man—a big man pulling a dark brown ski mask off his head. Then, as he noted the crowd of people in the room, the man's cheeks turned a dark red, and I realized it wasn't even a man at all—it was a great big boy.

"Sorry," he mumbled. "Didn't know you all was here."

Bobby Lee had risen and was standing beside the big boy. "Jim, Helen, you remember my little brother, Caleb?"

Daddy rose to shake the bear-boy's hand. With his ski mask off, I could see that Caleb looked a bit like Bobby Lee—younger and not so handsome, but with the same dark brown eyes, the same straight nose, the same shock of black curly hair falling across his forehead. But where Bobby Lee carried the features with a confident, slightly macho grace, Caleb looked like a hulking bear—his eyes glancing kind of sideways at you, dark with suspicion.

"Caleb's stayin' with us for a piece, till Mama gets herself settled somewhere. He's been a big help around the house, what with my schedule pickin' up so. I don't know what Jolene would do without him these days." Bobby Lee flopped back down onto the picnic bench beside Jolene. "Ain't that right, sugar?"

"Oh yeah." Jolene smiled back at him. "He's a great helper all right."

Then she glanced at my mother, just for an instant, and I could see in that look she was lying. Her green cat-eyes were narrowed slightly, her mouth drawn into a tight line. Funny, when she looked that way, she seemed suddenly old—lines creasing her forehead, small crow's feet around her eyes. Then she turned back to Bobby Lee, and she was herself again—pretty, plump Jolene. "I just wish your schedule would let up some, that's all."

Bobby Lee laughed, looking away from her. "If I'm gonna build you that loft you keep naggin' about, I gotta be doin' more long hauls to pay for it, now, don't I?" He grinned at my father and shook his head. "Jolene says she's gotta have a upstairs loft like you all got here, so Reana Mae can have her some privacy. With an extra body about, it's gettin' a might crowded at home."

"Especially when the body's so dang big," Jolene added, glancing at Caleb, who was standing awkwardly by the cabin door, still wearing his coat.

Mother rose, offering her hand to Caleb. "Why don't you sit down here, Caleb, and I'll get you some cocoa."

"No, thank ye, ma'am," he mumbled. "I gotta get on back home. Got things to do, you know."

With that, he fumbled for the handle of the door.

"We'll be home shortly, Caleb," Bobby Lee called after him. "Don't be gettin' yourself into any nonsense, you hear?"

Daddy turned inquiring eyes to him, and Bobby Lee grinned sheepishly. "He's a handful, that one. Always into something or other, especially since Mama left. But he's a good kid, Jimmy. He's okay."

Jolene had joined Mother in the kitchen, where a new batch of rolls was coming out of the oven. From the couch, I could see the two women talking, but their voices didn't carry into the room. Jolene had that pained look again; Mother looked worried, too. I knew this was the trouble Jolene had not wanted in her house, and I wondered how Caleb had ended up with them. I'd always figured Jolene ruled the roost at home. Maybe she didn't, after all.

Nancy and Melinda had climbed the ladder to their loft. I could hear them above, putting their room to order. Nancy was particular about where everything went, and they always took a long time, setting things up just so. Tracy sat at Daddy's feet, listening to the men talk. She loved being part of the adult conversation, and she adored Bobby Lee. At home she would sometimes compare boys she knew at school to her grown-up cousin.

"Oh, he's okay," she would say about some pimply Romeo. "But he sure doesn't carry himself like Bobby Lee."

I knew she wouldn't move unless Daddy ordered her to. So I pulled Reana Mae into our room, figuring now was the time to catch up in private. Summers, we had the whole outdoors to wander. Wintertime on the river, privacy didn't come cheap.

I admired Essie's new ensemble again, then asked about all the people I could think of. Harley Boy had won the spelling bee at school, beating out a sixth grader even. Cousin Lottie was saying real words now. Lottie's older sister, Ruthann, had herself a real boyfriend.

"But," Reana whispered, grinning slyly, "she ain't kissed him yet. She's gonna make him wait till Christmas for that."

Ruthann was in the fourth grade with Reana Mae at the grade school in town. They rode the school bus together, an hour each way every day—except when it snowed. Then the bus didn't run and the kids along the river went to Ida Louise's house for their lessons. All things considered, they preferred school to Ida Louise.

"How about you?" I asked, grinning at her. "You got a boyfriend yet?"

Her cheeks colored and she shook her head. "Who'd look at me?"

"I always thought Harley Boy looked at you kinda sweet," I teased.

"Naw, Bethany," she mumbled, her cheeks getting redder. "I know I ain't pretty. Mama says she don't know how she got a daughter like me, and I reckon she's right. She figures I'll probably stick with her always, 'cause won't nobody else want me."

"That's not true, Reana Mae," I said, holding her hand. "You've got your mama's pretty eyes. And Mother says you're going to be beautiful when you get older."

It was true, Mother said that sometimes. I never understood how she could, seeing that Reana was certainly not pretty now. But Mother just smiled and said to wait, Reana Mae would surprise us all.

"Does she really? Does she say that?" Reana Mae's eyes widened. Then she smiled shyly. "Caleb says I'm pretty, too," she whispered.

I stared at her in amazement. What did that bear-boy know about pretty?

"What's he like?"

"Caleb? Oh, he's all right. He makes Mama mad a lot, 'cause he's so big and clumsy, and he breaks things sometimes. And he gets into trouble, too, and won't listen to Mama. Seems like only Daddy can make him mind, and Daddy ain't home much these days."

Reana Mae's brow furrowed as she straightened Essie's coat.

"He's real nice to me, though." She smiled. "He even bought me a scarf from the Woolworth in St. Albans, a pink woolly one for school. But Mama don't like me to wear it." She sighed unhappily.

"How long is he gonna live with you?" I asked.

"Well, Daddy says just for a while. Just till Mamaw gets a new place to live where Caleb can finish school. He's sixteen, you know, so he's supposed to go to school. And he don't go here, 'cause he can't get along with the teachers at the high school. He says they got it in for him 'cause he lived in the city before."

She smiled sidelong at me, and just for a minute, she did look almost pretty. She was nine now and had rounded out a bit, looking less like a reed and more like a healthy girl. She'd also started braiding her dark blond hair back, so it wasn't such a tangled mess.

"Anyway, Daddy says just for a while, but Mama thinks he's here to stay. She says Mamaw don't want Caleb with her 'cause she can't make him mind her no more." She laid the doll down and stretched. "I hope he does stay."

"Why?" I asked. "He looks so mean."

"Yeah," she agreed. "He does look mean. And he's got hisself a nasty temper, truth be told. Buttons is sore afraid of him, that's for sure." She laughed guiltily. Neither of us much liked Jolene's ill-tempered poodle. Both of us had felt her sharp little teeth.

"But he's kind mostly," she continued. "And he talks to me and asks me things like he really wants to know what I think. I like him."

Jolene appeared in the doorway to tell Reana it was time to go. We were going to Aunt Belle's for supper, and they had to get back home and check on Caleb.

"Lord knows," Jolene said with a sigh, "if we're gone too long he's like to burn the house down. Or worse."

Bobby Lee laughed. "Aw now, Jolene, he's just sowing him some oats. That's what boys his age is supposed to do." He winked at my daddy. "Boys is supposed to sow wild oats, ain't that so, Jimmy? It's in their nature, that's all."

Jolene turned away from him abruptly. "Reana Mae! What on God's green earth is takin' you so long?"

They bundled up and left, walking single-file down the tire tracks in the road. Mother and Daddy stood in the cabin doorway, watching them go.

"Lord have mercy." Daddy sighed, his arm around Mother's waist. "They sure have taken on a load."

"It's trouble," Mother agreed, shaking her head, her lips in a tight, thin line. "Nothing but trouble."

* * *

Aunt Belle's house on Thanksgiving was filled with family and laughter and good smells. All the women had been there since sunup, stirring, kneading, tasting, and gossiping. All but my mother had been nipping from the bottle a bit as well. By the time we ate in the early afternoon, their cheeks were pink from kitchen heat and the good Kentucky bourbon Aunt Belle kept on hand.

When Tracy and I came in with Daddy from chopping firewood, the smells of corn bread, pecan pies, smoked ham, hot biscuits, sage, and cinnamon nearly knocked us back out the door. My mouth watered just thinking of all the food. Best of all, I knew out back in the spare kitchen, Belle's housekeeper, Donna Jo, was roasting the biggest, juiciest turkey in the valley.

We sat down to tables spread with every good thing you could imagine. Loreen had made corn bread and sweet potatoes topped with sticky, melted marshmallows. Jolene brought candied carrots and green beans boiled to a pulp with bacon fat. Belle's offering—made with her own two hands, as she proclaimed loudly—was a silver tray piled high with bourbon balls, sweet concoctions heavily soaked in liquor and rolled in powdered sugar.

Uncle Joe, Bobby Lee's grandfather who had been married to my Great-Aunt Arathena before she died, had driven in from Tennessee, bringing boxed chocolates, bottles of Coca-Colas, and more bourbon. Nancy and Melinda had spent half the morning under Donna Jo's direction, mashing potatoes with butter, warm cream, and pepper until not a lump survived. Mother had made her fancy sugar cream pies and a big pot of cooked cranberries. Aunt Vera and Uncle Hobie brought two enormous hams smoked in their own smokehouse and smothered with brown sugar and caramelized sweet onions. Donna Jo supplied the rest—huge lard biscuits, stuffing rich with sage, roasted turkey, creamed corn, strong coffee, and a sweet mix of canned fruits, dried coconut, and tiny colored marshmallows in a sour cream sauce. Heaven!

Even Belle's big table wouldn't hold all her clan, so Donna Jo had set up card tables in the living room. After she carried in the turkey—to a round of applause—Donna Jo sat down with the rest of us to eat. Her own husband was long dead and her children had moved from the valley years before. Her rough red hands spoke eloquently of the hard work she did for Belle, but at mealtimes she was just another woman at the table.

My daddy stood to ask the blessing. "Lord God in Heaven," he intoned solemnly, "how grateful we are to be gathered together as a family today."

I peeked around—I never could keep my eyes closed for prayers—and saw Caleb at the next table, staring at the empty seat he had saved for his mother. Cleda Rae had said she would be with us today, and she hadn't even called Belle to say otherwise.

"We ask your blessings, Lord, upon those who are gathered here today, and upon those who could not be here with us . . . because of the snow or other circumstances we cannot know."

Then I knew my daddy was worrying about Caleb and Bobby Lee, too.

"Bless this food to our bodies, and us to thy service, O Lord. Amen."

"Amen," we all echoed. I saw Bobby Lee reach over to clap his hand on Caleb's shoulder.

Then we ate, and ate, and ate. And the grown-ups talked, and talked, and talked.

We didn't have a children's table at Aunt Belle's. Everyone just sat where they happened to sit—except for Belle, of course, who always sat at the head of the big table, a decanter of bourbon beside her plate. I sat with Reana Mae, Uncle Joe, and Loreen. At the card table next to us were Caleb, Bobby Lee, and Aunt Vera, with Cousin Lottie in the high chair. Farther on, Ruthann was sitting unhappily at a table with her daddy (my Uncle Hobie), Nancy, and Melinda. Ruthann was sulking because she had wanted to sit with Reana Mae and me, but by the time she got there, the table was full. Uncle Hobie was trying his best to involve Nancy and Melinda in a conversation, but they simply answered him as briefly as they could and then pointedly ignored him and Ruthann. Tracy, of course, had managed a seat at the big table between Mother and Daddy. Somehow, she always managed that. She sat next to Daddy, smiling sweetly, quiet as a church mouse—like she might just sprout a halo at any minute.

Cousin Lottie, when she had eaten all the sweet onions at her own table, toddled from table to table, begging for more. "Onon?" she burbled sweetly, and no one—not even her sister, Ruthann— could resist. I'm not sure Lottie ate much that day besides onions and sugar cream pie.

When we had eaten until we could not eat any more, Donna Jo brought out the pies and the bourbon balls and the fresh-whipped cream and the strong, black coffee, and we were persuaded to eat "just a mouthful" more. Aunt Belle was cutting the pies when the front door creaked open and Cleda Rae burst in, bundled from head to toe in some kind of dark purple fake fur and carrying a six-pack of beer. "Hey, ya'll, here I am!" she called out.

Caleb was on his feet in an instant, rising so suddenly he knocked his chair over—and very nearly the table, too. "Mama!" he called, and I stared in amazement. In that moment he didn't look like a bear at all, but just like any other boy. In the next instant, his features changed and he was once again dark, suspicious, looking for all the world like a great bear. I turned to see what could bring about such a transformation. A man stood just behind Cleda Rae, holding another six-pack of beer.

Bobby Lee was on his feet, too. In an instant he was at the door and had wrapped his mother in a tight embrace. The man stood quietly behind them, grinning uncertainly. Cleda Rae disengaged herself from her older son, set down her six-pack, smiled brightly, and exclaimed loudly, "I hope ya'll don't mind, I brought along a friend with me." She turned to the man standing behind her and took him by the arm, drawing him forward.

"Bobby Lee, Belle, everyone, this here is Mr. Ephraim Turner from up to Huntington. His folks are all away down south today, so I asked him to join us for the holiday. I hope that's all right with you, Belle," she added, turning to Aunt Belle, who was standing just behind Bobby Lee by this time.

"Course it is, Cleda Rae," Belle boomed. "We got plenty of room for friends today. Mr. Turner, why don't you just bring that beer on into the kitchen?" she continued, taking the man by the elbow and steering him into the other room.

"Cleda, let me take your coat." Jolene was there now, tugging the awful purple fur thing from Cleda Rae's shoulders.

"Ain't it just the smartest thing you ever seen?" Cleda simpered. "Ephraim bought it for me last week. He said that old coat I had before wouldn't keep a raccoon warm in summer. Jolene, honey, let me look at you. Puttin' on a little weight, sugar? Now, don't fret about it. It looks right good on you."

Turning from Jolene's grimace, Cleda Rae continued brightly, "Now, where's my Caleb?"

Caleb still stood where he had risen, never taking his eyes from his mother. His bushy brows seemed to meet in the middle of his forehead.

"Sugar boy, come on and give your mama a kiss." Cleda Rae held her arms out as she crossed the room toward him.

Caleb stood still for a second longer, then turned and bolted from the room, through the kitchen. An instant later, we heard the back door slam shut.

"He forgot his coat!" Reana cried, running to the front closet to retrieve it.

"Reana Mae! You sit yourself down this very instant!" Jolene's voice rang out, harsh and tinny.

"But, Mama . . ."

"He gets cold, he'll come for his coat," Jolene said flatly.

"Gracious glory," Cleda Rae exclaimed, frowning, "I don't understand that boy. Never have, never will. He's just like his daddy, that one, never does what he's supposed to."

"Mama, why don't you sit yourself down and get a plate of something to eat," Bobby Lee said, holding out a chair for his mother.

"Good Lord, no, honey. Ephraim and I, we done ate on the way down here—we got ourselves a hamburger at the Big Boy. I will have me a piece of that pie, though. Is that your sugar cream pie, Helen? I'd know it anywhere. Ephraim, honey, you come sit yourself down beside me and try a piece of Cousin Helen's sugar cream pie. If it ain't the best thing you ever ate, I'll tap-dance Dixie."

She cut a big slab of pie and put it down before the empty seat at the table, the one Caleb had just vacated. Mr. Ephraim Turner walked over uncertainly, righted the chair, and sat down. He ate the pie silently, never stopped smiling, and never said a word. Cleda Rae, on the other hand, never stopped talking.

"We'd have been here earlier, but poor Ephraim had to work today—on Thanksgiving Day, do you believe it? I thought it was a national holiday, but evidently some people still have to go to work. He works up to the hospital, you know. He's in charge of the whole, entire food service for the veterans hospital up in Hunting-ton." She smiled then, looking for all the world like a cat with a live mouse caught by the tail. "Imagine, the whole dang hospital!"

Cleda Rae was not over forty-five then, and still a pretty woman, though her years of hard living were beginning to show in the web of tiny lines around her eyes and mouth. She had dark brown, curly hair—though the curls were probably permed, even then. She was very thin and sharp-looking—all knees and elbows, it seemed. Her dark eyes never rested on any one place for long, and she chain-smoked unfiltered Camels from the day I met her until the day she died. She never stopped moving and she never stopped talking, and she never once seemed to care about anyone but Cleda Rae.

Mr. Ephraim Turner seemed a likely enough fellow—small, thin, smiling nervously. He wore a gray fedora, which he never re-moved throughout the day, and he didn't speak more than half a dozen words that day or any other time I saw him. Still, he was there and Cleda's no-good husband, Noah, was not, and that mat-tered enormously to Cleda Rae.

I didn't see Caleb again during that trip. He never came back to Aunt Belle's that day. Cleda Rae stayed until early evening, then bundled up in her purple fake fur and headed back to Huntington with her smiling, silent gentleman friend. Reana Mae and I watched them go with relief—I figure everyone there was relieved. Cleda's nonstop chatter made my head ache, and I knew Reana Mae and Bobby Lee were fretting over Caleb's conspicuous absence.

Once his mother and Mr. Turner had gone, Bobby Lee took Caleb's coat and went out to find him. Reana told me the next day they hadn't come back until late at night, and that Caleb had come home with a hacking cough and a fever.

"Can't you just reckon on how miserable he is, with his mama showin' up like that with a sugar daddy?" she said, shaking her head.

"A what?"

Reana smiled at me then the way a grown-up smiles at a child.

"A sugar daddy," she explained, "is a man who buys things for a woman and pays her rent and stuff, so she'll be nice to him. Like Mr. Turner buying Cleda Rae that coat and hat. He must have a whole pile of money. Why else would she be hanging on him like she was? My mama says it's just like Cleda Rae to find a sugar daddy to take care of her while we take care of Caleb."

I stared at her silently. Suddenly, she seemed older than me—not just my little cousin Reana Mae, but an initiate in the mysterious ways of adults. I shook my head and frowned. "Maybe she just likes him."

"Naw." Reana seemed sure. "He's her sugar daddy, all right. She probably lets him kiss her and touch her titties and everything, just to get that coat."

I was silent again. This was a Reana I didn't know and I wasn't sure I liked, either. Then, abruptly, she was herself again—just nine-year-old Reana Mae, sitting on a red-checkered bedspread, brushing Essie's hair with a round blue brush.

"I just worry about Caleb, that's all. Can't you imagine how sorry he must be for his mama's shame? He knows she don't want him with her, and that's bad enough. Then she comes down here with that man. She ain't even divorced from Noah yet. It's just purely hard on him, that's all."

I nodded sagely. It must, indeed, be hard. Caleb was just a boy, after all—I had seen that in his face when his mother first arrived. For that one instant, he looked like any other boy eager to see his mama. And then the way she'd behaved . . . even though he was big and gruff, I still felt sorry for him.

My conversations with Reana Mae that week were peppered with stories about Caleb. He had swum all the way across the river in September. Buttons wouldn't come near him because he'd kicked her clean across the room one day—by accident, he said, but Reana didn't believe it. He used Bobby Lee's shotgun to hunt with Uncle Ray, and he caught more fish than anyone else in the valley. He got in a fistfight with another boy at the high school, and then quit going to school. He could eat eleven pancakes at one sitting, and drink a whole pitcher of Tang. By the time we packed the car to head back for Indiana, I knew more about Caleb Colvin than I'd ever wanted to know.

Bobby Lee had already left on another long haul, so Jolene and Reana Mae came alone to wave good-bye. Mother hugged Jolene tight and I heard her whisper, "You just call us if you need anything, you hear?"

I was sitting in the back of the station wagon, watching through the window in amazement as Jolene hugged Mother back. Mother often hugged Jolene, but I'd never seen Jolene cling to Mother before. She had that tight, strained look again. It scared me.

I watched them out the back window of the car as we bumped down the snowy ruts in the road. Jolene had her arm around Reana's shoulders, and both of them were waving. Standing there like that, they looked more like mother and daughter than they ever had before. I realized with a start that Mother was right. Reana Mae was going to be beautiful someday.

7

The Innocent

In early January, I received my first letter from Reana Mae.

> Dear Bethany,
> Hi. How are you? I am doing very fine. I got this pretty paper and envelops for Christmas from Aunt Bell. She says I got a gift for writing because she read my school papers that Ida Lues gave to her. She said I got to practice my writing all the time, so I can grow up to be a famus writer some day. What do you think of that!!!!
> I got a very nice present from my mama and daddy. It is a radio for my own room, so I can listen to music when I am in bed. I can get the radio station from Charleston, and last night they played Strawberry Feilds by the Beetles. Do you know that song? It is so pretty it almost makes me cry ever time I here it.
> Caleb gave me some color pencils he got at the store in Sant Albans. There are lots of colors, so I can make you a picture at the bottom of this letter. What did you get from Christmas? Write back to me, and I will write back to you tow.
> Love your cousin
> Reana Mae Colvin

When I showed the letter to Mother, she took me right down to Murphy's and let me choose a box of stationery, so I could write back to Reana. I chose pale pink paper with dark pink lines and a cluster of strawberries in the bottom corner of each sheet. The envelopes had strawberries, too. Of course, when Tracy saw the box, she pitched such a fit that Mother drove back to Murphy's and let her pick out some stationery, too. I don't know who Tracy ever wrote to, but Reana Mae and I wrote letters back and forth that winter and for years afterward.

In February, I was the first one to hear about Jolene's pregnancy—and I announced it to the rest of the family over dinner.

"Jolene is having a baby."

Everyone turned to stare. Even Daddy put down the paper and looked. Mother stopped passing rolls in mid-motion, her arm outstretched like a statue.

"What did you say, Bethany?"

"Jolene is going to have a new baby." I smiled.

"How do you know?" Tracy jeered.

"Reana Mae wrote me a letter about it." At this, I whipped the letter out of my pocket and waved it in the air with a small flourish.

"Let me see that, honey." Mother took the letter from my hand, scanned the first few lines, then read out loud:

"I got some really great news for you. Mama is going to have a baby this fall, so I will be a big sister! She is feeling awful sick now, but I know she is happy because she sings a lot and she pats her tummy sometimes. Her tummy is getting big! And she says daddy will build the new loft for sure now, so we will have room for the baby."

Mother stopped reading and smiled. "Well, that is big news!"

"She's lying!" Tracy's face was white.

"Tracy! Why would you say something like that?" Mother handed the letter to my father to read.

"Because I know Bobby Lee isn't having any more babies with Jolene." Tracy smiled smugly.

"And just how would you know something like that?" Daddy's voice was calm, amused even.

"Everyone knows it, Daddy," Tracy continued contentedly. "Everyone knows Bobby Lee has a girlfriend in St. Albans."

"Tracy Janelle Wylie!" Mother's face was furious. "Where did you hear such a thing?"

Nancy and Melinda gazed steadily down at their plates, never raising their eyes.

"It's true!" Tracy insisted, her voice rising. "It's true! Ask Nancy, she knows! Everyone knows!" Her voice was shrill now. "Bobby Lee's got a girlfriend, and she's prettier than Jolene, and he's probably going to leave Jolene any day. It's true! Ask Nancy!"

Nancy only shook her head.

Mother simply stared at Tracy, her face ashen, her lips moving silently. Daddy slammed his fist down on the table so hard the silverware rattled. "That will be enough of that, young lady. You are excused from the table!"

But Tracy had already left the table. She pounded up the stairs to the attic room we shared, and we heard the door slam shut. Then the screaming started—long, terrible shrieks punctuated by the slamming of drawers and the thudding of books being thrown across the room.

Nancy and Melinda and I sat as quietly as we could. Whatever the truth was about Bobby Lee didn't matter now. Tracy had lost control again.

Mother sat frozen for a moment, then rose abruptly and walked into the kitchen. "I think I forgot to turn off the oven," she murmured. I knew she was lying—we all did.

Daddy looked at the three of us and smiled wanly. "Well, girls, eat your supper now."

He spooned mashed potatoes onto his plate and ladled pan gravy on top. We ate in silence until Mother returned. She was composed, but her eyes sparkled suspiciously and her nose was red. She gave Daddy an impenetrable stare, then sat back down at the table and took up Reana Mae's letter again.

"Let's see what else Reana Mae has to say," she said brightly. She read the letter out loud, so everyone heard how Ruthann had finally let her beau kiss her cheek and how Caleb had argued with Ray over a hunting knife that was missing. Normally, I wouldn't have let anyone else read Reana Mae's letter—especially the part about

Ruthann, who would be mortified if she knew her first kiss had been talked about all the way to Indiana. But tonight I didn't make a peep.

Tracy's fits were the subject of many whispered discussions in our house in those days. She'd always been moody, explosive even, but since starting junior high school, she'd become a living time bomb, as if reaching adolescence had set off something dangerous inside her. She seemed happy enough at school. She was on the student council, she made the honor roll every semester, and she was a cheerleader. She hung out with the right crowd, flirted in the school yard at lunch, and had a steady stream of friends calling on the phone.

At home, however, she was completely unpredictable. It seemed like she held it together through the school day and then just had to let loose when she hit the front steps of our house. We never knew what would set her off—an interrupted phone call, a perceived slight, a giggle at the wrong time. She said we were out to get her, and her beautiful hazel eyes radiated suspicion and hostility most of the time—except, of course, when she was being charming. And the change from charming to rage could come as suddenly as lightning.

It was a terrible rage when it came. When Tracy was raging, the only thing to do was get out of her way, fast. She poured red fingernail polish on Melinda's white bedspread because Melinda laughed at her platform shoes. She wadded Nancy's clothes into a pillowcase and lit them in the trash-burning pit because Nancy wouldn't let her borrow a blouse. Even Mother wasn't above abuse. One time when Tracy had to miss a party because of a church dinner, she took the kitchen scissors and cut Mother's best party dress into shreds.

Tracy and I shared the attic of our small house. The room ran the entire length of the house, and Daddy had let us choose the décor—an explosion of bright, primary colors. Crazy quilts covered the beds; posters of Mac Davis, Glen Campbell, and Bobby Sherman plastered the walls; stuffed animals and trolls with neon hair filled every available surface of the shelves, the beds, and the dressers.

I had been thrilled two years before when Daddy and some men from the church had finally finished the attic into a bedroom for us. But now I spent as little time there as possible. I lived in fear of setting off one of Tracy's fits. At nights I lay awake, waiting for her to fall asleep, afraid that if I slept first, she might kill me in my sleep— I'd never forgotten what she said about Mother's kitchen knife. Sometimes it got so bad I crept downstairs and crawled into bed with Melinda.

None of us understood why Tracy was the way she was. She could be kind one minute and vengeful the next, looking like an angel and then the devil's own stepchild, all in the space of a heartbeat. But we all had our theories.

Daddy opined loudly and often that it was hormones—typical adolescent shenanigans. "We were lucky with the first two," he'd laugh. "Now we're paying for it big-time!"

Mother didn't try to explain away Tracy's behavior. In fact, she didn't talk about it at all. But we all knew it scared her. She watched Tracy with a kind of panic on her face, her eyes wide, her mouth set in a tight line. As Tracy's fits grew fiercer and more frequent, Mother's hair turned an ashy gray and she began the bimonthly ritual of having it colored black again. Crow's feet edged her eyes, and the furrow in her brow sometimes looked so deep you wondered if you couldn't plant potatoes in it. She was always patient with Tracy, crooning in a singsong voice that everything was okay, would be okay. But I don't think she believed it. I know I didn't.

Nancy and Melinda said Tracy was crazy, like Kelly Morgan's crazy grandma who had to go live in a hospital—but they never said it to Mother and Daddy. They whispered it to each other and sometimes to me, and I believed them.

But none of us ever mentioned Tracy's fits outside our family. Mother had a saying: "You don't hang underwear on the outside line." Our family's underwear hung neatly and properly on a clothesline in the basement to dry. And our secrets stayed neatly cloistered within the family, where they belonged. That was our way for a long time, until we couldn't hide them anymore.

January 25, 1970
Dear Bethany
Hi! I got your letter you wrote today. I never got any
mail before that was for me. I like the straberrys on your
paper. Tell Aunt Helen I said thanks from me for getting
you that. Now I will know when I look in the mail box if
there is a letter from you.

Daddy is working on the loft at our house. It will have
2 rooms. 1 is for Caleb and 1 is for me. The baby will have
my old room and Caleb will finally have his one room
insted of sleeping on the sofa. He is helping Daddy bild it.
Rite now there is a big hole covered with blue plastick
over the living room. Mama hates the mess. But she will
be glad to have the loft done. She is sick a lot and she is
looking fat in the tummy. Caleb said she looks like she's
been streched out like a rubber band. Mama smacked him
on the hed when he said that. He just laffed at her. He
sure does make her mad.

That is all from here. Write back to me soon. Tell Tracy
and Malinda and Nancy I said HI!

Love your cousin
Reana Mae
P.S. Buttons died, but Mama is so happy, she don't even
care much.

"How's Reana Mae?" Mother asked when I came downstairs.

"She's just fine," I answered, flopping down beside her on the couch.

"Watch out for my yarn," she warned. I pushed her skeins of yarn aside, brown and gold. She was knitting a sweater for Nancy in the high school's team colors. Nancy was a varsity cheerleader, and we all went to the basketball games on Friday nights. All of us except Melinda, who told us every week that basketball games were for pork-heads. None of the really cool kids went, she said. Of course, Melinda had not made the cheerleading squad, so her opinion might have been biased.

"Bobby Lee is building the loft, and Reana Mae and Caleb will have their rooms upstairs. Caleb is helping."

Mother's brow furrowed slightly. "I wonder how long Caleb will be staying with them?" she said, looking up at my father. He was sitting in his La-Z-Boy watching the evening news.

"Did you say something?" he asked, never taking his eyes from the screen.

"I was just wondering how long Bobby Lee and Jolene are going to have Caleb with them," she repeated, sighing softly and raising her eyebrows at me. Daddy often didn't hear us when he was watching the news.

"Hmmm," he said. Then silence, until Walter Cronkite's grandfatherly face was replaced by the Hawaiian Punch man floating on a pineapple in a pool of red punch. Daddy finally turned to Mother. "My guess is, he's there for good. If Cleda Rae hasn't come for him by now, she's not coming."

He shook his head and ran his hand through his thinning hair. "That whole family is a mess, and it all boils down to Noah. That man ought to be horsewhipped!"

"Jimmy, not in front of Bethany, please." Mother frowned.

"Oh, Helen, she knows Noah ran out on his family. And she ought to know it's wrong. Just plain wrong for a man to do that."

"Is that why Cleda Rae's got a sugar daddy?" I asked.

"Bethany Marie!" Mother's shocked face stared at me over knitting needles frozen in mid-stitch. "Where in the world did you hear such a thing?"

"Reana Mae says that's what Jolene calls Mr. Ephraim Turner," I murmured, knowing I shouldn't have told. Then I heard my father snort. Abruptly he rose and walked into the kitchen. A moment later, we heard him laughing.

"Jimmy," Mother called to him. "Will you take the trash out, please?"

The back door swung shut and we couldn't hear the laughing anymore.

"Bethany, that is not a term I ever want to hear you use again. It's crass and rude and inappropriate for a young lady."

"But Reana Mae said . . ."

"Reana Mae doesn't know any better. She hasn't had the advantages you do, and she hears Jolene talk like that. Jolene ought to know better, too, but then she's had such a hard life." Mother sighed heavily. "But you, miss, you do know better. I will not tolerate that kind of talk from you. Do you understand me?"

"Yes, ma'am," I said meekly.

She smiled then, so I knew I was forgiven. "What else does Reana say?"

"She said thank you from her for getting me the stationery. She never had a letter before."

"Well, you'll have to write to her again."

"Yes, ma'am, I was just going to do that."

In fact, I had my box of stationery in my hand and was looking for a quiet place to write. Tracy was upstairs with her friend Lynette, so that was out.

"Would you like to use my desk?" Mother asked.

"Yes, ma'am!" I could hardly believe my ears. She never let us use her desk, or even touch the things on it. It was in her room—the one she shared with Daddy, of course, but we always called it Mother's room. And that room was off-limits, unless we were sick. Then we slept in Mother's bed and she brought us 7UP and potato soup and Ritz crackers with cream cheese.

She cleared a place on the desk for me to write, turned on the small hurricane lamp, and left me alone, closing the door behind her. For several moments I simply sat and looked around. It was strange being in Mother's room when I wasn't sick in bed. I rose and walked to the vanity. I stared at myself in the mirror, pulling my hair up on top of my head and sucking in my cheeks, the way I'd seen Nancy do. I touched Mother's jewelry box, wishing I had the nerve to open it.

I picked up a lipstick and opened it, screwing the pale peach waxy stick up and down, up and down. Then I opened all of the perfume bottles and sniffed them, one by one. I knew by smell which ones she wore for what occasions—White Shoulders for church, soft lilac for home, and Chanel No. 5 for special nights out with my father. I wished I could put some Chanel behind my ears, the way my mother did. I imagined myself sitting at this vanity, putting on the peach lipstick and the Revlon powder and dabbing Chanel on my throat and wrists.

I heard Tracy and Lynette clomping down the stairs into the kitchen, Tracy calling to Mother that they were going to Lynette's and she'd be home for dinner. I sat down at the desk and started writing hurriedly. If Tracy was gone, Mother might want me to go back upstairs. By the time I realized she wasn't coming for me, I'd written half a page.

> *February 8, 1970*
> *Dear Reana Mae,*
> *Hi yourself! Thanks for writing to me. I like getting letters, and I like notes too. Do you write notes at school? I write them to my freind Susan Lewis and she writes them to me. We like to fold them in triangels or little squares. But we have to be careful passing them, because if Mrs. Hanson our teacher catches us, it is big trouble! One time, Mrs. Hanson made Susan read her note out loud to the hole class. And it was when Susan had a crush on Don Heizer. So she had to read it out loud, and he heard!!! Boy, was she embarased!*
> *Nothing much is happening here. Fifth grade is really hard. And Mrs. Hanson is really hard. But at least she lets us read good books. I am reading Little Women by Louisa May Alcott (she's got your middle name!!!), and I really, really love it. Its got a sad part where one of the girls dies. I cried when I read it. But its really good.*
> *Mother is knitting a blanket for Jolene's baby. It is pink and blue and yellow and green, all soft and pretty. I bet the baby will love it!*
> *Write to me soon.*
> *Love,*
> *Bethany*

I proudly folded the letter and addressed the envelope. I had written a whole page and a half. Mother found a stamp and told me I could walk to the mailbox to mail it. That night at bedtime when she gave me my usual kiss on the forehead, she said, "I'm glad you're writing to Reana Mae. You're a good friend to her, Bethany. And she needs that."

I went to bed happy that night.

Two weeks passed before I heard from Reana again. The pale blue envelope was waiting on the kitchen table when I got home from school.

> *Feb. 26*
> *Dear Bethany,*
> *Im sorry I did not write befor. Things are just awful! Mama lost the baby, and she is so sad I am afraid she mite die! She just stays in bed all day and cries and she don't want to eat or nothing. And daddy is gone off to drive the truck to Oragon so he can't help her. And Caleb is gone too. And mama won't let granma and granpa come in the house cus she says they make her nervus. So it is just me to help mama. And I don't know how to.*
>
> *What happened is last week mama was looking for Caleb cus he was supposed to be at Ida Louis house for his lessons but Ida came and said he never showed up. So mama went hunting for him and she spotted him down by the dock. He had granpa's knife that was lost, and he was carving a stick with it. So mama got real mad and she started down to get him. But there was ice on the steps and she fell down them—almost the hole way from the top to the bottom. I was at school, but Ida says mama scremed terribel. And then she was bleeding and the baby was born, but it was way to erly for the baby to born and it died. I saw it in the dish pan on the porch when I got home. It wasn't any bigger than my hand, but it had little tiny hands and feet. It was a boy. Granpa buried it out back. Me and granma put some plastik flowers on the grave from granpa's store, but mama wouldnt come out there. She just stayed in bed and cried. And she told Caleb he had to go away. She said it is his falt the baby died, cus he is so mean he made her loose the baby. Granma tried to*

tell her she was being rong headed, but mama would not lissen to her.

So Caleb took his stuff and he left. I dont even know where he went to. Granpa says probably he went to Hunington to find his mama but I dont think that he went to find Cleda becaus he dont like her boyfriend.

Daddy dont even know yet about the baby becus we have not herd from him this week. He will get back from Oragon tomorow or the next day and I think he will be tore up to. Expecially becus the baby was a boy. He reelly wanted a boy. I hope he will not be mad at Caleb to. I hope he goes to find him. I am woried about him. And I am woried about mama. I wish you all were here. I think aunt Helen could help mama more then me.

Write to me soon. And say your prayers for mama to.
Love
Reana Mae

I read the letter twice, my hands trembling. "Mother!" I cried. "Mother, come quick."

"What is it?" she asked, coming up the stairs two at a time. I guess she could hear the panic in my voice.

I was crying by then. All I could do was hand her the letter. I watched her as she read it. Her face grew very white and still. She looked like a little old woman standing there. Her hand holding the letter shook so that she finally sat down, laid the letter on the bed, and leaned over to read it again. "Dear Lord," she whispered, shaking her head. "Oh no."

"Mama," I whimpered. "Is Jolene gonna be okay?"

She wrapped me in a hug and held me tight while we both cried. "Yes, honey," she finally said, pushing my bangs from my forehead to kiss me. "Jolene will be okay. And so will Reana Mae. And you know what?"

She stood as she said it.

"What?"

"We're going down there and make sure they're okay."

She said it firmly and quietly. She wasn't shaking now. She had decided what to do, and she was calm and steady.

"What about school?"

"You'll just have to miss a few days," she declared. "Because right now, Jolene and Reana Mae need us, and family comes first. So"—she was walking briskly around the room now—"you need to get some things together. Your pajamas and toothbrush, some clothes and socks and panties. Can you get your things together, Bethany?"

"Yes, Mother." I was already pulling things out of my drawers. "Yes, I can get my things ready."

"That's my good girl." She was heading down the stairs. "I'll call the school and see if we can get some work for you to take with us, so you won't fall behind. And I'll have to cancel my meeting tomorrow night." Her voice faded as she walked down the stairs.

"And, Bethany," she called up from the bottom. "You might just put some of your old books in a bag for Reana Mae. Just a few that you're done with. I'll bet Reana could use an escape right now."

"Yes, Mother!" I began pulling books from the shelves. What would Reana like? Trixie Belden mysteries? Nancy Drew? Definitely *Little Women*. I was sorting piles of books on the floor when Tracy came up the steps.

"What are you doing?" She stared at the room. My clothes were spread out on the bed. Books were scattered across the floor in small stacks.

"I'm getting some books for Reana Mae," I answered, not looking up from my work.

"What?"

"Some books for Reana Mae. To take with us."

Tracy stood for a moment, then pounded down the stairs. "Mother!" I heard her yelling. "Mother, what's going on?"

A few minutes later, Tracy stormed back up the stairs, her face white, her eyes red, her nostrils flared. I shrank away from her, but she swept past me, flung herself down on her bed, and wailed. I sat uncertainly for a moment, then cautiously walked to the side of the bed.

"Are you okay, Tracy?"

"Leave me alone!"

"Are you crying for the baby?"

She sat up and stared at me, her face twisted in fury. "You just go on down to that hillbilly river, you little bitch. Go on down and be with your trashy twin and her whore mama! I don't care if you never come back—either one of you! I hate you!"

Then I realized Tracy wasn't coming with us. Only Mother and I were going. I stood before her silently. I didn't know what to say. She stared back at me, shaking with rage. Finally, she flung herself down onto the bed again and wailed some more. I returned to my stacks of books, deciding on Beverly Cleary and Nancy Drew. Then I took my clothes and books down to Mother. She was packing in her room. She smiled wanly when I walked into the room, looking pale and very tired.

"Thank you, sweetheart." She put my clothes in the suitcase with hers and found a bag for the books. Daddy came home then, and I was shooed outside so they could talk. I sat on the back porch glider with our cocker spaniel, Skipper, scratching his soft ears and shivering in the weak March sun until dinner.

We gathered at the kitchen table for supper. Melinda and Nancy were unusually quiet. They had been looking forward to baby-sitting next summer at the river. Nancy had even been knitting booties. Pink ones, because she was sure the baby was a girl. Tracy's chair was empty as we bowed our heads for grace. And then, there she was—smiling, laughing, apologizing loudly for being late. She slid into her chair and helped herself to meat and noodles.

"Tracy," my father began cautiously. "Your mother and I have been talking, and we were wondering if you'd like to spend a few days at Lynette's while she and Bethany are gone. Would you like that?"

"Oh no, Daddy." She smiled at him. "If I go to Lynette's, who will take care of you?"

"Well, Nancy and Melinda will be here," Mother said.

Tracy cut her off. "Oh, they can't make tuna noodle casserole like me," she said with a smile. "Besides, Nancy always has cheer-leading practice, and Melinda has track. I'll stay here and take care of Daddy." She fairly beamed at him, her eyes sparkling like an angel's.

"Well, all right. If that's what you want to do," Mother said hesitantly.

"Good, then. That's settled." Daddy grinned. "You all go on down and take care of poor Jolene. Tracy will stay here and take care of her old man."

Nancy and Melinda said nothing, just rolled their eyes at each other. At least their schedules wouldn't be affected.

I went to bed early that night. Mother and I would leave first thing in the morning. But I couldn't sleep until I heard Tracy's even breathing. I was still in shock. Tomorrow, I was going to West Virginia with my mother . . . just the two of us in the middle of the school year. Would wonders never cease?

8

Spring Storms

We left the house before the sun rose. I sat proudly on the front seat beside Mother, my pillow and blanket bundled around me, and waved to Daddy and the girls as we backed out of the driveway. Tracy's arm was wrapped through Daddy's, and she smiled brightly as we drove down the street. Mother blew a kiss to them, then sighed. "I hope they'll be all right," she said.

She turned on the radio to the easy-listening station and reached over to pat my arm. "Why don't you go back to sleep, sweetheart? It's early, and we have a long trip ahead of us."

I snuggled down in my seat, wrapping the blanket around me, and watched the familiar scenery pass. By the time we got on the interstate, I was asleep.

By mid-morning we were following the Ohio River, now catching glimpses of the water, now seeing only the grimy industry that lined the river's edge. At noon we crossed the Ohio into West Virginia and began following the Kanawha River south. Now the road got rougher, the hills higher, the houses farther apart, and the tobacco barns more ramshackle. We were coming home.

* * *

Aunt Belle threw open the front door and pulled Mother into a hug. Then she reached for me, and I was enveloped in her soft, ample embrace. Belle gave the best hugs I've ever had.

"Come in, come in, you two." She laughed. "Come in out of the cold. Helen, you must be stiff as a rod after that drive. It's a shame Jimmy couldn't come with you. Bethany Marie, let me look at you. Lands, child, you've grown a foot! Donna Jo, come and lay your eyes on my Bethany. If she ain't grown a foot, you can call me a nigger! What are we standing here for? Come in, come in."

Donna Jo appeared from the kitchen, wiping her hands on her apron, smiling warmly. She hugged us, then took our suitcase from the porch and carried it upstairs.

I ran up the stairs and down the long, carpeted hall to the funny little wooden door at the very end. I turned the skeleton key in the lock, opened the door, and ran up the steep steps to the attic room. At the top I stopped and stared happily. This room was my favorite place in the world. It was L-shaped, each side furnished with a small, black iron bed, a bedside table with its own Bible, a three-drawer chest, and a round-backed upholstered rocking chair. Hand-stitched quilts adorned the beds, and a rag rug lay beside each.

Every summer we girls took turns spending nights at Aunt Belle's—as many as Mother would allow. We always went in twos—Nancy and Melinda one weekend, Tracy and me the next. And we always slept in the attic room.

The room had two windows—one at each end of the L. You could lie in bed and look out at night and see a million stars in the heavens. But one window overlooked the road, while the other commanded the best view of the river in the whole valley. And that's the window Tracy always demanded. Sometimes she let me climb into bed with her to watch out the window at night. But she never once let me sleep there myself. It was her bed, she said, because she was older.

Well, this time Tracy was in Indiana. The river window was mine. I ran back downstairs to get my clothes from the suitcase Mother was unpacking in the guest bedroom at the front of the house. The canopied bed was so tall, you had to use a step stool to climb into it. Mother looked like a little girl standing beside that tall bed. I climbed the step stool and plopped onto the feather mattress, relishing freedom after eight hours in the car.

"Mother, I get to sleep in the bed by the river window since Tracy's not here!" I said happily, watching her unpack. "I've never slept in it before."

She turned to look at me. "Never?"

I shook my head. "Tracy gets that bed, because she's older. But this time I get it!"

She smiled at me, then bent over and kissed my forehead. "Sweetheart, you and Tracy were supposed to take turns."

"Well, but she always wants it. And you know how she is. . . ." I trailed off.

Mother sighed. "Yes, honey. I know how she is." She put down the blouse she was holding, climbed up on the bed, and lay down beside me, pulling me close. "You must be patient with your sister, Bethany. I know she can be . . . well, hard. But you must always be patient with her. She may not seem like it, but Tracy is fragile. Do you know what that means?"

"You mean like your china cups?" I asked.

"Yes, that's just exactly what I mean. Tracy is fragile like a china cup. She takes things so hard and feels things so very much, and sometimes I'm afraid . . . well, we all must be very patient with her. And very kind."

"Yes, Mother." I nodded, impatient to get back to the river window upstairs.

"Now," she said, sitting up and surveying the room. "Take your things up and put them away. We'll have lunch with Aunt Belle, and then we'll go see Jolene and Reana Mae."

After a late lunch of cold ham, cottage cheese, and macaroni salad, we put on our coats and walked to Bobby Lee and Jolene's. Aunt Belle offered to drive us, but Mother and I wanted to walk.

"Tell Jolene I'm here if she needs anything," Belle called after us. "She can't be so stubborn that she don't need her family now."

In the March chill against a steel-gray sky, Jolene's cabin looked smaller and drearier than I remembered. Plastic sheets were nailed over the windows, a metal trash can overflowed on the porch, and a huge sheet of blue plastic flapped from the roof in the wind. When we opened the gate to the yard, Bo loped around the corner of the house, woofed once at us, and wagged his tail hopefully. His coat was matted and dirty.

"Hey, Bo," I said, patting his head. "Hey, buddy. How're you?"

As if in response, he trotted to the porch and pawed at his empty bowl.

"Okay, buddy." I nodded. "Don't worry. I'll get you some dinner."

Mother rapped briskly at the front door. She waited a moment, then knocked again. When no one answered, she called out, "Jolene! Reana Mae! It's Helen. Are you home?"

I heard feet pounding on the wooden floor, and the door swung open. Reana Mae flew into Mother's outstretched arms and began sobbing. "Aunt Helen! I knew you'd come. I knew you'd come help Mama."

Mother stroked her tangled hair and kissed her upturned face. "It's all right now, Reana Mae. I'll help you take care of your mama."

"Hey, Reana," I said, suddenly shy. I'd never had to deal with trouble like Reana Mae was facing. I didn't know how to help.

"Hey, Bethany!" She ran to hug me, too. Bo's tail thumped the porch hopefully.

"Oh, Bo!" Reana Mae's hand flew to her mouth and her cheeks reddened. "You poor thing, I forgot to feed you yesterday, didn't I?" She stroked the dog's head. "I'll get you something right now, Bo."

I looked back to the door and saw that Mother had walked into the cabin. I waited for Reana Mae and we followed her.

Inside the cabin was dark and cold. Mother stood silently in the front room, looking about uncertainly.

"Oh, Aunt Helen, I'm so glad you're here," Reana Mae said as she ran into the kitchen. "I can't make the fire stay lit, and Mama won't eat hardly nothing, and I don't know how to make the washing machine work, and she won't let me ask Granma for help."

She reemerged, dragging a huge bag of dog food. "I got to feed Bo," she said. "Mama's in her room in bed. But I bet she's awake. You can go on in."

She went out on the porch again, and I followed. I didn't want to stay inside the cabin.

Reana Mae filled Bo's dish and we watched him wolf down the food as if he were starving.

"Poor thing," she murmured. "I didn't feed him yesterday. I can't remember if I fed him the day before, either. It's been so hard, Bethany," she said, turning to me. "Mama won't get out of bed at all, and I don't know how to make her better. I'm afraid she's gonna die of pure sadness."

"Where's your daddy?" I asked.

"He's gone to look for Caleb." She sat down on the front step and cupped her chin in her hands. "He came home and Granma told him about the baby. And he cried, Bethany. I never seen Daddy cry before. And then he went in to talk to Mama, and I heard them both crying. And I thought maybe Daddy would take care of Mama, and I could go back to school. But then it all blew up."

She rubbed the back of her hand across her eyes. Her hands were red and chapped. Her fingernails had been chewed to the quick.

"What do you mean, it all blew up?"

"Daddy asked Mama how it happened, and she told him it was Caleb's fault. She got real upset and started yellin' that Caleb was wicked, like the devil's own stepchild, and that's why she lost the baby. So Daddy asked where Caleb was, and Mama told him how she sent him off. She was hollerin' and cryin' like she was being whipped. She kept saying Caleb was wicked, and it was his fault the baby died."

She fell silent for a moment, her eyes staring at nothing. I reached over to hold her hand. "What did Bobby Lee say?" I asked.

"He kept trying to ease her, telling her it was all right, that they'd make another baby. And then, finally, she did quiet down. But then Daddy asked her where Caleb had gone to, and she started hollerin' again. Said she didn't rightly care where he'd gone to, that probably he'd gone back to hell where he came from. And then Daddy started getting mad at her. You know, Daddy and Caleb get along real good 'cause they're brothers. And Daddy said she'd better stop talking like that. He said she sounded crazy. And she did, Bethany," she said, turning to stare at me. "She sounded flat-out crazy."

She fell silent again, chewing the bits of fingernail left on her fingers.

"So that's when Bobby went to look for Caleb?" I asked.

"Not that day. He got Mama quiet again and then he made us some soup. And I went to bed that night and I thought it would be all right. But then in the morning he went and talked to Granpa. I don't know what Granpa told him, but Daddy came back looking mad. I ain't never seen him look like that, Bethany. I seen Mama mad before lots, but not Daddy.

"He looked like someone else, not like Daddy at all. He came in and slammed the door and told me to go on outside. So I came out here and sat with Bo. But I could hear him yelling at her. He said she was the wicked one, that she never gave Caleb a chance in hell. He said if she hadn't been so mean to Caleb, she wouldn't be in this mess. And then Mama started screaming again that it was Caleb that was wicked. And they both screamed at each other so much, even Bo was scared.

"Then he hit her. He smacked her real hard. I heard it. And she stopped screaming. He told her he was gonna go find his little brother and bring him home. Mama said if Caleb came back, she wouldn't stay here. And he said she could leave, then."

I was still holding Reana Mae's hand. Her face was sickly white, her dirty hair limp. She looked much older than nine—like she'd lived a whole lifetime since Thanksgiving.

"He left that very morning," she continued softly. "That was almost a week ago, right after I wrote to you, and he ain't come home yet." She sighed. "Mama don't get out of bed at all, and she won't let nobody come in to help us. And I don't know when Daddy will get back, or if he'll find Caleb. And I don't know what Mama will do if he brings Caleb back."

I sat awkwardly holding her hand. I couldn't think of a thing to say.

She leaned against me heavily. "I'm glad you're here, Bethany. I been praying every night that you and Aunt Helen would come. Mama will listen to her. I know she will. Aunt Helen will make it all right."

I nodded, putting my arm around her thin shoulders. But I wondered how Mother could ever make things all right for Jolene and Bobby Lee.

Mother opened the door then. She stepped out onto the porch and began shaking a rug over the rail. "You two will freeze sitting out here. Come inside now, there's work to be done."

"Yes, ma'am," we said in unison.

The room looked brighter already. Mother had started a fire in the woodstove, opened all the curtains, and turned on the little radio in the kitchen. I could hear the washing machine chugging away on the back porch. The curtain was still drawn closed across the doorway to Jolene's room, and the blue plastic still flapped above the gaping hole in the corner of the roof, but the cabin felt more alive than before.

I dusted, Reana Mae swept, and Mother washed the dishes that were stacked all around the kitchen, while Bo scratched and scratched at the front door. When we'd finished cleaning, Mother made a list, gave us a five-dollar bill, and sent us up the road to Ray's store. "You can each have a dime to get a treat," she said as we left.

Reana Mae fairly danced down the stairs. "You see?" she said, grinning. "I told you Aunt Helen would make it all right."

I nodded again, hoping she was right.

Mother fried pork chops and potatoes and baked corn bread in Jolene's tiny kitchen. She carried a tray to Jolene, then joined Reana Mae and me at the table. Reana ate like a half-starved orphan—two pork chops, two helpings of potatoes with ketchup, and three pieces of corn bread with syrup. "Thank you, Aunt Helen," she said when she was finally full. "We been living on cereal and tomato soup."

"Well, I know your mama appreciates all the hard work you've been doing since her accident, Reana Mae," Mother said as she carried dishes to the sink. "Tomorrow, it's back to school for you."

I looked up forlornly. "What'll I do while Reana's in school?"

"You can help me with chores, Bethy. There's a lot to be done."

Reana and I washed dishes while Mother folded and put away laundry. Then we sat down to watch the news on the little black-and-white television Ray and Loreen had given Jolene for Christmas. At the first commercial break, we looked up to see Jolene standing in the doorway. I started in surprise. She didn't look like herself at all. I recognized her short pink robe, but her face looked years older than it had at Thanksgiving. Her skin was blotchy, and dark bags hung beneath her puffy eyes. Her beautiful red hair hung in limp, dirty ringlets. She leaned heavily against the door frame.

Reana Mae jumped up and ran to support her as Mother rose, saying, "Jolene, honey, I'm so glad you're up. Here, sit on the couch and I'll get you some tea."

Jolene smiled wanly at Mother as she draped her arm over Reana Mae's shoulders. She walked slowly to the couch, then sank down beside where I sat. "Hey, Bethany," she said to me. "How you doing?" She leaned over and kissed my cheek.

"Fine, Jolene. I'm just fine."

She patted my cheek, but her eyes were on the television. "What're they saying today?" she asked Mother, who returned from the kitchen with a mug of steaming water, a tea bag dangling down its side.

"More war news, I'm sorry to say," Mother replied.

"I still can't understand what it's all about," Jolene said, "but I'm surely glad Bobby Lee ain't over there."

We sat silently until the news was done. Then Jolene returned to bed, leaning on Reana Mae again. Soon after, Mother and I walked back to Aunt Belle's.

"What's wrong with her, Mama?" I asked. "Is she gonna be okay?"

"Yes, honey, she'll be okay."

"She looks so sickly."

"Well, Jolene's had a big loss, and she took a mighty hard fall, too. I think her body has mostly recovered, but her spirit hasn't. That's going to take a while. She'll be all right once Bobby Lee comes home."

I stared down at the road. "Reana Mae said they fought about Caleb before he left."

"Yes, Jolene told me. But I'm sure that will pass, too." She paused a moment, then squeezed my hand. "People say all kinds of things they don't mean when they're grieving, Bethy. Bobby Lee and Jolene are both grieving hard. But they need each other to get past the grieving. Once they realize that, they'll be okay."

By that time, we were at Aunt Belle's front steps. "You just be an extra-good friend to Reana Mae, okay? She really needs a friend right now."

I nodded, and we went inside to a barrage of questions and solicitude from Belle.

I lay awake that night watching clouds drift across the night sky, now hiding the moon, now sweeping away. The river below was as black as the coal it hid. When the clouds cleared, the river seemed to come alive—shiny black currents sweeping southward in a never-ending, always-changing pattern. Then the moon would disappear and the water's surface became matte black again, the patterns disappearing in the night. It was mesmerizing and a little scary. I'd never slept alone in the attic room before. The shadows seemed longer and darker than I remembered. The light from the hallway far below barely edged into the corner of the room by the stairway.

I stared longingly at the empty bed—the despised road-facing window bed—its neatly made covers hanging down, concealing . . . what? Had the rocker moved? I rubbed my eyes, staring into the darkness. Wind creaked in the eaves. I was afraid to move, afraid to call out for Mother. Was that a thump on the roof?

I crept from the bed and padded down the curved stairway, toward light and Mother and safety. I ran down the long hallway, and then down the steps toward the entry hall. I stopped on the landing, hearing Mother and Aunt Belle in the front room. Would they be upset with me for getting out of bed? I hesitated on the landing, listening.

"But why would Ray tell Bobby Lee something like that?" I heard Mother ask.

"Because it's true," Belle said. "It's true, and Bobby had a right to know."

"Oh, Belle, not really," Mother protested. "Jolene wouldn't do something like that."

Belle laughed. "Helen, you never will get used to other folks' wicked ways."

"But why would she? Why would Jolene . . . take an interest in her husband's brother? And while she's pregnant! No, Belle, I just cannot believe that."

"Well," Belle said, "I figure it's like this. Now Jolene, she never had much going for her except her looks. No, I'm not attacking her, Helen, just stating God's plain truth. Jolene hooked Bobby Lee because she was sexy—everyone knows that. That's how she's gotten everything—it's the only way she knows how to get anything. And now Bobby's gone most all the time, and folks are whispering he's got a fancy girl up in St. Albans, so she gets herself pregnant, thinking she'll keep him home with a son."

"Oh, Belle, don't say that. She's lost the baby. At least give her credit for wanting it."

"Oh, she wanted it. Because it was a boy, that's why. Look here, Helen. I know what it's like to lose a baby. I been there. But Jolene just ain't the mothering kind, you know that as well as I do. Hell, look at how she treats the child she's already got. She treats Reana Mae like hired help—and you know that's the truth."

"But still . . ."

"Still nothing. She wanted a boy to keep hold of Bobby, because she's getting older now. Not ancient, like us, of course." She laughed. "But not eighteen no more, either. The bloom is off that rose, Helen, and we all know it, and so does she."

I listened, transfixed at this bit of adult lore.

"So now here she's pregnant, and Bobby Lee's still gone, and folks are still whispering, and she's getting fat—not just a little pouch like she got herself with Reana Mae. I mean she's getting *fat*.

So she has to prove to herself she's still got it, you know? And who is there around here to prove it with but the boy? And Lord knows, Caleb's all boy. And he used to have it mighty bad for Jolene, back when he was a little one."

"But, Belle, what did she . . . I mean, how . . . ?" Mother's voice trailed away. I could feel her embarrassment wafting up the stairwell.

"You're blushing now, Helen, but you'd have died to see how she carried on. The fatter she got, the shorter her dresses got. She took to wearing halter tops and shorts around the house, even when it was freezing outside. And she'd lean herself over in front of the boy when he was sitting at the table—you could see everything she had then. She was always touching him or brushing up against him. It was purely revolting."

"What did he do?" Mother whispered.

"Caleb?" Belle laughed again. "Lord, Helen, he was so embarrassed he like to died. He ignored her mostly. Then later, he got snappish with her. Started making little digs at her, about how fat she was. I heard him one time tell her she looked like a trailer park queen—only he said trailer pork queen. And then he laughed."

"Poor Jolene," Mother said.

"Well, now, I don't rightly know about 'poor Jolene.' She has reaped what she has sowed, Helen, flaunting herself in front of a sixteen-year-old boy . . . her husband's own brother, at that."

"I know it's shameful, Arabella. But think how awful it must be for her."

"Think how awful it was for poor Caleb, once she caught on he wasn't interested. She tore into that boy like a hound on a rabbit. Everywhere he went, she dogged him. Everything he did, she was after him for it. I seen her take a switch and whip that boy's back till it bled, just because he left the screen door open. It wasn't right, Helen. She was acting like she had that bad blood."

There was a pause. I could hear a spoon stirring in a teacup. What, I wondered, was bad blood? Before I could think much about it, Belle was talking again.

"That last day, when Ida Louise came to the house looking for him, she said Jolene was in a devil's fury. She grabbed a cane and lit

out down them steps to beat the tar out of him, and she wasn't paying attention to where she was stepping, and she fell. I heard her
screaming all the way up here, and I ran down to see what happened—everyone on the road was running. I got to the top of them
steps and seen her lying at the bottom. Ida was trying to help her
up, but she wouldn't get up. She was screaming like a banshee,
swinging that cane at Caleb. He kept trying to help her, and she just
kept swinging at him, screaming that he was the devil hisself. It was
awful, Helen, just awful.

"Then, when we finally got her up to the house and she was
bleeding and we knew she was going to lose the baby, she made
Loreen bring her Bobby Lee's shotgun. And don't you know that
girl got herself up out of her bed and dragged herself onto the
porch, where Caleb was sitting. That poor boy was crying, and trying real hard not to show it. And Jolene pointed that gun straight at
his head and told him to clear off—that it was his fault she was losing the baby, and if he ever showed his face at her door again, she'd
blow his head off. I'm telling you, Helen, it was like she was crazy."

"Dear Lord," Mother whispered. "What will she do now?"

"If she's got the sense the good Lord gave a coonhound, she'll
tuck her tail between her legs and beg Bobby Lee's forgiveness
when he comes back. *If* he comes back."

"Do you suppose he'll find Caleb?"

"I don't know, Helen. I just don't know."

I crept back up the stairs then, to think things over. But I didn't
go back to the attic room. Instead, I climbed into Mother's bed,
grateful for the pool of light from the hallway. When she came in a
little while later, I closed my eyes and pretended to sleep.

Mother changed into her nightgown and kneeled beside the big
bed for a long time, saying her evening prayers. I squeezed my eyes
tight and prayed, too. I prayed hard for Reana Mae and for the
baby that was dead and gone away to Heaven. I prayed for Jolene
and for Bobby Lee. I even prayed for Caleb.

Finally, Mother climbed into the bed, kissed my forehead, and
pulled the quilt snug under our chins. Then we both finally slept. It
had been a long day.

9

News and Prattle

The next day, Reana Mae went back to school. I stood on the porch and waved at her and Ruthann and Harley Boy as the dirty yellow bus rumbled down the rutted road. Mother put her hand on my shoulder and squeezed gently.

"All right, then," she said, cheerfully. "Are you ready to do some chores?"

"Yes, ma'am." I sighed. I hadn't counted on Reana Mae going to school while I was here. But of course she'd been out of school for nearly three weeks. It was time for her to go back.

I followed Mother into the cabin and helped her take down the blue curtains in the front room and kitchen. We were going to clean Jolene's house from top to bottom, and I knew better than to argue about it. Mother was in spring-cleaning mode. It happened every April at home, and we all dreaded it. She got a kind of half-crazed gleam in her eyes when the south wind started blowing warm and the first daffodils poked up through the late snow. All of us scrubbed and scoured and dusted and waxed every surface in the house until the whole place sparkled clean and smelled of bleach. Today, Mother's eyes had that gleam, and she'd come armed with buckets, scrub brushes, scouring powder, and a big mop she'd borrowed from Donna Jo. I knew it would be another long day.

Jolene was still asleep when we started working. By the time she staggered out of her room at ten, we had scrubbed down the whole kitchen, walls and all, and were starting on the front room.

"Hey, Jolene!" I called out when I saw her.

Mother looked up from the spot she was scrubbing on the wooden floor and smiled. "Good morning, Jolene. How are you feeling today?"

"What the hell are you doing?" Jolene scowled. She swayed slightly, then clutched the table to support herself. She looked as bad this morning as she had the night before—worse, maybe, because the morning sun streaming through the newly washed windows showed every line on her face, every sag in her neck. She looked like a rag doll that had been wrung out wet and hung to dry—like Essie after her ordeal in the mud, I realized with a start.

Mother rose from her knees and walked into the kitchen, reemerging with a mug of steaming, black coffee. "Why don't you sit down, honey? Sit down, drink some coffee, and just relax."

Jolene stood still, clutching the table, ignoring the mug Mother held out to her.

"I said, what the hell are you doing, Helen?"

"Why, we're just cleaning up a bit. I thought it might cheer you up if the place was a little . . . brighter, that's all." Mother set the mug down on the table before Jolene and pulled out a chair. "Here, you just sit down and relax. Bethany and I will take care of it all. We'll have this place bright and shiny in no time."

Jolene stared at her in silence. I could see her jaw clench tightly, and I wondered if she was going to yell. I looked down at the floor and scrubbed furiously.

"I don't need you to clean my house, Helen," she said finally, in a sad, weary voice. "I don't need you or no one else taking care of me and my family."

"I know you don't, Jolene. It's just that, after all you've been through . . . well, I want so much to help, and this is the only way I know how." Mother's voice was soft, cajoling. She smiled at Jolene and gestured at the chair again. "Please, honey, sit down and relax. Bethany and I came all the way down here to be helpful. Let us do *something* for you."

Jolene sighed and sank onto the chrome and red vinyl chair. She sipped at her coffee, pulled a pack of Marlboros from her robe pocket, lit one, dragged heavily, and finally sighed again. "Whatever," she said flatly. "Lord knows them windows ain't been that clean in a generation."

Mother found an ashtray in the kitchen cabinet and placed it on the table. "When did you start smoking again? I thought you gave that up years ago."

Jolene just shrugged her shoulders and dragged on her cigarette. Mother's lips pressed together in a tight line. She walked briskly out the back door. I kept scrubbing the floor in silence, wondering where she'd gone, when I saw her at the kitchen window, tearing at the plastic that had been nailed over it. When she had the whole sheet down, she came back into the house, leaned across Jolene, and shoved the window open.

"If you're going to smoke in the house with Bethany here—or Reana Mae, either—you ought to at least open a window."

Jolene shrugged again. She stared out the window, ignoring my mother and me. She sat silently in her short pink robe, smoking her cigarette and drinking her coffee. I found myself staring at her again and again when I thought she wasn't looking. I couldn't believe how different she looked. She had been plumpish at Thanksgiving—prettily so—but she had gained a lot of weight during the pregnancy. Her stomach still bulged under the robe, her ankles looked thick, and her neck rolled slightly under her drooping chin. Was this the same Jolene I'd seen just last fall sporting a black leather miniskirt and white go-go boots? Slumped in the chair before me, she looked like a balloon that had been overstretched and then partly deflated.

She stubbed out her cigarette and stretched, yawning hugely. Looking down at me, she smiled tightly. "Well, I reckon you're glad to be out of school in the middle of the week, anyway."

I smiled back and nodded. I wasn't sure what to say. Abruptly she rose and her robe fell open to show her distended belly and sagging breasts beneath her sheer nightgown. I dropped my head and pretended not to notice.

When I looked up again, Jolene was gone. She'd gone back to

bed, and we didn't see her again until lunch, when she staggered into the kitchen to tuck away two platefuls of scrambled eggs, hash browns, biscuits, and bacon. When she'd finished eating, Jolene sat back in her chair, lit another cigarette, and sighed.

"You know," she said, "my whole damned life I been starvin' myself, just so some man or another would look at me." She plucked another strip of bacon from the plate.

"And what's it got me?" she demanded, staring straight at Mother. "What in God's own name has it got me? A goddamned shack in a goddamned hick valley with an ugly kid that don't much like me and a husband who ain't never at home."

Mother and I sat quietly watching her while she chewed the bacon noisily. "A goddamned shack," she repeated, wiping her fingers on her robe. "Well." She smiled at Mother—it was not a pretty smile. "The hell with that!"

She took the last strip of bacon from the plate and held it up like a trophy.

"From now on, Jolene Darling Colvin is lookin' out for herself first. Startin' with food, goddamn it! From now on, if I want to eat bacon, I'll goddamn well eat bacon—and plenty of it! And if some goddamned man don't like the way I look, that's just too goddamned bad for him!"

Mother's lips formed a thin line as she looked at me and said quietly, "Bethany, will you please go to the store and pick up some dish soap? Ask Uncle Ray to put it on my account."

I nodded and scampered for the front door, grabbing my jacket on the way out. I didn't want to hang around and hear what Mother might have to say to Jolene just now.

I stopped in briefly at Aunt Belle's, to ask Donna Jo if she needed anything from the store. She said no, she surely didn't—but since I was such a thoughtful little thing, why didn't I take a dime from the change jar and get myself a little treat? I smiled as I continued down the road. Some grown-ups, at least, were predictable.

"Bethany Marie!" Loreen hollered gladly when I entered the store. "You surely are a sight for these old, tired eyes. Ray told me you was in here with Reana Mae yesterday. God bless you and your precious mama for coming down here to help my little girl."

With that she pulled me into a suffocating embrace. Squirming slightly, I pulled back as soon as she loosened her grip.

"Hi, Aunt Loreen." I smiled at her.

I hadn't counted on Loreen being here. Usually, Ray minded the store. But here she was, her short, squat body nearly bursting the seams of her cotton housedress, her nearsighted green eyes watering behind her eyeglasses.

"You sweet thing," she said, still holding tight on to my hand. "You sweet, sweet thing. Ain't you just the sweetest thing, coming down here with your mama to help. The good Lord will have a rich reward waiting for you both someday," she gushed. "And don't we all deserve a rich reward, with all the troubles of this world?"

She shook her head sadly as she continued. "How are you, Bethany? And how's your dear mama? Ya'll have a good trip? Roads okay? You stayin' at Belle's? She's got plenty of room, of course. But ya'll know you're more than welcome to stay with me and Ray any time. Especially since you're down here to help my little girl.

"The good Lord," she continued, removing her glasses and wiping the back of her hand across her eyes, "He knows she surely does need some help right about now. God Hisself knows we have tried, me and Ray. We tried awful hard to raise her up right after her mama died. We done all we could for her. But she's a wild one, Jolene is, and now she's got herself in a whole mess of trouble. Lord knows how she's gonna get herself out of this mess. But we'll do everything we can, me and Ray, 'cause we love her just like we loved her mama.

"You remember EmmaJane? No, of course you don't. My poor EmmaJane, she's with Jesus up in Heaven. Wasn't any older than Jolene is now when she died. Course, it was a accident, her dying. Or maybe even murder, I think sometimes. She was so pretty, my sweet EmmaJane. I think someone maybe just got so jealous of her beauty they killed her. But she died, rightly enough. And poor little Jolene, hardly older than you are now and left all alone up there in Huntington, without her mama or any daddy either. But me and Ray, we tried. We surely tried. We gave her a home and took as good a care of her as we knew how to. But now"—she sighed, shaking her head—"I don't know what she's gonna do now."

She paused to take a breath, so I blurted out, "Mother wants some dish soap, and she says just put it on our account."

Loreen waddled to the back of the store. "Is she over there washing Jolene's dishes? She shouldn't be doing that! I told Jolene over and over again, she's got to keep her house up better. If she spent as much time makin' a comfortable home as she did makin' up her face, maybe Bobby Lee would want to be at home. The good Lord knows, we all of us start out pretty, just like Miss Jolene. But sooner or later, time catches up with us all.

"That's what I always say. Time catches up. Then it's the home, not the woman that brings 'em back. That's what I kept tellin' Jolene, but she wouldn't listen to me. She thinks she's different than everyone else . . . that the Lord's gonna keep her beautiful till the day she lays herself down and dies. Well, I got news for her. We all start out beautiful, but it don't last. That girl's gotta start makin' a good home for her husband. That's what'll bring Bobby Lee home. That's what he wants. It's what they all want in the end.

"Oh, they might take up with some fancy girl on the road now and then, but it's a home they mostly want. Someplace nice and clean to come home to, someplace they can be king of the castle. Course, she tried to give him a son, I'll say that for her. She tried. But I'm sore afraid her childbearing years are done with now. Lord knows, she took this pregnancy hard. She better not try again. She better just start trying to make a nice home for Bobby Lee. That'll keep him home."

During this last barrage, Loreen had located a bottle of Palmolive and put it into a small sack.

"Mother says put it on our account," I repeated as soon as she paused again for breath.

"Oh, Lord, no, honey! This here is on me and Ray. Does your mama think we're gonna charge her cash money to clean our granddaughter's kitchen? That ain't the kind of folks we are. We'd be over there ourselves helpin' out, if only Jolene would let us.

"I told Ray to keep his big trap shut. It wasn't none of his business talking to Bobby Lee about his own wife. What goes on between married folks is their own business, not no one else's. I told Ray, but he wouldn't listen to me. Had to go flappin' his jaw to Bobby Lee. Got him all riled up. Not but what he said ain't true. Ray don't tell lies. But he shouldn't ought to have told Bobby Lee, that's all.

"Do you want a little piece of candy, sugar? You pick yourself out a little treat. No, darlin'! Don't you try to pay me for that. You just tuck that dime right back into your pocket. You think I'd charge you for a Snickers bar? After you come all the way down here to help my girls? No sirree, it's on me and Ray. You take that on home and you enjoy it, darlin'. And you give your mama a kiss from me, you hear? You tell her poor old Loreen blesses her every night in prayer. She's a saint, your mama, you hear?"

I could hear Loreen still calling after me as I escaped with my dish soap and candy bar out the screen door. I was down the steps, congratulating myself on a clean getaway, when she burst through the door behind me.

"Oh, sweet Lord, I nearly forgot!" she called. "You tell your mama and Jolene, too, that Bobby Lee is on his way home!"

I stopped dead and swung around, staring at her. "What?"

"He called last night on the telephone here at the store. Ray talked to him. I didn't get a chance to talk to him. I told Ray to give me the phone, but he wouldn't. Said it was a long-distance call and I didn't need to waste poor Bobby Lee's money. As if I would! I know how to keep a conversation short. I told Ray . . ."

"Aunt Loreen," I blurted out. "When is he coming home?"

"What? Oh, he'll be back tomorrow morning. He's found Caleb! Found him at the YMCA in Cincinnati, Ohio. Can you believe it? That boy got hisself all the way up to Cincinnati, Ohio. That takes some gumption, don't you think? I never would have reckoned on it myself. But he's got hisself some smarts in that thick head of his, after all. And Bobby Lee, now, how he tracked that boy down, I'll never reckon on. Ray said he asked lots of people at the bus station in St. Albans, and one of them ticket agents looked at Caleb's picture and said he remembered him buyin' a ticket to Cincinnati. So Bobby Lee, he rode up to Cincinnati and he went right down to the YMCA, 'cause he remembered that's where his daddy stayed the first time he left Cleda Rae—Lord, that was all the way back in 1963, the first time Noah left. Course, he didn't stay gone that time. He came on home again after a while, with his tail tucked, outta money. And Cleda Rae took him back, too. I don't know why she took him back. I said to Ray . . ."

"Aunt Loreen," I started to interrupt again.

"Oh yes, anyways, that's where he found Caleb—at the YMCA. Don't that beat all? And now they're comin' home. You tell Jolene that, okay, darlin'? You tell Jolene her husband is on his way home. And he's bringing that poor boy with him. You tell her that, too.

"And tell her she better get herself busy makin' a home for both of them, and she better watch her step or she ain't gonna have no home to keep clean at all. Lord knows what we'll do if he kicks her out. I reckon she'll have to come back to me and Ray. How we'll manage then, I don't rightly know. Herself and Reana Mae both . . . the good Lord knows that's too much for me and Ray at our age. But I reckon the Lord don't give more than we can take."

By this time I was edging away again. As soon as it seemed decent, I turned and ran headlong down the road. I could still hear Loreen hollering behind me, "You'll tell your mama and Jolene, won't you, darlin'? That's a sweet girl."

❧ 10 ❧

Hail the
Conquering Hero

Mother, Reana, and I stood with Jolene on the front porch of the scrubbed-clean cabin. Reana Mae was home from school again to wait for Bobby Lee's homecoming. Jolene had tied her hair back with a black ribbon and put on some makeup. Her face was ashen and her clothes were far too tight, but she didn't wobble or chain-smoke as she stood on the sagging porch. She just stood silently, twisting her hands before her.

When we heard the roar of the motorcycle, Mother smiled reassuringly at her. "I think Bethany and I will scoot on back to Belle's now," she said.

But Jolene grabbed her by the hand and held tight. "Stay, Helen," she pleaded. "Just stay a little while, okay? I know Bobby will want to see you."

By this time, Bobby Lee had pulled in front of the house, as I'd seen him do countless times before. He tugged the helmet from his head, shaking his curly black hair. Behind him, Caleb removed his helmet, too, shaking his head the same way. Sitting there together on the bike, they looked more alike than I'd remembered.

As Bobby Lee swung himself off the huge motorcycle, Reana Mae ran down the steps and into his arms, her long braid flapping behind her. She was scrubbed clean, too, and wearing her Sunday dress. "Daddy! I knew you'd come home! And I knew you'd find Caleb, too! I just knew it!"

She turned to Caleb as he climbed off the motorcycle. "Hey, Caleb." She grinned, throwing her spindly arms around him. "I'm glad you came back."

Caleb wrapped his arms awkwardly around her slight frame and buried his face in her hair. I couldn't hear what he said to her, but I could see his shoulders shaking slightly, even from the porch.

"Hey, Helen." Bobby Lee nodded to my mother as he strode up the porch steps. "What are you doin' here? Everything okay?"

"Yes, Bobby Lee, everything's just fine." Mother hugged Bobby Lee lightly. "Bethany and I came down to help Jolene get back on her feet."

At the mention of Jolene, Caleb abruptly released Reana Mae and stood stiffly, staring at the group on the porch. Then he reached into his back pocket, pulled out a small plastic comb, and began yanking it furiously through his tangled black curls.

Bobby Lee reached out and ruffled my hair. "Hey, Bethany. You've growed a foot since last summer."

"Hey, Bobby Lee." I smiled shyly.

We all stood in awkward silence. Finally, Bobby Lee turned to his wife.

"You still here?" he demanded. He did not move toward her.

"Yeah, Bobby Lee. I'm still here," she said, not meeting his gaze. She shifted from one foot to the other and wrapped her arms tightly around her swollen middle.

"I brought Caleb home." He stared hard at his wife.

Jolene still looked down at the floor.

Suddenly, Bobby Lee reached out and grabbed her by the arm. Mother stepped back, pulling me with her. Jolene finally looked up into Bobby's unsmiling face.

"Did you hear what I said? I brought Caleb back home, where he belongs."

"Yes, Bobby," she whispered. "I heard."

"And he's here to stay. My little brother is gonna live right here in this house—in *my* house—with me. You hear me?"

Jolene simply nodded, her face growing redder with each passing minute. Mother still held me tightly by the hand. I didn't make a sound. I'd never seen Bobby Lee so angry, so quiet, so menacing.

"All right, then," he continued grimly. "You think you can live with that and behave like a decent woman instead of actin' like some two-dollar whore, you can stay, too."

Jolene stared hard at the ground for a long minute. Then she raised her eyes and whispered, "Okay, Bobby."

I could barely hear her words, standing as close as I was. Tears streamed down her red face. Jolene Darling Colvin had been thoroughly humbled.

"Go on inside, then, and get some coffee going. We got us a lot of talkin' to do," Bobby Lee said.

"Yes, Bobby," she whispered, disappearing into the cabin.

He looked at Mother and me. "I'm sorry, Helen, that your little one had to hear that."

Mother nodded, then reached out and touched his arm. "I'm glad you're home, Bobby Lee." She turned to look at Caleb, still standing in the yard. "You, too, Caleb. I'm glad to see you home."

Caleb ambled up onto the porch, staring all the while at the ground.

"Thank you, ma'am," he mumbled.

"Caleb got hisself a job up in the city, workin' at a drugstore. The manager said he done real good work." Bobby Lee draped his arm over his brother's shoulders. "Ain't that something?"

"It certainly is," Mother said. "That's something to be proud of, Caleb."

Bobby Lee smiled at his brother. "Yeah, he done hisself proud, all right." He looked toward the cabin door, his smile fading.

"Reana Mae," he said, reaching into his pocket and pulling out a five-dollar bill, "why don't you and Caleb walk on down to Ray's and pick us up a six-pack of Bud? Ya'll get yourself a treat, too."

I stood with Mother and watched Reana Mae and Caleb as they walked down the road. Reana was chattering the way she did when she was excited. I was disappointed she hadn't asked me to go with them. When I turned back to Mother, Bobby Lee had already disappeared into the cabin.

Mother smiled as if she understood. "She's excited to have her family back, sweetheart. But she's awfully glad to have you, too."

As we walked back to Aunt Belle's, we were both quiet. I felt a jumble of emotions—relief at escaping the tension, disappointment at Reana's betrayal, and curiosity at what might be happening in the little cabin.

"Is it going to be all right now, Mother?" I asked.

"I hope so, Bethany. I hope so," she said.

The next day was Saturday—our day to head back home. After we had packed our suitcase and stripped the sheets from the bed we'd shared, Mother and I sat down to breakfast with Belle, Donna Jo, Bobby Lee, Jolene, Reana Mae, and Caleb. Belle's big mahogany table shone dark under a white lace cloth. Whether it was Thanksgiving dinner, a simple lunch, or even breakfast like this, Belle's table was always perfect. The morning sunlight glinted off polished silver, white china plates, and cut-crystal drinking glasses.

We consumed huge quantities of Donna Jo's eggs, ham, grits, biscuits, gravy, and fried apples. Reana Mae was more animated than I'd ever seen her, joking with Aunt Belle about her strong coffee—for Reana drank coffee even as a child, and she liked it strong and black—and jumping up from time to time to help Donna Jo carry things to and from the kitchen. Once again it struck me that she had somehow made the leap from childhood to the mysterious adult world, leaving me behind.

"Let me get you some more of them grits, Caleb," she said, reaching for his bowl.

"Sit yourself down, Reana Mae," Bobby said in a soft but steely voice. "Your mama can fetch Caleb his breakfast."

He turned and looked pointedly at his wife. Jolene had been nearly silent all morning. She had made up her face more heavily than usual, curled her red hair, and squeezed herself into one of her short skirts. She looked like a sad parody of her former self, stuffed too tightly into Jolene's skin. She'd held Bobby Lee's hand when they arrived, sat beside him quietly, served him his breakfast, poured his coffee, and stared at her lap a great deal. Not once had she lit a cigarette.

Now she returned his stare for a long moment. I held my breath and felt my stomach clench—I think we all did. Jolene looked like she might just punch her husband right in the jaw. I know the old Jolene would have. Instead, she rose, smoothed her tight skirt, smiled grimly, and said, "Can I get you some more grits, Caleb?"

"Yes, ma'am," Caleb said, not looking up at her. "That'd be nice, ma'am."

Jolene walked into the kitchen and returned with his china bowl filled to the brim with steaming hominy grits. She set the dish in front of him. "Do you need anything else, Caleb?"

"No, ma'am. Thank you, ma'am," Caleb mumbled. His face was the color of a dirty brick.

Mother reached over and tapped my knee. I realized I was staring, openmouthed. I had never seen anyone tell Jolene what to do before. I hadn't believed it possible. Yet here she was, waiting on Caleb as meekly as a housemaid.

As Jolene sat back down, pulling her skirt over her knees, I saw Caleb glance sidelong at Reana Mae and wink.

After we had helped Donna Jo clean up the breakfast dishes, Reana Mae and I walked down to the riverbank to say our goodbyes.

"Mama promised Daddy she'll be nicer to Caleb from now on," Reana told me, smiling brightly. "And she said she won't hit me no more, neither."

"Does she hit you a lot?" I asked. I had wondered about that in the months since the doll episode.

"Just sometimes, when I'm bad or mouthy . . . or when she's had too many beers," Reana said, dropping her eyes to the willow branch she was holding in her hand. She threw it into the river abruptly. "Anyhow, she won't do it no more. She promised Daddy. Besides"—she dropped her voice to a whisper—"Caleb said he won't let her hit me no more neither."

I stared at her in silence. Maybe I had been wrong about Caleb. Maybe we all had.

"Daddy said he'll try to be home more, too. He said he's gonna ask for shorter hauls—maybe even take a regular route. He never wanted to do that before, but now he might. Then he'd be home every single weekend, and maybe sometimes during the week, too."

She was chattering again. I watched her quietly, trying to assess this new, talkative Reana Mae.

"And he's gonna finish the loft, too, even though the baby's gone. So me and Caleb can have rooms upstairs, and Mama and Daddy can have them some privacy downstairs. And Caleb's gonna work at Granpa Ray's store, so he can earn hisself some cash money and help out with the bills. He was workin' in a drugstore when Daddy found him in Cincinnati, so he knows all about workin' in a store."

She smiled at me and shyly held out her arm.

"See what he brought me from the city?"

I stared at the silver charm bracelet that sparkled around her thin wrist. A single charm dangled from it—a silver heart.

"Your daddy?" I asked.

"No, Caleb. He bought it for me at the store he was workin' at. It's genuine sterling silver. Ain't it pretty?"

"Yeah, Reana. It's real pretty."

"He brought Mama a present, too," Reana Mae said. "It's a new purse—a black one that looks just like real leather. He told Mama he was real sorry about her losin' the baby. And she said she was sorry she whupped him and made him leave."

She shook her head, her long braid swinging from side to side. "I never thought I'd live to see Mama apologizing to Caleb."

She smiled again. "You see? I told you your mama would make it all right."

"What did Mother have to do with it?" I asked. "Your daddy would have come home even if she wasn't here."

"But it was Aunt Helen who made Mama see things right."

Reana Mae's voice dropped to a whisper again.

"The other night after I went to bed, Aunt Helen came to the house. I heard her tell Mama that if she didn't straighten herself up, she'd lose my daddy for good. And then Mama and me would have to move in with Granma Loreen, 'cause Mama ain't got no business skills—that's what Aunt Helen said. Mama can't type or teach school or be a nurse or nothin'. So she'd better stay with my daddy, Aunt Helen said, 'cause she surely don't want to live with Granma again—that's for damn certain!

"Mama argued back some, you know. She said she'd move us away to Dunbar and be a fancy girl before she ever let Caleb set foot in her house again. But she didn't call him Caleb—she called him 'that sneaky bastard.' I don't know why she hates Caleb so much."

"A fancy girl?" I was puzzled at the term.

"You know, a prostitute." She said it matter-of-factly, bending to pick up a small stone and toss it into the river.

"What's a prostitute?" I asked, my face coloring. I had a pretty good idea already.

"You know, a woman that lets men have sex on her and then they give her money for it." Reana Mae smiled at me smugly—the way she had when she'd explained about Cleda Rae's sugar daddy.

"Aunt Helen 'bout died when Mama said that." She laughed. "She smacked Mama hard. I heard it even in my room with the door closed. And then Mama cried, and Aunt Helen said she'd better straighten up and fly right, or she wouldn't have no house, no family, no husband, no nothin'. And that must have scared Mama, 'cause she promised Aunt Helen she'd try. And she is, don't ya know."

Reana Mae smiled broadly. "Did you see her fetchin' Caleb his grits this morning? I like to died!"

I smiled, too, for it had been a sight. But I wondered how long it would last. I could not imagine Jolene catering to Caleb for very long. Jolene was many things, but she was not meek. She was too headstrong, too hard-edged, too much Jolene to continue this way. I didn't say that to Reana Mae. Why spoil her happiness? But I knew it couldn't last.

Just then, Mother called to say it was time to go. As I hugged Reana Mae tight, I felt a lump in my throat and tears stinging my eyes.

I had the sudden notion that I might never see Reana Mae again. And in a way, I was right. The shy little girl I had teased and loved and shared so many secrets with would be gone before I returned to the Coal River Valley. In her place would be a pretty young woman with secrets she did not share with me—or with anyone— for a long, long time.

The drive home was long and dull. Mother was as lost in her thoughts as I was in mine. I stared out the window as the scenery changed from tobacco barns and rolling hills to flat farmland.

It was suppertime when Mother finally pulled the station wagon into the gravel driveway. She honked the horn, and Daddy immediately appeared on the front steps, followed by Nancy and Melinda.

"I'm sure glad you're home." Daddy grinned, enveloping Mother in a hug. "I don't like you being on the road all by yourself."

"I wasn't by myself," Mother said with a smile. "I had Bethy with me."

Daddy laughed and turned to hug me. "Sure enough you did! I'm glad you were along to keep your mama company, Bethany. I imagine you were a real help to Reana Mae."

"Yes, she was, Jimmy," Mother said, smiling down at me. "She surely was."

"How's Jolene, Mother?" Melinda asked as she pulled the big suitcase from the back of the car.

"She's going to be all right, honey. She just needed a little help getting back on her feet. But Bobby Lee is home now, and he's brought Caleb home. I think they'll work it out."

I saw Mother looking at Daddy as she said this. Her look belied her words. I knew she didn't believe in Jolene's new attitude any more than I did. Daddy took her by the hand and they walked into the house together, her head resting lightly on his shoulder. I stood in the driveway, holding my pillow and blanket, and watched them.

Nancy and Melinda walked into the house, too, and I trailed after them. As I came in the front door, the first thing I heard was Tracy's voice chirping, "Oh no, we didn't miss you at all. I took good care of Daddy, just like I said I would. Didn't I, Daddy?"

She turned to my father and took his arm in hers.

"Yes, darlin', you sure did." Daddy grinned down at her.

"But," he continued, drawing Mother close, "I sure did miss you, Helen."

Tracy turned on her heel and walked into the kitchen, calling over her shoulder, "Dinner will be ready in a few minutes."

Mother looked inquiringly at Daddy and he grinned again.

"She's been cooking every night." He laughed. "I think she's found her calling."

"Well, she certainly thinks she's an expert chef, that's for sure," Nancy said tartly. "Every time Melinda and I went in the kitchen, she chased us out like she owned the place."

Mother laughed and gave Nancy a quick hug. "I imagine it wasn't *too* hard, was it, having someone else do the cooking?"

Nancy's cheeks colored and she grinned. "No, it wasn't too hard, I guess."

"Anyway," Melinda chimed in, "Tracy's not a bad cook. But she sure is a messy one. We didn't have to do the cooking, but we had to clean up after her."

At that moment Tracy's voice trilled from the kitchen. "Dinner's ready. Come on and eat before it gets cold."

The kitchen table was set for four. I stared as Tracy sat down in Mother's chair. Then I noted the two chairs set back from the table under the window.

"Tracy, you forget to set places for Mother and Bethany," Daddy said.

"Oh yes, I suppose I did," she said. But she didn't move from Mother's chair.

"That's all right, Jimmy," Mother said, "I'll get it."

Nancy and Melinda scooted their chairs over to make room for Mother and me. I stared at Tracy, sitting at the head of the table, holding a serving spoon poised over a big dish of egg noodles.

"Would you like some noodles, Daddy?" she asked sweetly.

Melinda rolled her eyes at Nancy and both of them giggled.

As we ate, Mother told Daddy what had happened in West Virginia. She didn't tell him everything, of course. I knew she was saving the details until they were alone.

"Well, I don't blame Jolene for not wanting that big oaf in her house," Nancy opined. "I bet it's a nuisance having him around."

"Now, Nancy, don't be that way," Mother scolded. "Caleb is just a boy, and he needs a home. He's Bobby Lee's family, and family matters more than anything else. You know that."

I didn't say anything. I wasn't sure how I felt about Caleb, but I thought Mother was probably right. He was just a big boy, and he was good to Reana Mae. Maybe he just needed to feel at home someplace.

After supper, I retrieved my pillow and blanket from the sofa and trudged up the stairs to the attic room. At the top of the steps, I stopped in amazement. Everything had changed. The furniture had been rearranged so that Tracy's things occupied the front of the room and mine were squeezed into the small alcove at the back. My books, my pictures, my stuffed animals and dolls were stuffed willy-nilly into a small bookcase. Even my clothes had been moved from the big closet we had shared into the small closet at the far end of the room.

I stood in stunned silence for a moment. Then I began yelling, "Mother, Mother! Come look what Tracy's done!"

Mother came up the stairs with Tracy right behind her. She stood staring, too, as Tracy said in the same sharp, bright voice she'd used since we got home, "I rearranged things. Doesn't it look nice, Mother? See, all of my things are here at this end, and Bethany's are at that end. That way we each have a space of our own. Doesn't it look nice?" she repeated, looking up at Mother.

"Well, Tracy . . . I think maybe you should have waited until we were home and let Bethany have some say, too."

"But I wanted to surprise her," Tracy said sweetly, her hazel eyes sparkling innocently.

"Don't you like it, Bethy?" She turned to me now. "See, all of your stuff is together now. And you have your own closet, too, so we don't have to share anymore. And look," she said triumphantly, lifting the quilt on my bed, "look what Daddy got for you to keep your extra things in."

Under the bed was a large, flat wooden box with a hinged lid. Tracy pulled it out and lifted the lid. Inside I saw my summer clothes, folded neatly.

"Daddy helped you do this?" Mother asked incredulously.

"Oh yes, Mother. When I told him how I wanted to surprise Bethy and give her some space of her own, he said that was just the nicest idea he'd ever heard. He helped me move all the furniture around. I certainly couldn't have done it myself."

Tracy turned back toward her side of the room. I noted grimly that she commanded the lion's share of the space, and that my posters had been removed from all the walls.

"Don't you like it, Bethy?" She looked at me again, and I could see the spite in her eyes. "It will be so much nicer if we don't have to step over each other all the time, don't you think?"

Mother was looking at me, too, waiting to see what I would say. We all made allowances for Tracy. And even though it wasn't fair, I knew Mother would go along with it if I would—as long as it kept Tracy happy.

I looked around the room again. My stomach churned; my fists and teeth clenched tightly. Just for once, I wondered what would happen if *I* threw a fit, if I lost control and screamed and threw things out the window.

But even as the thought arose, I knew it would never happen.

I sighed. "Sure, Tracy. I like it just fine, I guess."

"Are you sure, Bethany?" Mother asked softly.

"Yes, Mother." I nodded. "It's fine."

I carried my pillow and blanket to the bed at the far end of the room. That's when I realized that Patsy wasn't in her usual place on the bed. I had put her there when we left for our trip. I knew she had been there, tucked under the quilt in her flannel nightgown. I turned in a panic to look at Tracy and caught just a trace of a smile on her face before her eyes widened in mock dismay.

"Oh, Bethy, I'm so sorry," she gushed. "When Daddy was moving your bed, Patsy fell off and her head broke wide open . . . just shattered right there on the floor."

I stared at the spot on the floor where she was pointing, as if I might see some remnant of my Patsy. Of course there was none.

"He felt so bad about it, Bethy, he really did. I don't know how it could have happened. I guess she must have been right at the edge of the bed."

I shook my head. Patsy hadn't been on the edge of the bed. I had tucked her in myself in the early morning before we left.

"Don't be mad at Daddy," Tracy continued, her voice sweetly pleading. "He felt so bad about it. He really did."

"Daddy moved the bed?" Mother asked quietly.

"Well, of course," Tracy said, looking right into Mother's face. "I couldn't move it on my own, so he came up to help me."

"So you both moved it?"

"Well, I was helping Daddy," Tracy said flatly, her eyes still wide and staring straight up at Mother. "But he's the one that pushed the bed. And he feels just terrible about it."

"I'm sure he does," Mother said, watching Tracy's face closely. Then she turned to me. "I'm so sorry, sweetheart. We'll get you a new doll."

It wasn't until Mother hugged me that I began to cry. My tears came in great, gulping sobs, and once I started, I couldn't seem to stop.

I cried for Jolene's lost baby, and for Reana Mae. I cried from anger and confusion and sheer exhaustion. And I cried for Patsy— my beautiful doll. I hadn't actually played with Patsy much in the last year. But losing her felt like losing part of myself.

Mother held me until I had worn myself out with crying. Then she helped me change into my nightgown, washed my face, and tucked me into bed.

She sat on the edge of the bed and stroked my hot, flushed face, until my eyes finally closed. And as she stroked she sang, "All night, all day, angels watching over me, my Lord. All night, all day, angels watching over me."

As I drifted off into a restless, uncomfortable sleep, I wondered what kind of angels they were to let such awful things happen on their watch.

❧ 11 ❧

Demons and Ghosts

"I know, Helen, I know." I could barely hear my father's voice. It seemed to come from inside a deep well. "She's a handful now. But it'll pass. Just you wait and see. She'll grow out of it."

"What if she doesn't, Jimmy?" My mother's voice sounded equally far away and very worried. I struggled to wake myself from the fog of sleep. Where was I? Oh yes, at the far corner of the attic room, where Tracy and Daddy had pushed my bed. I could see stars in the night sky out the window over my bed, and I could hear my parents' voices through the heat vent that now lay directly under the bed. I must be right over their room.

"She will, Helen. She's just upset by this whole business with Bobby Lee and Jolene, that's all."

"Jimmy, did you move Bethany's bed?" Mother asked abruptly. "Or did Tracy?"

"Well . . ." Daddy hesitated. I sat up in my bed, listening intently now. At the other end of the room, Tracy snored.

"Well," he continued, "Tracy wanted to surprise you all, moving the furniture all by herself, so she and Bethany would both have some space. And she started out on her own, but then when she tried to move the bed . . . well, she came running downstairs in a panic, saying she'd broken Bethany's doll. You should've seen her, Helen. She was so scared. She thought you would blame her for it. And she was just crying to beat the band. I thought she'd never stop. So I said I'd help her with the rest, and then I moved the bed where it is now."

"So Tracy broke Bethany's doll?" Mother asked.

"It was an accident, Helen. Honestly, you should have seen how sorry she was." Daddy was pacing now. I could hear the floorboards squeaking.

"I'm sure she was," Mother said grimly.

"Now, don't be that way," Daddy was pleading. "She really was sorry. And she was so afraid you'd be mad at her. Honestly, Helen, it was pitiful."

There was a long pause. I slid to the floor, rolled myself under the bed, and laid my ear against the vent. Finally, Mother spoke.

"Jimmy, we've put this off for a long time," she said. "But we both know something is not . . . right with Tracy."

I could hear Daddy's pacing. One particular board squeaked loudly each time he stepped on it.

"Jimmy? Are you hearing me?" Mother's voice was sad and tired. "I know it's not something we wanted to believe. But, Jimmy, look what she's doing to Bethy."

"No!" Daddy's voice was so loud it made me jump. At the far end of the room, Tracy sighed and rolled over in her sleep. "I'm not going to let you make this into a crisis. So she broke a doll, so what? It was an accident, for God's sake. And even if it wasn't . . . even if it wasn't completely an accident . . . Helen, is it any wonder she's so resentful?

"Just look at it from Tracy's perspective. First, you pay all kinds of attention to that little girl down there, not that she don't need it, God knows. But Tracy . . . she just needs a little more attention from you, that's all. That's all she's ever needed. And then you take off in the middle of the week—in the middle of the school year, for God's sake—and you take Bethany with you, but you don't take her. How did you think she was going to feel, Helen?

"Tracy would be just fine if you spent as much time worrying over her as you do over Jolene and Reana Mae. I'm sorry I ever took you back to West Virginia! When are you going to start putting your own family first, Helen?"

The door slammed, and I knew he'd left. A moment later, I heard the car start in the driveway. Then I heard my mother sobbing. She was still crying when I heard the bedsprings creak under her weight. Finally, a long time later, I fell asleep there on the floor to the sounds of my mother's muffled sobs.

❦ 12 ❦

Pilgrimage

We didn't go to the Coal River that summer. Instead, we spent the long vacation at home in Indiana. Nancy and Melinda were delighted by this change; they both had boyfriends and belonged to sororities, and they spent less and less time at home those days. Nancy took a summer job at a store in the mall, earning extra money and a big discount on clothes. I don't know which she valued more, but my parents were amazed at how well she did at work. Nancy had never been much of a student, but she was a marvel at sales. Soon, she had customers who wouldn't buy from any other salesclerk.

"That girl could sell ice to Eskimos," my father crowed at dinner one night. "Who knew she'd have such a head for business?"

"I bet I could sell things, too," Tracy trilled. "Don't you think I'd be a good salesman, Daddy?"

"Probably so, baby." Daddy smiled. "But you've got a ways to go before you can get a job."

The very next day, Tracy announced she had taken a paper route. For the next two years, she diligently delivered newspapers after school every day, dragging the large canvas bag full of rolled papers in a wagon behind her. Sometimes she paid me a penny a paper to help her roll them. Her customers loved her, often tipping her far more than any of the other carriers received, and Daddy beamed when he talked about his two budding business tycoons.

Melinda spent her days at the YMCA. She was on the swimming and diving teams, and she worked long hours on her rolls and butterfly stroke. Daddy went to all the meets, cheering himself hoarse from the side of the pool. All of Melinda's ribbons hung from a corkboard in his office, and he proudly boasted of his future Olympian, too.

I spent the summer reading, writing letters to Reana Mae, and whining at Mother. I didn't remember a summer when we hadn't gone south, and I didn't know what to do with myself. I went to the pool with Melinda sometimes, but I didn't want to swim on the team. I followed Tracy on her paper route, rode my bike to the park, drew chalk pictures on the sidewalk, and bitterly resented my father for keeping us at home.

"I don't know why we can't go to the river," I complained daily. "I think Daddy is just mean to make us stay home."

After a week or so of this, Mother's patience wore thin and she told me that every time I complained about staying home, I would have to put a dime in the gripe jar she made and set out on the kitchen counter. After losing a dollar's worth of dimes, I stopped griping out loud. But I was not happy.

Part of my unhappiness stemmed from Reana's irregular letters. I wrote to her diligently, twice a week at least, bemoaning my fate and maligning my father. Her letters came less and less frequently that summer, and she seemed not to miss me at all. In fact, Reana Mae sounded happier than I'd ever known her to be. In June she wrote,

> *Today we had the biggest game of kick-the-can you ever saw. Every kid on the river played, and Caleb was IT. Just when he thought he had everybody, I ran in and kicked the can over. Harley Boy swore he let me kick it, but I don't think so. Caleb don't let nobody beat him.*

Two weeks later,

*Bethany, you are missing the best summer ever! Caleb
and me cut a real path all the way to the beach. Boy was
Harley Boy suprised! He even got mad and said he was
going to do that and we took his idea. But Caleb just laffed
at him and said Harley was jelus cause we did it with out
him.*

In July,

*I swam all the way across the river today!!! I was
scared to at first but Caleb swam with me the hole way.
When he is not working at granpa's store we swim all the
time. And mama don't even yell when I come home late
like she used to. She just smokes her cigs and don't say
anything.*

The only dark cloud on Reana's summer parade seemed to be
her daddy's long absences. Despite his promises in March, Bobby
Lee was taking longer and more frequent hauls. Reana Mae wrote
that he hadn't been home more than four days all summer. Still, on
the whole she seemed to be having the time of her life. Without me.

Near the end of July, Daddy announced that he was taking a
two-week vacation. We sat in stunned silence, gaping at him.
Daddy had never taken a whole two weeks of vacation before.

"Are we going to the river?" I asked, already planning in my
head all the things I wanted to do with Reana Mae.

"Not this year." He grinned, winking at Mother. "This summer
the whole family's going to . . ." He paused just long enough for us
to get impatient. "Florida!"

He beamed proudly, Mother smiled, and the other girls
squealed in excitement.

"Florida! Oh, Daddy, that's so cool!"

"Are we staying at the beach?"

"Will the hotel have a pool?"

"We'll get so tanned!"

I sat sullenly, watching them.

"What's wrong, Bethany? Don't you want to go to Florida? Land of the golden sun!" Daddy tweaked my chin.

Mother stood behind him, watching me. She smiled hopefully and nodded.

So I nodded, too.

"Yes, Daddy. I want to go." I could hardly get the words past the lump in my throat, but I smiled and blinked back the tears stinging my eyes. "That'll be great."

Satisfied, he turned to the others, who were peppering him with questions. Mother touched my cheek lightly and smiled. I ran upstairs to write to Reana Mae.

We drove to Florida in the big old station wagon, each of us commanding her usual spot. Mother and Daddy sat up front, of course. Nancy and Melinda laid out their blankets and pillows in the backseat. Tracy and I took the back end. Daddy laid out all the suitcases, then spread several blankets over them. Tracy and I sprawled on top of these, amusing ourselves by sticking our feet out the back window, making faces at the drivers of cars behind us, and bickering.

Our destination was Bonita Springs on the Gulf Coast. We were going to see our Grandmother Araminta. I didn't remember having seen her before, though Daddy swore I had. Now she had lung cancer, and Daddy was bringing his girls to visit her before she died. I wondered, as we drove, what I would feel for this woman who was my daddy's mother but wasn't my Aunt Belle. I wondered what Daddy felt for her, too. If he was worried at all, it didn't show. He sang nonsense songs, teased my mother, and ate jelly beans as he drove over the speed limit through Tennessee, slowing to obey the signs in Georgia, then speeding again when we hit the Florida state line.

On this special pilgrimage, we didn't pack our meals. We ate in real restaurants and stayed in real motels—which turned out to be not nearly so glamorous as we'd imagined. Six people in a single motel room did not lend itself much to glamour. Mother and Daddy slept in one bed, Nancy and Melinda in the other, and Tracy and I spread the blankets from the back of the car on the floor to sleep.

We unloaded the car just after lunch on the third day at a small motel six blocks from the ocean, raced for the bathroom to change into our swimsuits, then waited impatiently while Mother donned her suit and Daddy found the cameras. Finally, we climbed back into the car and drove to the beach, where Daddy fumed at the injustice of paying fifty cents for a parking place, and we swam in the ocean, letting the waves knock us about, screaming at the cool water, while Mother fussed about sunscreen and sharks.

The next morning, we showered and shampooed and donned the Easter dresses mother had draped so carefully across the motel beds. Daddy paced about the small room, barking orders and checking the cameras again and again.

"Nancy, you are not wearing those green stockings. Helen, did you see Nancy's stockings? She can't wear those today.

"Melinda, tie your hair back, for Pete's sake! You look like you just got out of bed.

"Bethany, where are your shoes? No, you can't wear your sandals. Where are your nice shoes? I know your mother packed them. Get them on your feet . . . now, Bethany!

"Tracy, where are you? Helen, where's Tracy? What's she doing in the bathroom? We've got to go, ladies. Come on, we're late!"

I'd never seen my father so nervous. Mother moved wordlessly from suitcase to suitcase, finding stockings and hair bows and patent leather shoes. Finally, we lined up for inspection. Daddy looked us over critically, pronounced us fit to be seen, snapped a couple of pictures, and herded us to the car.

"No, girls, you can't ride in the back in your nice dresses. Tracy, you sit up front with us. Bethy, you're with Nancy and Melinda. Everyone ready? Okay, let's go."

The apartment my grandmother shared with her daughter was in a gated village called Green Palm Estates. It seemed like everyone who lived there was old—white-haired men toddled around the lake; leathered old women lay like so many raisins by the pool. I'd never seen so many old people.

The buildings were pink stucco, the railings on the walkways dark green. The August sun glared down so hot and white, it washed out the colors to faded pastels. The humidity was unbelievable. By the time we'd trudged around the man-made lake to our grandmother's door, the curls Mother had so carefully crafted in my hair clung limply to my neck. My bangs stuck to my forehead like wet tissue. Daddy mopped his bald spot repeatedly. Only Mother looked cool and collected, as she always did.

Before Daddy even knocked on the door, it swung open and a tall, thin redheaded woman stepped out and flung her arms around him. She kissed Daddy on both cheeks, then drew back to look at his face. She had more freckles than any human being I had ever seen, more than Melinda—more than could ever be counted, I thought.

"Hello, Jimmy! Hello! We're so glad you're here. And, Helen." She turned to Mother. "It's wonderful to see you. And look at your girls." She breathed deeply, apparently enraptured at the sight of us. "My goodness, you all have grown up into such fine young ladies. Why, the last time I saw you, you were just little girls. And now look at you all."

So we did. We looked at one another, to see if we really were fine ladies. But we were still only us—dressed in our finest, to be sure, but sunburned red and drenched in sweat.

"Girls, you remember your Aunt DarlaJean?" Daddy pointed to each of us in turn. "DJ, that's Nancy, Melinda, Tracy, and Bethany."

"Why, that cannot possibly be Bethany Marie!" the woman cried, apparently disbelieving her brother's words. "Darlin', you come over here and give your Aunt DJ a hug."

She scooped me in with her long thin arms and crushed me to her bony self.

"The last time I saw you, you were just a little baby! Suckin' on a pacifier and hangin' on to your mama's skirts. And look at you now! Look at all of you. Well, my soul and salvation, I'd never have known you could be so grown up. Sakes alive, Jimmy, where does the time go to?

"Well, come on in, come in, all of you. You must be wilting in this heat. August is *not* the time to visit Florida!"

We stepped into a delicious burst of cold air.

"We keep the AC running nonstop during the summer. It's just unbearable outside, you know. Did you see the ladies down by the pool? How they stand this heat, I will never fathom! But they're down there every blessed day!

"Now, you all just sit down and make yourselves at home. I'll get us some nice, cold lemonade. You like lemonade, Bethany?"

I nodded, smiling.

She bustled out of the room, and I sank down onto the couch beside my sisters. The room was cool and dark, the shades drawn against the sun. Once my eyes had adjusted to the abrupt change, I saw that the room was decorated in the same colors as the outside buildings. The sofa and chairs were patterned with huge pink peonies and dark green leaves; the walls were pink, the carpet dark green.

And then I spotted the memorial wall. That's all I can call it, really. At the end of the room the furniture simply ended and the wall stood blank—except for the pictures. There must have been a hundred of them framed on the wall. Each photo was matted in pink and framed in dark green. The effect was dizzying.

I rose and went to take a closer look, then nearly dropped back into my seat. The pictures were of us—me and my sisters and my parents—all of them. In one lower corner, I even saw a photo of our dog, Skipper. There were baby pictures and school pictures and Nancy's latest prom picture. Snapshots of family picnics, Melinda with her swimming ribbons, Tracy with her friend Lynette, me opening birthday presents. In the middle of it all, smack in the center of the wall, was a huge black-and-white portrait of my parents on their wedding day—Daddy grinning with a full head of reddish-blond hair, Mother smiling shyly in her long white dress.

I turned back to see Mother smiling at my reaction, as my aunt reentered the room, carrying a tray of glasses and a pitcher of lemonade.

"That's right, Bethany. There you are." She beamed, pointing at my baby picture. "There you all are."

She sat down in the rocking chair across from the sofa and began pouring lemonade. "Your daddy sends us all kinds of pictures, you know. Why, we hear all about you girls, so we feel like we almost know you already."

I sat back down on the couch as Daddy asked, "Where's Mother, DJ?"

"She's resting in her room, Jimmy. She always takes a nap late morning. She don't sleep much at night."

"How's she doing?"

"Well, she's been better, Jimmy. She's been better." Aunt DJ sighed. "Some days are good, some not. But we go on as best we can. What else can you do, after all? Helen, would you like a sugar cube in your lemonade?"

"But, DarlaJean, what do the doctors say?" Daddy leaned forward, his brow creased.

"Oh, Jimmy, you know how doctors are. They're always pestering her to come to the hospital. They want to stick her with needles and fill her full of drugs. And she don't want any of it, no, sir! And neither do I, you know. I can take care of her just fine here. We do fine together, the two of us. We always have, you know."

Daddy's brow furrowed deeper. "But what kind of treatment is she getting, then?"

"Well, right now she ain't doing that, Jimmy. She just wants to stay home and let me take care of her. And I do, you know. I take care of her, just like always." She smiled proudly.

"Is she taking chemotherapy?" Daddy asked. "Are they trying any drugs? What are they doing for her?"

"Well, Jimmy, it's like I told you, Mama don't want those drugs no more. They made her sick as a dog, I can tell you. She was sicker on 'em than she was before. It was just awful! Now she just wants to stay here and let me take care of her."

Daddy's face was red as he tried again. "But, DarlaJean," he said, his teeth clenched now, too.

Mother touched his arm gently and leaned forward. "What about pain, DarlaJean? Is she in much pain?"

Aunt DJ sat back, relaxing at Mother's gentle tone. "Well, now, sometimes the pain gets pretty bad, Helen. Not always, of course. She has some good days, some bad. But when it gets too bad, why, I just pour her some peach schnapps, and that seems to help her a lot." She smiled, looking back at my father. "She's always liked her schnapps."

Daddy rose abruptly and said he was going to walk outside for a few minutes. When he'd gone, Aunt DJ talked to us about the Florida weather, the price of groceries, and the alligators that sometimes came to stay in the lake. She seemed painfully anxious to please us, and kept glancing at Mother for approval.

"I do take real good care of her, Helen," I heard her whisper once.

Mother reached over to pat her hand and said, "Yes, DarlaJean. I know you do. And Jimmy knows it, too. He's just anxious, that's all."

DarlaJean nodded and smiled, then began pouring yet another glass of lemonade for Melinda.

"Have a cookie, sweetheart," she cooed, handing the pink plate to Tracy. "I made them myself, just for you all."

"Thank you, ma'am." Tracy smiled up at her aunt in the heartbreakingly beautiful way she sometimes had.

"What an angel," Aunt DJ crooned in delight. "Helen, you have such angels."

∞13∞

Araminta Lee

Daddy came back from his walk smelling of pipe tobacco and looking calmer. I knew he would hear from Mother later about the tobacco. Just now, however, he was drinking lemonade and listening to Aunt DJ talk about her Saturday night bingo game. Apparently she and Grandma Araminta were masters of bingo.

Suddenly, Aunt DJ grew silent, holding up a finger to shush us all. Then she rose, setting aside her knitting. "I do believe Mama is awake," she said, disappearing down the hall.

Daddy looked at Mother and began mopping his forehead again. Mother looked sternly at the four of us squeezed together on the couch and said quietly, "All right, girls. Best behavior now, you hear?"

We all nodded miserably.

Aunt DJ returned with the tiniest, whitest-haired lady I had ever seen. You could hardly believe she was Aunt Belle's sister, she looked so small and fragile, holding her daughter's arm, walking unsteadily to the upholstered rocking chair that had sat empty the entire morning. We all stood quietly, waiting for something, I suppose. Daddy leaned forward and kissed his mother on her pale, creased cheek, then Mother did the same. Finally, Aunt DJ helped the old lady sit down, and we all sat, too.

I stared in wonder at my grandmother's tiny frame and snow-white hair. She didn't look a thing like Belle, or like anybody else I knew. Then she turned her head to look me square in the face, her eyes catching mine and holding them as though she were sizing me up. And I could see that her eyes were Belle's eyes and Melinda's, too—sharp, clear, and bright blue. And when she smiled at me, those eyes crinkled at the corners just like Belle's.

"So, Jimmy, here are your girls."

Daddy smiled, pointing at each of us in turn. "Here's Nancy, she's seventeen. And Melinda, she's fifteen now."

Araminta peered closely at my sisters, then smiled. "Why, this one," she said, pointing to Melinda, "looks just like DarlaJean did when she was younger. Ain't that so, DarlaJean?"

DarlaJean blushed. "Well, Mother, I don't think I was ever that pretty."

"And here is Bethany. She's eleven."

The blue eyes settled on me briefly. "You look just like your mama, little one." She smiled at Mother.

"And this is Tracy."

Araminta gazed at Tracy in silence for a long minute, her eyes filling with tears.

"Mother?" DarlaJean leaned down to touch the old lady's hand.

"Why, it's like looking in a mirror," Araminta whispered, smiling at Tracy. "A very old mirror . . . She looks just like me."

Tracy smiled as the old lady reached out her hand. She walked to Araminta's chair and kneeled before it. Araminta laid her hand on Tracy's cheek, then pulled her close and buried her face in Tracy's hair. Her thin shoulders shook.

When she finally looked up, her eyes shone. She held Tracy's hands in her own. "Jimmy, it's like she's my own granddaughter."

"Well, of course she's your granddaughter." Daddy smiled. "They're all your granddaughters."

Araminta didn't answer. She simply stroked Tracy's hair and held her hand tightly. Tracy smiled at her, glancing back toward the rest of us triumphantly.

"I hope you're feeling better, Mother," Daddy said.

My father seemed unlike himself in this pink and green room.

He talked like he did when the preacher came calling, polite and formal.

"Well, Jimmy, I tell you now, some days is good and some bad. But I still got life, and I got DarlaJean here to care for me. That's more than some folks got, I guess." She winked at my mother. "Specially the dead ones."

"DarlaJean says you're not taking treatments anymore," my mother said. "What do your doctors say about it all?"

"Well, they fuss at me, you know." She smiled down at Tracy, stroking her hair. "Tell me I need to take this treatment and that one."

She sighed heavily. "I'm too old, Helen. When it's my time, I'm ready. I reckon Arathena will be waiting for me on the other side . . . and my Winston. He's been gone such a long time. It will be a blessing to see him again."

She paused, staring into space, then smiled.

"When it's my time to go, I want to die right here in my own home. I want to meet my Maker in my navy blue dress and pumps with my makeup and hair done up real nice. DarlaJean knows how; she'll take care of me. I don't want to go in the hospital."

"Now, then." DarlaJean was on her feet, gesturing toward the door. "Mama and I are taking you all out for lunch . . . no, don't you argue with me, Jimmy. We are taking you to lunch. We know just the place. The girls will love it."

We piled back into the car and followed DarlaJean's Chevy down a busy street toward the ocean, to have lunch at a small restaurant by the beach. Nancy, Melinda, and I gazed longingly toward the water, counting the moments until we could go back to the hotel, change into our swimsuits, and play in the waves. But Tracy seemed perfectly content sitting quietly by our grandmother, offering her tartar sauce for her fish, retrieving Araminta's napkin when it fell to the floor. She looked like the cat that swallowed the canary.

In the next few days, we visited with Araminta and DarlaJean every morning, sitting dutifully on the couch, paging through photo albums stuffed with pictures of our family. It seemed Araminta had a copy of every photo ever taken of each of us, and hundreds more of Mother and Daddy from before we were born.

"There must be a million pictures here." Tracy smiled at our grandmother.

"Well, I don't know about a million, Tracy. But we've got a lot." DarlaJean grinned. "Mama and I like to know what's going on with you girls. Your daddy sends us lots of pictures."

Tracy grinned back at her. "It's sort of like we're movie stars," she said.

DarlaJean beamed.

"Now, these here are of your mother and daddy's wedding day," she said, pulling out yet another album. "Wasn't Helen a beautiful bride? Everyone said she was just the prettiest bride Charleston ever did see. They got married up in Charleston, you know. Everyone drove up there for the wedding. Even Mama and I came all the way from Florida on a Greyhound bus. We stayed at the Holiday Inn. It was just lovely." She smiled, remembering the adventure.

"Mother did look beautiful, didn't she?" Tracy whispered.

I nodded, staring at the two people in the photographs. Daddy looked like Daddy, even then. Younger, of course, but tall and freckled and handsome. Mother looked like a beauty queen in her long white gown. She even wore a small tiara on her head, just like a princess. Her smile was brilliant. I'd never seen her smile like that.

Araminta leaned in to look at the album.

"Belle put on a fine show, all right." She sighed. "Big church, lots of flowers, even a singer in the balcony. I'll say that for her; she gave my boy a fine wedding. Even paid for me and DarlaJean to come up and stay at a hotel. Course, what else could she do? He is my son, after all."

The old lady grew silent. She sipped her coffee and stared at the wall behind Tracy and me, as if she could see her boy there.

With each visit, it became clearer that Tracy was in love. It wasn't just the longing for adult attention she displayed with most people. Tracy was fascinated by Araminta. Each time we visited, Tracy sat close by our grandmother, fetching her pillow, pouring her coffee, asking for stories about her life in Florida.

Araminta seemed to enjoy the attention. On our last visit, she rested her hand on Tracy's soft hair and smiled. "You really do favor me, young lady."

"I hope so, ma'am." Tracy smiled back at her.

Araminta kissed Tracy's forehead and smiled up at my father. "Jimmy, it's like she's my own granddaughter," she said again.

"Well, of course she is, Mother!" Daddy said, laughing. "She and Bethany and Melinda and Nancy—they're all four your granddaughters."

Araminta shook her head and smiled at Tracy. "No," she said softly. "This one is mine."

Tracy's face fairly radiated pride.

Later that day, as we bickered over a blanket in the back end of the station wagon, Tracy thrust her angry face toward me and hissed, "I wish someone would come take you away like Belle took Daddy. I wish I never had any sisters at all."

Relinquishing the blanket, I wished fervently that Aunt Belle would take me, too. But I didn't think it would make Tracy any happier.

❧ 14 ❧

Growing Pains

Istarted sixth grade that fall, moving from the elementary wing of the school into junior high. I felt I had arrived. I was almost grown up now. Even Tracy's taunting on the playground after lunch couldn't dampen my spirits—although she certainly tried. Tracy resented my presence in her domain. Tracy was in eighth grade that year and captain of the cheerleading squad. She had a boyfriend—a tall, blond boy named Paul who was on the freshman basketball team at the high school. All of that didn't make her any nicer to us at home, of course, but she seemed to enjoy herself at school.

Still, the junior high was mine now, too. I had my own friends, my own place on the blacktop, my own secrets and stories. And even if I was never going to be a cheerleader like Nancy or Tracy, I had my own measures of social success. I signed up to help with the yearbook. I sang in the sixth-grade choir. And I had my own admirer—not a high school big shot like Tracy's beau, but Mark McGinty was nothing to sneeze at. He was easily the smartest kid in the sixth grade, he rode a brand-new ten-speed bike, and he was very cute, even if he was a little bit shorter than me. All in all, I was satisfied with my position in life.

I wrote about all of this to Reana Mae in early September. I sent another letter mid-month, and yet another at the start of October. But I didn't hear from my cousin until nearly Halloween.

> *October 26, 1970*
> *Dear Bethany,*
> *I'm sorry I didn't write sooner. I have been real busy sense school started. I don't like 5th grade!!! I don't like my teacher and the other kids are flat out stupid. I don't know how they ever were my friends. I wish I coud just quit school and work like Caleb does. He is working at granpa's store all the time now since he does not have to go to school any more. Granpa says he don't know what he ever did before Caleb came. He even lets Caleb run the store by hisself sometimes.*
> *Daddy is gone away a lot. I thout he was going to stay home more like he promised. But he is not. Caleb says its cause he can't stand being around mama and I think maybe he is right. Mama is still fat from the baby. And she is smoking lots and drinking a lot of beers. But at least she is keeping her promise. She don't hit me any more. And she don't yell at Caleb much at all. Mostly she just sits on the sofa and watches the TV and drinks beers. She likes the soap operas, Days of Our Lives is her favorit. She don't even cook no more. I been doing all the cooking since summer. And me and Caleb even do the washing up. I think she wood get better if daddy came home more.*
> *Write to me soon. Tell aunt Helen I said hi!*
> *Love,*
> *Reana Mae*

The letter worried me, especially the part about Bobby Lee being gone so much. I wanted to talk with Mother about it, but I didn't want to worry her. And I didn't think Reana Mae would want me sharing her letters with anyone. Instead, I wrote to her every week and prayed for her every night.

Mother always said prayer was the most powerful force there is. And our Sunday school teacher that year told us if you prayed hard enough, God would answer your prayer. She allowed that the answer you got might not be the one you wanted, but she promised He would answer. So every night, after I knew Tracy was asleep, I knelt by my bed and prayed as hard as I could. I prayed for Reana Mae, so she would be happier at school. And for Jolene, so she would stop drinking beer and become a good mother. And for Bobby Lee, so he would come home more. And for the baby who died.

At Christmastime I sent Reana a new box of stationery and some stamps.

> *December 30, 1970*
> *Dear Bethany,*
> *Thank you for the new writing paper. I love it!!! Did you have a good Xmas? Daddy came home and we had a real nice time. He brout me a record player and some records of my own!!! I got 3 Dog Night and a Patsy Cline. I asked for the Jackson 5 too, but he didn't get me that record because he said they are black. Mama was mad he got me 3 Dog Night. She said they are trashy but they are not! She just don't like them cause they are not country. She and daddy had a fight about it before he left. But I still like the record.*
>
> *Caleb gave me a necklass to wear and also my own subscripshun to National Geographic magazine, cause he knows how much I love that magazine. Isn't that the nicest thing you ever herd of? He is so good to me. I made him a Christmas card and a pine-apple upside down cake. Granma helped me make it. I wish I had some mony to buy presents for him and for you too. But Caleb said he liked the cake just fine.*
>
> *What did you get for Xmas? Write to me soon.*
> *Love,*
> *Reana Mae*

In February, Tracy was voted Sweetheart Queen at the Valentine's dance at school. Her boyfriend, Paul, looked very proud when she got her crown. Even I was proud, being her sister. Until after the dance, when she told me she wished I wasn't her sister. We were in our room, and I told her I thought she looked beautiful when she got her crown. She looked straight at me and told me she wished I wasn't her sister. And then she said that nobody at school liked me, but they were nice to me just because I was her sister.

All I could think of was how much I hated her. I wrote about it to Reana Mae, like I wrote to her about everything. But I didn't hear back from her until spring.

> *May 5, 1971*
> *Dear Bethany,*
> *I am verry sorry I have not ansered all your letters. I got so much work to do now it seems like I can never get it all done. I been helping at granpa's store to make some spending mony. And I am doing all the cooking now cause mama don't cook at all no more. And I still have to go to school even tho I hate it. Mama said she didn't care if I don't go no more, but Aunt Bell says I have to go or she will call the police in St Albans and have them take me away from mama and put in a good home. She says I got to go to school so I can make something of my self. But I alredy am something. Why don't she know that?*
> *Daddy has not been home since Xmas. But we are doing ok without him. Caleb is doing all the mans work around the house. He is still working at granpa's store too. I try to do mama's work but it is hard sense I have to go to school all day. Granma is teaching me to bake bread. We had some I made for dinner last night and Caleb said it was the best bread he ever ate. Mama didn't eat any till this morning cause she was asleep at dinner. She does that some days. Caleb says its cause she is a drunk. I used to get sad over it but I don't any more cause at least she leavs us alone now.*
> *Did you like 5th grade? Its awful boring here.*
> *Love,*
> *Reana Mae*

One day in May, Tracy asked Mother if she could invite a boy to come for dinner.

"I don't know, Tracy," Mother fretted as she stirred Chef Boyardee spaghetti sauce with hamburger over the stove, her black curls clinging to her forehead. "You know how I feel about boyfriends."

"I know, Mother." Tracy sat at the table, chopping lettuce for a salad and smiling brightly. "But it's not a date, after all. We'll just be here with you and Daddy. And this way you can get to know him. Paul is so nice, Mother . . . really! I think if you just spend some time with him, you'll see how nice he is."

"I'm sure he's nice, honey. I just think you're too young . . ."

"But I've already asked him! And he's so excited about meeting you. Oh, Mother, if you'll just meet him, I know you'll see it's okay."

"What's okay?" The screen door slammed shut behind Daddy. He loosened his tie, dropped his briefcase on the kitchen table, and kissed Mother on her forehead, pushing the damp curls back with his fingers.

"Tracy asked a boy to come for dinner." Mother frowned at Daddy.

"But it's okay, Daddy," Tracy trilled. "It's Paul. You know, the boy you met last month?"

Mother stared hard at Daddy. Daddy stared back, his face reddening. I stared at Mother, then at Daddy, and finally at Tracy, who was smiling smugly.

"You've met this boy?" Mother spoke in the soft, dangerous kind of voice she used sometimes when we were in big trouble.

"You girls go on upstairs now," Daddy said to us briskly.

"But, Daddy . . ." Tracy rose as she spoke. She was still smiling.

"Go on now, baby. You, too, Bethany. Go upstairs and finish your homework."

We walked into the living room, then stopped, both of us straining to hear our parents in the kitchen.

"Well, Jimmy?"

"Now, Helen, don't take that tone." Daddy's voice was soft and cajoling. "It's nothing, really. Just listen for a minute."

He cleared his throat. "I did meet Tracy's young man last month."

Tracy glanced sidewise at me, smirking.

"And he's a nice young man. He's a freshman at the high school, and I know you think that's too old for Tracy, but I talked with him, and I think he's all right. He's hardworking and smart as a whip. Why, he's at the top of his class in school. And he's respectful, Helen . . . real respectful. I think he might be good for Tracy."

"Jimmy, you know how I feel . . ."

"I know, Helen. I do know. But Tracy asked him to come for a reason. She wants you to know him. And that's a good thing, honey, ain't it?"

"Isn't it." Mother's reply was automatic, even when she was angry.

"I mean, she's not sneaking around behind our backs. She wants us to meet him . . . Paul is his name," Daddy continued without pause.

"Apparently, you've already met him, Jimmy."

"But she wants you to meet him, too. She's thirteen years old, Helen, nearly fourteen. Why, she's only a couple years younger than you were when we first met. "

"Tracy is not fifteen, Jimmy," Mother replied firmly. "And she's not me."

"Tracy is a good girl, and she's trying to make things right with you. Let her bring her young man to dinner. You meet him, and you'll see he's a good boy."

Mother sighed. "You know best, Jimmy," she said, in a tone that implied he did not know best at all. "I'm sure you know best."

Tracy smiled at me triumphantly. She had won and she knew it—and not just this once. She knew how to work our father against our mother. She knew how to win.

I wondered how she knew how to do that. It would never have occurred to me to use Daddy against Mother. It seemed wrong and dishonest. And it made me mad at my father. Why did he always side with Tracy . . . even against Mother? Did he just not see how mean she was?

Of course, Tracy knew how to be charming. She could smile so sweetly, and even make herself cry when she needed to. And then, she was so pretty. Was that why Daddy favored her so? Or was it just that she seemed to need him so much?

Whatever the reason, it was a fact that Daddy favored Tracy, a fact as set as the sun rising in the east every morning. There was nothing to be done for it.

✤ 15 ✤

Childish Things

In June, Daddy told us we would be going to the river. I wrote a letter to Reana Mae as soon as I heard.

We loaded the station wagon and headed south, toward home. Daddy drove, singing his nonsense songs and telling bad jokes along the way. Mother sat beside him, knitting a baby blanket for the church ladies' auxiliary. Nancy and Melinda sat in the backseat, looking at magazines and whispering. Tracy and I lay on blankets in the back end of the car. I was excited to be going back to the river, but Tracy was miserable. She wrote a six-page letter to Paul before we even reached the Ohio River, sighing heavily every ten minutes or so.

As we rounded the final turn and reached the dirt road, I strained my eyes for Reana Mae, Jolene, or Bobby Lee, but they were nowhere to be seen. Tracy scanned the horizon, too, before saying dully, "Well, I guess your trash-can twin finally found something better to do."

We pulled to a dusty stop in front of the cabin and piled out of the car. No one stood on the porch to greet us; no fire burned brightly in the stove. No one had even unlocked the door for us. Daddy and Mother stood beside the car, exchanging indecipherable looks.

"Good thing I brought the extra key," Daddy said. "Okay, ladies. Let's get going! No one uses the bathroom till we're unpacked!"

We hauled boxes and bags onto the porch as Daddy unlocked the door, opening it to the damp, cold darkness of long neglect.

Daddy carried in wood from the pile out back while Mother searched our bags for matches. Finally, she lit a fire in the woodstove and opened the shutters on all the windows, letting sunlight stream in on the plank floors and musty furniture.

"There!" Mother sounded triumphant as she turned from the stove. "Now we can make some supper. Bethany, Tracy, find the bags with the groceries."

As we began shoving aside bag after bag, we heard a tramping on the porch out front. Looking up, I saw a slim figure backlit in the doorway. It might be Reana Mae, but it seemed much older, tall and sleek, with a flowering figure. Then the figure spoke, and I sprang up to greet her.

"Hey, y'all! I'm mighty glad you're here!"

I ran to hug Reana Mae, pulling her slight frame to mine fiercely.

"Hey, yourself!" I hollered. "How are you?"

Mother joined us, scooping Reana into a hug and kissing her blond head. "Where's your mama, Reana Mae?"

"Oh, you know." Reana waved her hand vaguely. "She'll be along soon enough."

Daddy came in with another load of boxes, and Reana Mae set about helping us unpack. Finally, she winked at me. "How 'bout a walk, Bethany?"

I glanced at Mother. She nodded and smiled. "Come back soon, though, you hear? There's lots to do yet."

I slipped gratefully into the early evening shadows with my cousin. Silently, we walked around the cabin toward the river—the dark, smooth, silent river winding its way toward the Gulf of Mexico and my Grandmother Araminta. I stared at the water for a minute before sliding down the hill on my bottom behind Reana.

I'll pray for Grandma and Aunt DJ later, I promised silently. Those days I felt guilty if I thought of someone and didn't pray for them right away—like they might just die from a lapse in God's mercy. It was exhausting, being responsible for all those lives.

Sitting at the river's edge, I dipped my toes in the cool water and grinned at Reana Mae sitting beside me.

"So," I ventured. "How're things?"

"Great," she murmured. "Just great."

We sat in silence for several moments—the first silence I ever remember between us.

"How's school?" I tried again.

"It sucks!" she hissed with such vehemence, I jumped. "I hate it!"

I sat quietly for a moment before asking, "Why?"

"They're just a bunch of jackasses, Bethany. You know? It's like Caleb says, just a bunch of jackasses!"

I nodded wisely. Of course I didn't know, but I didn't want to admit it just yet.

"And they don't know nothin' about nothin'!" Reana continued.

"Like what?" I asked.

"Like about life!" She nodded sagely, her braid bobbing behind her. "Or about love. Or about nothin'!"

I sat in silence again.

"Anyways," she continued brightly, "you just got to know Caleb, Bethany. He's so much fun! And he's smart! Why, I bet he knows more that's useful than anyone else you ever met in your life."

Reana Mae beamed at me. I stared back, feeling stupid and very, very young.

"You know how people say nothin' makes sense till you're grown up? Well," she babbled along quickly now, "Caleb, he knows all about it. He makes sense of all kinds of things. I reckon that's 'cause he had to grow up fast, you know? Just like me. His mama, well, she's a tramp and a drunk . . . just like mine. And his daddy, well, he ran out on 'em. He ran off just like my daddy did. So that's why Caleb understands it all. You see, Bethany? He understands 'cause he's just like me!"

But I didn't see. All I saw was my eleven-year-old cousin—her dark blond hair pulled back in a tight braid, her shorts too tight and far too short. Reana Mae, who suddenly seemed light-years older than me, was raving about her uncle—her own blood relative—who was older even than Nancy. Too old even to be talking about. I sat dangling my feet in the river, feeling a headache coming on.

"Bethany!" Daddy's voice pierced the heavy silence of the valley. "Time to come in now!"

I stood uncertainly. Reana Mae stood, too, and I made a grim assessment of her appearance. She wore short shorts and a midriff-baring top that had been Jolene's once. She was tanned and taut and sleek like I'd never seen her before, and her figure was definitely filling out. I hadn't seen Reana for more than a year, after all. Not since Jolene lost the baby. And in that time, Reana Mae had grown up in a way that I hadn't. For all my junior high maturity, Reana Mae had left me in the dust. She was a small but complete woman-in-training, while I was still a child. And there was nothing to be done about that.

"You'll stay and have supper with us, Reana Mae," Mother said as we reached the cabin.

"Oh no, thanks, Aunt Helen. I got a stew on the stove at home. I better get on back before it burns."

Mother and I stood on the porch, watching her run up the road, her long braid flapping behind her. Mother's lips were set tight and her forehead furrowed. Her hand, resting on my shoulder, tightened slightly as Reana rounded the bend in the road and left our sight.

"You pray for her, Bethy, okay? You keep Reana Mae in your prayers."

"Yes, ma'am," I whispered. I already did that, of course. But I knew then I'd have to pray harder.

The next day, I waited until mid-morning for Reana to come. Nancy, Melinda, and Tracy had already left for the beach, and Daddy had driven into St. Albans with Aunt Belle to get groceries. Finally, Mother took my hand and pulled me toward the door, saying, "Come on. Let's go see how they are."

We walked up the road, stopping here and there to pull a handful of lilac blooms from the bushes.

"Mother?"

"Yes, Bethany?"

"Why do you suppose Reana Mae didn't come this morning?"

"Well, she probably has chores to do." She smiled down at me, brushing my bangs from my eyes. "But I know she's glad you're here."

We stopped at the gate and stared for a moment at the little house. The curtains were drawn, green paint peeled from the walls, and torn blue plastic still flapped from the roof. Finally, Mother pulled me forward by the hand and we climbed the broken step to the porch and knocked. No reply came from within.

"Jolene?" Mother called. "Reana Mae? It's Helen and Bethany."

We knocked again, but no one answered. Even Bo seemed to be gone away. Finally, Mother said, "I'll bet they're at the store."

So we walked on up the road toward the store. Mother hummed as we walked, her hand still holding mine.

We opened the screen door to the familiar smells of smoked ham and vinegar. Ray's store always smelled of vinegar. I guess it was the pickles.

"Hello?" Mother called out.

"Well, hey there, Helen! How're you, honey?" Ray appeared behind the counter, wiping his hands on a gray apron. "And Bethany Marie! Lord, child, I'da hardly knowed you. Look at how growed up you are."

He hugged Mother and patted my hair. "You all have a good trip down? What can I get for you? Bethany, how 'bout a Snickers bar?"

"We had a fine trip, Ray, just fine. And I do need a few things. But mostly we're looking for Jolene and Reana Mae. I thought they might be here." Mother glanced around the store.

"Nope, Helen. Not today." Ray handed me a candy bar. I glanced at Mother and she nodded, so I took it.

"I expect Reana Mae's somewheres about with Caleb. He's got the day off. Maybe they're fishing out behind the house," he suggested.

"What about Jolene?" Mother asked. "Any idea where she might be?"

Ray shook his head, frowning. "Ain't no tellin', Helen. Just no tellin' where that fool girl is." He glanced down at me the way grown-ups do when they don't want you to hear something.

"Bethany, why don't you go on out to the porch and eat your candy," Mother suggested. "I'll be done here soon, and we'll walk to the beach."

I sat as close to the screen door as I could without them seeing me and listened intently.

"It's bad, Helen, real bad. Bobby Lee ain't been home for months, and I hear tell he's got an apartment in Charleston with some woman. And Jolene is takin' it hard. Either lyin' in bed stone-cold drunk or goin' out God knows where drinkin' whiskey with God knows who. She don't talk to nobody 'round here—especially me and Loreen. Don't cook, don't clean, don't take care of Reana Mae." I heard him sigh. "Lord knows we tried. We been tryin' all these years. But Jolene, she just don't seem to care about no one but her own self."

"What about Reana Mae?" Mother asked.

"Well, me and Loreen look out for her as best we can. She's growin' up fast, that one. Does all the cookin' and cleanin' that gets done down there. Course, there's Caleb, too. He watches out for her. Between the two of 'em, they keep the house goin'. He works for me most days. Does a good job, too. Works hard. And Bobby Lee sends money now and then. He don't come home hisself at all, but he does send money. I'll give him that.

"Me and Loreen try to help out. But Jolene, she don't want no help from us. Blames me for her troubles with Bobby Lee, you know. Won't let us do nothin' for her. Damned, bullheaded fool—just like her mama."

"Well, we won't give up on her just yet, Ray. We'll keep praying and trying, and someday we'll get through to her. She's not a bad person, you know. She just had a hard start, that's all." Mother's voice was firm.

"Well, I reckon we'll see, Helen." Ray sounded doubtful. "I reckon we'll see. . . . Now, what can I get for you and yours today?"

Five minutes later, Mother and I were walking toward the beach, each carrying a bag from Ray's store. By the river's edge, we saw Nancy and Melinda lying on their towels, their portable radio blaring. Tracy sat on her towel, pen and paper in hand, composing another letter to Paul. Out in the water we could see two heads bobbing toward shore. As we got closer, I saw it was Harley Boy and Ruthann. I waved as they neared the shore, running down to meet them.

"Hey, Bethany!" Ruthann slogged onto the beach and gave me a wet hug. "You're here!"

I grinned at her. At least someone was glad to see me. Harley Boy trudged up beside her, his eyes carefully avoiding Nancy and Melinda's oiled-up bodies stretched out on the ground.

"Hey, Bethany, how's it goin'?" he mumbled.

"Fine, Harley Boy." I smiled at him. "Just fine."

"It's H.B.," he mumbled again.

"What?"

"He likes to be called H.B. these days," Ruthann explained. "Thinks it makes him sound older." She laughed as his cheeks reddened.

I hadn't seen Ruthann or Harley for nearly two years, but they looked about like I remembered them. Taller and older, but still like themselves. Still kids, like me.

"Did you bring your swimmin' suit with you?" Ruthann asked, flicking me with water as she toweled her dark hair.

"It's back at the house. But I'll go get it."

Mother smiled and told me to go ahead. She was going to sit a while with the girls. I took both grocery bags and ran down the road, my bare feet stumbling now and then against a rock or stick. My feet hadn't toughened up like they did every summer. Coming around the last bend toward our cabin, I caught sight of Reana Mae disappearing into the woods at the end of the road. I ran faster, calling out to her, until she finally turned. She wore tight shorts again, this time with a tiny bathing suit top. She smiled as I arrived before her, panting heavily.

"Hey," I said, smiling. "Where you been?"

"I had chores to do," she answered, not meeting my eyes.

"You wanna go swimming? Ruthann and Harley, I mean H.B., are down at the beach."

"H.B.," she snorted. "Like that makes him a man."

I simply stared at her, trying to catch my breath. I'd always thought she liked Harley Boy. I knew he liked her.

"Anyway," I finally gasped. "You wanna come?"

"No." She shook her head, glancing back toward the woods. "I'm gonna take a walk."

"But you've already got your bathing suit on," I began. She shook her head adamantly.

"Maybe later," she said, edging away. "I'll come later."

"Where you going, Reana Mae?"

"Like I said, I'm gonna take a walk."

"You want me to come with you?" I asked, knowing the answer would be no.

"Naw, that's okay, Bethany. You go on down to the beach with the kids. I'll come later."

Looking up, she suddenly colored slightly, grabbed my hands with both of hers, and said earnestly, "I promise! I'll be there in just a little while."

Then she turned and ran toward the woods, disappearing almost immediately into the thick brush.

I stood in the road and watched her go. Where was she going in the woods? Why didn't she want me to go with her? Where had the old Reana Mae gone? And who was this new girl-woman in her place? I shook my head as I pulled on my bathing suit. Well, at least Ruthann and Harley Boy seemed glad I was there. At least they still wanted me.

"What's up with Reana Mae?" I asked cautiously, lying on the wooden raft that floated halfway out in the river.

Ruthann leaned up on one elbow to look down at me. "Caleb Colvin," she spat. "That's what's up." She grimaced at his name. "Ever since he came back, Reana Mae don't do nothing with us anymore. It's always Caleb. I reckon she's purely in love with him."

I laughed. "Oh, Ruthann, that's just silly. She's not in love with Caleb!"

Ruthann didn't answer. She just shook her head knowingly.

"Oh, come on," I pleaded. "He's way older than her. Why, he must be eighteen, at least. Plus," I added triumphantly, "he's her uncle. How could she be in love with her own uncle?"

"Happens," Ruthann said grimly. "Happens sometimes. Anyways, it's God's own truth, Bethany. Ever since he came back, Reana Mae don't want nothin' to do with me . . . or with H.B." She glanced down at Harley floating on his back in the water. "Poor Harley Boy," she continued in a whisper. "He's plain crazy 'bout Reana Mae, always has been. And she won't even look his way. Not since Caleb came around, leastwise."

"She sure seems different," I muttered.

"You got that right. She *is* different, and that's the Lord's own truth. She don't like school no more—not even English class—and she don't even go half the time. Hides out in the woods till the bus is gone."

I stared in disbelief. "She skips school? What does Jolene do?"

Ruthann snorted. "Jolene? Well, she drinks liquor, that's what she does. She drinks herself dead drunk."

Ruthann sighed, shaking her head. "I guess it must be hard on Reana Mae, what with her mama bein' that way and her daddy always gone. Still," her voice sharpened as it rose, "she don't need to be so hard on poor H.B. It surely ain't his fault."

Late in the afternoon, just as I was thinking of heading home, Reana Mae walked onto the beach, stripped off her shorts, and dove into the river, swimming cleanly out to the raft.

"Hey, ya'll," she said, not even out of breath as she pulled herself onto the raft.

"Hey, yourself." I smiled at her. With her hair plastered to her head and her bony hips showing, she looked more like the Reana Mae I knew. More like a little girl. Then she arched her back to squeeze out her braid, and her small breasts stood erect, straining against the tiny bra of her bikini. On her other side I could see Harley Boy staring at them intently. I looked away.

"Where you been all day?" Ruthann asked, squinting at Reana Mae in the late afternoon sun.

"Helpin' out at the store."

She said it so smoothly, so easily, it sounded just like the truth. I stared at her, my mouth slightly open, and she returned my gaze steadily.

"Granpa needed some extra help today."

I saw Ruthann shoot a glance at Harley Boy, and I knew they didn't believe her.

"Ruthann says there's a new drugstore open up by Crayville. You wanna walk up there tomorrow and see if they have any good comic books?" I asked, praying she'd say yes.

"Sure," she said lightly, dropping her arm across her eyes as she lay back on the raft. "That'd be fun. They got real good makeup there. I need some new eye shadow."

"You know your daddy wouldn't let you wear that." H.B. leaned over her. "You know he wouldn't want you to."

"Well, if he ever comes back home, he can tell me that hisself, Harley *Boy*. Meantime, why don't you keep your big ole nose in your own goddamned business?"

The anger in her voice hit me like a shock wave. I could only stare at her.

H.B. looked at her miserably for a minute, his cheeks reddening. Then he rose abruptly and dove into the dark water, swimming furiously for the shore.

Ruthann eyed Reana Mae coldly. "Why do you have to treat him like that?"

"Why does he think he has to pry into other folks' business?" Reana spat back.

Ruthann stood, too. "I'll see you later, Bethany."

She dove into the water and swam toward shore.

I sat quietly for a long minute before venturing, "I think he's right, though, Reana. I think Bobby Lee wouldn't like it if he saw you wearing eye shadow."

She turned to squint at me, shading her eyes against the sun's slanting rays. "I reckon you're right. Probably he'd hate it. But he ain't here, is he? He ain't here to tell me nothin'. And Harley Boy." She sighed, flopping back onto the raft. "Well, he just needs to stop pesterin' me, that's all. Always followin' me around, tellin' me I'm going to hell if I don't straighten up. He's got just like Ida Louise."

"I think he just likes you."

"Yeah, well, he better get over that, right quick. 'Cause I ain't never gonna like him, not like that." She laughed derisively.

We sat on the raft a while longer, neither of us speaking. I felt like I was in a foreign land, unsure of the landscape. Why was Reana so angry with Harley? Why had she been so mean? She of all people knew what it felt like to crave affection. This angry young woman was a stranger to me.

We finally swam back to shore as the sun dipped behind the hills.

"You wanna come home with me for supper?" I asked, toweling myself dry.

"No, thanks. I gotta cook dinner at home. If I don't cook, dinner don't get made."

"But if you come home with me, you don't need to cook dinner. Jolene's not there, is she? You can just eat with us."

"Bethany Marie, if I don't cook, what'll Caleb do for supper? A woman's gotta cook, or a man don't eat." She smiled. "That's what Caleb says."

I shook my head in frustration. I wanted to shake this woman-child and demand the return of my Reana Mae. She must have seen something in my face that reached her, because suddenly she broke into her old grin and grabbed my hand. "Come on! Let's race!"

We ran headlong down the road, laughing like little girls, until we came to the cabin she shared with Caleb and Jolene. Panting slightly, she grabbed me in a quick, tight hug.

"I'll see you tomorrow, Bethany. Okay? I promise!"

I watched her disappear into the house, her small hips swaying. When had she gotten so grown up? And why was she doing it so fast?

I shook my head hard, my wet hair slapping my cheeks. Then I ran toward home and supper, where everything still seemed familiar.

∽ 16 ∽

Another World

A few nights later, Mother convinced Reana Mae and Caleb to eat supper with us. Daddy had already gone back home, so Caleb was the lone male at our table, a position he seemed not to mind. He ate four helpings of meat loaf and mashed potatoes before pushing himself back from the table.

"Thank you, ma'am," he mumbled toward my mother. "That was real good."

"I'm glad you enjoyed it." Mother smiled.

"Lord knows he ate enough of it," Melinda whispered at Nancy as Caleb rose.

Mother shot a quick warning glance at them before continuing, "I hope you saved room for some pie."

Caleb grinned at her then—the first smile we'd seen from him all evening—and sat back down. He didn't look menacing at all when he smiled. In fact, he looked almost like Bobby Lee. Glancing across the table toward Reana Mae, I was startled to see Nancy's eyes scanning Caleb quickly, as if reappraising him.

"Let me help you with those dishes, Aunt Helen." Reana Mae rose and began stacking plates.

"Now, you just sit down, Reana Mae. You're our guest tonight—no dishes for you!"

Mother turned and looked meaningfully at Tracy and me. Tracy pretended not to notice as I rose and took the plates from Reana.

Sighing, Mother tried again. "Tracy, will you go out and get some water from the pump, please?"

"I'm not finished with my dinner, Mother." Tracy smiled sweetly at Mother and pushed a small puddle of potatoes, peas, and butter around her plate.

Mother frowned slightly, then turned to the older girls. Before she could speak, Nancy rose gracefully, laying her napkin on the table. "I'll go, Mother."

She smiled down at Caleb and said, "Apparently, my little sisters need to brush up on their company manners."

Tracy stared at her balefully, but she still made no move to rise. I stifled my own protest at being included in the indictment. After all, wasn't I carrying dishes to the sink at that very moment? And wasn't it Nancy herself who sidestepped chores at every opportunity?

Nancy took the chipped enamel dishpan from Mother, then turned and asked in a breathy little voice, "Caleb, would you pump the water for me? That darned thing is so rusty, it really needs a man to work it."

All of us were staring now. Why, I could make that pump work with just one hand. Nancy had certainly never had trouble with it before.

Caleb rose and grinned down at her. "Sure," he agreed. "I'll get it goin' for you."

I glanced back at Reana Mae, who sat frowning slightly as she watched them walk out the door. Nancy had turned eighteen that spring and was just done with high school. She was very pretty, with a small but curvy frame, dark hair, and flashing black eyes. Nancy had broken off with her latest beau just after the senior prom. It seemed like she was always breaking some boy's heart. For the moment, at least, she was unattached. And Caleb apparently had just registered on her feminine radar.

When they returned from the pump, Caleb was carrying the dishpan splashing full of water, and Nancy smiled brilliantly up at him.

"Thank you, Caleb," Mother said as she took the dishpan from him. "But you're company tonight. No more chores for you."

She handed Nancy a dishrag and slightly shoved her toward the kitchen. "Now, how about some pie?"

So Caleb and Reana Mae ate pecan pie while Nancy and I washed the dishes. That is, I washed dishes. Nancy rinsed and stacked them haphazardly on the counter, fuming at Mother. By the time we finished, Caleb and Reana Mae had risen from the table and were edging toward the door.

I had just cut myself a piece of pie when Mother asked, "Where's your mama tonight, Reana Mae?"

Reana glanced at Caleb first, then shrugged. "Oh, you know, Aunt Helen. She's got herself some friends up in Crayville. She's probably havin' supper with them."

"Will you tell her I'd like to see her tomorrow?"

Reana Mae nodded quickly, then leaned over to kiss Mother's cheek. "I'll tell her, Aunt Helen. But I can't make you a promise she'll come."

With that they left, walking back up the road toward the cabin they both called home. Mother watched them from the porch, her eyebrows knit tightly together. I watched her watching them, then turned toward Nancy.

"Reana Mae said Caleb helped her swim all the way across the river. You should ask him to help you do it, too."

Nancy had never been a strong swimmer, and she had taken loads of grief from Melinda every summer because she couldn't swim across the river. Melinda had even formed a "there-and-back" club, just for kids who could swim across the river and back—a club Nancy couldn't join.

"Maybe I'll do that, Bethy," Nancy purred at me, smiling.

Good, I thought grimly. *Take all the time in the world. Just keep him away from Reana Mae.*

But Nancy didn't seem overly anxious to join the there-and-back club. For most of June, at least, she seemed content to bask in the sun, reading fan magazines and drinking Tab colas. Some days Caleb joined us by the river, cutting cleanly through the dark water, throwing younger kids out into the deep, diving off the wooden raft, then dropping down beside Nancy and staring hungrily at her tiny waist and rounded breasts when he thought she wasn't looking.

Whenever Caleb came to the beach, Reana Mae was right behind him. She struggled to keep up with him in the water, matching him dive for dive from the ramp. But back on the shore, she could only sit unhappily in her own tiny bikini—the kind Mother would never let any of us wear—and watch Caleb stare at Nancy's breasts rising under the tight black nylon of her swimsuit.

Otherwise, I didn't see much of Reana Mae. Most days she worked, either at Ray's store or at home. I stopped by her house almost every day, anyway, sometimes staying to help with laundry or cleaning. Once I even helped her bake bread, and took a loaf home to Mother, receiving a kiss in return. Some days, though, Reana was neither at the store nor at home. Invariably, those were the days Caleb had off work. Sometimes on those days the two of them would show up in the late afternoon at the beach. But sometimes they never came at all. We didn't know where they were, and I never asked.

Jolene finally showed up at our house a couple weeks after our dinner with Reana Mae and Caleb. It was late morning and I was at home, nursing cramps with a hot water bottle and aspirin. I'd been having my period for several months now. It was the only time when Mother let me lie about in bed, reading or listening to the radio, while she brought me crackers and hot tea.

Mother was in the front room snapping green beans for supper and listening to the radio, and I was lying miserably on my bed, feeling very sorry for myself, when I heard a loud thudding on the porch. I sat up, hearing Mother open the screen door and say, "Why, Jolene! Are you all right?"

I sat quietly, listening to shuffling sounds. Then I heard the screen door screech closed again and Jolene's voice saying, "Why, sure, Helen, I'm okay. Your damned step's crooked, that's all."

"I'll ask Jimmy to look at it next time he's down." Mother's voice was so soft I had to strain to hear her.

"Reana Mae said you wanted to see me." Jolene's voice sounded muffled, like she was talking with a mitten in her mouth.

"I just wanted to visit with you. We've been down here almost a month now, and I was missing you."

"You got any coffee made, Helen?"

"I'll put the water on right now."

I heard Mother bustle around in the kitchen for a minute, then return to the couch.

"How are you, Jolene?"

"I'm just fine. I'm all right." Jolene's voice had a sharp edge. "You shouldn't go believin' half what you hear down here, you know. Damned valley's nothin' but a bunch of gossips and liars, Helen. That's what they are. Just gossips and liars!"

"I hadn't heard anything at all, Jolene. I was just wondering how you are."

An uncomfortable silence followed, broken finally by the teakettle's whistle.

"I'll get us some coffee." Mother's voice was unnaturally bright, like chrome on a new bike.

"Now, then," she said, "do you want cream or sugar? . . . Okay, then, how about some banana bread? Melinda made it just this morning."

"Well, thanks, Helen." Jolene sounded like she'd swallowed an entire sheep now. "I didn't get me no breakfast. Reana Mae's workin' down to the store today, so she left before I got up."

"Reana certainly is growing up," Mother ventured. "Why, I hardly would have recognized her, she's gotten so grown up."

She paused, waiting for a response, I guess, then plowed ahead.

"Why, she looks almost like a little woman these days. Jimmy and I both noticed it. The girls have, too. . . . In fact, Jolene, I . . . that is we, me and Jimmy, I mean . . . well, we were wondering if Reana Mae isn't growing up too fast? Of course," Mother continued quickly, "of course, she's bound to grow up sooner or later. But my goodness, Jolene! She seems older even than Nancy sometimes. Years older than Bethany and Tracy."

Mother paused to catch her breath. Still, Jolene said nothing except, "You got any more of that bread, Helen? That's real good."

"Jolene!" Mother sounded angry now. "Are you hearing what I'm saying? We're worried about Reana Mae, Jimmy and me. And about you, too, honey. Reana is too young to be taking on all this responsibility. And you . . . Jolene, I do believe you've been drinking even this early in the day. Good gracious, it's not even noon!"

Jolene sighed heavily—so heavily I heard it in the bedroom. Then she answered in a dull, flat voice, "Helen, you don't know nothin' about it—nothin' at all. Hell, you don't know nothin' at all about real troubles . . . with your rich husband and your nice house. . . . But I do, Helen. I surely do know. And I guess Reana Mae's gotta know, too. I want that girl to know how to take care of herself, 'cause ain't nobody in the world gonna do it for her. That's the devil's own truth. And Reana Mae's gotta learn it now, so it don't kill her later."

A loud crash made me sit up straight.

"Oh, Lord Almighty, Helen! I went and broke one of your nice teacups. I'll pay for it. . . . No! I will! I'll pay for the damned cup! I don't need no charity from you or from no one else, either! I'll pay for the goddamned cup, and I'll take care of my own goddamned kid, too!

"You just stay outta what you don't understand, Helen, you hear me? You stay outta my life and outta my business! I'll raise my own goddamned kid any goddamned way I want to! I don't need no help from you!"

A scraping of chairs and the banging of the screen door told me she was leaving.

"You just leave me be, Helen! Leave me and Reana Mae alone! You hear me?!"

She thumped down the step and I heard her voice grow faint as she stumbled down the road. Then I heard the springs of the old sofa in the front room, as Mother sank back down, sobbing softly.

I tiptoed into the front room to sit beside her on the couch. Wrapping my arms around her bent neck, I crooned to her the way I'd heard her do all my life.

"It's okay, Mother. It's okay. They'll be all right. I know they will. I'm sure Bobby Lee will come home soon and make it all okay. You'll see."

She sat quietly for a long moment, then raised her head, wiped her eyes, and kissed me on the forehead.

"Yes, Bethy, it will be okay. Whatever happens, it will be all right. We'll just keep praying for them, okay? You keep praying for Reana Mae and for Jolene and Bobby Lee, and it will be all right."

In late June, Melinda solemnly inducted me into the there-and-back club, while Nancy stared at us bitterly.

The next day, as I set out for Ray's store on an errand for Mother, Nancy fell into step beside me.

"Whatcha up to, Bethy?" She smiled down at me sweetly. I half expected her to pat me on the head.

"Going to the store for Mother."

"I'll come with you."

I stared at her a moment before elaborately shrugging my shoulders. "If you want," I said as casually as I could.

We walked in silence most of the way. Just before we reached the store, Nancy touched my arm, saying, "Did Caleb really help Reana Mae swim all the way across the river?"

I nodded in relief. Life made sense again.

As we entered the store, I heard Reana Mae's voice from the back.

"That there's a fondue pot, Mrs. Perkins. You fill that little pot at the bottom with lamp oil, and then you light it up. And that heats the cooking oil in the big pot up top. And then you cook yourself up some meat in the big pot, right at the table! Ain't that somethin'? Folks out in California use 'em all the time—three meals a day, I hear tell!"

I knew if Reana Mae was there, Caleb would be, too. Sure enough, we hadn't been there more than a minute before his hulking shadow overtook us.

"What're you lookin' for today, ladies?" he asked, smiling down at Nancy.

"Well, Bethany is looking for some things for Mother," she cooed at him. "But I came looking for you."

A sudden break in the conversation at the back of the store told me that Reana Mae had heard them.

"Well!" Caleb sounded mighty pleased with himself, and mighty pleased with Nancy, too. "Then what can I do for *you*?"

Nancy took him by the elbow and steered him deftly toward the front door. I knew she wouldn't ask for help in front of me. Smiling, I began filling my basket. I had just checked shampoo off the list when I felt rather than heard Reana Mae behind me. Starting slightly, I turned to see her staring at me mutely, her green cat-eyes open wide, her mouth set grimly.

"Where'd they go?" she whispered.

I shrugged. I did not care where they had gone. And I didn't understand why Reana Mae should care, either. I certainly was not going to be drawn into some soap opera triangle consisting of my sister, my cousin, and her eighteen-year-old uncle.

Reana Mae left me in the aisle, heading for the front door to find Caleb and Nancy. I went on about my shopping, refusing to give in to the temptation to follow her.

By the time my basket was full, Caleb was back at the cash register. Reana Mae stood behind him, looking miserable.

I handed Caleb the money as quickly as I could, smiled uncertainly at Reana Mae, and fled with my shopping toward home and Mother.

∽17∾

Independence Day

July Fourth brought a festival kind of feeling to the valley. Of course, up in Charleston they had a real celebration, complete with a big fireworks display. But along the Coal River, the Fourth of July meant picnics, Roman candles, and free-flowing beer. Every year, we walked to the beach to cook hot dogs and marshmallows over a huge open fire and watch Bobby Lee and the other men set off illegal fireworks from across the river. This year, Bobby Lee was conspicuously absent—gone away to Phoenix in his rig, Reana Mae said. But Uncle Hobie, Albus Greenaway, and even old Uncle Ray were planning a big display, and us kids were all excited.

That morning, I met Ruthann early and we walked to the beach to swim in the gloriously cool water. I couldn't remember such a muggy, steamy summer as we were having. I had spent most days at the beach with Ruthann, staving off the suffocating heat in the muddy river, emerging only after the midday sun's rays had diffused and the mosquitoes started swarming.

We laid out our towels near the water, staking out spots early for the fireworks. I wondered briefly if Reana Mae would join us, then remembered she was helping in Ray's store that day. Sighing, I stared at the water swirling slowly past, wondering idly how long it took to reach the Gulf of Mexico.

"Hey there."

Harley Boy dropped down beside me, his sunburned nose reflecting the morning sun.

I smiled up at him. H.B. joined us almost every day. Ruthann and I were poor substitutes for Reana Mae, but I suppose we were better than nothing.

"You gonna swim across tonight?" Ruthann asked him, leaning on one elbow.

"Grandmaw says I can't," H.B. fumed. "Granddad's goin', and he said I could go with him. But she says no."

I raised my eyebrows at Ruthann. She smiled back, saying innocently, "I guess she thinks it's too dangerous for you over there."

H.B. grimaced. "Naw, she just don't want me over there 'cause she knows they'll be drinkin' spirits."

Ruthann laughed. "Just beer," she said. "My daddy always takes over some beers."

"I know." H.B. nodded. "But Grandmaw don't want me around even that." He kicked absently at the sand. "She wouldn't let Granddad go neither, if she could help it. But she can't stop him."

We leaned back in one, unison movement, covering our eyes against the sun's gathering strength. For a while, no one spoke. I heard my sisters' voices on the road. They'd be joining us soon.

Sure enough, within minutes Nancy, Melinda, and Tracy were spreading their towels on the ground behind us. Melinda and Nancy were discussing the latest news on Mick Jagger. Tracy began scribbling yet another letter to Paul.

Ruthann grinned at me. "Wanna go?" she said.

I nodded and we walked into the river, squealing at the cold water until we were waist-deep. Then we dove under and swam out to the raft, H.B. close behind us. Pulling ourselves onto the raft, we congratulated each other on escaping the crowd, then dropped down on our stomachs in silence again.

Along toward noon, H.B. sat up abruptly, saying impatiently, "Let's do somethin'!"

Ruthann nodded. "It's purely dull out here."

"Okay," I agreed. "What?"

H.B. was standing on the edge of the raft, shading his eyes with one hand. "Last summer, Reana Mae said her and Caleb had cut a path all the way from her house down to the beach."

"Yeah, but we never found it," Ruthann said. "I don't believe they really did it."

"Let's go look for it," H.B. said, setting his shoulders. "Maybe we'll find it. If not," he added, staring into the woods darkly, "maybe we'll just make one of our own."

We swam back to shore, grabbing up our towels and drying off.

"Where are you going?" Tracy frowned at me as we walked toward the woods.

"For a hike," I said over my shoulder.

"Lord God Almighty, does she think she's your mama?" Ruthann whispered viciously. I laughed.

We followed H.B. as he hacked through the brush with a large stick. The last time I tried to make my own path, I'd seen Tracy burying Essie in the mud. It seemed so long ago.

Within minutes, my legs were scratched and bleeding. Ruthann and I struggled to keep up with H.B. Finally, Ruthann called out, "H.B., wait up! You're goin' too fast!"

But he didn't stop. We watched him whacking at the bushes furiously, as if he held a personal grudge against each one. Ruthann smiled at me uncertainly. "He's been fumin' over that path all year," she explained. "It's something he and Reana Mae always talked about when we were kids, and then she and Caleb went and did it without him."

I nodded grimly, swiping at the sweat dripping into my eyes.

"Okay, then, let's find it," I said.

We trudged along behind him, shoving aside the brush as best we could with our bare hands. Suddenly, Harley stopped so abruptly that Ruthann nearly plowed into him. Drawing close behind them, I heard Harley's quick intake of breath. Ruthann turned to stare at me, her eyes wide. Peering over Ruthann's shoulder, I gripped her arm tightly.

In a small clearing before us lay an old mattress covered with a blue and white quilt we all recognized as Reana Mae's—Loreen had sewn it for her before she was born, when everyone hoped she'd be a boy. Reana used to carry it everywhere when she was little. A small portable radio sat on a wooden box beside the mattress. The ground was littered with small squares of plastic packages, each torn through at the top.

Harley picked one of the plastic squares up from the ground. Over his shoulder I read the word *Trojan*. Even I knew what they were. Melinda had told me once when we found a package like that in the alley near our house. I stared at the package, trying to understand what I already knew but couldn't believe.

Harley Boy's hands shook as he threw the package to the ground. He dropped to his knees on the mattress and pulled the blanket off, then lifted the pillow, as if he thought he might find Reana Mae hiding beneath it. Finally, he rocked back onto his haunches and looked up at us. His face was red and tight.

"I'll kill him," he hissed.

"Come on, H.B.," Ruthann whispered, reaching for his hand. "Let's go." She looked to me for support. "Let's go now, before anyone comes down here."

I could only nod, my eyes stinging back tears. This is where Reana Mae came when she disappeared into the woods. This is where she'd spent so much time all summer, instead of going to the beach with me. This . . . this is what she'd been doing. My stomach lurched and I thought I might just throw up.

"Come on!" Ruthann urged again, pulling at Harley's shoulder. But he didn't move. He sat still clutching the pillow, staring at the ground.

Suddenly, he leaned forward, reaching for something behind where Ruthann and I stood.

"What's that?" Ruthann asked as he sat back on the mattress. He was holding a small book.

Still Harley said nothing. Ruthann looked at me again, as if I might answer her question. But I was as confused as she was. Both of us dropped to the ground beside Harley Boy, neither of us touching the mattress. He held the book out so we could see it, then silently opened it.

The lined pages were filled with a familiar handwriting in purple ink. It was Reana Mae's.

March 6
Dear Diary,
Today is my birthday. I am 11 yrs old now. Only 2 more years til I can marry Caleb. He says I am almost a real woman.
Aunt Belle said I shoud write every day so I can practise. She thinks I will be a writer some day. I read about William Falkner in a magazine once. He was a famus writer and he lived in a hore house. I told Caleb that and he laffed. He said it would be ok to live in a hore house. He says stuff like that some times.
Caleb gave me a pretty nitegown for my birthday. It is green and short and has lace on it. I can't wear it when mama is at home. She wood not like it. But next time she stays out I will wear it for Caleb. It is a sexy nitegown. He says I will look sexy in it. I hope I do.

"Sweet Jesus," Ruthann whispered. "Put it back, Harley Boy."
She tried to take the book from him, but he shoved her hand away and began turning the pages fast. When he stopped turning, Ruthann and I both leaned in to read.

June 6
Dear Diary,
Today Caleb put his mouth on my brests without my shirt on. He says they are beutiful. He says that I am beutiful. More than my mama ever was. He says she is trashy but I am not. I was real scared when he took off my shirt. I was scared some one wood see us. But no one did.
Caleb kissed my brests and then he put his teeth on them. It hurt some. But I didnt make him stop. He was breething real hard. I know he liked it. Now maybe he will stop looking at Nancys tits all the time.

I felt my throat constrict. Tears ran down my face. Why, oh why, couldn't Nancy have sparked Caleb's interest earlier? Before . . . this?

Ruthann held my hand tightly. Harley Boy's face was dark and angry as he flipped pages.

> *June 12*
> *Dear Diary,*
> *Yesterday Caleb put his fingers inside me. It hurt at first but I didn't cry or nothing. He said since I am 11 now and getting some brests I am ready to be a woman. He has been asking since I let him put his mouth on my brests. He says I am ready now. First he put 1 finger in. Then he put 2. He says when he can put 3 in that he can love me like he wants to.*
>
> *Then he made me put my mouth on his thing again. I don't like that but Caleb says it is what women do when they love a man. And I do love him. So he said I had to proov it. But I don't like it.*

> *June 20*
> *Dear Diary,*
> *Today I am a real woman. It was not like I thout it wood be. It hurt and I bled some. But I love him. And I know he loves me to. And that is what people do who love each other. He used a rubber so I won't get pregnent. I don't want a baby til we are married. Then I want a little boy baby. I will be a good mother.*
>
> *Caleb said next time it wont hurt so bad. And he kissed me all over my face when I cried. So I know he loves me true.*
>
> *But it did hurt.*

"Stop!" I heard the words come from my mouth before I even knew I was speaking. "Put it back, Harley." I was desperate to leave this place, to return to the beach, to safety, to ignorance.

Harley just turned the page. He didn't even look up.

June 26
Dear Diary,

I told Caleb today that I want to do it lots of times so it will stop hurting sooner. This morning was are 3rd time but I still bled some. He said thats because he is so big he has to strech me out. I hope it happens soon.

The best part is after he is done and then he holds me tite and he talks real sweet. I like resting my head on his arm and he has his other arm around me. Its the best thing ever.

Mama came home early last nite and almost caught us in my bed with my pants off. Caleb says from now on we can only do it here til I am 13 and we can get married.

June 28
Dear Diary,

I wish aunt Helen would go home and take Nancy back with her. Today she came in the store and was hanging all over Caleb. And he liked it. I saw he did. I got mad at him and told him he sholdn't act like that with Nancy if he loves me. Then he got mad and told me to shut my mouth. He said I was just a little girl and not his wife. And he can do what he wants. That made me cry.

So then I came here and then he came to. And he told me he loves me. But he said he is a man and I cant understand what he needs becuse I am just a little girl. But I told him I am a woman, and I took off his pants and put my mouth on him and sucked on him til he came in my mouth. So that shows him I am not a little girl. But I still wish Nancy was not around here.

June 30
Dear Diary,

I dont think I am going to like sex very much if I have to do it like today. Caleb told me get down on my knees and bend over like a dog. And then he got behind me and I coldn't see him in the face or anything. I hated it.

> *But I still liked after it because he layed down and held me tité and said he loves me and wants to marry me when I am 13. I love him so much.*

Harley slammed the small book into the hard dirt with a strangled kind of sound in his throat. His face was brick red, and a small muscle twitched on one side of his neck. Ruthann leaned toward him with her arms open, but he shoved her away with such force that she fell backward onto the mattress. I backed away from him, away from the mattress and the diary and the clearing and the knowing. I wanted to run as fast and as far away as I could. Before I could move, Harley Boy let out a roar I was sure they heard all the way to Huntington. Then he turned and ran deeper into the woods, straight through the brambles and bushes. We watched until he was out of sight.

Ruthann rose silently and began rearranging the little clearing, trying to erase any trace of our being there. She straightened the pillow and blanket, then placed the diary under the bush where Harley Boy had found it. I stood mutely, watching her, willing myself not to throw up. When she had finished, we ran as fast as we could back the way we had come. We didn't stop or speak until we reached the road. Then Ruthann took my hand, squeezed it hard, and whispered, "Don't say nothing to no one, you hear? I got to find Harley Boy."

With that, she turned and padded down the dirt road. I didn't follow her. I figured she knew where to find him. I'd just be in the way.

I walked back toward the beach. When I got there, I headed straight for the cold, dark water—not stopping to answer my sisters' questions about the scratches and blood on my legs. I swam straight across the river, heaving myself onto the shore on the far side, away from everyone else. There, I collapsed to the ground and cried—huge, gasping sobs that shook me to my toes.

❧ 18 ❧

Fireworks

When I swam back across the river, it was early evening and a crowd had gathered on the beach. Uncle Hobie had lit the bonfire, and some of the little kids were cooking hot dogs on sticks, their faces glowing red with the heat.

Ruthann was sitting on a towel, squeezing ketchup onto a hot dog for her little sister. Lottie was an energetic four-year-old now—full of piss and vinegar, as Belle liked to say. I dropped down beside them. "Where's Harley Boy?"

Ruthann just shook her head grimly.

"There," she said, handing the hot dog to her sister. "Don't drop this one."

Lottie toddled away, her mouth happily stuffed full of bun and ketchup.

"I don't know where he is," Ruthann whispered. "I looked everywhere I could think this side of Beckley, but I couldn't find him."

"Maybe he just needs some time to think," I said hopefully.

"I just hope he don't think up something evil, that's all."

"Well, here you are, Bethany." Mother stood over us, smiling. "I was beginning to wonder where you'd gone to."

"I swam across." I smiled back.

"Our hamper is over there." She pointed to the big picnic basket sitting under a nearby tree. "Why don't you get something to eat?"

"I will," I lied. I wasn't at all hungry. I felt like something heavy was camped out in my belly.

"Reana Mae was looking for you a while ago," Mother said. "When you see her, you make sure she gets something to eat. Caleb, too," she added as she turned away.

Ruthann and I stared at each other glumly. "Oh, Lord," she whispered. "I didn't reckon on him bein' here."

"Maybe it's a good thing Harley Boy's not," I said.

"Probably you're right," she agreed. "But I wish I knew where he was."

"Hey, ya'll!" Reana Mae's voice was bright. She dropped down onto the sand beside me. "I been lookin' for you."

"Oh! Uh, hey, Reana," I stammered, not meeting her eyes. "Where you been?"

"Oh, you know, I had to work at the store today. Lots of folks in buying stuff for the picnic."

Ruthann rose abruptly and stalked away, dragging her towel behind her.

"What's eatin' her shorts?" Reana asked, grinning at me. "Can't she find ole Harley Boy? I swear, that girl better learn to hide her heart away before she makes a fool outta herself."

I bit my lip, my mind spinning. Should I tell her what we'd found? That we knew? She leaned back on her elbows, arching her back slightly, and smiled at me. I thought again about how grown up she looked. It made my stomach churn.

"What's wrong, Bethany? You look like you seen a spirit."

I shook my head, letting my wet hair hang over my face. "Nothing," I lied. "Mother said to tell you she packed stuff for you . . . and Caleb, too," I added reluctantly.

"Did she? That was real nice of her. I got us some wieners at the store, but that's all I brought," she said, holding out a small bag. She rose and stuck her hand out to me. "Come on, then, lazybones. Let's eat."

I let myself be pulled to my feet and followed her to the hamper.

We skewered a couple hot dogs and pushed our way in close to the fire. It was roaring now, the flames dancing orange against the deepening indigo sky. Beside me, Reana Mae leaned close to the fire, her face flushed red. I watched her closely, looking for some sign of . . . I don't even know what. And she looked just like herself right then, just like my own cousin, my own Reana Mae. I closed my eyes and breathed heavily, willing my stomach to quiet down.

"Well, hey there, you!" Reana's voice purred happily.

I looked up to see Caleb standing over Reana Mae, grinning down at her.

"I cooked you a wiener," Reana said. "And Aunt Helen packed us a whole bunch of food."

She rose, extending the sizzling wiener toward him. He took the skewer from her and turned without a word, knowing she would follow him. I watched them walk to the hamper, then stared as Reana Mae fixed a plate for her uncle, her lover. She piled on potato salad and coleslaw, loaded ketchup, mustard, and relish on the hot dog, and poured him a soda. Finally, she took another hot dog from the cooler, skewered it, and walked back toward me.

"Lord God Almighty, Bethany." She laughed. "Are you fixin' to eat that thing?"

The hot dog on my stick was black, its skin split wide, dripping fat into the fire.

"Here, you take this one." Reana took the skewer from me and handed me hers. "I'll get me another one."

She ran back to the hamper while I absently stuck the hot dog into the flames. When she returned, she squatted next to me and laughed. "Are you okay, Bethany? 'Cause you're acting like one of them voodoo zombies."

"I guess I'm just tired," I said. I wanted to slap her hard, to shake her, to drag her away from the river and the damned valley and most of all from Caleb. Instead, I turned my hot dog on the skewer so it would cook evenly.

When our dogs were done, we walked back to the hamper to fill our plates. Reana Mae's eyes scanned the beach quickly. I knew she was looking for Caleb.

"There he is," I said dully. My throat felt tight, like someone was squeezing it. I pointed to where Caleb sat with Nancy and Melinda, laughing at something. Reana Mae drew her breath in sharply. She grabbed a can of soda and walked quickly toward the threesome. I trailed behind her.

"Hey, ya'll," I heard my cousin say as she dropped onto the sand next to Caleb.

"Oh, hi, Reana Mae." Melinda's voice was surprised. "Can't you find Bethany?"

"I'm here," I said miserably, dropping down beside my cousin. I don't know why I followed her. Maybe I thought I could protect her—maybe I just had to see what would happen next.

"Anyway," Nancy cooed toward Caleb, "I told that boy he could take his ring right back, if that was how he was going to be."

Caleb laughed, his eyes never leaving Nancy's face.

"But you never did give the ring back," Melinda added.

"Of course not!" Nancy was indignant. "It's just a figure of speech, you know, 'Take the ring back.' No one ever actually gives back the ring. It's mine. He gave it to me for keeps."

She leaned toward Caleb and placed her hand on his shoulder. "You wouldn't expect a girl to give you back a ring, would you, Caleb? I mean, it's not like you can give it to some other girl, right?"

"Why not?" He grinned at her.

"Well, because, silly"—she laughed, her black curls tumbling about her lovely face—"no girl in her right mind is going to accept a ring you bought for some other girl." Her hand still rested on his shoulder.

"Hey, Caleb." Reana Mae laid her hand high up on her uncle's thigh, almost to his crotch. I could see her fingernails digging into his leg. "You want another soda pop?"

"No, thanks," he said, his eyes never leaving Nancy's.

"How 'bout some more corn chips, then?"

"No." He shook his head.

Nancy leaned back on her elbows, her breasts arching toward the darkening sky. "Hey, Reana Mae," she cooed. "If you really want to do something nice, how about cooking me a hot dog?"

Even in the gathering dusk, I could see Reana Mae's face turn a deep, dark red. Her lips formed a thin line. I held my breath, watching her nails dig deeper into Caleb's flesh.

"Yeah." Caleb turned toward us finally. "Why don't you cook me another wiener, too?"

I could see the struggle going on inside Reana Mae. She pulled back from Caleb, her hands clenching and unclenching. Her breath came in ragged little gasps. She laid her plate down on the sand and rose, walking briskly back toward the hamper to skewer two more hot dogs. I knew she was furious, and probably hurt badly. But I didn't follow her. I couldn't. Instead, I sat with my big sisters and Caleb, crunching potato chips.

"Hey!"

Reana Mae's voice rang through the air, startled and angry. I turned to see her pulling her arm from Harley Boy's grip. His face in the firelight was frightening. His red hair hung low over his forehead; his mouth was set in a furious grimace; and high on his cheeks, two spots of red glowed.

"Let go of me, Harley Boy! What the hell is wrong with you?"

"You better just come with me, Reana Mae." Harley Boy grabbed her arm again, pulling Reana toward him.

"I said let go!"

Reana Mae jerked herself backward, stumbling dangerously close to the fire. Everyone on the beach stared from her to Harley Boy. Even Caleb had pried his eyes from Nancy, although he made no move to intervene.

"You better just come on with me right now!" Harley Boy's voice was loud, his speech slightly slurred. He didn't sound at all like himself.

I looked around for someone to help, but most of the men had already rowed across the river to set up the fireworks. Down the beach behind Harley Boy, I saw Ruthann running toward the fire. I rose to join her, but before either of us could get there, Ida Louise reached Harley Boy, grabbing him by his red hair and his sunburned shoulder.

"What has gotten into you, boy?" the old woman barked. "You're actin' like you been possessed by Lucifer hisself."

Harley Boy tried to shake himself loose, but Ida Louise was deceptively strong—tiny but wiry, her hands accustomed to strangling the life out of chickens. She dragged Harley Boy away from the bonfire, finally turning him so that he faced her.

"Have you been drinking?" she shrieked.

Harley simply stared at her, his red face moving furiously.

"I said, have you been drinking?" Ida Louise jerked her grandson forward by the hair. "I told them men they shouldn't buy that liquor. I told them they're working in league with the devil's own. And now look at you! My own grandson! Look at what you done!"

She dragged Harley Boy across the dirt beach by his hair. He stumbled along behind her, but he didn't struggle. He just stared balefully at Reana Mae, shouting back at her, "You better straighten yourself up, girl! You better start doin' right! You're goin' to hell for sure, Reana Mae! You're goin' to hell for sure!"

Reana Mae sank to her knees, shaking furiously. I ran to her and wrapped my arms around her thin frame. Then Mother joined us, holding us both in a close embrace. In the distance, I watched Ruthann following along behind Ida Louise and Harley Boy. Numbly, I wondered if Harley and Ruthann would tell the old woman about Reana Mae and Caleb. At that moment, I didn't even care. I looked around to see where Caleb had gone to. Surely he would come to help Reana Mae now?

But he sat still beside Nancy, both of them whispering and laughing. Melinda sat beside them, staring at us with wide eyes. Behind her, I saw Tracy walking toward us. Dear God in Heaven, I prayed silently, just keep her away from us now. Reana Mae surely did not need Tracy gloating over her now. Neither of us did.

"Are you okay?" Mother whispered, burying her face in Reana's hair.

"I'm fine, Aunt Helen." Reana abruptly pulled away from her, staring after Harley Boy's retreating figure. She stood slowly, still clutching her hot dog skewer.

"What do you suppose has gotten into Harley Boy?" Mother sat back on her haunches, watching Ida Louise pull Harley along the road.

"He's crazy, that's all." Reana Mae's voice was dead calm. It made me shiver to hear her. "He's got his daddy's bad blood in him."

Mother nodded her head sadly. Harley Boy's father—Reverend Harley's son—had disappeared shortly after his son's birth—drifting away on a sea of cheap bourbon. His young wife, Evie Rose, had given the baby to Reverend Harley and Ida Louise to raise. Evie Rose was only seventeen. Everyone agreed it was the right thing to do. At nineteen, Evie left for a job in Louisville, Kentucky, without her young son. She had made a life for herself in the city, and she visited the valley sometimes, but Harley Boy had never lived with his mother. And he'd never met his father. Could he have his father's bad blood? I shook my head. It was aching now with so many worries.

"Damn it!" Reana Mae's voice came sharply. "Look at them wieners."

The hot dogs she'd been grilling had dropped directly into the coals and were charred black. Glaring at Nancy and Caleb, she trudged to the hamper for more. I stayed beside her while she grilled them. Mother, still frowning, rejoined Aunt Vera and Lottie.

Finally, we walked back to where my sisters sat with Caleb. Tracy had joined them now, but she didn't say a word as we approached. Reana Mae handed Nancy her hot dog in silence.

"Thank you, sweetheart." Nancy's voiced dripped sugary syrup.

"Where's the fixin's?" Caleb handed his hot dog back to Reana Mae. Obediently, she took the sandwich back to the hamper and added ketchup, mustard, and relish. Even from where I sat, I could see her hands shake.

When she returned, Caleb took the hot dog from her without even looking up.

"What was that all about, Reana Mae?" Tracy leaned forward eagerly. "Was Harley Boy drunk?"

"Looked like a lovers' quarrel to me." Nancy laughed.

"It wasn't no lovers' quarrel!" Reana Mae snapped back. "We ain't lovers at all." She paused, staring angrily from Nancy to Caleb. "Ask Caleb! He knows the truth!"

Nancy arched her eyebrows at Caleb, smiling. His cheeks reddened.

"How the hell would I know?" He shrugged. "I can't keep up with every little thing you kids get into."

Reana Mae sat back in a stunned silence. Then she rose and ran headlong toward the road.

"You're just hateful," I hissed at Caleb. As I ran after Reana Mae, I could hear them laughing behind me—my sisters and Reana Mae's lover. I hated them all.

"Reana Mae!" I called out, grabbing at her arm as we reached the dirt road. "Wait up."

She shook her arm loose from my grip, but slowed down to walk beside me. Tears dripped from her chin. I walked beside her silently.

Earlier that year, Mother had signed me up for cotillion, so I would learn proper etiquette and manners. I had learned how to hold my salad fork and dance the fox-trot. But old Miss Sheldon never told me what to say at a time like this. Finally, I reached over and grabbed Reana's hand, holding it tightly in mine.

"Lord God, Bethany. How can he be that way?" She stopped in the road. "Oh, God. Bethy, it hurts so bad," she whispered, collapsing against me.

I wrapped my arms around her, and she cried until it seemed like she surely should run out of tears. Finally, she pulled away, straightened her shoulders, and snuffled loudly; we walked up the road, still holding hands, until we reached the dark little house she shared with Jolene and Caleb—her mother and her father's brother. Latching the gate behind us, I followed her to the back of the house, and we sat down at the top of the steep stone steps that led down to the black, swirling river below. Neither of us spoke.

Yawning mightily, Bo rose from where he'd been sleeping and lumbered over to lay his head on Reana Mae's lap. She promptly buried her face in the dog's fur and began crying again. I sat watching her, wondering what I could possibly say to ever make it better.

Suddenly, an explosion filled the sky overhead, and then another. Across the river, the men had begun setting off fireworks. I watched in silence, while Reana Mae sat hunched over Bobby Lee's old dog. Every time a rainbow exploded in the sky, poor Bo whimpered pitifully.

Finally, after what seemed like a long time, the huge blasts stopped, the acrid smell of gunpowder drifted across the river, and the stars reappeared in their usual places, blinking as if blinded by their brighter cousins below.

Reana Mae raised her head from Bo's fur and wiped her arm across her eyes, sniffing. "How can he be so mean, Bethany?" she said, staring into the dark night. "How can he act that way to me?"

"I don't know, Reana Mae," I whispered back, casting about for a reason, an explanation about it all. "Maybe he's just playing with Nancy, you know?"

"You don't know nothin', Bethany Marie," she hissed savagely. "You don't know nothin' about it."

I sat up straight, pulling away from her, my feelings hurt. After all, wasn't I the one sitting beside her in the night? Wasn't I the one who had been defending her all summer long? Wasn't it me that came when her baby brother had died, and me that wrote to her every week, and me that prayed for her every blessed night?

"Oh, I know, Reana Mae," I whispered, half to myself. "I do know."

I felt rather than saw her turn to look at me, felt her wide eyes staring at me in the dark.

"You know what?"

"I know all about it, Reana Mae," I continued, still not looking at her, not wanting to see her eyes staring back at me. "We found your spot in the woods . . . me and Ruthann and poor Harley Boy. We found your blanket and the mattress and the packages . . . and your diary, too. We all know."

I heard her suck her breath in sharply.

"Are you gonna tell?" she whispered the question finally—cementing the knowledge in my heart. For probably the hundredth time that day, I thought I might throw up.

I sat there for a long minute, staring straight ahead of me, not looking at my cousin. It felt like a whole eternity. I wanted more than anything right then to be at home in my own bed in my mother's tidy white house on a quiet street in Indianapolis. I wanted to be far away from Reana Mae and her terrible family. Far away from the Coal River Valley.

Then, finally, I shook my head. Of course, I knew I should tell. I knew it's what Mother would want me to do. I even knew it would be the right thing to do for Reana Mae. I knew my confession would take Reana far away from Caleb and Jolene—that it would be for her own good. But we were cousins, Reana and me . . . hell, we were sisters. And I knew I couldn't tell, not then and not ever, no matter what.

"No, I won't tell," I said.

"Ruthann and Harley Boy?" Reana whispered.

"I don't know what they're gonna do. I think Ruthann won't say anything unless Harley Boy does. But if Harley Boy tells, you know Ruthann will back him up."

"They can't tell, Bethany!" Reana Mae rose suddenly, pushing Bo aside as she stood. "I gotta find Harley Boy . . . I gotta find him right now."

"But Ida Louise took Harley home. You know you can't get to him tonight."

Reana Mae stared down at me steadily for what seemed like a long time, then turned and ran toward the front of the tiny, shabby house. I stood uncertainly for a moment, then sighed heavily and followed her.

We ran down the hard-packed dirt road, Reana Mae and I, finally turning onto a path that led up the hill toward Brother Harley's parsonage and Christ the King Baptist Church. Panting and swearing mightily at my bruised, bare feet, I struggled to keep pace with my cousin. She ran like she was in a race for her life, and I guess she probably was. When we reached the church, we veered left and ran toward the small parsonage. Silently, I watched as my cousin deftly climbed the tidy wooden fence that surrounded the house. I stayed behind on the dirt road while Reana Mae padded across the yard, stooped to pick up a handful of pebbles, and climbed into the stunted, gnarled apple tree in the yard. She moved gracefully and quickly, finding foothold after sure foothold. I could tell she'd climbed that tree before.

Holding my breath, I watched as she crawled out onto the narrow limb nearest the house and pitched a stone at a darkened window on the second floor. Downstairs, several lights burned brightly.

I could see Ida Louise moving about in the kitchen, dishrag in hand. I saw Reana Mae throw a second pebble at the second-floor window. Then I saw him.

Harley Boy opened the window slowly—it creaked loudly, and I glanced again toward the kitchen below. But Ida Louise kept right on washing dishes.

"Come out, Harley Boy," I heard Reana Mae's voice pleading. "Come on out and talk to me."

"I can't," he hissed at her. "Grandmaw's downstairs. And anyway, why should I?"

"Because you want to," Reana Mae's voice was soft and cajoling now. "And because I want you to," she whispered urgently. "Come on down and let me talk to you . . . just for a minute?"

Just then, the light in the kitchen went dark. Reana Mae crawled farther out onto the limb. "She's gone into the front room now, Harley. Come out . . . please?"

Harley Boy's face disappeared from the window, and Reana Mae edged carefully back toward the tree trunk. By the time she had climbed down from the tree, Harley was rounding the back of the house. The two of them walked quickly away from the house, toward the darkened church and its even darker graveyard. Unable to take my eyes from them, I followed along the dark road.

"She beat you bad?"

Reana Mae reached out to touch Harley Boy's face just below the purple, swollen eye. He pulled away from her.

"She's done worse, I guess."

They dropped down onto the church steps. Still, I watched them from the road. Neither of them ever once looked my way. I think Reana Mae had forgotten I was there.

"You acted like a damned fool tonight, Harley Boy. You know that? You acted crazy."

"You're the one who's crazy!" Harley's voice sounded sharp and hurt. "You're the one who's goin' right straight to hell! What are you doin' with that man, with your own blood-uncle? That man is old enough to be your daddy!"

"But I love him, Harley." Reana Mae's voice carried across the dark yard, calm and steady. "I know I ain't supposed to, and I know you think it's a sin. But I love him, anyways. He's the only one that truly knows me. He's the only one that loves me back."

"That ain't true." Harley Boy's voice shook. I nodded along with him. "It ain't true, and you know it—or at least you ought to! Belle loves you, and Helen and Bethany love you, and your daddy does, too."

"My daddy?" Reana laughed disdainfully. "Oh yeah, my daddy loves me right good! He loves me so damned much he can't stand even to be in the same state as me."

"That ain't because of you." Harley Boy spoke confidently now. "It ain't you he hates, and you know that, don't you?"

He leaned forward and took both of Reana's hands tightly in his. "It's your mama that he hates, Reana Mae. And you know why, don't you? Don't you even know why your daddy hates Jolene?"

Reana sat back, trying to pull her hands from his. But Harley Boy held on, staring straight into her eyes.

"He hates her—he hates his own wife—because of his own damned brother. It's all because of Caleb. It's because your mama acted like a whore with Caleb. That's what Bobby Lee can't abide. And now you, Reana Mae . . . now you're carrying on with Caleb, too? Can't you see how that's gonna hurt your daddy? Can't you see how that makes you just like your mama?"

Reana Mae stood abruptly, pushing Harley Boy away. "I ain't a bit like my mama," she spat at him. "You take that back right now!"

"But just look at it, Reana," Harley pleaded softly, urgently. "I ain't saying you're exactly like her. But you're carryin' on shameful-like. And can't you see how folks are talking about it, all up and down the river? Grandmaw says it's so, and that's the Lord's plain and honest truth. They're talking, and you ought to know it!"

"You think I give a shit what folks on this river say about me?" Reana Mae's voice rose.

"Well, you ought to give a shit. Lord knows, you ought to. 'Cause this time they're right. You're eleven years old, Reana Mae Colvin. And Caleb, why he's near onto nineteen, if he ain't already. He's a growed-up adult. Plus he's your own blood-kin. That's wrong, Reana. It's purely wrong."

"Okay, look, it ain't wrong." Her voice was soft and pleading now. "I promise you, Harley, it ain't so very wrong. 'Cause Caleb loves me. He's gonna marry me. Don't you know he's gonna marry me as soon as I get old enough?"

"Good gracious God, Reana Mae! He can't never marry you." Caleb sounded tired now. "Don't you know that the state of West Virginia won't never let you marry your daddy's own brother?"

"But Caleb says . . ."

"Oh, well, Caleb says . . . That's a real good one. Caleb says . . . like Caleb's word is worth a piece of shit . . . like it's just Caleb's mouth to God's own ear."

Harley Boy rose as he spat the words. He looked wiser and more grown up than I'd ever seen him.

"Listen, you cannot marry your own uncle. Not in West Virginia, and not anywhere else in the whole United States of America," Harley spoke confidently. "And Caleb damned well knows it! He just wants you to think he's gonna marry you so you'll let him do whatever he wants to you."

Harley Boy's words came tumbling out in a jumble of fury and pleading. He grabbed at Reana's hands again, pulling her close to him on the church steps.

"He ain't never gonna marry you. He just wants to do it with you. And you . . . dear God, Reana, actin' like you are . . . why, you're no better than your own sinful mama. You're actin' like a whore for him. And if you don't stop it right now, you're gonna go straight to hell, just like your grandma and your mama before you."

"You just leave them outta this, Harley Boy. Do you hear me? You leave my mama and her mama out of this."

Abruptly, Harley Boy dropped back onto the wooden steps of the church, burying his face in his hands. Reana Mae dropped down again beside him, touching his shoulder tentatively; then she leaned against him, her arm circling his back.

I held my breath in the dark, afraid even to breathe. Leaning heavily against the old wooden fence, I heard Reana Mae whisper, "Oh, Harley Boy, I know you love me. You told me so right and plain last winter. But, Harley, you just ain't the one for me, and you know that's true. You know straightaway that I'm meant for Caleb, and you're meant for Ruthann. That's just the way it is." She sighed then and leaned closer into him.

"But you can't tell on me, Harley. You can't tell your grandma or no one what you know. . . . Hush now, don't you go to arguin' with me."

Reana Mae knelt before him on the ground, raising his chin with her hands so that he had to look her straight in the face.

"Look, Harley, if I'm goin' straight to the devil's own hellfire . . . well, then, I'm goin' to hell. There ain't nothin' you can do about it. You know that's the Lord's own truth, don't you?" She was insistent now, knowing she had won.

Harley stared at her in a palpable mute anguish, but even I could see that Reana Mae was winning.

"You know that's the truth, and you know I'm right. I am who I am—and maybe I am my mama's own daughter and maybe I am going straight to hell. But I love him, Harley. I know it hurts you, and I'm sorry . . . truly and honestly I am. But I can't help it. I love Caleb with all my heart.

"So promise me, Harley. Promise me because you're my only real friend in the whole wide world. Promise me you won't tell. 'Cause if you tell, Aunt Belle will have them take me away to Charleston or Huntington or somewhere else, and then you won't never see me again. And I'll be living in some house with people who don't even know me, people who aren't my own."

He stared at her steadily now. I could see the pain written across his white, freckled face.

"Don't you see what will happen? They'll take me away . . . from the river and from Mama and from you. Don't do that to me, Harley. I'm beggin' you, don't do that to me."

"I won't." He whispered it so quietly I could barely hear him. "I won't let them take you away."

"You just keep your mouth shut, then, you hear me?" She leaned forward and kissed his freckled forehead, smiling at her victory.

Suddenly, he lunged toward her, grabbing her face in both his hands and pulling her toward him. I watched him kiss her hard on the lips, and she never struggled, not even once. She only leaned in, letting him kiss her again and again. When he finally released her, she sat back slightly, smiling.

"You just keep your mouth shut, okay?" she repeated, licking her lips quickly.

I saw Harley grimace, clench his fists tightly, and slowly nod.

He wouldn't tell. Not now, maybe not ever.

Reana Mae rose, smiling down at him. Kissing the top of his red hair, she turned and ran silently back toward the dirt road and me.

Joining her on the path, I turned back to see Harley Boy still sitting on the church steps, his head buried in his hands. He wouldn't tell on Reana Mae. I was sure of that, and so was she. But at what cost?

Turning briefly to smile at me, Reana grabbed my hand as we pounded down the path toward the road. For the moment, her agony over Caleb and Nancy was at bay. She had won Harley Boy's silence, and with it Ruthann's. And she knew she had mine.

She was safe, then, for the moment, in the love of her friends . . . if not safely in Caleb's.

~ 19 ~

Cool Water

The next morning, Ruthann knocked on our door early. Moments later, I was walking down the road with her toward the beach. Neither of us spoke about the day before, about Harley Boy or Reana Mae or the mattress in the woods. Instead, we talked about the fireworks and the cookout and, briefly, about Nancy and Caleb.

"He surely seems taken with her," Ruthann said, glancing sidelong toward me.

I shrugged my shoulders. "Who knows?" I said as lightly as I could.

"I wonder what Reana Mae thinks about that?"

I stopped to pull a small rock from my sandal, unsure what to say. Thankfully, I was spared a response when Harley Boy came running down the path toward us.

"Hey, ya'll," he said, pulling up short beside us. "What are you up to?"

Ruthann glanced silently from him toward me, waiting for some kind of signal, I guess. Then she shrugged elaborately. "Nothing, I guess. Just goin' to the beach."

I straightened up and smiled at Harley as we walked toward the beach. When we passed Reana Mae's house, I glanced at Harley and saw him looking toward the cottage and trying not to. I wanted to touch his arm, but I didn't dare. Instead, I said brightly, "Those sure were some fireworks last night, H.B. What did your grandpa say about them?"

He shook his head, red hair hanging thickly over his forehead. "I went to sleep before he got home. But I know they was good, 'cause I helped pack them." He knelt down to pick up a small, flat stone. "Did ya'll like them?"

"Sure," Ruthann lied smoothly, glancing at me. "They was plain gorgeous."

I simply nodded in agreement. I certainly did not want him to know that I'd been with Reana Mae the night before in the church-yard.

We spent that morning as we had every morning—lying on the beach, swimming out to the raft, lying in the sun there, then swimming back to the beach. By now, it was almost a ritual, but this morning it felt different. Every little while, I turned my eyes toward Harley Boy, wondering how often he had snuck out of his bedroom in the night to meet Reana Mae. I was certain the night before had not been the first time.

Along toward noon, I heard Melinda's voice float out toward the raft—the words unclear but the voice unmistakable. Ruthann raised her head, too, glancing toward Harley as she said, "Looks like the reinforcements are here. What do ya'll want to do about lunch?"

I watched as Harley leaned forward, straining his eyes toward the shore. In a minute, he flopped back down onto the raft. "I don't care." He sighed. "What do ya'll want to do?"

I lay in silence, knowing that if Reana Mae was on the beach, Harley would be up in an instant. Finally, Ruthann sighed loudly.

"Okay," she said, standing and pulling at her swimsuit, "let's swim back and eat."

I looked from Ruthann to Harley Boy, feeling sorry for both of them. I knew how Ruthann felt about Harley by then—it probably was clear to anyone who spent five minutes with them. And I knew how Harley felt about Reana Mae.

We swam back to the beach and unwrapped the peanut butter

sandwiches we'd packed. Nancy and Melinda were bickering over which radio station to listen to. Tracy was nowhere around.

We ate our sandwiches in silence, listening to "Mr. Bojangles" on the radio. Just as we were wiping away our crumbs, Tracy appeared, carrying her towel and stationery box. But instead of settling down beside Nancy and Melinda, she threw her towel down by me.

"What are you all doing?" Her voice was bright.

Ruthann and Harley Boy looked at each other, then at me.

Tracy never joined us. She never even spoke to us except to mock us for something.

"We was just fixin' to swim out to the raft," Ruthann said warily.

Tracy leaned back on her towel, shaded her eyes against the noonday sun, and smiled. "I thought you might be going hiking again."

I glanced at Ruthann, but she was watching Harley Boy. None of us spoke.

"Where'd you all go off to yesterday?" Tracy asked, eyebrows raised slightly above those clear hazel eyes.

"Just hiking . . . in the woods, you know. Back toward our house . . . or . . . I mean, toward Ray's store." My words came out in a jumble. Even to myself, my voice sounded unnaturally sharp.

"Nowhere in particular," Ruthann added.

"None of your damned business," Harley Boy growled.

"Why? Is it a secret?" Tracy leaned up on an elbow and smiled sweetly into Harley Boy's angry face, her beautiful eyes widening. "Some kind of national security secret?"

No one answered her.

"Oh, well, then . . . maybe it's a hillbilly secret." Tracy shrugged slightly, still smiling at Harley Boy. "Maybe a hillbilly love secret— the kind of love secret that only happens in West Virginia."

"Shut up, Tracy," I hissed.

"Oh, did I guess it right, then? It *is* a love secret." She sat up, lowering her sunglasses on her nose and smiling brightly.

Harley Boy stood up suddenly, kicking sand onto the rest of us in the process.

"You just stay out of what ain't your goddamned business, you hear?" He spoke quietly, but there was a dangerous edge in his voice.

"Well, maybe it is my business, Harley Boy." Tracy leaned toward him, her eyes gleaming the way they did sometimes when she was feeling especially mean. Or when she was about to cry. "Maybe you don't want it to be, but maybe it is anyway."

That made all of us jump. Tracy leaned back, her eyes narrowed, watching us closely.

"You just stay out of it, Tracy Wylie," Harley repeated. "You hear me? You better just stay out of what don't concern you . . . or else . . ." His voice rose, his hands were clenched into tight, white fists.

"Or else what?" She smiled, shading her eyes as she looked up at him.

"Or else . . . you'll make a whole lotta trouble for a lotta people . . . and for yourself, too. Goddamn it, just stay out of it . . . you hear?"

With that, Harley Boy turned and ran toward the cool, dark water. Ruthann looked at me briefly, then followed him. But I stayed put. If Tracy knew something about Caleb and Reana Mae, I had to find out what. Harley might think he could scare Tracy into staying quiet, but I knew my sister too well to believe that.

"Why are you so mean, Tracy?" I asked. "Why can't you just stay out of things that aren't yours to worry about?"

Tracy simply smiled, covering her eyes with her arm.

"I mean it, Tracy!" I hissed. "Why are you so mean all the time?"

She let out a soft laugh, dropping back onto her towel gracefully.

"Why can't you just be nice like a regular person for once?"

I felt like I might just hit her if she laughed again.

"Oh, chill out, Bethany," she said. Her voice was bored now. "Do you think I give a shit what you and your little friends do in the woods?"

She rolled onto her side facing me and rested her head on her hand. "You're just so . . . easy, Bethany, you know?" She wasn't laughing or even smirking now. In fact, she looked almost puzzled, staring at me.

I wanted to walk away, swim to the raft, and hate her just like always.

But she had never looked at me like that before. Like she actually was waiting to hear what I was going to say.

I shook my head, staring at her suspiciously.

"What does that mean?" I asked. "What does that mean . . . that I'm easy?"

She gazed at me unblinking, her eyes narrowed slightly. "I mean, you let yourself get hurt so easy," she said, in the same puzzled voice. "Why do you let everyone hurt you so much?"

"I don't," I snorted.

"Fine, then," she said, dropping back onto her towel, her voice contemptuous again. "You don't."

I sat a minute longer, waiting to see if she would say something else, but she was done. Whatever had caught her interest before was gone. She had no use for me now.

"Tracy?" I couldn't help it, I had to push it.

"What?"

"That hike we took yesterday, me and Ruthann and Harley Boy . . . it was just a hike. That's all." I stood, wiping sand from my legs, watching her closely.

"Whatever." She didn't even open her eyes.

"Okay, well . . . then, I'll see you later."

She lay silently, her eyes closed against the sun.

I swam slowly out to the raft, where Ruthann and Harley were waiting.

"Do you think she knows?" Ruthann asked as I pulled myself out of the water. Her eyes were wide and anxious. Harley Boy stared grimly toward the shore, as if ensuring Tracy's silence through sheer force of will.

"No," I said, wringing water from my hair. "She's just yanking our chain."

"You sure?" Harley asked, still staring at the beach.

"Yeah, I'm sure." I nodded. "If she knew, she'd have told Mother already."

"She wouldn't!" Ruthann sounded appalled.

"Yeah, she would." I nodded grimly. "She'd tell Mother, and she'd make it sound like she was doing it because she was worried about Reana Mae."

I grimaced, picturing the scene.

"Or . . ." I was thinking out loud now. "Or she'd let me know that she knew, and then she'd use it to make me do stuff."

"Like what?" Ruthann leaned toward me.

"Give her money. Do her chores." I shrugged. "Whatever she wanted, she'd make me do it. That's how she is."

"She oughtta be a politician," Harley Boy growled. "One of them senators up in Washington, D.C." His voice was contemptuous. "Maybe even president."

Ruthann laughed shortly. "Oh yeah, H.B.," she snorted. "Tracy for president."

He glared a minute longer at my sister's small form on the beach, then stood abruptly. "Well, as long as she don't know about . . ."

His cheeks reddened as his voice trailed away. Suddenly, he dove into the river, surfacing seconds later swimming toward the far shore, away from my sisters. Away from Ruthann and me.

Ruthann sat quietly, watching him while I watched her.

"Damn her," she whispered, her voice tight in her throat.

"She's mean, all right." I nodded. "But I don't think she can hurt us."

"Not Tracy!" Ruthann's voice came sharp and loud, startling both of us. "Not her," she said more quietly, jerking her head toward the beach.

Of course she meant Reana Mae.

I lay back on the raft, my stomach knotting tightly. I wished I was not on the Coal River, that I was back in my own house in Indiana . . . or back in Florida with Aunt DJ even . . . anywhere else but here.

Ruthann lay back, too. For a long time we didn't talk. I could almost feel the tension of her body next to mine. I knew she wanted to follow Harley Boy. Staying put was probably the hardest thing she'd ever done.

I cleared my throat, thinking I should say something. But no words came to mind. So we lay there in silence.

Ruthann and Harley Boy, Reana Mae and Caleb, Nancy and even terrible Tracy—all of them seemed like strangers this summer. All of them had changed. They'd gone on into a world I didn't know . . . one I didn't want to know.

After an hour or so, maybe longer, Ruthann said she ought to be getting on home to see if her mother needed help with Lottie.

I knew she was lying, of course. Aunt Vera hardly ever asked Ruthann to watch Lottie. Little Lottie Fern was the spark in Vera's engine. Born when Vera was past thirty, after a whole series of miscarriages, Lottie was the treasured joy of Vera and Hobie's lives. Vera had even quit working at the A&P in St. Albans after Lottie was born. Always before, Ruthann had stayed at Ida Louise's after school, playing checkers, working out math problems, and doing chores with Harley Boy. With Lottie's arrival, Ruthann had her own mother at home, whether it suited her or not. She bore it well, though she admitted to me that summer she often wished she could just go back to Ida's and be with Harley Boy.

After Ruthann had gone, I stayed on the raft, glad of being alone. I wondered where Reana Mae might be. Was she with Caleb? Had she told him we'd found their secret place? Would that be enough to make Caleb let her go? What if he simply took Reana and left the valley altogether? What if they rode away on a Greyhound bus, and I never saw Reana again? What if Jolene found them together in Reana's bed? Would she kill Caleb? Would she kill Reana Mae? Would she even care?

I was twelve years old. I did not want to think about my eleven-year-old cousin having sex with her uncle. I did not want to think about Jolene beating Reana Mae to death, or shooting her with Bobby Lee's hunting rifle. I did not want to think about how Bobby Lee might feel, knowing his own brother was having sex with his daughter. I did not want to think about any of that . . . but, of course, that's all I could think about.

Just as the sun was hedging away behind the trees on the south bank, I started awake, my neck aching in an awkward tilt.

Reana Mae pulled herself onto the raft, smiling uncertainly at me, dripping cold water on my legs.

"Hey, you," she panted, dropping down beside me.

"Hi." I forced my voice through my dry throat. How long had I been asleep?

"You got too much sun."

Reana Mae touched my chest lightly. I raised my head to see a white spot appear where her finger had been.

I rolled onto my stomach, turning my face away from her.

"Did you see Harley Boy today?"

Her voice was soft.

"Yeah," I said, not looking back at her. "He was here before."

She waited quietly, patiently.

"He swam on over to the far side," I said finally, sighing heavily.

"Was Ruthann with him?"

"No." I shifted slightly. "She went home."

"Did she talk to him since last night?" Reana Mae asked.

"I don't think so," I answered dully. "She didn't say so, anyway."

"You reckon she'll keep her mouth shut?" Her voice, still soft, sounded anxious.

"Yeah," I said, still not looking at her. "She'll keep quiet. As long as Harley stays quiet, Ruthann will, too."

I felt her relax, her breath slowing until it came deep and regular. As she relaxed, I felt my own body tense up, bile rising in my throat. Why should she be so calm, when the rest of us were so damned unhappy?

"Where's Caleb today?" My voice came out harsh—sharp and angry.

I sat up, staring down at her face, looking for some sign of discomfort.

"He's working in the store." She smiled slightly, shifting her hips.

"Does he know about yesterday?" I watched her face carefully, waiting a long time for her response. Finally, she sighed.

"No, Bethany," she said, raising her head to look me in the face. "He don't know that ya'll found . . . found out," she finished hesitantly.

"You didn't tell him?" I was stunned. How could she not tell him?

"Naw." She shook her head, her wet braid swinging heavily from side to side.

"But . . ."

My voice stuck in my throat. How could she not tell him? We knew—Harley and Ruthann and me—we all knew. Didn't that even matter?

I stared at her in disbelief. Somewhere in the back of my brain, I was aware how stupid I must look—my eyes round, my mouth hanging open. But I didn't care. Or at least, I couldn't help myself.

"Bethany," Reana Mae cooed, her hands cupping my chin so that I had to look at her. "Look . . . don't worry, you hear? Don't worry yourself over it."

She smiled, her eyes holding mine. I noted again how much older she seemed than the last time we'd been at the river. As if she'd lived a whole lifetime since then.

"Listen," her voice pleaded now, sweet and firm. "It's gonna be all right, you hear me?" She nodded firmly, her braid flapping silently in affirmation. "I promise you, Bethy, it's gonna be all right."

"How, Reana?" I found my voice finally. "How is it going to be all right?"

She looked away from me for a minute, then looked back, holding my eyes. "It just is," she said firmly. "Caleb . . . well, Caleb's gonna make it all right."

She touched my cheek.

"Honest, Bethy," she pleaded. "I know you don't believe me, but it's God's own truth. Caleb's gonna make it all right, you'll see."

She nodded again, not looking at my face now. "He's gonna make it all right . . . and then," she rushed ahead, holding my hands tight in hers, so tight it hurt. "Then, you'll see, Bethany. We'll have us a real house, me and Caleb. Not a shack like here, a real house like they have up in the city, with lacy curtains in the windows and air-conditioning and everything! And we'll have money to buy nice things." She nodded eagerly at me, as if nodding could make it so.

"We'll have a big house and a big car—bigger even than Aunt Belle's. And then we'll have babies . . . at least two." She smiled eagerly. "I want a boy for Caleb and a little baby girl for me. You know, Bethy?" She stared right in my eyes. "You know what I mean? I want me a little baby girl I can dress up and take shopping and spoil real bad."

I stared at her in disbelief, at my eleven-year-old cousin in her too-small bikini, her wet braid swinging from side to side as she spun fairy tales out of thin air.

"And she'll be real pretty, Bethy," Reana Mae continued eagerly. "She'll be a real pretty little baby, just like my grandma . . . my mama's mother, I mean. She'll look just like EmmaJane. Everyone knows she was flat-out gorgeous."

I stared at her, aghast.

I'd never heard Reana Mae mention Jolene's mother. EmmaJane had been dead for years before Reana even was born. Jolene hardly ever talked about her. Neither did anyone else, except sometimes Aunt Loreen. I couldn't fathom that Reana Mae would want any child of hers to take after old, crazy, dead EmmaJane.

"Course, she'll have more sense than EmmaJane," Reana Mae said quickly, watching my face. "But she'll be real pretty . . . pretty like EmmaJane—that's for damn certain." Her voice trailed off as she stared hard at me.

"My baby girl will be so pretty," she repeated firmly, her chin rising defiantly. "And me and Caleb, we'll be so happy then."

Her voice rose, till it carried far away down the river.

"You just wait, Bethany. Me and Caleb and our baby, we'll be real happy."

I nodded. What else could I do?

Three weeks later, I lay on my belly in the back of the station wagon, watching Reana Mae waving good-bye.

One evening the week before, Aunt Belle had burst into our cottage to announce that Daddy had called her house. He had a promotion!

He would be calling back in half an hour, so Mother had to come down to Belle's right away.

He wasn't going to be a regional director anymore. He was going to be a vice president at Morrison Brothers' Insurance Company.

That meant more money, Belle said. And a bigger office . . . even a secretary, probably.

But, most important, we all knew immediately, it meant he wouldn't have to travel. He wouldn't be gone all summer anymore.

Nancy, Melinda, and Tracy had erupted into joyous whoops and wild dancing at the news. Mother fairly beamed as she climbed into the big Lincoln to ride up to Aunt Belle's house so she'd be there when Daddy called again.

When she came back an hour later, she was smiling still. Her black eyes sparkled.

"It's a good promotion," she announced. "He'll have an office of his own and there will be more money. Best of all, he'll be home more."

Her voice quavered, and I saw tears well in her eyes as she repeated, "He'll be home more!"

The next few days we spent packing for the trip home.

My sisters were overjoyed, of course. None of them cared a whit for the Coal River.

Nancy was anxious to start packing for college. She was going away to Indiana University in the fall. Melinda was ready to get back to her regular swim practices before school started. And, of course, Tracy couldn't wait to get back to Paul.

Mother sang as she scoured the oven and washed the windows. Even Aunt Belle seemed elated, though I was sure she would miss us when we'd gone back north.

"You okay, honey?" she asked one day, watching as I folded towels and packed them into the cedar chest under the front window.

"I'm fine, Aunt Belle," I said.

And, to be honest, I was.

For the first time I could remember, I was ready to go back to Indiana.

Back to my reliable best friend, Cindy, and her grandma's soap operas. Back to old Skipper, who bayed when anyone knocked at the front door. Back to my own bed in my own attic room in my own tidy house on Lowell Street.

For the first time ever, I was ready to leave the river.

I watched Reana Mae's waving form retreat, ever smaller, from the back window.

Then we rounded a curve in the road, and I flopped back onto the blankets, staring at the car roof. I felt like an old towel, wrung out and hung up.

Beside me, Tracy sighed happily.

"I can't wait to get home," she said. "Can you?"

❦ 20 ❧

Truth Be Told

Fall brought changes for all of us. After many tears and a few screaming matches with my parents, Nancy finally left for college. From the fuss she made, you'd have thought she was moving to Mars instead of Bloomington, only an hour away. Melinda began her senior year in high school as captain of the swim team. Tracy started high school, winning a spot on the freshman cheerleading squad and catching the eye of a basketball player two years older than she was. With Tracy at a different school, I felt I had finally arrived. I was twelve. I was nearly grown up.

In November, Daddy and Mother drove to West Virginia for Aunt Loreen's funeral. She'd dropped dead one morning at the store, the telephone receiver still clutched in her hand. I felt very grown up, staying at home with Melinda and Tracy while my parents were gone.

On a Wednesday night the week before Christmas, I sat at the kitchen table, staring grimly at my math homework, wishing I could skip the next two days and get right to Christmas vacation. Two glorious weeks at home to bake cookies, wrap presents, and forget about fractions and long division.

I had been staring at the same problem for several minutes when the phone rang.

Glad of any diversion, I ran down the hallway, reaching the phone just ahead of Melinda.

"Hello?" I panted, smiling triumphantly at Melinda stalking back down the hall.

"Bethany Marie, is that you? It's me, child. It's Aunt Belle."

"Aunt Belle!" I cried out happily. Belle's phone calls sometimes lasted for hours. Maybe she would talk until bedtime, and I could skip my math homework altogether.

"How you doin', Bethy? You bein' a good girl for Santy Claus?"

"I'm trying," I said.

"Good, darling, that's real good."

Her voice was quieter than usual, and instead of prodding for every detail of my day, as she usually did, she asked abruptly, "Is your mama there?"

"No, ma'am," I said, surprised. Didn't she want to talk to me at all?

"How 'bout Jimmy, then? Is he there?"

"Yes, Aunt Belle," I said, laying down the receiver. "Daddy! Aunt Belle is on the phone."

Daddy padded down the hall in his slippers, his smoking pipe cupped in one hand, a folded newspaper in the other. He handed me the paper as he took the receiver.

"Hey there, Belle! How's my favorite lady?"

He was silent for several minutes. I stood watching as his grin froze, slowly dropping into a dark frown. Melinda had stopped in the hall behind me and was watching, too. Just from Daddy's face, we knew something was wrong, something bad.

"Hold on now, Belle. Slow down. Are you sure she . . . ?"

He paused again, the frown deepening across his face. Then he noticed us standing there, watching.

Cupping his hand over the mouthpiece, he said firmly, "You girls go on in the other room, now. This is nothing to do with you."

I followed Melinda into the living room. Then she motioned me to follow her down the hall into Mother's room.

She closed the door behind us quietly.

"What are you doing?" I whispered.

"Shhhhhh," she shushed me urgently, reaching for the phone by the bed.

My eyes widened in disbelief as she gently rocked the receiver from its cradle, lifted it to her ear, and motioned for me to come closer. Even from across the room, I could hear Belle's booming voice.

"Oh, it's bad, Jimmy, it's real bad. I put her in the car and drove her up to the doctor at St. Albans myself. She's got a broke wrist, of course. And he says probably some broke ribs, too. And the bruises are terrible, Jimmy. I never seen anyone so beat up before."

"Where is Jolene now?" Daddy's voice was grim.

"God alone knows, Jimmy." Belle sighed so deep I could almost feel it right through the phone line.

"After Ray pulled her off Reana Mae, she swung at him, too. Can you believe it? Swung at him hard, like she'd take his head right off, if she could. Then she tore off down the road, screamin' at the top of her lungs for everyone to hear how her own daughter ain't nothing but a tramp and a whore.

"I couldn't hardly believe it, Jimmy. I seen Jolene lose it before, but not like this. She kept yellin' about how everyone thought *she* was so bad, but at least *she* never had sex with her own kin-blood uncle. It was like she was possessed."

Melinda gasped quietly at this, her eyes widening in horror.

I was shaking all over, shaking so bad I had to sit down on Mother's bed.

Jolene had found out, then.

She knew about Reana Mae and Caleb. And Belle knew, too.

Probably everyone on the river knew.

"Well, it's bad, Belle. I'll give you that. But I don't know how we . . ."

"You got to, Jimmy." Aunt Belle's voice was urgent. I could almost see her gripping the phone, nodding her head firmly. "You know you got to. She's family. Just like you was family when I took you in to be my own."

"But I was just a baby, Belle. And you didn't have kids." Daddy's voice shook. "Reana Mae, why . . . she's a full-grown girl,

Belle. A full-grown girl who's got herself a whole boatload of troubles. I don't think she'd be good for my girls, living here with us. I mean . . . Lord, Belle! Bethany is only thirteen. . . ."

"Bethany is exactly why Reana Mae needs to be with you, son." Belle's voice was soft, but firm. "Why, Bethany and Helen are the only family Reana has, besides me. They're the only ones she trusts in the world."

"What about Ray?" Daddy asked weakly.

"Oh, Ray . . . Good Lord, Jimmy, Ray's an old man. He's about wore out hisself. He already raised two hellcats. He can't take on a third . . . not at his age. Not since Loreen died."

"But, Belle," Daddy started again, "what about . . ."

"Now you listen to me, James Winston Wylie. You and Helen are the only chance this child's got. I know it will be trouble. You don't have to tell me about that. But you got to do this. I can't, Jimmy, I'm too old . . . and Reana Mae, she's just too wild. But Helen can. And I know she'll want to. And you know it, too. You got to take her, son. That's all there is to it."

"Can't we wait and see if Jolene's gonna calm down?" Daddy pleaded. "Maybe once she's had some time to cool off, she'll . . ."

"Lord have mercy, Jimmy, what ocean are you swimmin' in? Jolene ain't never gonna cool off. She's got that bad blood, for sure. She's been mean to Reana Mae since the day she was born, and now she flat-out hates her. Jolene blames Reana as much as she blames Caleb."

"Where *is* Caleb?" Daddy asked this as if it had just occurred to him.

"Oh, he lit out right quick once he saw Jolene knew. Tore off down the road like lightning, never even looked back. Probably a good thing, too, 'cause she still has that gun. Bobby Lee's rifle, I mean. She'd killed him if she could."

I sat as still as I could, bunching Mother's clean white bedspread in my fists, listening hard and desperately fighting a tickle in my throat. I never have been able to sit in silence. Soon as it gets too quiet, I have to sneeze or cough or hiccup. It never fails.

Finally, I couldn't help it. I cleared my throat as quietly as I could. Of course, that soft clearing coincided with a short break in the conversation on the phone. Melinda stared at me in consternation as Daddy yelled, "Who's that on the line?"

Melinda returned the receiver to its cradle and we both ran for the door, but before we could reach it, Daddy flung it open.

"What in the hell do you two think you're doing?" he roared, his face a splotchy purple.

"You go to your rooms. Right now! And don't even *think* about coming out, you hear me?"

Melinda ran down the hall toward her room, and I pounded up the stairs to mine. After a while I heard the front door open downstairs. Mother was home. Soon after that, Tracy stomped loudly up the steps.

"What's going on?" she hissed, seeing me. "Daddy said I had to go right to my room. I didn't even do anything."

I gave her the vaguest answer I could think of.

"Aunt Belle called. Jolene beat up Reana Mae real bad, and Belle thinks we should bring her up here."

I didn't mention the reason for the beating. I really did not want Tracy to know about that.

"What?" Tracy stared at me, her mouth agape. "Why should we bring her here? Why can't she stay with Aunt Belle, or Uncle Ray, or . . . or somebody else down there?"

I shook my head and shrugged my shoulders. I knew Tracy wouldn't want Reana Mae to come.

"Jesus H. Christ," she spat, flopping back onto her bed. "It's bad enough having you here all the time. But that . . . that hillbilly . . . in my house . . . I might as well just dig myself a hole and never come out."

I turned my back to her and lay quietly on my bed, wishing Tracy would just go away. But of course she couldn't. We were stuck there together until Mother or Daddy said we could come down.

Just before nine, Mother's heels clicked up the stairs. Her face was pinched and creased like I'd never seen it before. Her beautiful dyed-black curls were flattened on one side of her head; her eyes were puffy and red.

She sat down on Tracy's bed, pulled both of us close, and explained in her soft, unwavering voice that tomorrow Daddy would be driving down to the Coal River to bring Reana Mae home to stay with us. After Christmas, Tracy would move into Nancy's room in the basement, when Nancy went back to college. Reana Mae would share the attic room with me.

"Can I go with him to get Reana?" I asked.

"Not this time, Bethany," Mother said firmly. "This time your daddy needs to go alone."

"But why did Jolene . . . ?" Tracy asked.

"It's no good even asking, Tracy," Mother said firmly. "It's not anything I want to talk with you about. Done is done. Jolene is sick, and Reana Mae needs us. She's family. That's all there is to it."

She turned to me and said, "That's all anyone needs to know."

"Yes, ma'am." I nodded. The lump in my throat felt so big I could hardly swallow.

Mother kissed both of us, then heard our prayers and clicked back down the stairs.

Daddy left early the next morning. I watched him pull away in the station wagon before the sun even came up. Then I dressed for school.

That night, Mother took me to the shopping center, where we bought sheets and blankets and a pillow for the bed she had ordered from Sears. We also picked out some Christmas gifts for Reana Mae, so she would have something to open on Christmas with the rest of us. Mother chose dark green pants and a matching sweater, a blue coat with a fur-lined hood, and some bright-colored hair ribbons. I found an Elvis Presley album I thought Reana would like and some cherry-flavored lip gloss. Finally, I put a small, locked journal on the pile at the sales counter. Mother smiled and nodded.

"That's very thoughtful of you, Bethany," she said as she counted out the money. "Your Aunt Belle says Reana Mae is quite a writer."

I wondered if Reana had been able to retrieve her old journal from its hiding place in the woods. She must have gone back for it. She wouldn't just leave it there. What if someone found it?

I realized then, with a lurch in my stomach, that it didn't matter, really, if someone found it now. Everyone knew anyway.

I swallowed hard, my eyes stinging again. If only she had listened to Harley Boy that night last July. If only she had stopped meeting Caleb then. If only Caleb had never come to live with Bobby Lee and Jolene.

If only I had told Mother last summer, maybe she could have stopped Reana Mae from getting hurt.

"Are you all right?"

Mother was staring at me, her hand reaching for my forehead. "You look like you're going to be sick, honey. Are you okay?"

I nodded, gulping and blinking furiously.

Mother picked up our bags, took my hand, and led me to the ladies' room. There, she felt my forehead again and told me we would stay a few minutes, just in case I needed to throw up.

"Goodness knows you're upset," she said, her own eyes bright with tears. "It's something you ought never to have even known about. Something that never should have happened."

"I already knew, Mama," I said.

Her hand, stroking my bangs, froze.

"What?"

"I knew already." I plunged ahead, my words tumbling out in a jumble of fear and relief. "I knew, and I didn't tell you."

"What are you talking about, Bethany?"

Mother leaned forward, her eyes staring straight into mine.

"I found out," I whispered, "last summer . . . on the Fourth of July. We . . . I mean, I . . . well, really, me and Ruthann and Harley Boy . . . we were in the woods, trying to make a path, you know? Trying to make a path from our house to the beach. And, we . . . that is, Harley . . . well, we found the place where . . . where . . ."

"Where what, Bethany?" Mother's voice was low, urgent. Her hands were on either side of my face, so I couldn't look away from her.

"Where Reana Mae and Caleb . . . where they did it."

My voice came out in a strangled kind of croak. Never in my

lifetime would I have imagined saying those words to my mother. My mother, who had worked so diligently to protect us from anything harsh or crass or painful. My mother, who prayed on her knees every blessed morning and night that her girls would grow up innocent, in grace and truth. My mother, whom I had never heard utter a swearword, who had never spoken ill of anyone in my hearing.

Frightened, I stared into my mother's familiar face and saw an expression there I had never seen before.

I stepped back, away from that face, pushing her hands from me and turning toward the wall.

She didn't say anything for a while. She didn't move, didn't speak, didn't even seem to breathe. Then, I felt her reach for me. And when I turned back, she was just Mother again, her dear, calm, familiar face staring sadly into mine. Tears dripped from her chin, but I don't think she realized it. At least, she didn't wipe them away.

"Oh, Bethy," she whispered. Her voice sounded like it came from someplace far away. "Why didn't you tell me? Why did you . . . oh, honey, I'm so sorry."

She pulled me to her, hugging me tight. And we both cried, right there in the ladies' room at the JC Penney store. I cried until my stomach hurt and my head ached. I was so glad, so relieved to finally tell her. The secret wasn't mine to carry anymore. I didn't have to lie, or hide, or worry. Mother would take care of it, just like she always did.

Eventually, we snuffled to a stop. Mother pulled a handkerchief from her purse and dabbed at her eyes and nose, then handed it to me. She turned toward the mirror and grimaced.

"Well, neither of us is fit to be seen. But I suppose we can't stay in here forever," she said firmly, touching her finger to her smudged lipstick.

We walked out of the ladies' room and straight through the store toward the exit and the bus stop. Mother never turned her eyes to the left or right, just stared straight ahead, her chin held high. I could see the saleslady in the lingerie department stare as we passed. Mother was puffy-eyed and blotchy, and I knew I must be a terrible sight . . . my eyes swollen, my nose a vivid crimson, my cheeks blotched. Still, Mother pulled me along and I followed.

When the bus arrived, she put the packages on the seat in front of us, unbuttoned her coat, then turned to me again.

"Bethany Marie," she said very quietly. "I'm sorry you had to know about this. It's the kind of thing I thought . . . well, the kind of thing we've tried hard to keep away from you girls."

She paused, breathing deeply and visibly steeling herself. But she never took her eyes from mine.

"Life can be so hard, Bethy, especially down there . . . down south, I mean. My mother . . . Lord, my mama had a real hard time, just even getting by. She struggled so hard, you know?"

Her voice had a soft twang, the kind I would recognize instantly as Belle's or Reana Mae's. I'd never heard my mother's voice twang like that. She usually spoke so carefully.

I nodded, as if I understood. But of course I didn't. I had never met my maternal grandmother. She had died a few months before I was born, and Mother didn't talk about her except to say things like "Oh, that was my mother's recipe" or "My mother always said, 'Clean house, clean heart.' "

In my own adolescent mind, then, my maternal grandmother was a cook of good food and a very clean housekeeper—nothing more. Daddy's family was my family. I had Aunt Belle. I had not thought much about Mother's past. She was just Mother, after all.

"My mama had a real hard time just keeping us fed." Mother sighed.

I wasn't sure who she meant by "us."

"It wasn't her fault," she added quickly, glancing away briefly, dabbing her eyes with her handkerchief again. "My father . . . well, he was . . ." She stopped, breathed heavily, and looked back at me.

"My daddy had a problem."

She looked at me expectantly, as if I might catch on. But I didn't. I had never even heard Mother mention her father. Of course, I knew she must have had one. Everyone did, after all. But I had never thought about him.

"My father had a problem . . . with alcohol," she said finally. "Just like Jolene does. He drank . . . too much."

She shifted in her seat, turning to stare out the window.

"He drank until he was wicked, really. I don't think he could help himself. It was the bad blood maybe. But he drank a lot."

I could see her face reflected in the dark window. Her eyes were huge, unfocused.

"And then he would come home," she said softly. "And he would hit my mother, and my little brother . . . and me, too, sometimes."

I stared at her openmouthed. My mother had a brother?

And her father . . . what about that?

My friend Cindy lived with her grandmother because her daddy had beaten her up once while he was drunk. I knew things like that happened in the world.

I just couldn't imagine it happening to my mother—my quiet, ladylike, oh-so-proper, God-fearing mother. How could anyone dare?

It was unthinkable.

"He was an alcoholic, Bethany." Mother's voice was dull, flat. "When he didn't drink, he was so smart, so handsome. He was . . ." Her voice trailed off.

"But he did drink," she continued finally. "And then he was . . . awful. Mama . . . my mother . . . she tried to keep it from us . . . tried to keep him away from us."

Mother sighed deeply, her shoulders rising almost imperceptibly.

"But she couldn't, of course. She couldn't keep us from knowing about him. She couldn't keep him away all the time."

She sighed again and looked at me, her eyes clear and dry now.

"And I have tried hard . . . I've tried so hard to keep you girls from knowing just how mean life can be. I wanted you to grow up away from all that. I just wanted you all to grow up happy."

She said it so quietly I had to lean forward to hear her.

She touched my cheek. "But I can't, Bethy. I can't do it any more than my mama could keep it from me.

"Damn it!"

Her voice cracked as she said it, so it came out in a staccato burst.

I drew back, as far away from her in the seat as I could get. Her face was unfamiliar again, pinched and hard and angry.

Then, almost immediately, she seemed to deflate like a balloon, to soften, to relax into my own mother's body again.

"We shouldn't have taken you girls down there," she said finally.

"I told him, I told your daddy," she whispered. "We got out, after all. We should've stayed clean away."

She looked old, then . . . older than I could even imagine. As old as Grandmother Araminta, almost. I tried to picture her as a girl. My mother, a little girl, with an alcoholic father who sometimes hit her. Mother, living in a house like the ones on the Coal River, worrying about her father the way Reana Mae worried about Jolene.

Thinking of Reana made me sit up straight.

"But, Mother," I said, touching her arm. "If we didn't go to the river, who would take care of Reana Mae?"

She turned toward me again, her face lit by the traffic lights outside. She stared for a minute and then seemed to gather herself up, until she sat straight-backed on the bus seat, calm and regal.

"You're right, Bethany," she said, her voice steady again. "And Reana Mae certainly does need us now."

She leaned over to kiss the top of my head.

"You're a good girl, Bethy. You can help Reana Mae more than anyone else. And you will, won't you, honey? You'll help her just like she was your sister."

I nodded proudly. Of course I would help Reana. She was my sister, after all. The only sister I ever really had.

✎ 21 ✎

Coming Home

On Friday afternoon, I paced the living room, around and around the coffee table, watching out the front window for the station wagon. I had run straight home from school, arriving just in time to see the Sears delivery truck pull away. Mother and I made up Reana Mae's bed next to mine in the attic, while Tracy packed her own things into boxes to move downstairs to Nancy's room.

Tracy still wasn't happy about Reana Mae moving in with us. But she was happy to move into a room of her own, even if it was in the basement. Of course, she wouldn't actually move downstairs until after Christmas, when Nancy went back to college. But she was packing up now, she told me outside of Mother's hearing, "So that hillbilly won't touch any of my things."

Mother had bought Tracy a new bedspread and throw rug. Tracy's old crazy quilt was now on the bed we'd bought for Reana Mae.

I hoped Reana would like the bed, the room, our house. But I wasn't sure she would.

I had not talked to Reana Mae, or written to her even, since we'd come home from West Virginia in July. She had written to me once, in November, to tell me about Loreen's funeral. How Jolene had shown up drunk and cried and wailed and thrown handfuls of dirt down onto the coffin until Uncle Ray had to pull her away. And about how much Reana hated sixth grade. And how she was working in Ray's store most days after school, now that Loreen was gone. And how Caleb was in charge at the store most days, because Ray was staying home a lot. But I hadn't written back. I didn't know what to write to my cousin anymore.

I was in the seventh grade now, and I loved school more all the time. I was on the student council and I helped with the school newspaper. I had discovered Jane Austen, and was working my way steadily through her novels—*Mansfield Park* was my favorite. I had helped with makeup for the school play, and I thought I might try out for a part myself in the spring production of *Our Town*.

But I didn't think Reana Mae would be interested in any of that.

She had moved beyond middle school, after all, into the world of adults. Every time I sat down to write to her, I ended up throwing away a page of stationery, knowing that everything I wrote would seem childish to Reana Mae.

Now I wished I had written.

Just before five o'clock, I heard the car crunch into the gravel driveway.

"They're here!" I yelled.

Mother and Melinda came into the living room as I opened the front door. Then I stopped, rooted to the front porch, suddenly feeling shy.

Mother's arm on my shoulder felt warm and safe. I looked up at her, waiting for her to tell me what to do next.

"Hey, Bethany!"

Reana Mae's voice rang across the snowy yard, familiar, loud. Just like always.

I ran down the steps and grabbed her in a tight hug.

"Hey, yourself," I said, grinning. Then she stepped back and I saw her face. She had a nasty-looking black eye, and her upper lip was an ugly, swollen mass of dark purple.

"I know, I'm a mess," she said, her smile faltering. "But I looked a hell of a lot worse a couple days back."

Mother came up behind me and enveloped Reana Mae in a warm, tight embrace.

"Helen?" Daddy's voice was soft. He sounded uncertain.

Mother turned to him, smiling brightly.

But before he could say anything else, Reana Mae had opened the back door of the car and a huge, furry beast bounded out, leaping up at Reana and then at me, then running in circles, barking furiously.

"Bo!" Reana Mae hollered. "Bo, damn it! Stop! Come here, you stupid dog!"

She grabbed the huge hound by the collar, holding tight as he dragged her along behind him.

"Bo, damn it! Stay still!"

Swearing again, she struggled to attach a leash to the dog with one hand. Her other hand was in a cast—Jolene's awful handiwork.

But Bo was having none of it. He bayed and ran and squatted, then ran some more.

Mother stared openmouthed for a minute, then turned to my father.

"I had to bring him." He smiled sheepishly. "She wouldn't come without him."

"Oh, Aunt Helen," Reana Mae called over her shoulder, still struggling with the dog. "He won't be no trouble at all, I promise . . . Bo, damn you! Sit! Sit! Damn it, I said *sit*!"

The dog squatted again, peeing furiously as Reana Mae finally attached the leash to his collar.

"Well," Mother said weakly, looking from Reana Mae to the dog to Daddy.

"Well," she repeated, her voice faltering.

"Oh, Aunt Helen." Reana dragged poor Bo along behind her as she struggled toward Mother. "I couldn't leave him behind. I just couldn't."

She gripped Bo's leash so tight her knuckles whitened.

"Granpa wouldn't take him, 'cause of Granma's stupid cats." She hissed out this last, obviously incensed. "You know, Granma had all them cats, and Granpa won't get rid of 'em since Granma died." She shook her head fiercely.

"And Mama don't even feed Bo no more," she continued, nodding anxiously. "So I had to bring him, Aunt Helen. He needs me."

She looked straight up into Mother's face, her own face wide-eyed and sincere. A tear rolled down her swollen cheek.

"Poor ole Bo, he ain't got nobody but me," Reana continued. "Mama don't even like him. And Daddy . . . well, he ain't been home since Granma's funeral. I reckon Bo wouldn't even know Daddy no more."

Reana Mae dropped onto her knees in the snow and wrapped her good arm around the dog's thick neck, even as Bo pulled away from her, his nose snuffling madly at some scent carried on the cold winter air.

Mother looked at Daddy again. But he only shrugged his shoulders.

"Well," she said finally, trying hard to smile, managing a small grimace. "I guess we could build him a doghouse out back."

"Oh, thank you, Aunt Helen! He'll be real good, I promise," Reana Mae said. She smiled up at Mother, revealing a jaggedly chipped front tooth.

"I promise," she repeated, nodding firmly. "He'll be real good. Won't you, Bo? Won't you, boy?"

The dog stopped struggling against the leash long enough to sniff her face, then gave her a sloppy lick.

Daddy had opened the car's tailgate, so we all grabbed armfuls of brown paper bags and carried them into the house. It seemed like a very small load for such a permanent move. But then, I guessed, Reana Mae didn't have many things of her own to move, besides Bobby Lee's old hunting dog.

Nancy met us at the door, staring doubtfully at Bo as she said, "Hey, Reana Mae, how are you?"

"I'm okay, Nancy," Reana Mae said, holding tight to the dog's leash.

She didn't look up at Nancy as she spoke.

"I'm okay," she repeated.

Just then, Bo lurched forward into the house, wrenching the leash from Reana's hand.

Skipper was scratching furiously at the back door, whimpering frantically.

Snorting loudly, Bo ran through the house toward the back door, until his nose was separated from Skipper's only by a thin pane of glass.

"Melinda," Daddy yelled. "Go on out back and calm that dog down."

Melinda opened the back door a crack—just wide enough for Skipper to shove his way into the house, barking loudly. Bo bayed back, circling the smaller dog, his nose in the air, coat ruffled ominously.

"Melinda!" Daddy shouted above the barking. "Take Skipper out back!"

Melinda grabbed Skipper by the collar and dragged him unceremoniously out to the back porch again.

As soon as Skipper had gone, Bo turned his nose to the rest of us, sniffing each of us up and down, then burying his snout in the carpet and running furiously through the house, stopping here and there to bay piteously.

"Bo, damn it! Shut up!" Reana Mae called after him.

But Bo's nose was on the move, and all Reana could do was follow him from room to room, grabbing at his collar and yelling.

When he got back into the living room, the old coonhound stood quietly for an instant . . . just long enough for all of us to catch our breath . . . before heading directly for the Christmas tree, his nose snuffling loudly.

And then, as we all stood lamely by, poor old Bo hiked his leg against the one natural element in the room and peed onto the brightly colored gifts beneath the tree.

"Bo!" Reana Mae screamed, lunging forward. "No!"

But it was too late. The presents dripped with warm, yellow liquid. Christmas had been peed upon, thoroughly and completely.

Reana Mae grabbed the dog by his collar and hauled him away from the tree while Daddy hollered and Tracy shrieked.

Mother stood completely still for a moment, then said quietly, "Pick those packages up, girls, and unwrap them."

Then, as we stood dumbly, her voice rose. "Don't just stand there. Unwrap those packages now!"

So, five days before Christmas, we unwrapped every single package underneath the Christmas tree. Wrinkling our noses at the wet and the smell, we tore away the beautiful bows and gift wrap, shoving the wet mess into the garbage bags Mother brought from the kitchen.

We piled the packages on the couch.

"Oh, Mother!" Melinda squealed, scooping up a hardbound book. "*Bleak House!* Thank you so much!"

Nancy's voice echoed Melinda's as she lifted the lid from a box and pulled out a turquoise sweater.

"It's just the one I wanted, Mother! Thank you!"

Tracy said nothing. She just stared wide-eyed and furious at the mess that was Christmas.

I stood uncertainly for a minute, watching Reana Mae yank at Bo's collar. Then I grabbed his collar, too, and helped her drag the hound toward the back door.

Together, we shoved Bo onto the back porch, where he and Skipper engaged in a thorough sniff fest, each circling the other's backside.

"Bethany, why don't you take Reana Mae upstairs and get her settled in?" Mother said. "Then we'll have some supper. Girls, leave those packages alone. We'll open them after supper."

Reana followed me upstairs.

"Lord God above, Bethany," she breathed, standing at the top of the steps. "Is all this yours?"

"Mine and yours, too," I said, dropping two grocery bags onto her new bed.

"This room is almost as big as our whole house, back home," she said.

I helped her put her clothes away in the new chest of drawers. At the bottom of one bag, carefully wrapped in a dish towel, lay Essie, Reana Mae's old doll. I smiled when I saw her. Maybe Reana hadn't completely crossed over to the grown-up world yet.

I showed her the space I'd cleared in the closet and told her Tracy's stuff would get moved out after Christmas.

"Good!" she said firmly. "I was wondering if I'd have to share a room with her. I reckon she'd hate that."

We sat down to a supper of tuna casserole and good, hot bread.

"This is real good, Aunt Helen," Reana said, buttering a third slice of bread. "Donna Jo taught me to make bread, but mine ain't usually this good. That old cookstove we got burns the bottoms most times."

Tracy stared at her disdainfully, wrinkling her nose slightly.

"I guess you'd better not try cooking here," she said, smirking. "Our kitchen probably is a lot different than you're used to."

"It sure is." Reana nodded, ignoring or missing the snub. "But I guess I could learn to use it."

"Of course you can, Reana Mae." Mother scowled slightly at Tracy. "This is your home now, so you just think of it that way and make yourself comfortable."

"Thanks, Aunt Helen," Reana said, chewing her bread slowly. "But I reckon once Mama calms herself down, I'll go back home."

Mother and Daddy exchanged a worried look. My sisters kept their eyes fixed firmly on their plates. I simply stared at Reana in amazement. She must know she wasn't going back to the river. She couldn't . . . not now that everyone knew. I couldn't imagine Jolene would ever forgive Reana Mae for growing up to be so pretty, and for attracting Caleb's attention when Jolene herself couldn't. And Ida Louise would surely not let her come back to church, ever.

"Well, we'll see, Reana," Mother said.

"Or else Caleb will come and get me," Reana continued, smiling now. "I figure once he gets hisself a job, he'll come for me, 'cause he loves me true, you know. And he'll need me to take care of him and cook his dinners and wash the laundry. He ain't too good at that stuff."

Silence hung over the table. I was afraid even to breathe, afraid the awful, unspoken truth would break over us like one of those big waves we saw in Florida, taking us under and pulling us out to sea.

I gaped at Reana's bruised and swollen face, her left arm in its cast, a set of long, ugly gashes down her neck from Jolene's fingernails. How could she even think that Mother and Daddy would let her go back to the river—or, worse, away with Caleb?

Daddy put down his fork very quietly and leaned toward Reana, looking her straight in the face.

"That boy is not coming to get you, Reana Mae. If he comes

anywhere near this house, I will call the police and have him arrested. Do you understand me?"

"You can't do that!" Reana said sharply. "You can't arrest Caleb. He ain't done nothin' wrong!"

Mother cleared her throat sharply and rose.

"Girls, why don't you clear the table? Your father and I need to have a talk with Reana Mae."

She offered her hand to Reana and led her toward the living room. My father followed, carrying his coffee cup.

"Good God," Nancy said. "What is she thinking?"

Melinda shook her head grimly. "I can't believe she thinks that . . . that *bastard* would come here for her. Or that Mother would let her go with him."

"Well, obviously she's stupid enough for almost anything," Tracy said, rising from her chair. "She's already proved how stupid she is, sleeping with her own uncle. I mean, *my God!*"

I stared at her, openmouthed. How did she know about Reana Mae and Caleb? Melinda rose abruptly, her cheeks reddening. She didn't meet my eyes. I realized then she had told Tracy and Nancy.

"Well," Melinda said, gathering up a stack of plates. "She's only eleven, after all. She's just a kid. But he . . . well, he ought to be hanged!"

"Nancy didn't think so last summer!" Tracy smiled maliciously. "I guess she thought he was all right then."

"You just shut your mouth, Tracy Janelle!" Nancy snapped. "I never so much as looked at that pervert."

Tracy laughed, rolling her eyes.

"Reana Mae looks like she's been in a car wreck, doesn't she?" Melinda said. "I can't believe Jolene did that to her."

"Well," Tracy snapped, "I hope to God she looks better than that before school starts. Lord knows, she's embarrassing enough just by herself. If she goes to school looking like that, I'll just die."

"God, Tracy." Melinda's voice rose sharply. "It's not her fault!"

"It most certainly is," Tracy snapped back. "If she hadn't been screwing her own daddy's brother . . . well, I don't blame Jolene for beating her. I'm surprised she didn't kill her for being such a tramp."

"Shut up, Tracy," I said. "You just leave Reana Mae alone."

"Oh, don't worry, Bethany. I plan to leave her alone."

Tracy flipped her auburn curls, shooting me a look of pure disdain.

"Lord knows, I don't want anything to do with her. The further away she stays from me, the better."

Just then I heard feet pounding up the stairs to the attic. Mother appeared in the kitchen, her face tense.

"Bethany, why don't you go upstairs and help Reana Mae get settled in," she said, picking up a dish towel and wringing it absently.

As I left the room, I heard her say, "Tracy, if I hear you talk about your cousin that way again, I will ground you for a month."

Upstairs, Reana Mae was curled up in a tiny ball on her bed, Essie's lumpy little body cradled in her uninjured arm.

"You okay?" I asked.

She didn't say anything, didn't even look at me.

I sat down on the bed beside her.

"I'm sorry, Reana Mae."

It was the only thing I could think of to say. I wasn't even sure what I was sorry about—Jolene's beating her, Bobby Lee's continued absence, her disastrous love for Caleb . . . there were just so many things to be sorry for.

"They can't keep him away from me," she said, speaking so quietly I had to lean down to hear her.

"He'll come for me, and they can't keep him away."

She cried then, softly at first, then big, gulping sobs. I sat on the bed, holding her hand, and watched her cry until finally she cried herself out and drifted off to sleep. Even then, I sat beside her, as if somehow I could protect her just by being there.

But I couldn't protect Reana Mae. Not then, not later.

I couldn't protect her from Tracy, or from the hurtful things people said about her. I couldn't protect her from the pain of waiting day after long day for a lover who was never going to come. I couldn't protect her from her loneliness or her anger.

I could only love her, like I always had, and hope it was enough.

New Beginnings and Old Baggage

Christmas morning came quietly. We'd opened most of our gifts days before, though Mother had held back a few. I had a new record player and several albums. Reana and I spent long hours in the attic room listening to Three Dog Night and the Temptations. Sometimes Cindy joined us, though she didn't quite know how to talk to Reana Mae. Mostly, she stared as if Reana were from another planet, listening carefully to everything Reana Mae said, watching for some sign that Reana was joking when she talked about life on the river.

Tracy whined to Mother daily, but we had already laid claim to the room. Tracy had been effectively moved out, and until Nancy went back to college, she couldn't move downstairs. So she slept on the couch in the living room and complained bitterly.

Reana Mae had a new camera from Mother and Daddy, and we took dozens of pictures during winter break. Years later, I looked through those photos often, searching the faces of the two little girls on the brink of adolescence, looking for signs of things to come. Reana's face stared back, her lip swollen fat, her eye dark and puffy, her grin snaggletoothed. Except for the bruises and the cast on her arm, she looked like any other twelve-year-old. But of course, she wasn't. She knew things most twelve-year-olds hadn't even dreamed about. Things I certainly didn't know.

Three days before school started, Mother took Reana Mae to the dentist to get a cap put on her broken tooth.

"See," she grinned at me afterward, "you can't even tell it's broke."

So at least when she started middle school in Indianapolis, her teeth were okay, though she still looked like she'd been in a car wreck. The swelling had receded, but her upper lip still showed cut marks from the garnet in Jolene's wedding ring, and her eye was ringed in a faint greenish-yellow.

We stood at the bus stop, bundled against the blowing snow, and I tried to tell her everything I could think of that she might need to know about school.

"Miss Hancock is nice, but she gives lots of homework. Just don't talk in her class. And Mr. Burke . . . well, he's just gross. He always has spit on his mouth and his breath stinks! And he paddles, so be careful with him."

Reana Mae stroked the fur of her parka hood, seemingly unfazed by this information.

"And if Mr. McCormack calls on you and you don't know the answer, just ask him a question about another problem. That always gets him off the subject. He's pretty easy, as long as you do the homework."

Still, she said nothing.

"Aren't you nervous?" I asked finally. My stomach had been churning all morning.

She smiled at me in that smug-adult way she had sometimes.

"Naw, I ain't scared," she said airily. "I figure I ain't gonna be here long enough to worry about it."

I didn't reply.

She still expected Caleb to show up and whisk her away to her fairy-tale life, in a big house with air-conditioning and lace curtains. No matter what Mother or Daddy or I said, she refused to believe that he wasn't coming.

She liked her new clothes, of course, and her new coat. She

liked the bed and dresser Mother had bought, and our room in the attic. She liked Mother's cooking, and she had pitched in with housework cheerfully. She seemed to look on the entire episode as a vacation, a lark away from her mother and the disapproval of her kinfolk on the river.

I didn't see Reana all day. Sixth graders were in a separate part of the school building. When the bell rang, I ran to the bus, anxious to hear how her first day had been. But she wasn't on the bus. Ten minutes later, when the bus pulled away from the school, she still wasn't on it. I tried to convince Mr. Gonzalez, the driver, to wait, but he just told me to sit back down.

I ran home from the bus stop. I had to tell Mother that Reana Mae had missed the bus. But when I opened the door, Reana was already there, sitting bolt upright on the couch, her cheeks red and her eyes bright.

Mother turned away from her when she heard me.

"Bethany, go upstairs and get started on your homework."

I looked from her face to Reana's. Neither looked happy.

"But, Mother . . ." I began.

"Don't argue with me, now. You go on up to your room."

Upstairs, I lay on my bed, straining to catch any sound from downstairs. But Mother's voice didn't carry up the stairs.

After a while, Reana Mae came up. She didn't look at me or say anything, just flopped down on her unmade bed with a huge sigh.

"What happened?"

"I ain't never goin' back to that school," she hissed.

"But, Reana Mae." I walked over to sit on her bed. "What happened?"

"It wasn't my fault, Bethany." She rolled over, punched her pillow hard, and flopped back down. "Those stuck-up girls just kept doggin' me and doggin' me till I couldn't stand it no more."

"What girls?"

"I don't know their names," she said, staring at me as if I were stupid. "These three girls that are in all my classes . . . they started in first thing, and they kept at it all damned day."

"What did they do?"

"Called me a hillbilly, first off. Made fun of the way I talk. Said I was a goddamned charity case, 'cause Aunt Helen and Uncle Jimmy brought me up here."

She blinked furiously, trying to hold back tears.

"Then in gym class, they told everyone I was a whore. Said I had sex with my uncle, and probably lots of other men. Said that's what hillbillies do . . . have sex with their own kinfolk."

I stared at her, openmouthed. How had they known about Caleb?

Then I realized, it had to be Tracy.

"Those girls," I said, "was one of them short, with blond hair about down to here?" I gestured at my waist.

Reana Mae nodded. "That's the worst one. She said I was trash and belonged in a reform school."

"That's Jenny Spangler," I said. "And the others were probably Amy Adams and Patty O'Hearn."

Reana didn't answer. She just stared at me.

"How'd they know, Bethany?" she asked, not taking her eyes from mine.

"Oh, God, Reana, I didn't tell them!" I couldn't believe she would even think that. "Jenny's big sister is Lynette. That's Tracy's best friend."

Reana Mae nodded solemnly. "That's what I figured," she said. "No one else could be so goddamn mean."

"So, what happened then? When they kept teasing you, I mean."

"Well, I ignored them for a while, you know. But at lunchtime one of them—the one with real short hair—she dumped her whole tray of food on me! Got macaroni and cheese all over my new sweater. And then they all just laughed, like it was so goddamned funny."

"I'm so sorry," I said, reaching for her hand.

"Well, you don't have to be sorry for me, Bethany Marie. No one has to be sorry for me! I can take care of myself."

"What did you do?"

"I knocked her flat on her ass."

"Oh, Reana, no! You didn't!"

"Oh yes, I did." She smiled grimly. "I got her with one to the

202 • *Sherri Wood Emmons*

chin. Hit her so hard she went right down. Then I hit the blond one, too."

"Oh my God! You hit Jenny Spangler?"

"I guess she's got a shiner worse than this one." Reana Mae smiled again, pointing to her own eye.

I couldn't believe what I was hearing. Every once in a while, boys got in a fight in the lunchroom or in gym. But girls never fought—never! What would everyone think? God, what did Mother think?

"The tall one, the one with the long nose, she ran off and told a teacher. So here came this big old fat bastard, no hair on his head, looking fit to be tied."

"Mr. Burke," I breathed. "Oh, God!"

"And he grabbed my arm so hard I like to died. So I told him to get his goddamn hands off me, or I'd kill him.

"So he hauled me off to the principal's office, and she came in and hollered for a while and then she called Aunt Helen, and she came in and cried, and then she brought me home and cried some more and gave me what-for."

"Poor Aunt Helen." Reana shook her head. "I figure she got more than she bargained for with me. Maybe she won't want me here no more."

"Don't be silly," I said. "She's just mad."

"That's just it, Bethany. She didn't act mad at all. She just cried and told me she was sorry. What does she have to be sorry about? She didn't tell them girls about me and Caleb."

I wasn't sure what to make of Mother's reaction. If one of us had punched someone at school, I was dead certain Mother would have raised the roof before turning the culprit over to Daddy for a spanking.

"Well," I said uncertainly. "Probably she's sorry you had such a bad first day. But I'm sure tomorrow will be lots better," I added hopefully.

"I wouldn't count on that," Reana said. "If they make me go back to that school, I surely will kill someone."

"But, Reana Mae, you have to go to school."

"I don't know why," she said, her chin raised slightly. "Caleb didn't finish school, and he done just fine workin' at Granpa's store."

The stubborn chin began to tremble then.

"I wish I knew where he's gone to," she whispered. "Why don't he come?"

"I don't know. Maybe he can't."

"Yeah," she said, wiping the back of her hand across her eyes. "That's probably right. He's probably gettin' hisself set up with a job and an apartment first, so we'll have us a place to live."

"Mother and Daddy will never let you go away with him, though."

"They can't stop me!" She said it loudly, defiantly. "I ain't theirs to boss around. When Caleb comes, I'm goin' with him, and there ain't a damned thing they can do about it!"

Downstairs, we heard the front door slam. Then Mother's voice calling Tracy to her room.

"She's gonna get it now," I said to Reana Mae.

"She ain't gonna get nothin' from Aunt Helen, compared to what I'm gonna give her."

I stared at my cousin, watching her fist clench tightly.

"She's gonna pay for what she done to me, Bethany. That's for certain."

Reana Mae did go back to school the next day. She and her tormenters were called into Mrs. Watson's office and made to apologize—Jenny and her cohorts for tormenting Reana Mae, Reana for hitting Jenny and Amy. None of them meant a word they uttered, but they all went through the motions.

Reana Mae's burst of furious temper had earned her a good bit of notoriety at school . . . and several admirers. She hadn't, after all, been Jenny Spangler's first or only victim. Lots of other sixth graders hated Jenny and her crew. Most were delighted to see them knocked down. Within a week, Reana Mae had a new set of friends—not the cheerleaders and prep girls, of course, but an assortment of loners, stoners, nerds, and other outcasts for whom she had become a kind of instant hero.

Tracy had earned herself a monthlong grounding for telling people about Reana's background. This, coupled with Reana Mae's newly elevated status, infuriated her as I'd never seen before. She sulked in her basement room, listening to Led Zeppelin and Black Sabbath on her stereo and talking on the phone to Lynette and her new boyfriend, a dark-haired basketball player named Mark. When she emerged for dinner or school, she stared balefully at Reana and me, snarled at Mother and Daddy, and muttered under her breath a lot.

One morning, just before she left the house for school, I saw her hiss something at Reana Mae as she walked past. After she had gone, I asked Reana what she'd said.

"Just the usual." Reana grinned. "That I'm gonna pay for what I done to her. What *I* done to *her!*"

She shook her head, and her hair swung around her face. Mother had bobbed her hair, so that what had been a long, tangled mane was now a sleek, shiny curtain framing her face.

"I reckon she's dead crazy, Bethany," she continued. "She don't even know how mean she is, she's so crazy."

I nodded.

"Anyways," she continued, "I ain't worried about what Tracy's gonna do. She can't hurt me none."

I stared in admiration. I believed every word she said, that Tracy couldn't hurt her anymore. I wasn't sure how Reana Mae had come to a place where that was true, but I knew it was.

I only wished I knew how to get to that place myself.

Reana Mae was finding her way into our Indiana world. But every night at bedtime, she knelt on the rag rug beside her bed and prayed so hard her lips moved. And I could see what she was praying for—she prayed every single night that Caleb would come tomorrow and take her away.

ꙮ 23 ꙮ

Waiting for Princes, 1974

"Hey." Reana Mae looked up from the letter she was reading. "Harley Boy's got hisself a car!"

"He's not old enough for a car." I grabbed the page from her hand.

"Look." She pointed. "Right there, it says he got a 1968 Plymouth Duster, blue."

"He's only fifteen," I sputtered. "He can't even drive yet."

"He can back home." She smiled. "Hell, I bet he's been driving his granddad's car for years."

"So, maybe now he can take Ruthann out on dates." I laughed.

"Get real, Bethany." She rolled her eyes. "Harley Boy ain't no more taken with poor Ruthann than he was back when we were kids. I reckon he won't never be in love with her like she is with him."

It was true. Ruthann was still in love with Harley. She wrote to me every few months, always telling me everything Harley Boy had been up to . . . how well he was doing at school, how tall he was getting. She never asked about Reana Mae. But I guess that was probably natural.

Harley wrote to Reana Mae every month, and she always wrote back. They both knew he still loved her. They both knew she didn't love him. But still they wrote. I think Reana always hoped Harley would have some news about Caleb, but he never did. Caleb hadn't come back to the river since Jolene chased him off with Bobby Lee's gun.

But we did hear about other folks, from Harley Boy and from Ruthann and sometimes from eavesdropping when Aunt Belle called.

Jolene had finally come back home, several weeks after she'd beat Reana Mae so bad. No one knew where she'd gone to or what she'd done while she was gone. One day, she was just back in her house. She was fatter and she'd stopped dying her hair red, so now the gray showed through. But she didn't drink all the time anymore . . . at least, not so folks could tell.

She'd taken to doing jigsaw puzzles. She had one going of the Last Supper, one with twenty thousand pieces. Said by the time she finished it, she'd probably be ready to see the Lord Himself. And she went to church every Sunday and sat right up front by Aunt Belle. She'd taken to reading the Bible with a vengeance, and she quoted verses at anyone who'd stop to listen, especially the verses about hell and damnation. Belle said her eyes fairly lit up when she talked about the hellfire waiting for earthly sinners.

Of course, Jolene counted her husband and child among those sinners. She told folks that's why she'd sent them away, Bobby Lee and Reana Mae. They were sinners, and they had kept her from finding the Lord. They had to go away, she said, so she could find her way home.

Reana Mae read every letter that Harley Boy or Ruthann sent as soon as it came. She scanned them quickly first, looking for Caleb's name. Then she read them slowly, searching for any hint of his presence. Once I even heard her ask Aunt Belle on the phone if she knew where Caleb had gone to. But Belle said she didn't know.

Of course, Reana assumed Belle was lying, but what could she do?

At fourteen, Reana Mae was finally what Mother always knew she'd be—beautiful. Her skin was creamy pale, with a light sprinkle of freckles. Her brilliant green eyes were fringed with dark lashes, her dark blond hair smooth and soft. She was taller than me and much curvier, her breasts and hips rounded softly under her tight T-shirts and Levi's jeans.

I was still waiting for my own transformation. I was fifteen, after all, a sophomore in high school . . . and still flat as a board and skinny as a rail. Daddy called me beanpole, which I hated. And while Reana Mae said I was lucky because I didn't have to wear a bra and no one would even notice, I envied her curves, as well as her clear complexion, blond hair, and green eyes. My own dark curls and darker eyes seemed plain by comparison.

In three years, Reana Mae had settled herself into our lives completely. After her disastrous first day of middle school, she hadn't gotten into any more fights—although Mother did have to make several more trips to Mrs. Watson's office to hear about Reana's smart mouth. Mother bore this shame quietly, pleading in vain with Reana Mae to watch her temper and her mouth, but never meting out the punishment such behavior would have earned the rest of us.

Reana Mae was stubborn and willful, but schoolwork came easily for her—too easily, my father said. Teachers either loved her or hated her, but they couldn't fault her work—that is, when she did it. She coasted along with Cs and sometimes Ds for class work. She never studied and rarely did her homework. But she always got As on her tests.

The only class she seemed to care about was English. She devoured every assigned book, making trips to the library to check out other books by authors she particularly liked.

Lots of nights, we sat up late in our attic room, arguing the merits of Mr. Darcy and Mr. Bingley, debating the justice of Becky Sharp's fate, bemoaning poor Tess's sad outcome. By then, Melinda had followed Nancy down to Bloomington for college. Reana Mae could have moved into Melinda's old room, but we were content sharing the attic.

When she started high school, I'd hoped she would join the school newspaper with me. But she seemed uninterested in news writing. She wanted to write just what she wanted to write, assignments be damned.

She changed her mind when she found out that as a staff photographer she could use the newspaper's Nikon camera and darkroom. After that, she could be found almost every afternoon in the *Weekly Post* darkroom, learning to develop photos from Mr. Koontz, the journalism teacher.

She was not as reliable a photographer as we could have hoped for. Sometimes she showed up late for assignments, sometimes not at all. But her photos were gorgeous, and Mr. Koontz said she was the best student photographer he'd ever had—which didn't say as much as you might think, since he'd only been teaching for two years. Still, everyone agreed, Reana Mae was good with a camera. She had a knack for getting unusual shots—catching Jenny Spangler just as she fell off the balance beam, for example, or Brent Macy's face just as he got his knees cut out from under him by a linebacker.

Brent Macy had been after Reana almost from her first day in the sixth grade. He was a year older than her—a jock who played on the football and baseball teams. All the girls eyed him appreciatively. But Reana Mae was unimpressed, as she was by all the boys who called our house or bought her valentines or sent her notes.

"They're just boys," she sniffed derisively. "What do I want with a boy, when I already got a man?"

She only said this to me, of course. Outside of our room, she never mentioned Caleb to anyone, especially not around Mother and Daddy, who seemed to believe she had finally gotten over her disastrous relationship with her uncle. I knew better. I watched her night after night, scribbling away in her journal. I didn't have to read it to know she was pouring out her love for Caleb.

Someday, she still believed, he would come.

Reana Mae was just biding her time.

In late October, the entire high school became consumed with the homecoming football game. Howe High School was playing its archrival, Tech. Both teams had played well all season, and both were ranked in the state's top twenty.

And then there was the homecoming dance. Tracy had long since picked out her dress at the mall. She'd worked overtime at

the grocery store to earn the money for it, and it was beautiful—
pale, sea-foam green with spaghetti straps and a short matching
jacket. She looked like a beauty queen in it, and she'd already told
Mark exactly what kind of flowers to buy for her corsage. Tracy was
an old hand at dances; she'd been to every one since her freshman
year.

On the Tuesday before the game, Brian Hutson stood beside me
in the news office, watching critically as I aligned and cropped photos. He was a junior, the associate editor of the paper, and he made
me very nervous. He was so handsome.

"Damn!"

I had scored the photo a full pica too narrow. It was ruined.

"Here, let me."

Brian reached across me, turned the photo, and cropped the top
slightly.

"There, we'll just enlarge it a pica, and it'll be fine."

"Thanks." I smiled at him. "Sorry I messed it up."

He looked down at me for a long minute, then pushed his
glasses up on his narrow nose and blurted out, "Do you want to go
to the dance with me?"

I stared at him stupidly, blushing deeply, and finally said, "Okay."
God, I thought. *How stupid can I sound?*

"Good." He smiled, looking relieved. "I'll pick you up at seven,
and we'll have dinner first."

"Okay."

"And let me know what color you're wearing," he said, still
smiling. "For the flowers, you know."

"Okay."

*God! He must think I'm a total jerk. He's probably sorry he even
asked me now.*

I felt like I might keel over in embarrassment. Why couldn't I
ever think of anything funny or smart to say? I'd seen my sisters do
this . . . even Melinda was good at it. But all I could croak was
"Okay."

Then, without warning, Brian leaned toward me, lifted my chin
with his hand, and kissed me lightly on the mouth.

"See you later," he said.

"Okay."

He walked out of the office as the bell rang, and I stood gripping the table, my cheeks hot and flushed.

"Well, good for you, Bethy!"

I turned to find Reana Mae watching me from the door to the darkroom, smiling broadly.

"Your first kiss." She laughed, darting forward and grabbing my hands. "How was it?"

"God, I sounded like an idiot!"

"Yup, you surely did." She laughed again. "But he didn't seem to notice."

"Do you think Mother will let me go?" I asked, suddenly sure she wouldn't.

"Of course she will."

"What will I wear? I don't have a dress!"

"You leave that to me."

With that, she squeezed my hands, grabbed her books, and shoved me toward the door. "Come on, you're gonna be late."

After school, Reana and I boarded a bus to the mall. I had no idea how we could buy a dress. I had all of twenty dollars in saved allowance, and even I knew that wasn't enough for a gown. But Reana kept saying, "Just leave it to me," so I did.

When we got to the mall, she put her arm through mine and pulled me toward L. S. Ayres, the most expensive store there.

"What are we doing here?" I whispered as she dragged me past the makeup counters and racks of business suits.

"Gettin' you a drop-dead gorgeous dress," she said lightly.

"But, Reana." I stopped abruptly, yanking her hand till she stopped, too. "You know I can't afford anything in here. Hell, I can't afford a dress at Lerner's!"

"Maybe *you* can't," she grinned, opening her purse and pulling out a thick wad of cash. "But *I* can!"

I stared at the money, wide-eyed. "Where did you get that?"

I was half afraid to hear her answer.

"I earned it," she said, pulling me forward again. "I was saving up to buy those boots I wanted, but this here's more important."

"How did you earn that much money?"

I knew she didn't have a regular job, though she sometimes babysat for neighbors.

"That ain't none of your business, Miss Nosy." She smiled again.

"Seriously, Reana." I stopped again, my voice rising. "How did you earn that much money?"

A saleslady at the jewelry counter turned to glare at us.

"Shush up," Reana hissed. "If you have to know, I got it for helping people with their homework." She didn't meet my eyes when she said this, turning to look toward the dress department.

"Who?"

"Lots of people."

"I've never seen you helping anyone with homework."

"God, Bethany, you're worse than Aunt Helen!"

She turned to face me.

"I been writing people's papers, that's all."

"You mean, for school?"

"Of course, for school. What else do you write papers for?"

"You write them, and they turn them in?"

"Yup." She nodded, smiling. "I got a whole rate system, too. Twenty dollars for an A, fifteen for a B, ten for a C. If they don't get a C, I don't charge 'em at all. But that ain't happened yet."

I stared at her, torn between horror and admiration.

"But what if you get caught?"

"Don't worry." She was laughing now, pulling me toward the dresses again. "I ain't gonna get caught. It's all strictly business. Why, I bet Aunt Belle'd say I'm an entrepreneur!"

"How many have you done?"

"Lots." She grinned. "So we got plenty of cash to get you a really fine dress. Oh, Lord, Bethany." She stopped suddenly, pointing. "Look at that one. Ain't it gorgeous?"

She touched the soft silver fabric lightly, then held it to my cheek. "Don't that feel good?"

"It's real pretty." I nodded. "But I couldn't wear something like that."

"Why not?"

"Mother would never let me out of the house! Look at the back."

I held the dress out so she could take in the plunging back.

"Lord God Almighty," she crowed. "I bet even Nancy couldn't talk her into that!"

We paraded slowly up and down the aisles of dresses, cooing over one, then another. They all were beautiful, but none looked right for me, small and slight as I was.

Then we saw it. A simple ruby-colored gown—plain scoop neckline, small capped sleeves, and empire waist, the soft skirt falling straight to the ground. Perfect.

"Oh, Bethany, that's it. That's the one for you."

She held it up to me.

"Look, it's the right length and everything. Come on." She shoved me toward the dressing room. "Try it on."

We crowded into the small, mirrored room, and I pulled the gown over my head, letting it fall softly around me. Then I turned to the mirror and gasped.

My hair looked darker and fuller against the deep crimson. My eyes looked almost black. The gathering just under my breasts gave the illusion of a bosom. With a pair of high heels, the hem would just touch my toes. I looked beautiful!

"It's perfect!" Reana crowed. "Tracy will just die!"

"How much is it?" I asked, still staring at myself dreamily, thinking I could probably pass for royalty in this dress, in the right light.

"A hundred and twenty dollars," she said, studying the price tag carefully.

"A hundred and twenty dollars! God, Reana, help me get it off before I tear it or something!"

I had never had anything worth even half that much. There was no way I could buy this dress. Pulling it back over my head, I stared ruefully at the silky folds of the skirt and sighed.

"Bethany, you just got to have this here dress," Reana said, draping the gown carefully over her arm. "How much money have you got?"

"Twenty dollars," I muttered miserably. "Plus some quarters."

"Well, that's plenty, then." She grinned. "I got a hundred and fourteen. We got it covered!"

"But, Reana Mae," I said, sighing, "I can't take all that money from you. That's yours."

"Look here, Bethany," she said firmly. "It's my money, and I'll do whatever I damn well want to with it. And what I want is to buy you this dress."

"But what'll we tell Mother about the money?"

"I already thought of that," she said. "We'll tell her I been tutoring after school. It's almost true, anyways. She won't know the difference."

Riding the bus home, the gown in its plastic cover draped carefully across both our knees, I thought I might just die of pure delight. I was going to the homecoming dance with a junior, the associate editor of the newspaper, who was almost as tall as Tracy's boyfriend and certainly a lot smarter.

And I was going to wear the most beautiful dress in the world.

I squeezed my cousin's hand hard, my eyes stinging with tears.

"Shoot, Bethany, don't go to bawlin' now." She grinned. "It's just a dress."

She leaned over and gave me a quick hug. "I figure when my Prince Charming comes, you'll do right by me."

She was still smiling, but her eyes were staring past me into the dark outside the bus window.

"I reckon he'll come, sooner or later."

She leaned back abruptly and closed her eyes.

"Won't Tracy just die when she sees your dress?"

Tracy did have a fit when we arrived home, carrying my ruby red gown. But Mother was thrilled.

"Oh, Bethy," she breathed when I came out of her room wearing the dress and her black, high-heeled pumps. "Sweetheart, you're beautiful!"

Tracy sniffed loudly.

"No one wears red to homecoming," she sneered. "She looks like Jezebel herself!"

"Now, Tracy," Mother said, never taking her eyes from me. "Don't be jealous. Your dress is pretty, too."

214 · *Sherri Wood Emmons*

"Jealous?" she shrieked. "Jealous of Bethany? God, Mother! I'm not jealous of Bethany!"

"You watch your language, young lady, or you won't be going to the dance at all," Mother snapped.

"How much did this dress cost?" Mother asked, finally looking away from me to face Reana. "It looks very expensive."

"Oh, Aunt Helen, we got the best deal," Reana Mae burst out before I could say a word. "It was the last one like it, and it had been returned, so they cut the price almost in half! We only paid seventy-two dollars, plus tax."

She lied so smoothly I could only stare in awe.

"Well, that is a good price." Mother sighed happily. "It's a beautiful dress, honey." She cupped my chin, just the way Brian had done earlier, and kissed my nose. "And you are just beautiful in it!"

Tracy glared at Reana Mae. "Where did you get seventy-two dollars?" she sneered. "Where did you get any money at all? What did you do, steal it?"

"Tracy!" Mother was angry now. "What has gotten into you?"

"You can't tell me that hillbilly could come up with seventy-two dollars. Why, I'll bet they just stole the dress right out of the store."

"Go to your room!"

Tracy turned and stomped out of the room, through the kitchen, and down the stairs to her room. I knew she'd be calling Lynette within the minute to complain about my dress.

Lying in bed that night, I stared at the dark shape of the gown hanging from the top of the closet door.

"Reana Mae?" I whispered, long after I thought she was probably asleep.

"Yeah?"

"Thank you."

"It's okay."

"Reana?"

"Mmm-hmmm?"

"I'm sure your prince will come soon."

"I hope so, Bethy. 'Cause I'm gettin' awful tired of waiting on him."

❧ 24 ❧

Tracy's Way

I fairly floated to school the next day, thoughts of my beautiful gown crowding out everything else.

"You look like the cat that ate the canary," Reana Mae said with a laugh as we stood in the cafeteria line.

I smiled and felt my cheeks redden. "I still can't believe . . ."

"Hey!" Reana jumped suddenly and spun on her heel, her hand flying to her rear.

Behind her, Gary Newberg stood laughing. He'd just pinched her hard.

"What's wrong, honey? I thought you liked it rough," he said loudly, turning to grin at several boys standing with him.

Reana Mae stared at him, then raised her hand to slap him. He grabbed her wrist, wrenching her toward him.

"Come on, honey. Don't get mad. You know you like it."

He leaned forward and kissed her hard on the mouth.

"Stop it!"

Reana jerked away from him, pushing his chest. "What the hell is wrong with you?"

Laughing, Gary sauntered off with his friends.

Reana stood still, staring as they walked across the cafeteria, looking back at her now and then to laugh.

"Are you okay?" I asked.

"What a jerk!" she hissed. "What a goddamned jerk!"

We filled our trays and walked to our usual table, where Cindy sat waiting.

"What was that all about?" she asked, glancing from Reana's face to mine.

"Hell if I know," Reana said, her voice sharp.

She bit into her hamburger, staring down at her tray.

"Don't pay any attention to him," I said. "Everyone knows he's a jerk."

Reana's cheeks were red. She didn't look up from her meal.

When she rose to carry her tray to the back of the room, another boy sidled up beside her. He looked like a stoner—long hair, a flannel shirt baggy over a Black Sabbath T-shirt.

"Hey, Reana Mae, so I heard you like it . . . rough." He smirked at her.

"Well, you heard wrong." Reana set her tray back down on the table and clenched her fists.

"Come on, don't play hard to get." He leaned in toward her, his fingers stroking her cheek.

"Stop it!" Reana recoiled.

The boy laughed, leaning toward her again. Then suddenly, he was on the floor. Reana had punched him cleanly in the stomach and now stood over him, clenching and unclenching her fist.

"Hey," he grunted, looking up at her. "What the hell was that for?"

Teachers came running from all directions. Mrs. Riley grabbed Reana's arm and pulled her toward the stairs. Another teacher hauled the boy from the floor and dragged him in the same direction. Cindy stood staring, but I pushed my way after them. I wasn't sure what was going on, but I knew it wasn't Reana's fault.

In the principal's office, Reana and I sat across from the stoner boy. Mrs. Riley stood in the doorway, as if to prevent us from bolting. We waited what seemed like forever before Mr. Carmichael finally strode in. He sat behind his desk and glared at us.

"So, who wants to tell me what's going on here?"

Reana Mae simply stared at the floor, her cheeks red. I could see her hands shake in her lap.

"He just came up and started grabbing at her," I said. "Reana didn't do anything to start it."

Mr. Carmichael glared at the boy. "Is that true?"

The boy looked from Reana Mae to the principal and said, "She said she liked it rough."

"What?" Reana burst out. "I never said no such thing. I don't even know you."

Mr. Carmichael looked from her face to the boy, then shook his head.

"Mr. Boyden," he said finally, meeting the boy's eyes. "Miss Colvin here says she doesn't even know you. So how could she tell you anything?"

"She wrote it in the bathroom," the boy said, glaring at Reana. "Right on the wall, she wrote, 'For an easy lay, call Reana Mae. She likes a rough ride.' She even wrote her phone number."

He reached into his shirt pocket and produced a scrap of paper with our phone number written on it.

"I never wrote anything on no bathroom wall," Reana yelled.

Mr. Carmichael took the paper from the boy, crumpled it, and dropped it in the trash can.

"I think I can assure you, Mr. Boyden, that Reana Mae did not write her own phone number on the bathroom wall. It seems someone is playing a very mean trick."

He turned to Reana. "Do you have any idea who might have done this?"

Reana Mae looked up briefly at me, then shook her head.

Mr. Carmichael turned to me. "What about you, Miss Wylie? Do you know who did this?"

I knew, of course, just as Reana knew, who had written the ugly words. But like her, I shook my head.

"Well." Mr. Carmichael sighed. "I don't know who wrote it, but I know who is going to clean it up. You, Mr. Boyden, will spend afternoon detention scrubbing down the walls of that bathroom."

The boy glared again at Reana, then nodded.

"As for you, young lady." The principal turned now to Reana Mae. "I appreciate that you were upset, but I cannot condone fighting. You will spend detention in study hall, writing me an essay on the value of keeping your temper."

With that, we were dismissed.

Reana Mae arrived home from school at five. She spoke to no one, stomping up the stairs to our bedroom.

"What's up with her?" Tracy was sitting at the kitchen table doing homework. She smirked at me.

"You know darn well what's wrong!" I shouted. Mother appeared in the doorway.

"Bethany," she said sharply. "What are you yelling about?"

"Someone wrote a nasty thing about Reana in the boy's bathroom at school," I said, staring hard at Tracy. "They said she was an easy lay, and she likes it rough."

Mother's face blanched. "Is Reana okay?"

I shook my head, still staring at Tracy. "Two boys were grabbing at her at lunch, and she hit one of them and got detention.

"You did it!" I shouted at Tracy. "You wrote that because you're mad about my dress."

"I did not!" Tracy's eyes widened. "I would *never* write on the bathroom wall. And I certainly wouldn't put our phone number there!"

Mother looked from Tracy to me. "Someone wrote our phone number on the bathroom wall?"

"It was her, Mother! I know it was. How else did she know about the phone number?"

Mother looked hard at Tracy then, but she only looked back with her eyes wide.

"I heard about it," she said. "Everyone at school knows about it. God, Mother, I would never write our phone number in the bathroom! It just makes all of us look like cheap hillbillies."

Mother turned to me and said, "I know you're upset, Bethany. But I don't think Tracy would do something like that."

She turned toward the stairway. "I need to talk with Reana Mae," she said.

Behind her, Tracy smiled at me, her hazel eyes sparkling.

After dinner that night, Reana Mae followed Tracy down the stairs to her basement bedroom. I trailed behind.

At the bottom of the steps, Reana suddenly shoved Tracy into the wall.

"I know it was you," she hissed. "You can deny it all you want, but I know. And you're going to pay, Tracy Janelle Wylie. Just you wait, you'll pay."

Tracy smirked at her, her hazel eyes sparkling mean.

"Oh yeah?" she drawled. "Who's going to make me pay? You?" She laughed then, a nasty laugh. "What the hell can *you* do to *me*, you little tramp? You're nothing but trash!"

Before she could finish the word, Reana's hand shot out. Gripping Tracy by the throat, she pushed hard against the wall. Tracy's eyes widened. She grabbed at Reana's arm, trying to pull away. But Reana Mae would not let go. She leaned her entire weight against Tracy, squeezing Tracy's throat. She didn't say a word.

"Reana!" I grabbed her arm, trying to pull her back. "Let go!"

Tracy's face reddened as she scratched at Reana's arm.

"Stop, Reana!" I was afraid she would kill Tracy. I'd never seen anyone so angry before. "Stop, please."

Still Reana Mae didn't move. She didn't turn her head to look at me, or even acknowledge my presence. She stared straight into Tracy's face.

Finally, I grabbed her blond hair and yanked her head back.

Abruptly, she released Tracy's throat from her choke hold, turned to glare at me, and stormed up the stairs.

Tracy slumped against the wall, heaving great gulps of air.

"She's crazy," she finally whispered. "She's fucking nuts."

"Just leave her alone, Tracy," I pleaded. "Please, just let her be."

She glared at me, then disappeared into her bedroom, slamming the door behind her.

I was shaking so that I had to sit down on the stairs. I knew Reana Mae had a lot of anger inside, but I'd never seen her in such a fury. Should I tell Mother? What would she do?

No, I decided. I was probably overreacting. Reana Mae was mad and hurt, that was all. And now she'd blown up, and she'd be okay again.

I walked unsteadily up the stairs and onto the back porch. There I sat on the glider for a long time, wondering again at how Tracy could be so mean. And how Reana could be so violent. And why, oh why, God, was the world so hard?

～ 25 ～

Dancing on the Volcano

Brian arrived at our house carrying a white rose corsage. He shook Daddy's hand and explained exactly where he would be taking me for dinner. Then he assured Daddy that I would be home before midnight.

Mother snapped photos as Brian pinned the corsage to my dress, then as I fumbled about, trying hard to pin a boutonniere to his lapel. My hands shook so that Mother finally put down the camera and pinned the flower herself.

Tracy and Mark had already gone, but Reana Mae stood in the doorway, waving as we drove away. I felt like a fairy princess, whisked away in a dark green Pacer.

We joined another couple from the newspaper staff for dinner at a nearby steakhouse. Scared to death I'd drop something on my gown, I pushed the food around my plate, listening while the others chatted. Every once in a while, I glanced toward the large mirror on the opposite wall, just to reassure myself it really was me sitting there with Brian Hutson, having dinner in a restaurant.

The school gym had been transformed by a sea of crepe paper and ribbons. A disco ball hung from the ceiling, spinning lights onto the crowd below. We sat at a table with a group of friends, watching as one couple after another glided out to the dance floor.

Finally, Brian asked if I wanted to dance. And, again, all I could manage was "Okay."

I had never danced with a boy before, except for years before at cotillion . . . and I was pretty sure we wouldn't be doing the fox-trot. But Reana and I had practiced in our room all week. I hoped I wouldn't step on Brian's feet or trip on my gown. As we walked to the dance floor, I felt my cheeks burning. Surely everyone in the room must be staring to see me, Bethany Wylie, walking out to dance with Brian Hutson.

Then, he put his arms around my waist and I wrapped mine around his shoulders, and we joined the mass of slowly swaying couples, our feet shuffling as we circled around and around. This wasn't so hard, after all. I felt myself relaxing, leaning slightly into Brian's chest. It felt like magic.

We danced several slow numbers to Gordon Lightfoot, Barbra Streisand, and Jim Croce. Then, abruptly, the music changed. Couples pried themselves apart and started jostling and bumping and flailing about. Brian and I stood uncertainly for a minute, then he took my hand and we walked back toward our table. Nearly giddy with relief that I would not have to fast-dance, I didn't hear at first the high-pitched giggles and squeals coming from a table nearby.

Brian stopped short of our table and turned to see what the commotion was about. His hand tightened around mine as I turned and saw Tracy flouncing along behind us, making lewd gestures in our direction. When she saw we had stopped, she collapsed against a table, laughing shrilly . . . hysterically.

I stared in horror as she began dancing around Brian and me, her hips gyrating wildly, her arms flung out, her steps unsteady.

"See my li'l sister?" she cried out. "See the li'l Jeshabelle? She's a fucking whore . . . just like her twin. The trash-can twins, that's what they are . . . the fucking trash-can twins."

Behind her, Mark stood grinning, glassy-eyed, staring vacantly as Tracy spun around more and more unsteadily.

"They're drunk, or stoned," Brian said, putting his arm around my shoulder and pulling me close. "Just ignore her."

But I couldn't ignore her . . . my sister. Her auburn curls tumbled madly around her red-cheeked face, her eyes sparkled brighter than I'd ever seen them, her Kewpie-doll mouth was open in a horrible grimace. I couldn't move, couldn't turn away, couldn't take my eyes off her as she spun dizzily around, shrieking, "Whore! Whore! Whore!"

Then abruptly, she staggered to a stop, lurched forward, and vomited down the front of her pale green dress.

Mr. Landon, the freshman counselor, came running, took Tracy by the arm, and dragged her toward the bathrooms. The room was silent for an instant. And then everyone began talking at once.

Brian pulled me away from where we'd been standing, back toward the table where our friends sat in embarrassed silence. I picked up my purse and the shawl Mother had loaned me, and we walked to the car, staring ahead without a word.

Once inside the Pacer, however, I collapsed against the dashboard, allowing the tears I'd been fighting to stream down my face. It didn't matter; Brian was never going to ask me out again. Not after this.

We sat in the parking lot while I cried. Brian handed me tissue after tissue, but he never spoke.

Finally, I straightened up, looked into his kind face, and stammered, "I'm so sorry! She gets crazy sometimes, but she never does it in public. Usually it's just at home, when she's mad. And she just . . . she does crazy things, you know? Crazy things. She screams and throws things. She breaks stuff. Once she even cut up one of my mother's dresses. I don't know why she does it. I don't know what's wrong with her. But she's never been crazy in public before. I'm so sorry."

The words tumbled out, the most I'd ever spoken to him. I knew I was babbling, and I knew I shouldn't tell him about Tracy, but I couldn't help myself. Once my mouth opened, it all came out—my confusion, my fear, and my fury all tumbled together in a nonstop stream until I had finished. I had told him everything. And when I was done and there was nothing else to say, I simply sat with my hands folded in my lap and waited for him to tell me he never wanted to see me or talk to me again.

Instead, Brian leaned forward, took both my hands in his, and kissed me full on the mouth. Not a quick kiss like the one in the newspaper office. Now he gave me a long, slow, openmouthed kiss that left me catching vainly at my breath.

Then he smiled at me and said, very softly, "Look, you don't have anything to apologize for. So your sister's crazy. It's not like I didn't already know that. Hell, Bethany, everyone knows that. She's nuts . . . and your cousin slept with her uncle. And your dad looked at me tonight like he might just kill me. . . . And my brother is a druggie, and probably you'll hate my parents, because they're snobs."

He smiled again. I must have been staring stupidly.

"But you, Bethany, are sweet and pretty and smart," he said, still smiling. "And I hope you'll go out with me again."

"I'd like that," I said.

"Only maybe next time we'll go someplace where Tracy's not."

Then he drove me home, because I knew Mother and Daddy would be worried. I was sure Mr. Landon had already called them about Tracy.

What must Mother be thinking?

She was waiting on the front porch steps, absently scratching Bo's neck. When she saw the car pulling in, she ran down the walkway toward me.

"Are you okay?"

She grabbed me in a fierce hug.

"Are you okay?" she repeated, pulling back to look at my face.

I nodded, glancing toward Brian, embarrassed.

Mother extended her hand to him. "I'm very sorry your evening was spoiled," she said. "I hope you'll forgive Tracy. She has . . . well, I mean, she is . . ."

"That's all right, Mrs. Wylie."

He turned and smiled at me. "I'll call you tomorrow, okay?"

"Okay." I smiled back.

Then he got in the car and pulled away. Mother and I walked to the house, settling down on the front steps together. Her face was pinched and pale, her mascara smudged dark under her eyes.

"I'm so sorry, Bethy," she said. "And on your first date."

I sat quietly, not knowing what to say.

"I just don't understand what possessed her."

"I think she'd been drinking, Mother," I said. "Both her and Mark looked like they had. Brian said so, too."

"I'm sorry she ruined your first dance."

I sighed and leaned into her shoulder.

"But we had fun before Tracy went crazy," I said, smiling at the dark.

"I'm glad, honey," Mother said. Then, "Why don't you go on inside and take that dress off before it gets dirty."

"You coming?"

She shook her head. "I'm going to wait till your father gets back with Tracy."

So I left her sitting on the steps in the dark . . . waiting for her drunken, crazy daughter to come back home.

Reana Mae grabbed my hand as soon as I walked through the door. "What happened?" she asked, dragging me up the stairs. "Someone called and said Uncle Jimmy had to come get Tracy 'cause she got sick!"

I told her what had happened while I changed into my pajamas, lovingly draping my beautiful gown across the bed.

"I can't believe her!" Reana exclaimed when I told her what Tracy had done. "I cannot fucking believe her! Poor Aunt Helen like to died when that call came. And Uncle Jimmy tore outta here like Lucifer hisself was chasin' him."

She paced across the floor, then spat out, "Tracy don't even care what she does to them, does she? . . . And Lord God Almighty, Bethany, I bet you wanted to die, too, watchin' her act like that."

"Well," I whispered, "I guess she came out the worst in it, 'cause she threw up all over herself and everyone saw it. And then Mr. Landon came and got her, and I don't even know what Daddy's gonna do to her."

"Well, she deserves it, whatever it is."

Reana Mae shook her head.

"What do you reckon is wrong with her? I mean, she ain't stupid, and she's real pretty, and she's got herself this nice house. And Uncle Jimmy and Aunt Helen love her fit to gift wrap. Why can't she just be happy?"

She threw a pillow across the room.

"Why's she gotta be so damn mean?"

I shook my head, staring at my reflection in the dresser mirror, wondering if I could possibly be the same person I'd been this morning. Why, I didn't even look the same, did I? Now that Brian Hutson had kissed me like he did . . . and said he'd call me. Surely, I was changed through and through.

"Well, you don't seem too shook up over it," Reana Mae said, watching me closely. "You all right?"

I nodded, smiling at myself in the mirror.

"He kiss you again?"

I nodded again, feeling my cheeks redden.

"You reckon he's gonna call?"

I nodded yet again, still smiling at the mirror.

"Lord God, Bethany, you're lit up like a neon sign. I reckon you're right in love."

I flopped back onto my bed, smiling still. In love? That might be stretching it a bit. After all, I told myself sternly, I didn't know his favorite song. I didn't even know his phone number. But I knew what it felt like when he kissed me. And that was purely grand.

"Oh, Lord," Reana said suddenly. "There's Uncle Jimmy's car."

I sat up abruptly, listening to the slamming of one car door, then a second one. Reana Mae and I crept to the top of the stairs, trying hard to hear what would happen next.

The front door crashed open and Tracy's wails filled the house. I'd never heard anything like that shrill, ragged keening—not even from Tracy. She swore, she screamed, she crashed into things. We heard glass breaking, then a loud thud, but the wailing just went on and on.

"Tracy Janelle Wylie!" Daddy's voice boomed underneath the screaming. "Tracy, damn it! Stop it! Do you hear me? You stop that screaming right now!"

I couldn't hear Mother at all.

"I hate you! I hate you all!" Tracy shrieked. "Don't touch me! Don't you touch me! I can damn well do it myself!"

Another loud thud . . . then a momentary silence.

"Tracy, honey, let me help you get up." Mother's voice was soothing, cajoling.

"Nooooo! God damn it, keep your hands off me!"

She was sobbing now, wailing and hiccupping loudly.

I didn't hear Mother or Daddy for a minute, only Tracy's screaming. Then we heard the front door slam shut. Someone had left, but it certainly wasn't my sister. She was still wailing and, from the sound of it, trashing the living room. Whenever she paused to catch her breath, I could hear Mother's crooning voice trying to calm her.

After what seemed like an hour but was probably just a few minutes, the front door opened again and we heard Daddy's voice. "Now, Tracy, just calm down for a minute. Dr. Statton's here, honey. Dr. Statton is here, and he's got something that'll help you calm down."

"Nooooo!" she screamed louder than before. From the crashing, I guessed she was trying to rise from the floor, without much success.

"Get her arm, Helen." Daddy's voice sounded grim. "Now just calm down for a minute. Nobody's going to hurt you. It's Dr. Statton, Tracy. That's all."

After a few more minutes of screaming and thrashing about, Tracy suddenly went quiet. Reana Mae and I were halfway down the steps by then, sitting fearfully, holding hands.

"There you go, now." Dr. Statton's soft, soothing voice drifted up the stairs. "That's all right. You're all right. Helen, why don't you get her bed ready? She'll sleep for a while now. Okay, Jimmy, let's pick her up and carry her to her room. Ready? One, two, three."

We heard them grunt, then shuffle toward the basement. The house was still.

"Jesus Christ!" Reana Mae whispered, squeezing my hand. "She's gone crazy as a loon."

We heard Daddy's heavy footsteps, followed by Dr. Statton's.

"Thank you, John," Daddy was saying. "We didn't know what else to do."

"You did the right thing, Jimmy," Dr. Statton replied. "Best thing in the world for her is to sleep it off."

We heard the front door close behind the doctor, our neighbor across the street. Dr. Statton was actually an allergist, but he went to our church, and he and Daddy were on the same bowling team.

After a few minutes, we heard Mother come back up the stairs. Then we heard the swishing of a broom.

"Let's go help," Reana said, pulling me up by the hand.

We padded down to the living room. It looked like a tornado had been through. Chairs lay overturned, a lamp had smashed on the floor. Mother and Daddy's wedding picture had fallen from the wall, and a whole shelf of Mother's beautiful little glass figures had been overturned.

Mother didn't even look up as we began righting furniture and picking up glass bits. Daddy was nowhere to be seen.

It wasn't long before the room looked right again. I kissed Mother's cheek, and so did Reana Mae. Then we went back upstairs. Mother never spoke to us, just squeezed my hand and kissed us back.

"What do you reckon they'll do now?" Reana asked.

We were lying on our backs on my bed, staring at the sloping ceiling.

"I don't know," I said miserably.

"Maybe they'll put her in one of them places, you know . . . like a hospital for crazy people."

I turned to stare at her.

"Mother would never do that," I said firmly.

"You're probably right. I bet they won't let her see Mark no more."

"I'm not sure they can stop her," I said flatly. "I guess Tracy's gonna do what she wants, just like always."

"But even they got to see now, don't they? Even Uncle Jimmy's got to see that she's crazy."

I shook my head. I just didn't know. There were so many things I didn't know, didn't understand. Why was Tracy so mean? How could she do the things she did? How on earth could she cause so much pain for Mother? I thought about Mother's face, pinched and ashen, as she sat on the front steps, waiting for Daddy to bring Tracy home. My heart felt like it would break into pieces as I thought about what Mother must be going through.

I knew I should probably say a prayer for Mother. And for Tracy, too. But I couldn't bring myself to pray. What good did it do, after all? All those years I'd prayed for Tracy, and she just seemed to get meaner all the time. What kind of a God was he that he let my mother be so hurt? No, I didn't pray. I just lay in silence for a long time.

Finally, Reana Mae rolled onto her side, propped her head on her hand, and grinned.

"So," she said, poking at my stomach. "Tell me about the kiss."

❧ 26 ❧

A Changing Household

The next morning, I rose early and slipped quietly downstairs to the kitchen. Mother was already there, drinking coffee. She smiled at me wanly, gesturing toward the coffeepot.

"It's strong this morning," she said as I filled my cup. "I thought your father needed it, after last night."

I poured milk into my half-full cup, then spooned in sugar. "Where is Daddy?"

"He's taking a walk."

I sat down beside her, watching her carefully.

"Your daddy needs some time to think. We've got to make some decisions, and he just needs some time to think."

I nodded, as if I understood. What kinds of decisions? She didn't say.

Daddy didn't come home until after Reana Mae and I had left for Cindy's house. Tracy was still in bed when we left. I didn't want to be there when she got up. We spent the afternoon listening to records, painting our fingernails, and rehashing the events of the night before. Cindy had already heard most of it from Lori Bateman, but she wanted to hear it all again from me.

"Lori said everyone was talking about it after you left. They all felt real bad for you. Even Tracy's friends said she was nuts."

"She is, for certain." Reana Mae nodded. "She's gettin' loonier and loonier. I reckon now everybody knows."

"Poor Mother." I sighed unhappily. "She must just be dying."

I knew Mother was hurting. And that hurt me. But some part of me inside was strangely relieved. Everyone knew now. It wasn't a family secret anymore. I didn't have to pretend at school and at church that everything was fine. I was sorry for Mother, and for Daddy, too. But it was liberating, somehow, not to have to pretend anymore.

Tracy was crazy. And everyone knew it.

"Yeah," Reana agreed. "I guess Aunt Helen is plain miserable."

"I bet your dad blames it all on Mark," Cindy said.

I looked up at her, startled. She blushed.

"Come on, Bethany," she said quickly. "You know he never blames anything on Tracy."

Reana Mae was nodding. "That's the truth," she said. "Sure as sugar."

They were right, of course. If there was any way to blame Tracy's behavior on someone else, my father usually found it. In his eyes, Tracy could do no wrong.

Or maybe . . . maybe it wasn't that at all. I paused to consider something new. Maybe Daddy understood more than we knew about Tracy. Maybe he was so protective of her because he knew deep down that something was wrong with her. I let the thought roll around my head a bit.

"Well," I said finally, "he'll probably blame the liquor on Mark. But he can't blame Mark for the way she acted when she got home."

"Naw," Reana agreed. "He'll blame that on the liquor."

I shrugged. "Well, he might try. But Mother knows. She's known all along."

Of that, I was certain. I'd watched Mother watching Tracy for years. I'd seen the fear in her eyes as Tracy's tantrums grew more frequent and more violent.

"Poor Aunt Helen," Reana said, shaking her head.

We sat in silence for a while, brushing coral polish on our nails and blowing them dry.

"You didn't tell Cindy about the best part yet," Reana Mae said suddenly.

"What's that?" Cindy asked, looking up at me.

I felt my cheeks getting hot. Before I could answer, Reana Mae rose, laughing.

"She got herself kissed, good and proper!"

Cindy gaped. "Really?"

"Yes, she did," Reana continued. "Tell her about it, Bethany."

But she didn't give me a chance to tell, as she blurted out, "After Tracy puked, they went out to his car, you see, and then he kissed her on the mouth. Even French-kissed her, didn't he, Bethany?"

I nodded, my cheeks burning now.

"God, Bethany," Cindy stared at me, wide-eyed. "Did you like it?"

"Oh yeah, she liked it!" Reana Mae laughed again. "She came home lookin' like she might just float off to Heaven. She liked it, all right."

"And he used his tongue?"

Reana laughed again. I could only nod.

"What's it like?" Cindy asked, looking from Reana to me.

"It's . . . nice," I said, smiling now. "It's not gross at all, not like you'd think."

"Yeah." Reana Mae sighed. "It's not like you'd think at all. Mostly it's . . . well, it's hard to explain. But it's the best thing ever."

Cindy and I watched her silently. She'd never spoken to Cindy about Caleb at all. And while she'd often told me how much she loved and missed him, she'd never talked to me about kissing him or . . . anything else.

Reana Mae was staring out the window now, her hand poised in midair, holding the nail polish brush. She smiled, closing her eyes.

"When you're in love and someone loves you back . . . it's like you want him to kiss you like that. You want his tongue in your mouth. You want to just swallow him up so he's part of you and you can keep him with you always."

A drop of coral polish plopped onto her bare leg. She straightened herself abruptly, swiped at the spilled polish, and began fanning her hand, blowing on the nails intently. Her eyes were bright.

I realized, probably for the first time really, how much she did love Caleb. How much she missed him.

"Wow," Cindy breathed. "Is that what it was like for you, Bethany?"

"I don't know." I laughed uncomfortably. "I mean, I don't think Brian loves me or anything. But I liked it."

"And he's gonna call her again." Reana Mae smiled at me brightly. "So I guess he liked it, too."

We stayed at Cindy's until her grandmother shooed us home for dinner. I didn't want to be at home, and I guessed Reana didn't either.

"Do you really think they'd put her in one of those hospitals?" I had read *One Flew Over the Cuckoo's Nest* the previous summer. I couldn't imagine Tracy in a place like that.

"Naw." Reana shook her head. "I figure you're right about that. Aunt Helen wouldn't ever do that."

She kicked at a pile of leaves someone had raked, sending up a shower of red and gold.

"She'll get grounded, probably," she said. "I bet Uncle Jimmy grounds her for the rest of the school year, and by next weekend she'll have him convinced it wasn't her fault and he'll forget about it."

"You're probably right."

Tracy had always managed to escape serious punishment. Mother and Daddy made allowances for her. In our whole family life, I don't believe Nancy, Melinda, and I combined gave them so much to worry over as Tracy did.

I knew Mother worried a lot over Reana Mae, but since she'd moved in with us, even Reana hadn't given them too much to worry over. She'd had occasional run-ins with Jenny Spangler and her crew. One time she got sent home for two days after she punched Chuck Murphy in the gut for calling Cindy fat. But Reana Mae always said she was sorry, and she always *was* sorry for upsetting Mother, if not for her actions. And in the last year, she'd been better at school. Mother had yet to be called to the high school because of Reana Mae.

We turned the corner to find Daddy shoving a suitcase into the back of the station wagon.

"Whoa," Reana Mae exhaled. "They're taking her away."

I broke into a run, Reana just behind me.

Daddy slammed the tailgate and walked quickly toward the house. "Helen," he called as he opened the front door, "where's my sunglasses?"

We followed him inside. A notebook lay open on the coffee table. Daddy's briefcase was on the couch.

"Flight 254, nonstop to Miami," Reana read aloud.

"Uncle Jimmy is going to Florida." Mother walked into the room, holding Daddy's sunglasses.

Reana Mae glanced at me quickly. Were they sending Tracy to Florida?

"Your Aunt DJ had a stroke last night," Mother said, putting her hand on my shoulder. "She's in the hospital. It's very serious."

"Aunt DJ?" Surely Mother meant my grandmother. Why, Aunt DJ was just a year older than Daddy. She was too young to have a stroke.

"Your father is going down to see what he can do," she continued. "And to take care of your grandmother."

Oh, Lord, I thought. *If Aunt DJ dies, who'll take care of Grandmother Araminta?*

As if reading my mind, Mother sighed. "I suppose if DarlaJean can't take care of her, we'll have to bring your grandmother here."

Not long after, Mother and Daddy left for the airport. Only then did I think of Tracy. She wasn't upstairs. Was she still asleep?

Reana Mae tiptoed down the stairs to the basement and leaned her ear close to Tracy's bedroom door. Then she tiptoed back up.

"She's still sleepin', all right," she said. "Snorin', too."

She shook her head. "Even Mama didn't sleep till suppertime."

"Should we start dinner?"

A big pan of water sat on the stove. On the cutting board lay a dozen red tomatoes. Beside them was a bowl of chopped onions and peppers. "Looks like Mother was making spaghetti."

We chopped tomatoes and minced garlic, turned the heat on under the water, and sautéed the vegetables while I told Reana about DarlaJean and my Grandmother Araminta. By the time the station wagon crunched into the driveway, dinner was ready. Reana

Mae set the table while I drained the pasta. Mother's face brightened when she walked into the kitchen.

"Thank you, girls." She kissed each of us. "That's a big help."

"Should we get Tracy up?" I asked, watching Mother stir, then taste the spaghetti sauce.

"I think we'll just let her sleep," she said, sprinkling basil into the sauce.

So we sat down to supper, just the three of us.

"How long is Daddy gonna be in Florida?" I asked, buttering a saltine and dipping it in the sauce on my plate.

"I don't know, honey. I guess until DarlaJean gets out of the hospital."

"But what if . . . ?"

"I don't know," she repeated. "We won't know anything till Daddy gets down there."

Right then we heard a door creak open in the basement. A few minutes later, Tracy appeared, her face pale, her hair matted. She still wore her nightgown.

"Spaghetti for breakfast?" she asked, staring blankly at us.

"It's supper," Mother said quietly. "Sit down now and get some food in your tummy. You'll feel better."

So Tracy sat and ate spaghetti with butter and Parmesan cheese instead of sauce, like she always did. No one spoke for a while. I didn't look up from my plate, except to steal a glance at Reana Mae now and then. She was watching Tracy closely, like she might pounce on her at any minute.

"Where's Daddy?" Tracy finally asked, after her second plate of noodles.

So Mother told her about DarlaJean. Tracy sat quietly for a moment, then asked, "Will Grandmother come to live with us?"

"Maybe, I just don't know," Mother said.

"She'd better take Melinda's room," Tracy said firmly. "So she doesn't have to use the stairs."

"Let's not worry about that yet," Mother said.

Tracy pushed her chair from the table. "I gotta call Lynette," she said.

"Tracy, wait. I need to talk to you." Mother's voice was firm and soft. "Bethany, will you and Reana Mae clean up here?"

I nodded, even though we had cooked and it didn't seem fair that we had to wash the dishes, too.

Mother and Tracy walked down the hall toward Mother's room. We listened intently while we washed and dried the plates and pans, but we couldn't hear a word spoken. Finally, as I was putting away the last of the silverware, Tracy came back through the kitchen. She glared at us balefully, then disappeared down the stairs to her room again.

"Grounded," Reana said.

I nodded, hanging the dish towel to dry. "How long do you think?"

"Not as long as she deserves, that's for damn certain," Reana Mae said grimly as she switched off the light in the room. "Not nearly as long as she deserves."

Daddy called the next morning while we were dressing for church. I could hear Mother's voice rise and fall, then the clicking of her high heels in the hallway.

Tracy walked half a block behind us on the way to church, sulking and staring at Mother's back.

"What did Daddy say?" I asked.

"DarlaJean is very sick," Mother answered. "They're afraid she's not going to make it."

"How's Grandmother?" Tracy's voice came from just behind me now.

"She's very upset," Mother said. "She's so sick herself. This is very upsetting for her."

I spent Sunday morning at church, praying hard for Aunt DJ.

Mother sat quietly beside me. I wondered if she was praying for DarlaJean, too. Her eyes were closed, her head bent, her lips moving slightly. Mother always looked like that in church. Calm and serene, her back straight, her dark curls wound neatly, tightly in place. Church was her solace and her refuge. I'd read a story once about a woman who became a nun. We weren't Catholic, but I could see my mother as a nun, praying all day on a string of beads, kneeling on those little benches fastened to the pews in church. She'd have been good at that.

I squeezed my eyes closed, willing myself to at least look like I was praying. It was warm in the sanctuary. My sweater itched the back of my neck. The lady in front of us wore too much perfume. The heavy aroma tickled at my nose. I opened one eye to look at my sister beside me. Her angelic face fairly glowed, surrounded by her soft auburn tresses. Her long lashes fluttered now and then over her closed eyes. Her hands lay loosely in her lap. She didn't move at all. She might have been a statue—ANGEL AT PRAYER, the sign below her would read. And she looked like that. She really did. No one watching her in church could have imagined that just two nights before, she had been swearing at our parents, smashing lamps, and vomiting on her homecoming dress.

I couldn't see Reana Mae, sitting on the other side of Mother, but I knew what she would look like if I could. Her eyes would be open, staring straight ahead at the back of the old man's head before her. Her mouth would be set in a firm, flat line. She never bowed her head in church, never closed her eyes, never even sang the hymns. She wouldn't have come at all if Mother hadn't insisted on it.

Reana Mae did not believe in church or God or Jesus. "A load of crap," she called it, though not in front of Mother.

"All them people prayin' all them years, and look at the world," she said disdainfully. "Why don't God do something about all the wickedness, if he's real? Why don't he stop people killin' each other and all that?

"Plus," and this was the cornerstone of her argument, "why'd he let all them Jews get killed, if they were his chosen people? That just don't make sense."

She had given our Sunday school teacher fits in junior high with questions like that. Mrs. Russell was a nice old lady, but she wasn't prepared to discuss the theological ramifications of the Holocaust with a thirteen-year-old.

"Everything happens for a reason," she'd repeated again and again. "God has a plan. We just can't understand it yet."

"You got that right," Reana Mad hissed back at her more than once. "I don't understand it at all."

She was quiet in Sunday school these days. She liked the teacher better, for one thing. Velva Dreese had been a missionary to the

Philippines for years and years, and Reana Mae loved hearing about other places. But she still didn't believe in God.

That night, Daddy called to tell us that Aunt DJ had died during the afternoon.

"What about Grandmother?" Tracy asked. "How is she?"

"She's very upset." Mother sighed. "Daddy will bring her home on Thursday, after they get things settled there."

"Where will she sleep?" Tracy asked. "I think she better have Melinda's room."

"I think you're right." Mother's brow furrowed. "We'll have to put Melinda's things upstairs, with you girls."

She turned to Reana Mae and me.

"Will you two move your things so we can fit Melinda's bed up there?"

"Yes, ma'am," I answered.

I didn't much mind having Melinda move in with us. She hardly came home from college anyway, and she'd always been the easiest of my sisters to get along with. But I wondered how our house could absorb another person, even one as tiny as Grandmother Araminta.

Tracy, on the other hand, seemed thrilled. She helped Mother pack up Melinda's things and move them upstairs. Then she set to work with the vacuum cleaner and dust rag, cleaning the room Grandmother would take. She didn't even complain when Mother asked her to scrub the bathroom.

"Maybe we should get one of those toilet fresheners," she said as she scrubbed the toilet bowl. "The blue ones that make the room smell good. I bet Grandmother would like that."

Mother just nodded and smiled at her. She looked worried and tired.

By the end of the day, Melinda's bed had been moved upstairs, and her old room was spotless.

"We'll have to get a hospital bed," Mother said, writing in her notebook.

"I'll go with you, Mother," Tracy said, sitting beside her on the couch. She was watching Mother make her list, volunteering items she thought Grandmother might like.

"You are grounded, young lady," Mother reminded her.

"But I want to help," Tracy sputtered. "She's *my* grandmother, after all."

In the end, Mother relented and took Tracy with her to the Hook's Rehab store to look for a bed, then to the mall for sheets and blankets and pillows and new curtains. I thought about when I had accompanied her to the mall on a trip like that, when we knew Reana Mae was coming. That had been scary, but this was worse. I couldn't imagine our house with that old lady in it.

"Probably, we won't even be able to play the stereo," I fumed at Reana as we made up Melinda's bed. "No noise or anything fun."

"Well, now, Bethany," Reana Mae answered calmly, punching down the pillow. "That's just how things are with family. She's your granma, after all. And she ain't got any other family."

She sat down on Melinda's bed and looked at me sternly. "And family is all there is, you know."

She sounded just like Mother.

On Thursday evening, Mother and Tracy drove to the airport to meet Daddy and Araminta. Tracy had bought a bouquet of daisies at the grocery to take for Araminta.

Melinda's room looked like a hospital room. A new bed with rails sat against the wall. Reana Mae and I had already taken turns moving the head and foot up and down, turning a knob on the side. A picture of the Last Supper hung above the bed. Mother said Araminta had always had one like that in her apartment. A wheelchair sat waiting in the living room.

Reana Mae and I started supper. I was making hamburger Stroganoff and Reana had bread rising on the counter. She hummed to herself while she worked. Reana Mae loved making bread, pounding and kneading the dough till it felt just right, then letting it swell till she pounded it again. And her breads were always good. She didn't use a recipe, just threw in handfuls of flour and whatever else struck her fancy. Sometimes she added dried fruits or nuts, sometimes leftover mashed potatoes or applesauce. Even Tracy liked Reana Mae's bread.

Reana was just taking two perfect golden loaves from the oven when we heard the front door open and Tracy's voice chirp, "Here, Grandmother, let me carry that for you."

Reana Mae carefully dumped the loaves from their pans, wiped her hands on a dish towel, and walked into the living room to meet her great-aunt, who had been Loreen's aunt long before we were ever born.

"Araminta." I heard Mother's soft voice. "This is Reana Mae. She's Arathena's great-granddaughter."

"Well, now," Araminta said, smiling at Reana, "I can see that. She takes after Arathena, plain as day."

Her voice was low.

"So you're livin' here now, too?"

"Yes, ma'am." Reana sounded deferential.

"Well, that's best, I reckon. Can't have you down there with no one to look after you. Your mama couldn't, I reckon. She always was a wild one, your mama. I heard all about her from Loreen."

I stood at the stove, stirring sour cream into the Stroganoff.

"Bethany?"

Mother stood at the kitchen door.

"Come say hello to your grandmother."

So I put aside my wooden spoon and walked to the living room.

"And here's Bethany Marie."

Araminta smiled up at me from the couch, her bright blue eyes unclouded and clear.

"Hello, Grandmother," I whispered, kissing her soft, crinkly cheek.

"You've growed a foot," she said, inspecting me critically. "I reckon you'll be as tall as DarlaJean soon."

She looked away, out the window at the bare tree in the yard.

"My DarlaJean, why, she was five feet seven inches tall. Nearly as tall as her daddy, she was." She sighed heavily. "And now she's with him, I reckon."

Tracy sat down beside her and took her hand.

"First Winston, then Jimmy, and now my DarlaJean," she said. "I reckon I lost everyone I ever loved."

"I'm here, Mother," Daddy said anxiously, watching her. "You haven't lost me."

"Why, Jimmy, I lost you when you was just a baby," she said. "I lost you sure as I lost Winston."

She sighed again. "And now my DarlaJean, my own little girl. I never figured on losing her. I thought I'd have her with me till the end."

A tear slid down her cheek.

"You have me, Grandmother," Tracy said. "You'll always have me."

"You favor me, child." Araminta stroked Tracy's cheek. "You surely favor me."

I don't think I ever saw Tracy that gentle with anyone before or after. Reana Mae looked at me in surprise.

"Well, Mother, let's get you settled in."

Daddy picked up her big suitcase and offered his hand. "Let me show you your room."

"I'll take her, Daddy."

Tracy rose and helped Araminta to her feet, then walked slowly beside her down the hallway to Melinda's room.

"See, Grandmother? We found a picture for you."

"Well, that's a comfort, child. That's a real comfort."

Reana Mae and I escaped back to the kitchen to finish supper. Then we all sat down to eat, Grandmother Araminta in Mother's chair, Tracy perched right beside her.

"What's this?" The old lady stared at the Stroganoff before her.

Mother grimaced, then immediately regained her composure.

"That's beef Stroganoff, Araminta. Bethany made it."

"Well, I never had that before." She smiled at me, then looked back down at her plate. "I reckon I'll have to get used to lots of new things up here."

"How about some bread, Mother?" Daddy said, cutting a slice and slathering it with butter. "Reana Mae makes real good bread."

"Well, that's something I know about," Araminta said, taking the slice Daddy held out to her. "Me and DarlaJean, we always eat bread. DarlaJean, why, she bakes the best bread you ever ate."

She took a bite of the warm bread, chewed slowly, and looked around.

"Jimmy, I don't guess you got any schnapps?"

"I'll get it." Tracy rose immediately and disappeared down the hallway toward Melinda's room. She returned carrying a bottle of peach schnapps, then carefully poured a tumbler full and placed it before our grandmother.

"What a sweet girl you are." Araminta beamed at her. "Helen, this here child is an angel. It's like she's my own granddaughter."

I saw Daddy shoot Mother a pained look, then he cut another slice of bread for his mother.

"Lord God Almighty," Reana Mae said later, when we'd gone up to bed. "She's not a bit like Aunt Belle, is she?"

"No." I sighed. "She's not fun like Aunt Belle."

"She surely seems to favor Tracy."

I nodded. "She took to Tracy right from the start. I guess because Tracy looks like her . . . that's what she said in Florida, that Tracy looks like her when she was young."

"She looks real sick. I hope it ain't too hard on Aunt Helen, takin' care of her."

"Maybe if she gets too bad, she'll have to go to a nursing home," I said. Cindy's grandfather lived in a nursing home.

"No," Reana said, lying back on her bed. "Uncle Jimmy ain't gonna do that."

She rolled onto her stomach to look at me. "He won't never do that, on account of he's so guilty that he don't love her like he does Belle. And she knows it, too. She knows he loves Belle like his mama.

"What I can't get is why Tracy is so nice to her," she continued. "I'da never figured on that."

I didn't understand it either, but Tracy was wonderful with Araminta. Every day after school she came straight home to spend time with the old lady. They played hearts and euchre and even poker, when Mother wasn't home. And Tracy read to Araminta every night after supper. Araminta loved to hear the Bible read.

"Now, my DarlaJean, she's a real good girl. But she didn't read good like you do. That's a sad-sorry fact. That girl never read nothin' but them romance novels. Trash, I told her, nothin' but trash. But she read 'em anyways. Now you, child, you read them Bible stories real nice."

Tracy fairly beamed with pride.

❧ 27 ❧

I Seen Death

At Thanksgiving, Nancy announced that she was dropping out of college to get married. Daddy hollered and Mother cried, but they couldn't stop her. She'd been working in a jewelry store in Bloomington, and the owner had asked her to marry him. Neil Berkson must have been forty, but he was rich and he doted on Nancy, and she was determined to marry him, even though he was Jewish.

"He'll get baptized, Mother," she'd explained matter-of-factly. "So we can still get married in the church if you want."

Neil arrived the day after Thanksgiving, bearing flowers and cider and a gorgeous brooch for Mother.

Reana Mae and I gaped at his paunchy middle and the bald spot on the back of his head. Neither of us had ever met a Jew before. I don't know what we expected, but he seemed normal, just like everyone else, except old.

"I guess he's her sugar daddy," Reana Mae said that night, after Neil had left.

I started, remembering when she'd said that about Mr. Ephraim Turner, who had finally married Cleda. It seemed a world away.

"But I don't understand why she'd marry him," I said. "She could have anyone."

"Well," Reana Mae grinned, "maybe she wants a fat, bald, rich Jew."

I shook my head, remembering all the good-looking boys who'd been through our front door, pining after Nancy. Reana Mae must be right, I thought. Nancy must want a rich husband.

They got married just after Christmas in our church, Neil having dutifully been dunked in the baptismal the week before.

Nancy was stunning in an ivory, floor-length taffeta gown and fingertip veil. Melinda looked gangly in her peach bridesmaid dress, the ruffled skirt barely skimming her flat white shoes. Neil looked hot and uncomfortable in his black tuxedo, the cummerbund digging into his soft middle. But he looked happy, too—like a dying man who'd suddenly come across the fountain of youth. He paid for an extravagant reception at the Canterbury Hotel, with dinner and a swan made of ice and a champagne fountain and a live band.

Daddy seemed to have made his peace with the marriage, but Mother looked strained and tense. I'd heard her the night before the wedding, trying one last time to talk Nancy out of the marriage.

"Honey, you're so young. You have your whole life ahead of you. Can't you just wait until after graduation?"

"No, Mother, I can't," Nancy had replied firmly as she painted her fingernails pink. "I am *not* going to come home for Christmas break and share that basement room with Tracy. That's all there is to it. Why should I, when Neil has a big, beautiful house with a Jacuzzi hot tub?"

Reana Mae raised her eyebrows at me then in an "I told you so" kind of way. It seemed Nancy had indeed found her sugar daddy, and she was determined to marry him and get out of our tiny house.

When Nancy and her groom returned from their two-week honeymoon in the Virgin Islands, we drove down to Bloomington to see her new house. It was purely grand, with a sweeping staircase and a screened back porch, manicured lawn, and modern kitchen . . . and on the back patio, the prized Jacuzzi hot tub.

I stared at the tub, wondering how Nancy felt about sharing it with a middle-aged husband.

"Well, I guess she done better than Cleda Rae," Reana had whispered. "A hot tub beats a fake fur coat any day."

We both giggled as Nancy swept through the kitchen to tell us that dinner was ready. Not that she'd cooked it, of course. Neil had a housekeeper who cooked and cleaned and a lawn service to tend the yard. Balding and chubby he might be, but Nancy's husband was determined to give his young wife anything and everything she wanted.

Grandmother Araminta did not attend the wedding or the reception. She'd felt poorly, she said, and wanted to stay home. Tracy wanted to stay with her, but Mother made her come to the ceremony. They both made the trip to Bloomington, however, to see Nancy's house.

"Big as a mausoleum," Araminta said afterward. "And just about as warm."

Tracy laughed as she did whenever Araminta made a joke. And she repeated the assessment later at school, to Lynette's delight.

Tracy was calmer at home, with Araminta there. Her outbursts came far less often, and never in the old lady's presence. Reana and I wondered why she was so attached to her grandmother, but she truly was.

Poor Reana Mae often got stuck at home tending to Araminta on Friday nights. Tracy was dating yet another basketball player, this one named Luke. And most Fridays, I went with Brian to the movies or the mall or a friend's house. Sometimes I still couldn't believe that I was dating Brian Hutson. I thought I'd wake up and realize it had been a dream.

Sometimes I felt guilty leaving Reana Mae behind, but she didn't seem to mind.

"I been around old folks my whole life," she explained. "Hell, I took care of Granma Loreen for a long time before she died, and she was a goddamn yapper. At least Araminta don't talk, talk, talk at me all the time."

Reana Mae never accepted the dates she was offered by countless boys at school. Not one time did she go to a movie or a dance with a boy. Once I tried setting her up on a date with Brian's friend Chuck, who had just broken up with his girlfriend. But she said no, she was fine just by herself. And every blessed night she wrote in her journal about Caleb. I couldn't understand why she didn't let go of him. She hadn't seen him or heard from him since she'd left the Coal River. He'd never even tried to get in touch with her. But she still waited, expecting that someday he'd come for her.

One Friday afternoon in April, Mother asked Reana if she'd mind spending the evening with Araminta. Tracy had a date with Luke, and I was helping with the spring musical—sewing costumes and painting sets. Daddy was away on a trip to the home office, and Mother had a meeting at the church.

"I won't be out late," she said. "And I'll be right at the church if you need anything."

"Surely, Aunt Helen," Reana Mae said, smiling. "I don't mind. You go on to your meeting. Me and Araminta will play cards or watch TV or something.

"Long as she don't make me read that damned Bible," she whispered to me as Mother turned away.

I left the house at six, carrying an armload of freshly pressed skirts for the play. Reana Mae had set up the card table in the living room and was dealing a hand of poker.

"That ain't the way Tracy deals 'em," I heard the old woman's querulous voice as the screen door shut behind me.

I spent the evening dragging scenery on and off the stage and sewing a tear in the lead actress's dress. Finally, at eight thirty, I walked home in the cool, fresh April night. At nine I knew Brian would call. He called almost every night at nine. At the corner, I paused just long enough to see a shooting star streak across the sky. I wished that Brian would ask me to the junior prom—Mother always said if you wished on a shooting star, God would hear the wish.

I turned the corner onto our street and stared in confusion at a jumble of flashing red lights. They were in front of our house, and the front door was open. I began running, stumbling now and again over the skirts trailing from my arms. What was happening? Was Mother all right? Where was Reana Mae?

I bounded onto the porch and into the house, to find several men in uniforms standing about the living room. They stared at me as I paused, gasping, looking wildly around for Mother.

"Mother!" I called out. "Where are you?"

Then I heard the reassuring click of her high heels in the hallway.

"I'm here, Bethany, I'm fine. It's okay," she said, scooping me into a hug. "Reana Mae's fine, Tracy's fine, I'm fine."

"Why are they here?" I panted, pulling back to look at her face.

"Araminta has died," she said, stroking my hair.

"Died? Here? In my house?"

"Yes, honey, here in her own bed."

"But why?" I asked. "What happened?"

"Well, that's what the EMTs are trying to find out," she said, looking back down the hall. "But it looks as if she just died in her sleep."

"Where's Reana Mae?"

"She's upstairs," Mother said. "Why don't you go on up?"

She nodded toward the group of men standing awkwardly about the room. "They'll be gone soon."

Upstairs, Reana Mae was lying on her bed, staring at the ceiling.

"Hey," I said. "Are you okay?"

She nodded, turning to look at me.

"She just died, Bethany. Just like that. We was playing poker and I just won a hand, and she said she was tired, so I helped her get in bed. And when I went back to check on her, she was dead."

"What'd you do?" I asked.

"I called Aunt Helen at the church, and she came home and called for the ambulance. But I already knew she was dead. I seen death before."

"What did she look like?"

I'd never seen a dead person.

"Well, she was real still and her eyes were open, staring straight up at the ceiling. And then I touched her, you know, and she was real cold. So I knew she was dead."

"Were you scared?" I thought I would have been scared to death.

"Naw." She shook her head so that her blond hair brushed her chin. "She went real peaceful."

Downstairs we heard tramping boots. We looked out the window to see a hospital gurney being wheeled to the ambulance. A white sheet covered the shape on the gurney.

"Leastways she got to die at home," Reana Mae whispered. "She didn't want to go to no hospital. She told me that."

"And now she's with DarlaJean and Winston," I added.

She shot me a look of pure disdain then. Of course, Reana Mae did not believe in Heaven, or in hell either. "Dead's dead," she always said.

"Did Mother call Daddy yet?" I asked.

She nodded. "Right after she called the ambulance. He'll be home in the morning."

I wondered how he would feel, with his mother dying while he was out of town.

"Then she called Belle," Reana continued.

"Belle?"

"Course, silly. Belle is Araminta's sister, after all."

I hadn't thought about that. I had never seen the two of them together, and Araminta always spoke of Belle with anger.

"Is she coming?"

"She'll be here tomorrow night." Reana Mae smiled at me. "It'll be good to see Belle."

I nodded, watching silently as the men raised the gurney with my grandmother's body into the ambulance.

A car pulled up behind the ambulance, its headlights illuminating the scene.

"Oh, Lord," Reana Mae hissed. "There's Tracy come home. She'll have a fit!"

Sure enough, Tracy was out of the car before the driver even came to a complete stop. She ran toward the ambulance, as Mother ran down the walkway, trying to intercept her.

Tracy reached the gurney before Mother, shoved the EMT aside, and snatched at the white sheet, tearing it away to reveal Araminta's pale face, her eyes still wide open, staring at the sky.

"No!" Tracy screamed, elbowing away an ambulance attendant.

"No!" She slapped at my mother, who was trying to reach her.

I sat transfixed, watching as she fought off the paramedics, a police officer, my mother, and her date, who had left the car running behind them when he jumped out to follow her.

"No, no, no, no, noooooo!"

Her wails filled the quiet street. Neighbors came out to stand on their porches. The EMTs stood back, wary of Tracy's flying fists and fingernails, watching as Mother tried to subdue her. Even Tracy's boyfriend stood back, well out of reach of those hands. I looked to see what Reana Mae would say, but she was gone. In an instant I saw her running across the yard toward Mother and Tracy.

"No, no, no, no, nooooo!"

Still the wails came, until suddenly they were stilled by a loud slap.

Reana Mae had brushed past Mother and slapped Tracy hard across the face.

Tracy stood still, staring at Reana for an instant. In the silence, I heard Reana say, "Stop it, Tracy! Just stop that wailing right now! Can't you see what you're doing to Aunt Helen?"

Before Tracy could respond or begin screaming again, Mother had wrapped her arms around her shaking body and was walking her firmly back toward the house. Reana stood still for a minute, watching them, then followed them into the house. I ran down-stairs.

"Shall I go for Dr. Statton, Mother?"

Before she could answer, he was at the door, carrying his black bag. Fifteen minutes later, Mother and Reana Mae and I undressed Tracy and put her to bed. The sedative had knocked her out almost immediately. She would sleep for hours. That would give us time to think, to plan, to clean Araminta's room.

Daddy pulled in the next morning, unshaven and rumpled. His face was gray and he smelled of pipe tobacco. After a shower and shave, he and Mother sat down at the kitchen table to make arrangements. He would call the funeral home and the newspaper. Mother would pick out something for Araminta to wear at the viewing and go to the florist. Reana Mae and I were dispatched to the grocery. People would be coming to stay. We'd need more milk, more sodas, more eggs.

None of us spoke about Tracy, or what we would do when she woke up.

28

The Gathered Clan

Aunt Belle arrived that evening, bearing bourbon and a huge smoked ham. I felt better as soon as she walked in the door.

"Lord God Almighty, Bethany Marie! You've gone and blossomed into a beauty!"

Only Aunt Belle would say that.

She caught me in a tight hug, then turned to scoop in Reana Mae.

"And you, child. Look at you! All tall and growed up and pretty as a postcard. I bet the boys go damn-near wild over you."

Reana Mae grinned and kissed Belle's cheek.

"I don't know 'bout that." She laughed. "But I know one that's gone wild for Bethany."

"Well, now, Jimmy told me you got yourself a young man, Bethy. You bring him around one day so I can meet him." She laughed as she reached out to pinch my reddening cheek.

"Oh, I won't bite him or nothin'. I just got to make sure he's good enough for my little girl."

She plopped down onto the sofa.

"He ain't Jewish, is he?"

I shook my head and sank down beside her.

"Well, that's good." She nodded. "I don't think your mama could take another Jew in the family."

Mother walked in just then, carrying tea.

"Well, he's not a Jew anymore, Belle," she said firmly, setting the tea service on the table. "He got baptized before the wedding, you know."

"Once a Jew, always a Jew," Belle replied darkly, dropping sugar cube after sugar cube into her cup. "And he looks like a Jew. I imagine Nancy's babies will come out with hairy backs, that's all." She shook her head and sipped her tea. "Just like monkeys."

Aunt Belle had firm opinions about blacks, Mexicans, Asians, Jews, and Italians—anyone whose skin was a shade too dark or who spoke with an a "foreign" accent.

"Course, we always served them at the drugstores," she said. "Mason was firm about that. Even let 'em sit at the counter to buy a soda pop. We caught us some hell for that, you know. But Mason always said their money spends just like everyone else's, and I reckon he was right."

Mother's face was calm, but her eyes had a pained look.

"I don't suppose Nancy will have any children, Arabella. She says she doesn't want any."

"Oh, well, she'll change her mind. That urge will hit her, sooner or later."

Mother just smiled faintly and shook her head.

"Now, then." Belle set the teacup down and leaned forward. "What do ya'll need me to do? 'Cause I'm here to help. Minta and me, we didn't always get along, but she was my sister. And I'll do whatever you need me to do."

"I think we've got everything planned," Mother said. "Jimmy's made the arrangements with the funeral parlor, and we've bought a plot at the cemetery. And the ladies' auxiliary will cook the funeral meal."

"Well, then, I'll pay for it," Belle said firmly. "No, Helen, don't even think about arguing. I'll pay for the plot. She was my sister, after all. My mama would want me to take care of her now."

Aunt Belle settled into Araminta's room, unpacking her huge suitcase and folding her things neatly into the dresser.

"We'll just take these down to the Goodwill," she said, nodding at Araminta's clothes piled on the bed. "Someone will get some use out of 'em."

Tracy awoke just after Belle arrived, stumbling upstairs to the kitchen and drinking coffee with sugar and milk. She didn't rise to hug Aunt Belle, or even say hello when Belle hugged her. She just sat, staring at her coffee.

The kitchen was full of people coming and going, bringing more food than we could eat in a month. Church ladies came with casseroles and pies and loaf after loaf of banana bread.

"You'd think we was monkeys with all that banana bread," Reana Mae whispered. "Maybe them church folk is related to the apes."

I giggled, but my eyes never left Tracy. I was scared she might explode at any minute. But she simply sat and drank coffee, seemingly oblivious to the commotion around her.

Melinda and Nancy arrived without Neil. Melinda unpacked her suitcase in the attic room. Nancy would not be staying overnight, she said. Neil needed her at home. But they'd be back the next day for the viewing.

At ten o'clock, Tracy finally rose from the table, took a loaf of banana bread, and retreated to her room, closing the door behind her. She'd not spoken a word. Mother's tired eyes followed her anxiously, but she let Tracy go.

The next day we spent at the funeral home, sitting quietly beside the open casket where Araminta Lee Wylie lay in state. Mother had bought a beautiful new dress for her to be buried in, and the folks at the funeral home had made up her face. She didn't look like she was asleep, which is what Cindy had said. She looked like a department store mannequin or something you'd see at Ripley's Believe It or Not Wax Museum.

Mother moved smoothly around the hushed room, hugging people as they came and went, offering tea and comfort. Melinda stayed close by her, refilling the cookie plate and the teapot, smiling at people and saying, yes, she certainly did like college, and won't you have another cookie?

Nancy and Neil arrived mid-morning. Nancy wore a stunning black dress with white lace edging at the neck. A huge diamond pendant hung around her throat, and she spent most of the day waving her diamond ring in people's faces. She looked like she was going to the opera instead of a viewing. Neil trailed along behind her, watching her happily.

Daddy sat quietly beside the casket, firmly turned away so he didn't have to look at Araminta's still body. Tracy sat beside him, one hand in Daddy's, the other reaching out now and then to touch the old lady's face. She hadn't said more than ten words all day, just sat and stared at Araminta's body. It was creepy, Reana Mae said, seeing her stare and stare at Araminta . . . like she might just crawl in there with her.

Late morning, Uncle Ray arrived with Cleda Rae and Mr. Ephraim Turner. Cleda Rae walked straight to the coffin, leaned over to look at Araminta, then leaned farther down to kiss the old lady's cheek.

When she straightened up, she said to my father, "Well, Jimmy, leastways you took her in at the end. You done the right thing in the end. Lord knows, you didn't know her real well, but she was your mama, sure and true, and you done right by her at the end."

She turned to Reana Mae, holding open her scrawny arms and pulling Reana into a tight embrace.

"There's my little girl. How you doin', sugar? They treatin' you right up here? You gettin' along okay? You look like you've growed a foot! And that blond hair. I never will figure on where you got that hair. Lord knows it wasn't from your daddy, 'cause he's got Noah's black hair, sure and true. Him and Caleb both favor their daddy.

"How old are you now, sugar? Why, you must be fifteen! Lord, the time does fly by, don't it? Seems like yesterday you was just a little thing, scrawniest little thing I ever laid eyes on. And now look at you, a fine young woman. Bobby Lee'd be proud to see you, that's for certain. He couldn't come, you know. I told him he ought to be here, seeing as Minta was his aunt. But he's out in Nevada somewheres, drivin' that big ole truck of his. He ain't hardly ever home anymore, leastways that's what Ray says. Always gone somewheres in that truck."

She paused to breathe, her eyes scanning the room.

"Is Caleb coming?" Reana Mae asked quickly, watching Cleda Rae's face.

"Lord, no, honey, I don't expect so."

Reana seemed to wilt at this, but she asked, "Where is he, then?"

"Oh, Lord, sugar, I ain't seen that boy since he left the river. Course, I don't get down to the river much no more. Ephraim here, why he works harder than a Chinaman at that hospital. He don't get much time off for trips and vacations."

She put her arm through her husband's, as if staking a claim. "He works real hard so we can have us a nice apartment and a nice car. You gotta see my car, Belle," she said, turning to Aunt Belle. "I got me a Japanese car! A Toyota, is that right, Ephraim? Is that what it's called? Yes, a Toyota car all the way from Japan. Ephraim says they're the best at makin' cars, those Japs." She nodded earnestly.

"Well, that's fine, Cleda," Aunt Belle said. "I'm glad you got yourself everything you wanted."

"Well, it took long enough, Belle, that's all I got to say. Lord knows, I worked hard enough just to feed my boys all those years, 'cause their daddy surely didn't."

"But, Cleda Rae," Reana Mae interrupted. "Don't you know where Caleb is?"

From the corner of my eye, I could see Mother shaking her head at Cleda, as if she could stop Cleda Rae from saying anything that came into her head.

"Lord, no, sugar. I don't know where's he's got hisself to. He's a growed-up man now, and he don't come home to his mama no more."

She shook her head, then brightened. "Oh, and here's Brother Harley, come to pay his respects to Minta. Ain't that purely grand?"

I turned, startled, to see Reverend Harley standing in the doorway, Ida Louise by his side. Reana Mae's face whitened; she gripped my hand tight.

"Lord," she whispered. "I didn't count on Ida Louise bein' here."

Then a grin broke across her face and she dropped my hand and ran toward the door.

"Hey, Harley!" she called out, so loud that everyone in the room stopped to stare.

At sixteen, Harley Boy was tall, taller even than my father. His red hair hung low across his forehead. His face lit up when he saw Reana Mae.

"Hey, yourself," he said, wrapping his big arms around her and lifting her slightly off the ground.

Ida Louise's eyes narrowed as she watched them. She turned abruptly and walked to where my mother stood chatting with our minister.

I walked slowly toward Harley and Reana, feeling like an intruder. But Reana Mae turned toward me and said, "Here's Bethany, Harley. Ain't she growed up into a beauty?"

Harley grinned and hugged me lightly, but his eyes never left Reana Mae's face.

"Is Ruthann coming, too?" she asked, looking behind him expectantly.

"I reckon they'll get here later," he said. "Hobie had to work on the car before they left. Hey," he added brightly, "you wanna come see my car? I drove up in it myself, followed Grandpa in my own car, so you all could see it. Maybe we can take a drive."

"Sure, Harley." Reana Mae smiled. "Let me and Bethany tell Aunt Helen where we're goin' to, and we'll take us a drive in your car."

I don't think Harley meant for me to go along, but there was nothing he could say.

Mother frowned slightly, asked Ida Louise several questions about Harley's driving skills and his car, then relented. I felt Ida's sharp eyes on us as we walked out of the funeral home.

We admired Harley's blue Duster, then got in, Reana Mae up front with Harley, me in the backseat. Harley pulled out of the parking lot and let the tires squeal as he tore down Washington Street, going well over the speed limit.

"Ain't she a beauty?" he asked proudly.

"Sure enough she is." Reana Mae grinned. "And you drive just like Bobby Lee."

Harley grinned back at her. He didn't even try to hide his pleasure in looking at her, eyeing her curves and her sleek blond hair, watching her mouth as she talked. Reana directed him to drive past the high school, pointing out things along the way, but he never looked at anything she pointed at. He only looked at her.

Finally, Reana said we'd probably better get back to the viewing. She was wound tight, I could tell, and I knew why. Somehow, she expected Caleb to show up. I knew she believed Cleda Rae, when Cleda said she didn't know where Caleb was. Hell, she'd said to me that Cleda Rae didn't know where Caleb was long before now. But she was certain Aunt Belle could tell her Caleb's whereabouts, if only she would. And she was certain Caleb would come for the funeral.

"After all," she'd said the night before, "it ain't like Uncle Jimmy could throw him out of a funeral!"

When we got back to the viewing, Uncle Hobie and Aunt Vera were there with Ruthann and Lottie. Ruthann looked just like she always had—short, thin, and plain. Lottie was a pistol, just like always, Vera said. Never a dull moment with Lottie around. Just now she was clambering up the side of the casket to look inside at Araminta. Belle grabbed her just in time to prevent her tipping the casket right over.

"Hey, Ruthann," I said happily, hugging her. "I'm real glad to see you."

She hugged me back, then stepped toward Reana Mae, her face quietly studying Reana's.

"Hey, Reana Mae," she said finally, extending a hand for Reana to shake. "How are you doing?"

"Well, I'm just fine, Ruthann." Reana grinned at her, ignoring the outstretched hand and pulling Ruthann into a hug. "I'm glad to see you."

Ruthann allowed herself to be hugged, but I noticed she kept her arms at her sides.

The four of us sat at a table, eating banana bread and drinking sodas while Harley talked about everything and everyone on the river. He never mentioned Caleb once, but I wasn't surprised at that.

Finally, Reana Mae couldn't take it anymore. She leaned forward, put her hand over his, looked straight into his face, and asked, "Where's Caleb, Harley? Do you know where he is?"

Harley pulled away from her, his cheeks reddening just like they had when he was younger.

"No, I don't, Reana Mae. And you shouldn't even ask me that."

A heavy silence hung in the air, till I asked too loudly, "What grade's Lottie in now?"

Ruthann talked then about Lottie's adventures in school. Harley sat quietly watching Reana Mae with the same hurt, hopeful, adoring look he always had around her.

Ruthann's and Harley's families were both staying at the Best Western hotel near the cemetery. At suppertime, Reana Mae and I rode with them in Harley's car to the hotel, where we sat by the little outdoor pool and ate corn chips. It felt strange and familiar at the same time, watching Harley gaze at Reana Mae and Ruthann stare at Harley. We could have been on the raft in the river instead of sitting by a pool in Indianapolis.

Finally, Harley drove Reana Mae and me back to our house, stopping in shortly to shake my daddy's hand.

Later, when we were in bed, I asked Reana, "Did it feel strange to see Harley?"

"Naw." She smiled. "He's just like always."

"Well, he still loves you. That's pretty plain," I said.

"Poor Harley Boy." She nodded. "Why don't he just love Ruthann instead?"

But he didn't, not even then, and we all knew it.

❧ 29 ❧

A Funeral and First Love

Grandmother's funeral day dawned overcast but warm. We gathered in the church, where the casket sat in front of the altar, and the organist played softly mournful music. We waited in line to file past the open casket, each of us holding a white rose to put inside for Araminta to be buried with. It seemed like a waste of perfectly good roses to me, but it was important to Daddy.

I stood near the end of the line, holding my rose and whispering to Ruthann, when Brian walked into the church, carrying a small bouquet. After he gave me a quick kiss, I introduced him to Ruthann. Then he walked straight over to my father, held out his hand, and said quietly, "I'm sorry for your loss, sir." He turned to Mother and handed her the bouquet.

Ruthann stared wide-eyed at him, then looked to me and said, "My, he's a real gentleman, ain't he? Just like in a book or something."

Then she blushed as he came to stand with us in line, his hand holding mine tightly.

Ahead of us, Reana Mae leaned over to kiss Araminta's cheek. I was surprised to see her do that, because she hadn't even met Araminta till she moved to Indiana, but Reana was funny about family. She sounded just like Mother when she said that family was everything. It seemed odd to me, especially when you considered her own parents. Harley put his rose just next to hers in the casket, then followed her to a pew. Ruthann watched them sadly, holding her own rose in one hand and a handkerchief in the other.

The line moved along slowly. There must have been sixty people, because a lot of friends from church came to support Mother and Daddy. Then, we stopped moving entirely. I stepped to the side to see what the holdup could be, and there was Tracy, standing absolutely still in front of the casket, tears streaming down her face onto Araminta's body. She clutched her rose and leaned down to kiss our grandmother's face again and again. People began murmuring uncomfortably, and still she stood crying, unwilling to lay down her rose and move on.

Finally, Aunt Belle stepped out of line, walked toward her, took her firmly by the shoulders, and said in a low voice, "Come on now, honey. It's time to let other folks come up."

Tracy turned and pulled away from Belle sharply, bumping against the casket as she did so.

"Let go of me," she hissed so loudly I'm sure they heard her all the way at the back of the church. "Don't you touch me!"

Belle took a step back, staring into Tracy's spiteful eyes.

"What's got into you, child?" she asked, looking around for my parents. Mother was walking quickly up the center aisle toward them.

"You shouldn't even be here!" Tracy's voice rose. "She hated you! You took her own child away from her, her own son. You stole him away just like Reana Mae stole Mother. You shouldn't be here! She hated you!"

She was screaming now, shaking from head to foot. Mother grabbed for her, but she took another step back, knocking hard against the casket. It teetered a moment, then tipped, falling sideways off its pedestal, the lid swinging open and poor Araminta's tiny body half flopping onto the floor.

"Tracy Janelle Wylie!" Daddy's voice thundered in the shocked silence. "What the hell have you done?"

Tracy stared down at Araminta's face, now resting on the dark red carpet of the church. Then she turned and ran straight down the aisle, into the entryway, and out the front door of the church.

Several men stepped forward to right the casket. Mother and Aunt Belle straightened Araminta's dress and smoothed her white hair, the pastor said some soothing words, and Brian put his arm around me and pulled me close. Just behind us, poor Neil Berkson was staring aghast at the proceedings. I didn't know what Jewish funerals were like, but I was pretty certain they didn't include casket tipping.

Then the whispering died down, and we began filing past again. As I dropped my rose into the casket, I saw my father sitting slumped in the front pew, his shoulders shaking. Mother sat beside him, her cheeks a vivid crimson, her eyes staring straight ahead, her hand stroking his back.

"I never saw such a sight in all my life." Ruthann's eyes were wide and frightened.

We were sitting in the church banquet hall over plates of fried chicken, macaroni salad, and green beans.

"She's got the devil in her, for sure," Harley said grimly. "She's got that bad blood."

Ruthann nodded beside him, watching his face.

I pushed the food around my plate, staring unhappily at the floor.

"Lord knows how poor Helen must feel, her making such a scene like that," Harley continued.

I glanced at Mother. She sat next to Daddy, her back straight, her face composed. I knew she must be dying inside. There was no way to excuse or explain Tracy's actions. Everyone in the church had seen it. Everyone would talk about it. There was no hiding that something was seriously wrong.

Reana Mae sat quietly, pushing green beans around her plate with a fork. She hadn't said a word since we'd sat down. Just picked at her food and scanned the room continually, looking for Caleb, I guess.

Suddenly, she dropped her fork, leaned across the table toward Harley, and said, "Take me ridin' in your car, Harley."

He looked at her in startled silence for a minute, then pushed his chair back and stood. "Okay," he said, his eyes never leaving her face. "Let's go."

Ruthann watched them walk away, her eyes sparkling with tears. I held her hand and said with as much confidence as I could muster, "Probably she wants to talk about Caleb."

We all sat uncomfortably for a minute. Then Brian, bless his heart, moved his chair closer to Ruthann's and said, "I like the necklace you're wearing, Ruthann. Did your boyfriend give you that?"

Her cheeks reddened slightly as she shook her head no. But she tore her eyes from the door Harley had just opened for Reana Mae. Brian asked her all about the river and her family, just as if he were interviewing her for a story in the newspaper. And I could only watch him and love him with all my heart.

Brian walked with me back to the house after the funeral supper, holding my hand and telling me how interesting my family was.

"They're very . . . colorful," he said.

"You mean nuts," I mumbled, not looking up at him.

"No, Bethany, that's not what I meant. They're great."

I stared at him in surprise.

"Well, okay, maybe not all of them." He smiled then. "Maybe Tracy's not great. But your Aunt Belle is great. And I really liked Ruthann and Harley."

"Why?" I truly did not understand how he could. Brian was so smart. His manners were perfect. He seemed miles and years ahead of my river cousins.

"God, Bethany, don't you know why? Look at my family. They're so damned polite, so quiet and cold and . . . *polite*. But yours—your family is a real family. Sure, they fight sometimes, but they love each other. You can see it, just watching them. And they're funny and they have great stories. I really envy you."

My astonishment was complete.

I stood on my tiptoes and kissed him full on the mouth, right there on the street.

"I love you, Brian Hutson."

It was out of my mouth before I could swallow it.

"I love you, too, Bethany."

The sadness of the day and the shame of my sister and all my worries over Mother and Daddy and Tracy and Reana Mae and Harley Boy and Ruthann slipped right off my shoulders. I thought I might just float straight away to Heaven.

30

The Power and the Fury

I'd been home more than an hour before Harley brought Reana Mae back. She came straight upstairs and flopped down on the bed, staring up at the sloping ceiling. Her hair was a tumbled mess, her lipstick smudged, her blouse buttoned unevenly. Her pantyhose were nowhere to be seen.

"Where have you been?"

"I gave old Harley Boy a send-off he won't never forget."

She smiled, her cheeks flushed. "I guess today's the day he got to be a man."

I stared at her.

"You didn't . . ."

"Hell, yes, I did! We drove on down to the parking lot behind the high school and did it right there in his car."

"God, Reana! What if someone saw you?"

"Well, if they did, they didn't say nothin'. Besides." She laughed as she rolled onto her stomach. "I don't think they could see anything through them windows. We steamed 'em up real good."

"But why?" I asked. "You don't love Harley. You never did. Why did you let him . . . why did you do it?"

" 'Cause I wanted to, Bethany. I just flat-out wanted to. I wanted to fuck somebody, and Harley, well, you know he always wanted me. So we just did it."

She rose and began fumbling with the buttons on her blouse.

"Lord, they're all done up wrong, ain't they? Good thing Aunt Helen wasn't in the parlor."

I stared at her. What had possessed her to . . . do it with Harley Boy?

"God, Bethany, it felt good! And Harley, he liked it just fine, I can promise you that. Liked it so much, he did it twice. That's something."

She removed her blouse and I saw small bruises across her chest. She touched one with her fingertips and smiled. "He got goin' on me, that's for sure. I'da never figured him for a biter."

I thought back to the day Harley had found Reana Mae's diary, all those years ago, and read about Caleb biting her breasts.

"Did you use a condom?"

"Naw, we didn't have any. But it's okay," she said, pulling off her skirt. "I just got off my period, so I won't get pregnant or nothin'."

"Are you gonna marry him?"

She stared at me for a second, then began laughing, laughing so hard she had to sit down on the bed.

"Lord, Bethany, of course I ain't gonna marry him! Me, marry ole Harley Boy? That's a hoot!"

"Then why'd you do it?" I couldn't understand her at all.

"I told you, 'cause I wanted to. I wanted someone to fuck me. That's all."

"But . . ."

She sighed patiently and said more gently, "Okay, Bethy, it's like this. All these years, I been waitin'. Waitin' on Caleb to come. Waitin' on him to take me away, like he said he would. And when old Araminta moved up here, I thought, well, now, when she dies he'll have to come. I knew he'd come, 'cause then he wouldn't have to worry about Uncle Jimmy chasin' him off, you see?

"But he didn't come." Her voice grew softer. "He didn't come even when he could've. So I reckon he ain't never comin', after all."

She sat in silence for a minute, then stood and began pacing the room. "He ain't never comin'. He ain't comin' to get me, 'cause he don't love me. Not like he said he did. If he loved me, he'd of come a long time back—or at least today. 'Cause you know Belle told him about Araminta. Belle knows where he is, and I know she told him."

She paced some more before saying loudly, "Course he didn't come! Why, he's probably got hisself another girl by now. And he's fuckin' her instead of me. I bet he don't even think about me at all."

She stopped and looked at me.

"So why shouldn't I do it with Harley?" she demanded. "Caleb's out doin' it with someone else, why shouldn't I do it? And God knows"—she sighed as she flopped back down onto her bed—"Harley always wanted me. Everyone knew it. So I let him."

She slipped into a nightgown and pulled the sheet up over herself, then reached to turn out the light.

"And it did feel good." She sighed. "It felt real good."

After Reana Mae fell asleep, I put on my robe and went downstairs to the kitchen. I needed to think, and I needed to think in the light. Aunt Belle and Mother were drinking tea, though I was certain Belle's had been liberally laced with bourbon.

"Where's Daddy?"

"He's out walking," Mother said, pouring tea into a cup for me. "He needs to think."

"What about Tracy?"

"She's downstairs. I hope she's sleeping."

"Mother, what are we going to do about Tracy?"

I asked it before I could even think, then waited, expecting to be told not to worry, to let the grown-ups handle it, to go back to bed.

Instead, Mother sat down across from me, picked up her teacup, looked straight at me, and said quietly, "I don't know, honey. But we'll have to do something."

Aunt Belle nodded sagely beside her, her hand over Mother's.

"She needs a doctor, sure enough. Something's not right there."

Mother said nothing, but she didn't argue with Belle.

"You all take her to see one of them psychiatrists and see what they say," Belle said firmly. "I'll pay for it, you know, 'cause I hear them psychiatrists are expensive. But you all take her on to see one, and I'll pay for it."

Mother leaned into Aunt Belle's ample arm and said gratefully, "I believe that's what we'll have to do, Arabella. I believe even Jimmy knows that now."

I took my tea out to the back porch and sat on the glider. Skipper jumped up and laid his head in my lap so I could scratch his soft ears. Old Bo settled down on my feet, keeping them warm in the cool spring air. I sat for a long time, wondering what it was that made Tracy so crazy. And why Reana Mae would have sex with Harley in a car on a Sunday afternoon. And why God would let so many bad things happen to my family. Reana Mae always brought up the Jews when she was talking about God, how He'd let them die in the Holocaust. But that seemed awfully far away. What I couldn't understand was how He could let so many bad things happen to my Mother. Because she was more faithful than anyone else in the world.

I knew I should pray. I should pray for Reana Mae and for Tracy and for Harley and Ruthann, and especially for Mother. But I didn't. All those years Mother had prayed and prayed and prayed for her family—what good had it done?

I scratched Skipper's ears and refused to pray. Instead, I thought about Brian, his kiss, the way he liked my crazy family. He even loved me—he'd told me so himself.

God, if Brian knew everything about my family—about how bad Tracy really was, what Reana had done with Harley, how my grandfather was a mean drunk—he surely would not think they were wonderful. He'd probably run for the hills and never even look back.

The next day after school, Mother and Daddy took Tracy into their room and talked with the door closed for more than an hour. Daddy had taken the day off work just for this conversation.

Melinda had gone back to Bloomington by then, hugging Mother tightly when she left and whispering that she'd only be an hour away and Mother should call if they needed her.

Reana Mae and I took turns trying to listen outside Mother's bedroom door until Aunt Belle saw us and made us go outside. We sat on the glider, drinking iced tea and speculating about what might be happening inside.

"I guess Belle's right," Reana Mae said. "Tracy needs to see one of them doctors."

"What can the doctors do about it?" I wondered.

"Give her drugs, I expect," Reana Mae said knowingly. "Or do some kind of surgery on her head, like they did to that actress that was so crazy."

"Do you think they'll lock her up somewhere?" I thought about Ken Kesey and *One Flew Over the Cuckoo's Nest* again.

"Maybe," she said. "I reckon even Uncle Jimmy might go for that now."

Aunt Belle came out to join us, her tumbler filled with bourbon and Coke.

"You all just stop worryin' over it," she said. "Helen and Jimmy will figure it out. And I'll pay for it, whatever it is, I'll pay for it. So that's just fine."

We went inside to start supper. I made Stroganoff again, thinking grimly about the day Araminta had arrived and didn't want to eat it.

Aunt Belle laughed when I told her about it.

"Ain't that just like Minta?" she said. "She never liked to try nothin' new. Not like me and Arathena. Even Arathena liked to try different foods. One time, me and her went to a Chinese restaurant in Louisville, and I talked her into ordering that kung pao chicken. Lord God Almighty, you should've seen Thena's eyes water when she bit down on one of them peppers. She like to died!"

Mother and Daddy sat down for dinner quietly, but Tracy didn't join us. She was down in her room, Led Zeppelin blaring on the stereo.

Aunt Belle left on Wednesday. Reana Mae and I both went to the airport with Daddy, each of us carrying one of her big suitcases.

"Who's picking you up in Charleston?" Reana asked.

"Well, Brother Harley volunteered to come get me," Belle said. "I reckon any excuse is a good excuse to get away from Ida Louise." She laughed. "Especially after their trip up here in the car.

Even Harley Boy found a way out of that, drivin' his own car up. Ain't that something? Sixteen, and he's got hisself a car. That boy's gonna go far. You watch and see if he don't. He'll be a big man someday."

She glanced sideways at Reana Mae and smiled. "The girl that lands him will have herself a mighty fine husband."

Reana didn't even blush. She just said, "Well, that's what poor ole Ruthann is bankin' on."

Aunt Belle just shook her head and smiled. She knew as well as anyone else how Harley felt about Reana Mae. Of course, she couldn't know how much more he might feel today than he had just last week.

I wondered if he would write to her more often now, or maybe even call. I knew Ida Louise wouldn't let him come visit, though. She would keep her boy as far away from Reana Mae Colvin as she possibly could. Lord, she would rightly die if she knew they'd had sex in his car, and on a funeral day.

Reana Mae laughed as she walked beside Aunt Belle, her hips swaying. She had tied her hair back with a black ribbon, which showed off her long neck. I saw several men turn to watch her as we walked through the terminal. She looked like a sleek cat, ready to yowl at the moon. Every last vestige of little girl seemed gone. She was young, sexy, and very pretty, and she knew it. It showed in the way she walked and laughed and shook her hair, in the way she touched men on the arm just lightly when she talked to them, in the way she stared them straight in the eye, then let her eyes drop coyly.

Reana Mae Colvin had learned from her mama what Jolene learned from EmmaJane—she could use her looks, her smiles, and her body to get what she wanted from men. She had power.

✌ 31 ✌

Innocence Lost

Three weeks later, Mother and Daddy took Tracy to meet with a psychiatrist.

"He's good with teenagers," I heard Dr. Statton tell Daddy. "Has two daughters of his own, knows what's normal and what's not, and has the patience of Job himself. He'll know what to do for Tracy."

Tracy, of course, was furious about it. She'd spent the last several days screaming, crying, swearing at our parents, throwing dishes and one time a chair. Dr. Statton had been over several times to give her "a little something" to calm her down. She had been grounded since the funeral, although one day while Mother was at the grocery, she did slip out of the house and go to Lynette's. Daddy had to force her to come back home. Poor Mother looked so tired, I thought she might just die.

In the end, of course, Tracy had no choice but to go with them. But I knew she'd make it hell on them—and on the psychiatrist, too—as much as she possibly could.

Reana Mae and I sat on the front porch waiting for them to come home. Reana smoked a cigarette while we waited. I kept a nervous lookout for the car, terrified Mother would see her smoking. Reana Mae seemed not at all concerned.

"Everyone smokes, Bethany," she said, waving her Marlboro in my face. "Even Uncle Jimmy smokes sometimes."

"But Mother says . . ."

"Oh, Mother says . . . that's all you worry about, Bethany. Someday you got to stop worryin' so much and do some livin'. You got to loosen up—cut loose and have you some fun."

I simply shook my head. I had fun. I had fun at school and at the newspaper. I had fun with the church youth group and working on the school plays. And I had fun being with Brian. I just didn't smoke, or skip school, or flirt with boys the way Reana Mae did.

And Reana Mae had been doing a whole lot of flirting since the funeral. I saw her often at school, her arm draped across some boy or another, her hand resting on a thigh during lunch, leaned back against her locker pushing her breasts out. She seemed determined to flirt with every boy she met, and even with the teachers.

Just that morning, I'd seen her perched on Mr. McLean's desk, her short skirt shoved well up her thigh, resting her hand lightly on his arm as she bent down to watch him correct her math. Mr. McLean's face had been as purple as a Bermuda onion, but he'd smiled appreciatively at Reana Mae when she bent toward him, her breasts fairly bursting against her tight blouse. And Mr. McLean must have been at least forty.

Cindy told me she'd seen Reana Mae act that way with the gym teacher, too. We talked about it for hours, Cindy and I, wondering what to do. Should we try to talk to Reana about it? Should we tell Mother? Both of us knew Reana Mae could not go on like that for very long without getting a very bad reputation . . . and maybe worse. Cindy's cousin had been raped the year before while she was on a date. The boy who did it said she wanted it or she wouldn't have dressed the way she did. And everyone at school had nodded and agreed. She'd asked for it, after all. The girl had left school, and now she took night classes.

I didn't want that to happen to Reana Mae, but I didn't know how to talk to her about it. Since the funeral, I didn't know how to talk to her about a lot of things. She was sharper somehow, especially the way she talked. Reana had always been able to hold her own in a fight, but she'd never been cruel. But last week I'd seen

270 • *Sherri Wood Emmons*

her reduce Carrie Coats to tears, taunting her about her old clothes.

"Why did you do that?" I asked later.

"Oh, hell," she said, sounding bored. "I just felt like it. Carrie's such a whiny brat, and she was tap-dancin' on my last nerve today."

She'd sat quietly for a few minutes, then said, "I guess it was purely mean, though. I'll tell her I'm sorry tomorrow."

She did apologize to Carrie, but her tongue and her behavior both stayed sharp, even to me. She'd snapped at me the night before because I'd been on the phone with Brian and she wanted to make a call.

"I don't know what you got to talk about with him every night," she said. "It's not like you're lovers, after all."

I watched her smoke her cigarette and said, without thinking, "You look like your mama when you smoke."

She stood abruptly, ground out the cigarette under her heel, and said, "Don't you never say that again, Bethany Marie. I ain't nothing like my mama."

She turned and walked into the house.

When Daddy finally pulled the station wagon into the driveway, I rose, waiting to see what Tracy would be like. Had the doctor given her a shot? Did he make her take medicine, or maybe get a shock like Jack Nicholson in *One Flew Over the Cuckoo's Nest*?

She got out of the backseat, smoothed her skirt, and walked past me into the house without a word.

"Is she okay?" I asked Mother.

"She'll be fine. Don't you worry." Mother stopped to kiss my cheek. "The doctor gave her some pills to calm her nerves. She should be better now."

I searched Mother's face. She seemed calmer herself. Her eyes had lost the strained, unhappy look they'd had since the funeral.

Daddy grinned as he stepped onto the porch.

"Just her nerves," he said as he opened the door. "She'll be right as rain soon."

Tracy *was* calmer after that. She took a pill every morning at breakfast and every night at dinner, making a grand show of it. She had to have milk to take them, and the milk had to be right out of the fridge. Then she'd put a pill carefully on her tongue, take a big drink of milk, and throw her head back to swallow. Afterward, she always said, "I feel better already."

Valium made her calmer, but it did not make her any nicer. Tracy was still Tracy, after all. Still, she didn't scream or throw things or swear at my parents. She was quiet and subdued.

But she still hated me. And she still hated Reana Mae. And she still let us know about it, every chance she got.

One Tuesday afternoon, a month or so after Araminta's funeral, Tracy sauntered into the living room, where Reana and I were watching *General Hospital.*

Standing directly in front of the television, she flipped the channel.

"Hey," Reana snapped. "We were watching that."

Tracy turned toward her and smiled.

"Getting tips?" she smirked. "Like you need any help acting like a whore."

"Shut up, Tracy," I said.

"Why?" She laughed. "I'm just telling the truth. She acts like a whore at school. She's been a whore since she was eleven. Hell, she acted like a whore with her own uncle!"

Reana Mae rose, her fists clenched. But Tracy kept on.

"You stupid little bitch," she said. "Did you think he loved you? I guess you know better now. He never cared about you at all. You were just easy. You still are. You're just an easy whore!"

Reana shoved Tracy backward, and she stumbled against the television console.

"You shut your trap, Tracy!"

But Tracy just laughed and walked out of the room, leaving Reana Mae shaking with anger.

"Someday she's gonna pay for being so damned mean," Reana hissed before storming out of the house.

I remembered the time Reana had shoved Tracy against the wall and choked her. I wondered again whether I should talk to Mother about it. I worried at how much hatred there was between Reana and Tracy. But, I told myself, next year Tracy would be away at college. Then, things would be calmer for Reana Mae.

Tracy was finishing her senior year in high school. She was dating Paul again, the boy she'd brought home for dinner all those years ago. He was in college now at Butler University, and he drove a small black two-door Honda Civic. He knew Tracy took Valium, and he seemed to like her better now that she was more predictable. Paul had made a good impression on my parents. They seemed relieved that Tracy was dating him again, after some of the other boys she'd brought home.

Paul was unfailingly polite, like Brian, but less formal. Brian had a funny, old-fashioned way about him that I loved but Reana made fun of. Paul was more casual. And even though he was Tracy's boyfriend, Reana Mae liked to talk with him, joke around, and even flirt when Tracy was out of the room.

I came down the stairs one day to find Reana Mae perched on the sofa arm, right next to Paul, leaning across him so that her breasts lightly brushed his face, pretending to look for the *TV Guide*, which was on the table right behind her. It made me catch my breath, seeing her that way, and I immediately looked around for Tracy. I was certain that, even on Valium, Tracy would tear Reana Mae's hair right out of her head if she saw Reana draped over Paul like that.

I heard Tracy's voice in the kitchen, so I walked into the living room and grabbed Reana's arm, pulling her away from Paul and off the couch.

"What's that for?" Reana asked me crossly.

"I need to show you something . . . in Mother's room," I said, pulling her down the hallway.

"What the hell is wrong with you?" she demanded as soon as I'd shut the door behind us.

"What's wrong with *you*?" I hissed back. "You can't act that way with Paul. You know you can't."

"And why the hell not?"

"Because he's Tracy's boyfriend," I said as calmly as I could. "He's Tracy's boyfriend, and she'll have a fit if she sees you flirting with him like that."

"I hope she does." Reana Mae smiled smugly. "I hope she sees *him* flirting with *me*, 'cause he does, you know. He flirts right back."

"Reana Mae, you can't do that. It's trouble, that's all. Tracy would have a fit, and Mother would get upset, and . . . and you look like a tramp when you do things like that."

She glared at me for a minute as if she might slap me, then turned away and said flatly, "You don't know nothing about it, Bethany. You're just a little girl. You don't know nothing about it at all."

With that, she walked back into the living room. I heard her call out after Tracy and Paul, "Bye, ya'll. You have fun now, you hear?"

I told Cindy about it all, and then I told Brian. He listened, thought about it a while, and then told me to stay out of it.

"It's between Reana Mae and Tracy," he said. "One of them is going to end up getting hurt. And I don't want you to get hurt, too."

But I couldn't ignore what was going on. Reana Mae was my cousin, my best friend, and I felt like she was drifting away from me and from Mother. Like she was drifting out to sea, and I couldn't catch up with her or make her come back. She'd lost hope in Caleb, and it seemed to drain something out of her—her last shred of innocence or faith in anything good, even her faith in me. It cut me to the quick when she said I didn't understand her. I was the only one who had ever understood her. I was the only one who always stood by her. And now, she seemed not to need me or want me at all.

I tried to take Brian's advice. He was smart, after all, and he knew a lot about people. That's what made him such a good reporter. But it was hard watching Reana Mae drift away. Her friends had never really been mine, but now she was hanging out with a different crowd. They smoked outside the school doors and often came to class glassy-eyed and smelling of pot. The girls had a rough look about them, and the boys looked mostly dirty.

Reana Mae laughed when I told her I didn't think it was a good crowd. She told me to take care of myself and let her take care of herself.

She began dating a dark-haired boy named Doug who wore greasy jeans and black T-shirts every day of the week. He drove a motorcycle, too. Not as big as Bobby Lee's old bike, but a motorcycle nonetheless. Mother told Reana Mae she absolutely was not allowed to ride on Doug's bike, but of course Reana did, whenever Mother wasn't there.

I saw them sometimes leaving the school parking lot, the one where Reana and Harley had parked the day of the funeral. Doug leaned forward on the bike, driving fast, and Reana Mae leaned against him, her hands resting in his lap. They looked for all the world like Bobby Lee and Jolene.

I hated seeing them that way.

∽ 32 ∾

An Oncoming Train

At the end of May, Mother took Tracy to buy a dress for the prom. Brian had asked me, as well, but I said I would wear my ruby red gown again. I'd only ever worn it once, and then for just a little while. And Brian said I looked so beautiful in it, he'd love it if I wore that gown again.

Reana Mae loaned me her new black high heels to wear with the gown. She was not going to the prom. Doug was a junior, so he could have asked her, but he didn't want to go, and she didn't seem to mind.

Tracy came home with a stunning white gown with a strap over just one shoulder, like an ancient Roman goddess. She looked ethereal in it, heavenly, really. And while she could not bring herself to accept my compliment, or to compliment me on my own dress, at least she didn't say anything mean like she had the previous fall.

She told Paul he had to rent a white tuxedo and bring her white roses, and she bought a small tiara to wear in her hair. She had planned everything, down to which handbag she would carry and where they would eat.

Mother and Daddy smiled, watching her try on her new finery. Surely, the Valium was working.

They were so relieved over Tracy's transformation that they seemed not to notice Reana Mae's. Of course, Mother fretted over Reana's new boyfriend and actually yelled at her about the cigarettes. But mostly my parents seemed happy . . . happier than I'd seen them in a long time. Tracy was well.

A week before the prom, I spent a Tuesday evening at the high school, working on a story for the paper. Brian was there, working away on his weekly editorial, and Linda Murray was typing on the electric typewriter, swearing now and then at a typo she'd made. At eight, we decided to call it a night. Brian would drive me home, and maybe we'd spend some time kissing in the driveway. Mother and Daddy were gone for the evening, out with friends from Daddy's office.

As we walked toward the parking lot, I saw Tracy leaving the school. She was on the prom committee and had been working on decorations. Before I could stop him, Brian had called out to her, offering her a ride home. So much for kissing in the driveway, I thought unhappily. Still, that's how Brian was. He was always polite.

Tracy climbed into the backseat of the car and we drove straight home. She spoke briefly but relatively nicely to Brian and ignored me completely. Valium worked, but it didn't work miracles.

As we pulled into the driveway, where a Honda was parked, Tracy said, "Why, Paul's here!"

She was surprised, I could tell. And in an instant, my stomach lurched.

"Tracy, wait," I called to her. "Can you help me with these papers?"

But she was walking swiftly toward the house and never even paused.

Brian got out of the car and stood uncertainly. I ran up the walkway behind Tracy. I wanted to get to the door before her, to keep her from going inside. I knew—I don't know how or why—but I knew what she would see.

Tracy reached the door just ahead of me and pushed it open. Standing just behind her, I saw them as soon as she did. Paul was reclined on the couch, wearing only his unbuttoned shirt. Reana

Mae was completely naked, straddling him, her head thrown back, her eyes closed.

When he saw Tracy standing in the doorway, Paul froze, his eyes locked on hers. Then he tried to get up, but Reana sat firmly on top of him, grinding her groin into his. She didn't open her eyes, didn't stop grinding.

"Reana Mae!"

It came out in a strangled cry as I pushed past Tracy and grabbed at my cousin's arm. "Stop it! Stop it, Reana! Get off!"

I pulled hard at her arm and she opened her eyes, looking past me at Tracy. Then she smiled.

I stopped pulling at her, stunned by the smile on her face. It hit me then, hard, that she knew exactly what she'd done. She'd meant for Tracy to find them that way. She'd done it on purpose.

I backed away from her, staring at that smile, feeling sick. Behind me, Tracy made a single, small sound like a kitten mewing for its mama. When I turned toward her, she was already out the door, running down the porch steps and across the yard.

"Tracy, wait!" I ran after her into the yard, where Brian still stood by the car. She ran down the sidewalk and I pounded along behind her. I heard Brian running behind me, catching up and then passing me. He ran ahead, following Tracy, till he caught her arm just before the railroad tracks.

She swung around and began beating at him, slapping his face, his arms, his chest. But he held tight on to her until I caught up to them, panting and crying.

"Tracy, wait," I said, mimicking Mother's soothing tone. "Just wait a minute and calm down. Don't run off, please don't, Tracy. You'll get hurt. You need to sit down, just sit down here with me and Brian. Please, Tracy, please sit down."

Brian had pulled her toward him so he could wrap his arms around her, and she finally stopped hitting him and collapsed into his chest, heaving great sobs and clutching at his arms. He held her tight, stroking her hair and making shushing noises while he looked over her head at me, his eyes wide.

Then we saw Paul jogging toward us, his unbuttoned shirt flapping in the wind. At least he'd put his pants on.

I looked frantically from him to Brian and tried to wave him off. Tracy plainly did not need to see him, not now. But he kept coming.

"Tracy?" His voice was soft. "Tracy, honey, I'm so sorry. I'm so sorry."

She pulled back from Brian then, turning to stare at Paul as he stopped before her. Brian held her arms firmly, so she couldn't run away again.

"Please, honey, please let me talk to you. It was a mistake. I don't even know how it happened. I'm so sorry. I love you, Tracy. You know that, don't you? You know I love you."

With a sudden twist, Tracy lurched away from Brian, running toward Paul and screaming. She scratched at his face, leaving long red welts, then slapped him again and again until Brian caught hold of her arm. Then she wrenched her arm loose from Brian's grip and ran headlong toward the railroad tracks, toward the flashing red lights and the clanging bells and the whistle of a locomotive.

"Tracy, no!" I could hear myself screaming it over and over again. "No, Tracy, stop!"

Brian and Paul both ran after her, but I stood frozen to the sidewalk, watching my sister run toward the oncoming train.

"No, no, no, no!" I screamed, just as Tracy had done the night our grandmother died.

Brian tried to grab her arm as she reached the tracks, but she twisted away from him and threw herself onto the rails. The last thing I saw before the train hit her were her hazel eyes, staring up at Paul, wide and clear and beautiful. Then she was gone, and the huge engine rushed by, pulling car after car over her while Paul dropped to his knees by the tracks, and Brian sank to the ground, sobbing.

Daddy's car screeched into the driveway. The street was filled with flashing lights, policemen, a fire engine, and neighbors.

I ran down the porch steps toward him, toward Mother, who had just stepped out of the car, her eyes wide.

"What the hell is going on?" Daddy bellowed.

I couldn't even answer him. I ran straight to Mother and threw my arms around her. I wanted to protect her, to shield her from knowing what had happened.

A police officer carrying a small notebook stepped forward and said solemnly, "I'm afraid there's been an accident, Mr. Wylie."

Daddy stared at him for an instant, then asked, "What kind of accident?"

"I'm very sorry, sir, but your daughter was hit by a train."

"A train?" Daddy repeated it, uncomprehendingly. "What kind of train?"

"A freight train, sir. She ran onto the railroad tracks just in front of the train, and . . . and she's dead, sir. I'm very sorry."

The policeman looked kindly at my father, who still stared at him as if he didn't understand.

Mother stood absolutely still in my arms. She was staring at the policeman, too.

"Tracy?" she whispered.

"Yes, ma'am," the officer agreed. "Your daughter Tracy."

"Where is she?" Mother looked around the yard, as if she might spot Tracy.

"The ambulance took her, ma'am. She's at the hospital."

"Well, then, we've got to get to the hospital," Daddy said firmly. "We've got to see her. We've got to be there when she wakes up."

The officer shook his head sadly. "She's not going to wake up, Mr. Wylie. She was dead before the ambulance arrived."

"Sir?" Brian stood behind me, his voice shaking but sure.

"We tried to stop her," he said to my father. "Paul and Bethany and I all tried to stop her before she got to the tracks."

"Why?" Daddy asked, looking straight at me. "Why would she be on the tracks?"

"She and Paul had an argument," Brian said softly. "Bethany and I got home and they were arguing, and then Tracy just started running . . . toward the tracks. And when she got there, she didn't stop. I guess she thought she could beat the train. But she fell . . ."

At this, Mother sank to the ground. I tried to hold her up, but she slipped from my arms and fell in a huddle on the grass.

Daddy dropped to his knees beside her, and a police officer helped him carry her into the house.

On the porch, Paul sat shivering and crying. He'd thrown up twice and he looked like hell. He followed us into the house and watched in silence as Daddy and the policeman laid Mother on the couch. Her eyes were open and tears slid down her cheeks, but she didn't say a word. She looked as though she could be dead herself, except I could see her chest rising and falling.

Daddy stared from me to Brian to Paul, then back to Mother. Finally, he said, "Go get your mother a glass of water, Bethy."

Brian went with me to the kitchen, poured a glass of water, and took it back to Mother himself. I simply followed behind him. Daddy had stepped outside with the policeman.

I sat down on the couch by Mother and stroked her hair, the way she often stroked mine. She never looked at me. She just stared up at the ceiling and let the tears stream unchecked down her cheek.

After a little while, Daddy came back into the house. He looked as if he'd seen the Armageddon. His shoulders slumped, his eyes were puffed red, and he reeked of tobacco.

"I expect you boys better get yourselves on home," he said.

"I'm so sorry, sir," Paul whispered. "I'm so sorry I hurt her. I tried to stop her. . . ."

"I know you did, son. I heard the police report. It wasn't your fault." He sighed and ran his hand across his swollen eyes. "Hell, it wasn't anyone's fault, 'cept maybe mine."

He dropped into the recliner and stared sadly at Mother.

"Helen tried to tell me, all those years. But I wouldn't believe her. I kept saying she'd get better."

Paul watched him anxiously, then backed quietly out the door. I couldn't imagine how he must feel.

Brian stayed a while longer, helping me make a pot of tea, fetching a blanket to drape over Mother on the couch, asking my father again and again if there was anything he could do.

Finally, Daddy told him he'd done more than enough—more than anyone had a right to expect. And of course, Daddy was right even more than he knew.

It was Brian who'd lifted Tracy's mangled body from the railroad tracks and run back to the house with her—past Reana Mae, who was standing on the sidewalk, her fist shoved against her mouth, shaking uncontrollably, just the way Tracy had all those years ago when she'd watched Jolene beat Reana Mae with a belt.

It was Brian who'd called the police and the ambulance. Brian who'd run across the street for Dr. Statton, in case anything could be done to save Tracy.

Brian, covered in Tracy's blood, had talked to the police and the ambulance driver and the firemen. And he'd told them each the same story. He and I had just come home from school, he repeated over and over. Tracy and Paul were having an argument on the porch, and then Tracy lost control and began running down the street. And she'd tried to beat the train and had fallen.

Paul and I just listened at first. Then we repeated the same tale when it was our turn to talk. None of us said out loud that we would lie. We just did it. To protect Mother and Daddy from knowing that Tracy had done it on purpose. To shield them from her final pain.

None of us mentioned Reana Mae.

Daddy called Melinda and Nancy, then Aunt Belle. He led Mother by the hand to the bedroom and helped her into bed. Finally, he walked back out to the front porch, where a puddle of Tracy's blood was drying, and began to sob. I sat in the living room, watching him. I wanted to go out and help somehow, but I knew I couldn't. So I just watched him for a long, long time.

Finally, at about four in the morning, I walked upstairs to my bedroom. The lights were off, but I knew Reana Mae was there. She'd run upstairs hours earlier, after we knew that Tracy was dead, before the police came. I hadn't seen her since.

Once my eyes adjusted to the dark, I could see her, kneeling on the floor by her bed, her head dropped into her hands. She didn't move when she heard me, but I could see her breathe harder.

I got undressed in the dark and climbed into bed. I felt like I was in the middle of a movie—a horror film—or maybe a nightmare. Tracy was dead—beautiful, hateful, angelic, demonic Tracy. Her body had been crushed beneath a locomotive and seventeen freight cars. I'd counted each one as it passed. I couldn't help myself. It was as if I had to mark each car's passing, to acknowledge it.

When Brian picked her up, she looked like a rag doll. Her head lolled to one side, blood dripping from her mouth and nose, half her face looked entirely gone. And she looked small . . . too small to be Tracy. Small like a little girl.

I stood still in shock when Brian ran forward to pick her up off the tracks. And I could only follow him as he ran back toward the house, Tracy's blood drip, drip, dripping onto the sidewalk as he ran. He'd laid her on the porch and run inside to call the police. And all I could do was sit down on the porch by Tracy's bloody body and hold her hand. That's when Paul threw up the first time, right in the bushes by the front porch.

Tracy was dead. I'd watched them lift her onto the gurney and cover her with a white sheet, just like they'd done to Araminta. And when they drove away, it was to the morgue. Right now, right this very moment, my sister was lying dead in a morgue.

And it was because of Reana Mae.

I looked over to her bed, where she still knelt. And in the gathering early dawn light, I could see her lips moving. Reana Mae was praying. I hadn't seen her pray in years, not since she first came to live with us, when she prayed every night for Caleb to come.

I turned my back to her and cried then. I cried harder and longer than I'd ever cried before. I cried till I had to get out of bed and go into the little bathroom and puke.

Sisters and Cousins

For the second time in a month, our house was filled with mourners. Nancy and Melinda had arrived before I came downstairs the next morning. Melinda hugged me tight and said it was a blessing that Brian and I had been here. Nancy kissed my forehead and told me that she loved me and that I'd been a good sister to Tracy. Nancy's husband, Neil, sat quietly in the front room, watching anxiously for a chance to help.

Neighbors and church friends came and went, bringing casseroles and pies and banana bread.

Daddy and Mother had gone to the morgue to claim Tracy's body. I cried thinking of them seeing her like that.

Brian arrived around noon. He and I took a pan of soapy water out to the front porch and scrubbed at the dark stains in vain. We were still there when Mother and Daddy came home. Daddy held the car door open for Mother, then took her arm and helped her up the walkway toward the house. She looked very fragile, just as fragile as she always said Tracy was.

She stopped on the front porch to give me a kiss. Then she kissed Brian on his cheek and said, "Thank you for trying to help her."

Then she went inside, back to her bedroom, and closed the door behind her.

Daddy left soon after for the airport to pick up Aunt Belle. Melinda and Nancy drove to the grocery to buy milk.

Reana Mae stayed upstairs most of the day, venturing down around three in the afternoon. She looked like hell, but I guess we all did that day. Without a word to anyone, she put on her Windbreaker, pulled Bo's leash from the closet, and walked out the back door. She leashed Bobby Lee's old coonhound and left, walking slowly down the street, away from the railroad tracks, away from our house.

Brian asked if we should go after her, but I just shook my head. She needed to be alone, I thought.

And I didn't want to be around her.

Aunt Belle's arrival brought some life back into the house. She bustled in, took a tray of soup and crackers to Mother, sent Nancy and Neil out to arrange for flowers, supervised Melinda in the kitchen, then shooed Brian and me out to take a walk.

"Don't keep worryin' over them stains," she said, shaking her head sadly. "Bloodstains don't never come out."

We walked slowly, holding hands, quiet.

"Thank you," I finally said.

"It's okay," he said, squeezing my hand.

"I guess you aren't so envious of my family now."

"Not today," he said. "But your family will be all right. They love each other, and they'll get through this."

We walked in silence again. Then he said, "I'm worried about Reana Mae, though."

I shrugged.

"Bethany," he said, pulling me to a stop beside him. "I know it's her fault, hers and Paul's. But she didn't mean for this to happen. She didn't mean for Tracy to get hurt."

"I think she did," I said flatly. "I think she wanted to hurt Tracy."

"Okay, maybe she did want to hurt Tracy. She wanted to get back at her for all the times Tracy hurt her. But she couldn't have meant for *this* to happen. She couldn't have known Tracy would do what she did."

"I know."

And I did know. I knew she didn't mean for Tracy to die. Still, Tracy was dead.

"She must be pretty torn up about it."

"I guess so."

"Should we look for her?"

I shook my head again. "She'll come home when she's tired," I said. "Or when she gets hungry."

He looked at me sternly, straight in the eyes. "I don't know, Bethany. Maybe she'll think you don't want her there."

"I don't."

And that was true. I didn't want Reana Mae in my house, in my family's house, in Tracy's house. For the first time ever, I wondered about how hard it had been on Tracy to have Reana Mae there. I thought about what she'd said at Araminta's funeral, about Reana stealing Mother away.

I shook my head hard, trying to clear away the image of Reana Mae sitting atop Paul, smiling past me at Tracy. I'd known she hated Tracy. I'd seen how much anger she was holding inside. And I'd done nothing. Hadn't talked to her about it. Hadn't talked to Mother about it. I'd just pretended it would go away.

And now, Tracy was dead. My sister—the fragile, hateful stranger I'd shared a room and a family with all those years—was dead. And it was Reana Mae's fault . . . and maybe mine, too.

"I want it all to be like it was yesterday," I said. "I just want . . ." But the words caught in my throat.

Brian pulled me close and let me cry then, just let me cry against his chest. After a while, we walked back. I stared numbly at the bloodstains on the porch, then kissed Brian good-bye and sent him home. I figured he'd had enough of our family for one day . . . or for one lifetime.

We sat down to a quiet supper of split pea soup and bread. Of course, it was store-bought bread, because Reana Mae was still out. But it didn't matter. None of us ate much.

Belle poured some bourbon into Daddy's Coke and he drank it, but he didn't eat any of his soup. After a few minutes, he went back to the room where Mother still was, closing the door behind him.

I was cleaning up the dishes when Reana Mae finally came back. She fed Bo, kissed Aunt Belle, and went back upstairs to our room, never meeting my eyes. Belle watched her go, looking from Reana to me, but she didn't say a word.

Later, sitting in the living room with the evening news on TV, Aunt Belle turned to me and asked, "What's wrong between you and Reana Mae?"

"Nothing," I lied.

"Well, that's a load of horseshit, and you know it," she said briskly. "Whatever it is, now is *not* the time. You go right upstairs and make peace with your cousin."

I sat still, staring at the television.

"Bethany Marie!" Belle's voice was sharp. "You do what I say, child, and you do it right now. Your mama and daddy don't need no more drama in this house, 'specially between you and Reana Mae. Now you march yourself up them stairs and you make peace with your cousin, before I drag you up there myself!"

I wanted to scream at her, to tell her the truth. But I didn't. I couldn't. So I stood and walked slowly up the stairs to the attic, where Reana Mae was.

She was on the floor by her bed again, her head bowed, her lips moving silently.

"What the hell are you doing?" I asked.

She lifted her head to look at me.

"I'm prayin' for Tracy," she said softly.

"Like that's gonna do any good," I sniffed. "You don't even believe in God."

"But Aunt Helen does," she said. "Aunt Helen believes in God. And Tracy believed in God. And I figure, if there is a God, it can't hurt to pray for her."

I simply stared at her. All I could see when I looked at her was the smile on her face when she'd seen Tracy in the doorway.

"I ain't prayin' for myself. I know better than that. What I done is past prayin' for."

I said nothing.

"Look, Bethy." Her voice was pleading now. "I know what I done was wrong. Cruel, even. I know that. I wanted to hurt her. I wanted to hurt her like she always hurt me. I wanted to hurt her 'cause of all those things she said about Caleb, 'cause they were true, after all. And I hated that. I hated that she was right. I just wanted to hurt her."

Her voice broke into a strangled sob.

"But God, Bethany, I didn't want her to die! You know I didn't want that! You know I didn't!"

She was crying now, tears running down her chin.

"What I done was purely wicked, I know that. And God Hisself won't never forgive me. But *you* got to, Bethy. You got to forgive me. I ain't got nobody but you now. Caleb ain't comin' and Aunt Helen will probably send me away for what I done to Tracy. She'll send me back down to the river, or maybe to foster care. I know I don't deserve to live with her no more, not after what I done. I don't deserve to be in her house. Tracy's dead, and it's all my fault."

She was still on her knees, her face buried in her hands, her shoulders shaking furiously.

I dropped to my knees beside her and wrapped my arms around her, pulling her close. It was her fault that Tracy was dead, that was true. But I knew then she didn't mean for it to happen. Tracy was the way Tracy was, and that was all there was to it. Reana Mae was wrong, but I knew she was sorry for it.

I held her and told her that I loved her and that Mother loved her, too.

"She can't love me! How could she, after what I done?"

"She doesn't know. No one knows except me and Brian and Paul."

She stared at me, tears still dripping from her nose and chin.

"How come?"

"Brian told the police that we came home and saw Paul and Tracy having an argument. And that Tracy got mad and ran off and tripped on the tracks trying to beat the train. And that's what everyone thinks."

"Why did he do that?" she asked. "Why did he lie?"

"He didn't want Mother and Daddy to know she did it on purpose," I said. "They think it was an accident. They have to. They can't know the truth."

"But I got to tell them, then," she said urgently. "I got to tell them it was my fault. I can't stay here with them not knowin'. It's my fault, and they got to know that!"

"No, Reana!"

My voice was louder and sharper than I'd expected. She was on her feet, and I thought she might run straight for the stairs to tell Mother about her part in Tracy's death. I couldn't let her do that, not to Mother, not now.

Then we heard steps on the stairway and both of us froze. But it was only Aunt Belle carrying a plate of peanut butter crackers and two sodas.

"Bethany Marie," she hissed. "You keep your voice down, you hear me? Your mama needs her sleep now. She don't need you two up here yellin' at each other."

She set down the plate and sodas, plopped herself onto Reana Mae's bed, and held out her arms to us.

"Now, then, you two are going to sit right down here beside old Aunt Belle and tell her what's goin' on."

"Nothing's going on," I started, but she cut me off.

"Bethany Marie Wylie, I done changed your diapers when you was a baby—and yours, too, Reana Mae. I know when something's wrong with my girls, and I damn well know when I'm bein' lied to."

So we sat, one on either side of her, eating peanut butter crackers in silence. Finally, Reana Mae said very softly, "It's all my fault, Aunt Belle. It's my fault Tracy is dead."

Aunt Belle said nothing. She just brushed some crumbs from her waist and waited for Reana Mae to go on.

So Reana told her, she told her the whole truth. How she'd called Paul and asked him for help with her math homework. How she'd flirted and kissed him and teased him till he got undressed. How she knew when Tracy would be home to walk in on them. How Tracy's face had looked when she saw Reana Mae and Paul together.

"Oh, Lord, child." Belle sighed. "That ain't good."

Then I told the rest. About Tracy running down the street and Brian trying to stop her. And about how Tracy threw herself directly at the train.

Then we sat in silence for a long time, until Aunt Belle pulled both of us into a strong, warm hug and said, "Now listen here, you two. It's time you know the truth. I told Helen and Jimmy years ago you ought to know, but they didn't want to tell. Not that I fault them, mind you. They thought they were doin' the best thing. But these lies and secrets have tore this family apart, and it's time to set it all straight."

Reana Mae and I stared at her. What lies and secrets?

Belle pulled her ample weight farther up onto the bed and settled herself against Reana Mae's pillow, leaned against the headboard.

"Bethany," she said firmly, "go get my bourbon and a glass with some ice. This here is gonna take a while."

❧ 34 ❧

Secrets Told

"Did your mama ever tell you about her daddy?" Aunt Belle asked, after sipping her bourbon for a few minutes.

"Just that he wasn't very nice," I said. "And that he drank too much."

Reana Mae and I were both in our nightgowns, snuggled in on either side of Belle.

"Well, now, I reckon that's the understatement of the century." Belle smiled. "Danny O'Shea was purely wicked. He drank like a fish, and when he was good and drunk, he'd beat your grandma and your mama and her little brother. Parker's his name."

"I didn't know Aunt Helen had a brother," Reana Mae said. "What happened to him?"

"Just wait, child, just wait. I'll get to that."

She took a long drink and set the glass on the nightstand.

"Well, ole Danny, now, he was a handsome devil. Tall, dark hair like your mama's, and slick. Oh, he was real slick. He liked to drink, and he liked to gamble, and he liked his women. Had a whole string of 'em. The cheaper they was, the better he liked 'em. Nearly drove his poor wife to distraction. Olivia, that was her name. Olivia Harte, from down to Hurricane. Now, Olivia, she came from a real good family. Her daddy had a farm, and Olivia grew up knowin' how to work hard.

"Danny came into town when she was about fifteen years old. He was a salesman, in his twenties, I guess. And he looked at Olivia, and probably he looked at her daddy's farm, and he wanted 'em both. So he convinced that little girl to run off and get married.

"Well, Olivia's daddy wasn't havin' none of that. He told her she was dead to him, and he never let her come home again. I thought that was right mean, myself. Can't reckon on how a man could do that to his own child, especially with her bein' so young. But he was a Christian man, I guess, and he had his principles. Leastways, that's what Olivia said.

"So now here's poor Olivia married to a travelin' salesman. He moved her up to Huntington, where he lived, and got her pregnant right off. And that was your mama," she said, smiling down at me. "That was poor Helen.

"And then, two, three years later came Parker. Lord, he was a beautiful child. Like Helen, only chubby, with real dark eyes."

Belle sighed, closing her eyes for a minute.

"But what Olivia didn't know when she married Danny was, his family had bad blood."

She paused again, then looked into my eyes.

"You know about bad blood?"

Reana Mae nodded, her eyes wide, but I could only stare in horror. I'd heard of bad blood before, but not in my family . . . not in Mother's family!

"Well, Danny's mama, her name was Myra, she was the first one I know about for sure. Though I hear tell Myra's granny had the bad blood, too. I heard lots of stories about her, too. But Myra, that one I can tell you about for sure.

"Myra married Michael O'Shea, you see. Michael ran a ferry service on the river. He was a good man, Michael. I knew him a lotta years, and he was a real good man. Did the best he could by his family. Worked hard, read the Bible. But he was a joker, too. Liked a good joke. Kinda like Brother Harley that way."

292 · *Sherri Wood Emmons*

"But, Aunt Belle," I interrupted her. "I thought Mother's grand-parents were named Michael and LucyAnne."

"Well, you got it partly right. LucyAnne was Michael's second wife. And she's the one that was so good to Helen. Took her in just like she was her own daughter. Helped make Helen's wedding dress, when Helen married Jimmy."

She sighed, smiling. "LucyAnne was a real good woman. But she wasn't Helen's blood grandma. Danny's mother was Myra. Myra McCoy O'Shea. And she was . . . well, she was touched in the head. No two ways about it. She had bad blood.

"Ole Myra, why, she beat her boys black and blue. Beat 'em for nothin, just 'cause she felt like it. She drank whiskey and smoked a pipe and she swore like a sailor. Not at first, of course. When Michael first married her, I guess she was right enough. But after her boys was born, she was possessed by the devil hisself.

"I heard one time she took Danny and strung him up by his feet in the barn 'cause she couldn't find her pipe. Left him hangin' there for hours, till Michael came home and cut him down. The boy was halfway dead, they said. She strung him upside down and beat him with a horsewhip till he bled near to death.

"Another time, she took them out on the ferry, her own two sons, when they was just little 'uns, and threw 'em both into the water. They'da drowned if their daddy hadn't come just in time.

"And she just got worse as she got older. She used to stroll down the road stark naked sometimes. Naked as a jaybird! Folks on the river called her Crazy Myra, but someone always brought her home when she did that.

"Well, finally, she went too far. She shot her younger boy. Elbe was his name. Shot him right in the back with a shotgun. No par-ticular reason she could give. She just shot him, then sat herself down and drank whiskey."

I shook my head, trying to take it all in.

"So," Belle continued, "they put her away. Put her in jail for murderin' her own child. And she died there, a year or so later. She hanged herself. That's when Michael married LucyAnne. And LucyAnne was a good woman. She loved Michael and she tried to take care of Danny, too. But Danny, well he had the same bad blood."

She shook her head darkly.

"Danny strangled a boy one time 'cause he didn't like the way he was lookin' at him. Michael got him off that time. Paid the sheriff some money, told him Danny was in a sorry state, on account of his mama's death. Paid the dead boy's family something, too. But Danny had the blood.

"So now Danny marries Olivia and they have Helen and Parker. But Danny, he's drinkin' heavy and he loses his job. So he drinks some more and he beats his family. He keeps gettin' jobs, mind you, 'cause he's so danged handsome and slick. But he can't keep 'em, 'cause he's such a drunk.

"So poor Olivia, she sends the babies away. Sends Parker down to Georgia, to stay with a cousin. And she sends Helen to stay with Michael and LucyAnne on the river. That's when Helen and Jimmy met, you see."

She frowned slightly. "I was against the marriage at first, on account of the bad blood in Danny's family. But what could I do? Jimmy loved her true, and Helen . . . well, there's not a bad thing anyone can ever say 'bout Helen. She's as good as the day is long."

"What happened to Parker?" I asked.

"Poor Parker, he got the bad blood, too. He stayed down in Georgia for a long time . . . years, I guess. Olivia kept him down there till Danny had left for good. And when she got him back, he was . . . odd. Just odd, that's all. He couldn't hardly talk. He mumbled and sometimes he'd holler, but he never made any sense. And he had that same devil's temper. Killed a cat one time, just for fun. Beat it to death with a rock. That about killed poor Olivia. She loved little animals.

"But she kept Parker with her till she died. He ain't never worked at all. Can't get a job. Still can't hardly talk. And still just as mean as a snake."

"He's still alive?" I asked, surprised.

"Well, yes he is, darlin'. He lives in a hospital down to Georgia, a hospital run by the state, where he can't hurt nobody. He's been there since poor Olivia died. I pay for it, of course. I told Helen when Olivia died, I said, 'You're my family, just like Jimmy is. And family takes care of their own.' Yes sirree, I pay for ole Parker to stay in that hospital."

She paused to drink from her glass.

"So you see now, there's bad blood in Helen's family. Her grandma and her daddy and her brother, too. So we was always real concerned about her kids, you know . . . about you girls. Her and me, we always watched real close, lookin' for signs of the blood. Now Jimmy, he just laughed at us. Told us there's no such thing as bad blood. But your mama knew there was.

"And we worried 'bout poor Tracy. We worried even when she was a little thing. Her fits just weren't right. You know that, Bethany. She had her Grandpa Danny's temper. Course, she held herself together for a while, I'll say that for her. Your mama and daddy loved her and tried to raise her up right, and that's why she could. But in the end, that bad blood was in her veins. Ain't nothin' anyone could do about it."

She looked at Reana Mae then and took her chin in her hand.

"Ain't nothin' you did, and nothin' you coulda done, to make her do what she did. Tracy had the O'Shea blood, like ole Myra. Sooner or later, she'da done it, or worse. And it ain't your fault."

Then she turned to me.

"Nor your fault, neither," she said firmly.

We sat in silence for a while, letting it all sink in. Finally, I asked what I'd been wondering.

"Do I have the bad blood, too?"

"Lord, no! You ain't got it any more than Helen does."

"But if I have a baby, will she have it?"

"Well, now, Bethy, that I don't know. I just don't rightly know."

She shifted uncomfortably, then said, "I know Helen and Jimmy already told Nancy about it. They told her before she got married. Said they thought she ought to know the truth, just in case.

"And you, too," she said, turning to Reana Mae. "You got to know, too."

Reana looked at her in confusion. "But I ain't related to Helen's family. I'm only related through Jimmy."

"Well, now." Belle shifted again. "That's where you're wrong, Reana Mae. That's where you're dead wrong."

We both stared at her, not understanding.

"It's your grandpa." Belle sighed, looking down at her hands.

"You mean Ray?" Reana asked. "But Ray's not related to Helen."

"Not Ray, child," Belle said. "Your other grandpa . . . Jolene's daddy."

"You know my mama's father?" Reana Mae whispered. "Why didn't you never tell me? Why didn't you tell Mama? She always wondered, you know. She always wanted to know who her daddy was."

"Well, we thought it best not to tell."

"We who, Belle? Who else knew?"

"Helen, honey. Helen and Jimmy knew, and they told me."

"But why didn't they tell Mama? Why didn't Aunt Helen never tell her?"

"I expect she didn't want to cause Jolene no more pain. Helen always looked out for Jolene, you know. Loved her like a sister, really. And she surely didn't want to cause her no more pain."

I leaned forward slowly. My head ached, but I could see it now, like a puzzle coming together piece by piece. Why Mother had always loved Jolene so—like a sister, Aunt Belle said. Why she had taken Reana Mae in. Why she cared about them so much.

"It was Danny," I said. "Danny was Jolene's daddy."

"Aunt Helen's daddy?" Reana Mae said, puzzled. "Danny, who is Aunt Helen's daddy, is my mama's daddy, too?"

"That's right, Reana Mae." Belle nodded solemnly. "Danny O'Shea was a bad man, and he done some real bad things. But what he done to your Grandma EmmaJane . . . well, I guess that was just about the worst."

"That's right."

We all jumped. Mother's voice carried soft but clear across the room. None of us had heard her come up the stairs.

Her face was white and her eyes glistened, but she seemed calm. She walked to the bed, sat down, reached for Reana Mae's hands and held them tightly in her own. "Your grandfather was my father.

He met EmmaJane when she was just sixteen, and he got her pregnant."

"Your daddy had an affair with my grandmother?"

"It wasn't an affair, Reana. It was rape. My father raped EmmaJane."

Reana Mae stared at her.

"When I was fifteen, my father had been out of work for almost a year. We were living in Charleston, and he was drinking a lot, all the time really. He'd come home almost every night drunk and loud and mean. Mother was worried about Parker and me, so she sent us away. Parker went to Georgia, and I went to stay with my grandparents on the river. They knew about his drinking, and they tried to help Mother as best they could.

"So I moved to the river and helped out in the boardinghouse. I didn't even go home for Christmas. I worried about Mother all the time, but I couldn't write to her, because she didn't want Daddy to know where I was. It was the loneliest time of my life.

"Anyway, that's where I met your grandmother. EmmaJane worked for my Grandma LucyAnne. She helped with the laundry and cleaning during the week and went home on the weekends. We shared a room. She was sixteen then and as pretty as she could be. She had sandy-brown hair and big green eyes. You favor her, Reana Mae.

"We were the only girls around. It was pretty much a mining town, you know. And the miners mostly sent their children up to St. Albans for school. So we were friends. On our days off, Grandpa Michael took us upriver to visit EmmaJane's mother and father—Loreen and Ray, that is. EmmaJane had a boyfriend, too. He was Ida Louise's brother, Lloyd, and he was so sweet on her. He'd come sometimes and take EmmaJane and me riding in his daddy's car. EmmaJane liked him pretty well, but she had her heart set on moving to Charleston or Huntington and meeting a rich Prince Charming. She wanted someone older and sophisticated and wealthy. I suppose I did, too.

"One day in May, EmmaJane told me she had met a man—not a boy, mind you, a man. She said he was older and very handsome. He was staying at the hotel, he had a car of his own and lots of cash, and he took EmmaJane to the only restaurant in town and bought her pork chops and a beer. She made me promise not to tell my grandmother, because LucyAnne frowned on girls dating. She would have sent EmmaJane packing for home if she knew. So I didn't tell Grandma. I didn't tell anyone. I thought it was romantic and very grown up.

"That Friday night, I walked down to the river by myself. EmmaJane was going to meet her Romeo, and I was feeling kind of left out and lonely. Before I got to the clearing, I heard a voice—a man's voice—and I knew. I knew who EmmaJane had met.

"My father's voice was slurred. He was saying over and over, 'Helen, baby, don't cry. Daddy's here.'

"I looked through the bushes and saw him on top of Emma-Jane. He had his hand over her mouth so she couldn't scream. Her dress was torn. It was awful."

"What did you do?" Reana Mae asked, her eyes wide.

"Before I could do anything, it was over," Mother said. "My father got up, zipped up his pants, threw a whiskey bottle into the bushes, and walked up the path toward town. He just left Emma-Jane lying there on the ground with her dress all torn up.

"I went to her and helped her pull her dress together around her. I took her back to the house and got her inside and up the back stairs to our room without anyone seeing us. And I took care of her there. I told my grandmother that EmmaJane had gone home for a long weekend, and I did her chores and took food up to her and tried to take care of her. But we never talked about it, not even once. She just stayed in bed and ate what I brought her and then turned her face to the wall and slept.

"On Tuesday, she got up and got dressed and went downstairs and started working again. She never told anyone, so I didn't either.

"A few weeks later, she started having morning sickness. She tried to hide it—I think she was trying to ignore it. But then she began to show, and my grandmother made her leave. Grandma assumed the baby was Lloyd's, and EmmaJane never told her anything different.

"So EmmaJane packed her suitcase, got on a bus, and left. But she didn't go home. We didn't know that at first. We didn't know until a couple weeks later, when Lloyd drove down to see her. By then, she had a two-week start, and we didn't know where she'd gone. I still don't know where all she went—only that she ended up in Huntington with Jolene."

Mother looked at Reana Mae again. "I never told Jolene, because I thought she'd be happier not knowing. It's such an ugly story, and she'd already had such ugliness in her life."

She sat still then, watching my face and then Reana Mae's. I stared back at her, at her lovely, familiar face. I couldn't believe she had been through all that. And that I didn't know.

"Aunt Helen," Reana Mae said softly, holding tight to her hands. "It's my fault Tracy died."

Oh, God, I thought, *please don't do this. Not now, Reana! You can't tell Mother now! It will kill her.*

"I was playing around with Paul," she said, looking right into Mother's eyes. "I wanted her to see us. I wanted to hurt her. That's what she and Paul were fighting about when Bethany came home. That's why she ran away from him . . . when she fell."

Mother stared at Reana for a long minute, then wrapped her in a tight embrace.

"It's not your fault, Reana Mae. You wanted to hurt Tracy because she hurt you so much. But you didn't want her dead. And you know now that she didn't want to hurt you, either. Not really. She just couldn't help it. Poor Tracy couldn't help it. She had the bad blood."

❧ 35 ❧

No More Bad Blood

We buried Tracy next to Grandmother Araminta. The church was so crowded that some people had to stand at the back. Everyone from church came, and the folks from Daddy's office. It seemed like half the high school was there. Lynette sat next to Paul, who still looked as if he might throw up at any minute. He and Reana Mae avoided looking at each other at all. I heard later that Paul dropped out of college and moved away. I never saw him again after the funeral.

Mother and Daddy sat in the front pew with Aunt Belle. Mother sat straight and tall, her face pale, her eyes dull. Daddy slumped over, as he had at Araminta's funeral. He looked beaten down. Aunt Belle kept hold of them both, tightly by the hand. But even she looked small that day. And her face was an ashy gray.

Nancy sat behind them with her husband. *Poor Neil*, I thought, watching them at the funeral dinner. *He must be wondering what kind of family he's married into.* But Neil still seemed happy, watching his young bride. And Nancy seemed . . . well, if not happy, at least satisfied.

Melinda sat next to Nancy, holding her hand, but her eyes never left Mother. Melinda had been a godsend at home, cooking and cleaning and taking care of Mother. She was almost twenty, and while she might never be beautiful, she certainly was tall and tanned and healthy. And, of course, she was smart. Melinda read so much and understood so much, it seemed she could always find the right words at the right time. I envied her that.

Beside Melinda sat a young man named Barry, who was a sociology major at Indiana University. He'd arrived early in the morning, and Melinda seemed very glad to see him. He was tall and freckled, just like Melinda, and wore wire-rimmed glasses. He held Melinda's free hand and watched her just the way she watched Mother. I thought he seemed nice.

Reana Mae and I sat beside Mother. We held hands during the service and, for the first time ever in our church, Reana Mae prayed. She prayed along with the preacher when he led us in prayer, and she prayed silently during the communion service. She sang the hymns and prayed and cried through the entire service. I thought she'd never been prettier than she was that day.

I'm pretty sure Harley thought so, too. He'd driven up on his own for the funeral—without permission from his grandparents. We got a phone call at the house from Ida Louise just before we left for the church. Melinda took care of it, bless her heart. She told Ida that she'd watch out for Harley and send him back home the next day. Then she told Ida what a comfort and a blessing it was to have Harley at the house, and how much he was helping my parents. That was a lie, of course. Harley had shown up barely half an hour earlier and hadn't even seen my parents. But Melinda had a way with words, and she calmed Ida Louise down enough to get her off the phone. I was sure, though, that Harley would have hell to pay, once he got back home.

He sat behind us, in a pew with Ray and Uncle Hobie, Aunt Vera, Ruthann, and Lottie. His eyes never left the back of Reana Mae's head. I didn't look back, but I knew it was so.

Brian sat farther back, with some friends from school. He'd been to the house earlier, with flowers for Mother and some for me and some for Reana Mae. He kissed me, told me he loved me, and said he was glad Reana and I were okay again. I hadn't told him yet about what I'd learned the night before. But I knew I would tell him. I told Brian everything, even then.

So on a warm, sunny day in May, we laid Tracy in the ground, tossing our roses into the hole that had been dug to receive her. I thought about all the things she'd done, all the mean, hateful things she said, and about how sometimes she could be so kind. About how she'd buried Essie in the mud, and then how she'd bought a new dress for the little doll. About how she said she might kill me someday, and how she let me curl around her on cold nights in our attic. About how she'd told the kids at school about Reana Mae and Caleb, and how gentle and kind she was with our Grandmother Araminta.

I thought about the bad blood Aunt Belle had talked about, and how miserable Tracy had been so much of the time. And as I threw my rose onto her casket, I said the first prayer I'd prayed in a long, long time.

Dear God, please accept Tracy into Heaven. Let her be with Grandmother Araminta and Winston and DarlaJean. And please, God, let her be happy at last. Because really, God, when you think about it, it wasn't her fault. Tracy had the bad blood. And surely, in Heaven, that's all healed.

Epilogue

1982

The valley seems almost unchanged, as I sit on the porch swing, watching the dark water of the river. From here, you can't see the newly paved road, the vinyl-sided houses, the manicured lawns. Only the party lights draped on the back porches along the water look new from here.

The valley has become quaint, you see. People from Charleston started buying up the cottages for summer places a few years back. They painted and roofed, added window boxes and air-conditioning, landscaped the yards and refinished the floors. Or they simply tore down and started over. Brand-new houses now sit on double lots alongside cottages so prettified their original owners wouldn't recognize them.

A garbage truck rumbles through every Tuesday morning, followed by a recycling pickup service. A man from Cincinnati bought the beach and imported tons of white sand; then he built cabanas and a small restaurant. Now people drive in from St. Albans to swim and eat by the river. There are even plans for a boat launch, I hear, so weekend fishermen can ply the river.

There's a campground by the beach now, too, filled every weekend from May till September with nylon tents, pop-top campers, and huge RVs. Some nights I can hear the music from those RVs all the way down the river. Then one of the locals—a few still live hereabouts—calls the sheriff's office, and Harley has to drive down there and show his badge and ask the campers to please turn down the volume.

A nice retired couple lives in the cottage that was ours once upon a time. When Aunt Vera told them I had lived there before, they invited me to come see the place. I had dreaded that, but since there was no polite way around it, I walked down the road my second week here and knocked on the gray door. I needn't have worried, though, because inside was not a trace of the cottage I remembered. The walls had been papered, the windows and trim replaced, wall-to-wall beige carpeting hugged the floors, and a sparkling yellow kitchen filled what had been the back porch. It looked like any other house now. Only the loft remained the same. But, Mrs. Baker told me proudly, next summer they are putting in a real stairway and finishing the loft into a home office. I came home oddly relieved, then cried myself to sleep.

Aunt Vera still lives in her cottage, its dock now one of dozens dotting the river. Uncle Hobie is buried in the tiny hilltop cemetery, and Ruthann married a man from Tennessee two years back and moved away. But Lottie still lives with her mother. She's a pretty young woman now, working at the beach restaurant and engaged to Harley's deputy. She and her beau plan to buy the cottage from Vera when they marry. Vera will live with them. Lottie is still her mama's little girl.

Uncle Ray's store has reopened, much to the joy of the valley. After Loreen died, Ray talked about selling the place. Instead, he left it to Bobby Lee, who showed no sign of returning to run it in this lifetime or the next.

Two years ago, Bobby did come back for the first time since he left in 1972. But it was only to sign papers selling the shop to a man from Charleston, who runs it now.

The new owner has made a lot of changes to the store. Oh, he still sells bread and milk, hardware and cold beer. But the shop now carries gourmet coffee beans and expensive wines, plus seven different brands of suntan lotion, brie cheese, and lots of film. He's even added a coffee bar, serving latte and biscotti.

As for Bobby Lee, he's living in Dallas with a woman from California and her three kids. Last year, he visited Reana Mae and her husband, Mike, out in Idaho, and Reana says he took to the boys right away. She's been out there a while now, left right after college to work as a ranger in Yellowstone. She's finally living under that big western sky, married to a real-live cowboy and raising his three sons from his first marriage. She writes to me every week, and we talk on the phone most Sundays. She's happier than I ever thought she could be.

And I'm happy in my house. I haven't changed it much. The place still looks like Aunt Belle has just gone out to the store. Of course, it's dustier than Donna Jo would have let it get, and a port-a-crib graces the living room. But if Belle walked in tonight, she'd find her own pictures on the wall, her knickknacks on the shelves, even her brand of bourbon in the kitchen. She left the place—whole and full—to Daddy and Mother. But since Belle died, Daddy can't bring himself to be here. So, it stayed closed up.

Now it's mine. Brian and I bought it from Daddy two months back, and we've brought our Lily Belle to live in the valley where I always felt most at home. This is the only place I can imagine raising her. Even with the bad memories of Reana Mae and Caleb, of Jolene losing control, the valley is home for me . . . the only place I ever really fit. Belle's house is my house now. It's home.

Gazing at my tiny daughter's face as she sleeps in my arms, I know that.

Melinda and her brood came last week to see us. She and Barry have adopted a whole litter of kids. They've cobbled together a veritable United Nations—Rudy from Pakistan, Tyler from Nigeria, Kelsey from Guatemala, and now Alyssa from China. The kids hovered over Lily Belle, touching her tiny pink face with small brown fingers, recognizing her as their cousin—family, of course, being how you define it.

Melinda shook her head and sighed at how much Lily favors Tracy—her round hazel eyes sparkling over a slightly upturned nose. But she has my dark hair and a scattering of Melinda's freckles. And I know what Melinda doesn't about Lily . . . what I see in those hazel eyes.

Lily Belle is part me and part Brian. And between Brian and me, there is no bad blood.

Please turn the page for a very special
Q&A with Sherri Wood Emmons.

What motivated you to write a novel?

I didn't start out to write a novel, actually. I wanted to just write down some of my remembrances from childhood. My family spent several summers on the Coal River in West Virginia, and those are some of my favorite childhood memories. But in writing them down, I began to worry, "Did that really happen? Or did I make that up?" Finally, I gave myself permission to stop worrying and just write. And a novel came out.

How did you get the idea for this story?

In the beginning, I just had an idea of Reana Mae—a little girl, pretty much unwanted by her parents, raising herself as best she could. And her relationship with Bethany, a kind of sisterhood of misfits, saving them both from a pretty lonely existence. The story came as I was writing it. I really didn't know where it was going until it got there.

What made you decide to write in the voice of a child?

I started out writing in the third person, but it just didn't work. So then I tried writing from Reana's perspective, but there were too many secrets she had that I didn't want to give away. So, Bethany as the narrator made sense. She's close to Reana, but she's gone for periods of time. So she discovers Reana Mae's secrets over time, the way the reader does.

You have a couple of pretty unlikable characters, and yet in the end, both Tracy and Caleb generate some sympathy. How did that happen?

I did not mean for either of them to be sympathetic, really. But as I was writing, I couldn't seem to help it! Honestly, I would be writing about Caleb and all these "mitigating factors" just came out—his father abandoned the family, his mother has given up on him.

Those things don't excuse what he does, but they do explain it somewhat.

As for Tracy, she started out pretty hateful. But I think the more I wrote, the more I understood that she was mentally ill. And again, it doesn't excuse her actions, but it does explain them. When she died—when I was writing that scene—I actually was crying as I wrote. It surprised me how grief-stricken I was.

You write about the "bad blood" in Bethany's family. What is "bad blood"?

Bad blood is a strain of mental illness that runs through the family. I didn't try to define what the illness is. I don't know enough about psychology to even pretend to know. But I'm thinking it tends toward bipolar disorder or narcissism. Either way, it's not dealt with, it's hushed up, until the family can't ignore it anymore.

Why is the title "Prayers and Lies"?

Bethany starts out with a very naïve, Sunday school kind of belief in God. And that belief gets strained to the breaking point when bad things happen that she cannot rationalize or understand. In the end, I think, she comes to a more nuanced, shades-of-gray kind of faith. In the end, I guess most of us do.

Any advice for aspiring writers?

Write! I am living proof that a first novel can get published!

PRAYERS AND LIES

Sherri Wood Emmons

ABOUT THIS GUIDE

The suggested questions are included to enhance
your group's reading of Sherri Wood Emmons's
Prayers and Lies.

DISCUSSION QUESTIONS

1. Is there a villain in the story? Who is the villain? Is there anything that makes his or her actions understandable? Is that character redeemable?

2. Aunt Belle explains to Reana Mae and Bethany that Helen's family carries "bad blood." What is the bad blood? How might it be diagnosed today?

3. Does knowing about the bad blood change the way you view Tracy?

4. Do Helen and Jimmy bear responsibility for Tracy's death? What could they have done to prevent it?

5. Did Jolene have a right to know who her father was? Should Helen have told her? Why or why not?

6. Is there any good in the relationship between Reana Mae and Caleb? What good would that be?

7. Why did Reana Mae have sex with Harley Boy on the day of Araminta's funeral? What does her decision say about her attitude toward sex?

8. How might the story have changed if Jolene had not lost her baby?

9. What responsibility does Bobby Lee bear for Reana Mae's relationship with Caleb?

10. Were Harley Boy, Ruthann, and Bethany right to keep quiet after they found out about Reana Mae and Caleb? Should they have told their parents the truth?

11. What role does Neil play in the story?

12. Why is the book titled *Prayers and Lies*? Is there a faith element to the story?

13. Why is the story told from Bethany's perspective? Is that an effective narrative device? How might the story be different if it were told in the third person?

14. Was moving Reana Mae to Indianapolis the right decision for her? Was it the right decision for the rest of the family?

15. What enabled Helen to rise above the circumstances of her childhood and become a sane, loving mother?

16. Given the family history of "bad blood," is it irresponsible for Bethany to choose to have a child?